KT-461-419

*We Are Family*

*Also by Josie Lloyd & Emlyn Rees*

Come Together
Come Again
The Boy Next Door
Love Lives

# We Are Family

Josie Lloyd & Emlyn Rees

WILLIAM HEINEMANN : LONDON

Published in the United Kingdom in 2004 by William Heinemann

1  3  5  7  9  10  8  6  4  2

Copyright © Josie Lloyd & Emlyn Rees 2004

The right of Josie Lloyd & Emlyn Rees to be identified as the authors
of this work has been asserted by them in accordance with the
Copyright, Designs and Patents Act 1988

This book is sold subject to the condition that it shall not, by way of trade or
otherwise, be lent, resold, hired out, or otherwise circulated without the
publisher's prior consent in any form of binding or cover other than that in
which it is published and without a similar condition including this condition
being imposed on the subsequent purchaser

William Heinemann
The Random House Group Limited
20 Vauxhall Bridge Road, London, SW1V 2SA

Random House Australia (Pty) Limited
20 Alfred Street, Milsons Point, Sydney
New South Wales 2061, Australia

Random House New Zealand Limited
18 Poland Road, Glenfield
Auckland 10, New Zealand

Random House (Pty) Limited
Endulini, 5a Jubilee Road, Parktown 2193, South Africa

The Random House Group Limited Reg. No. 954009

www.randomhouse.co.uk

A CIP catalogue record for this book is available from the British Library

Papers used by Random House
are natural, recyclable products made from wood grown in
sustainable forests. The manufacturing processes conform to
the environmental regulations of the country of origin

ISBN 0 434 01144 4

Typeset by Palimpsest Book Production Limited,
Polmont, Stirlingshire
Printed and bound in Great Britain by
Clays Ltd, St Ives plc

For Roxie – welcome and enjoy!

# Acknowledgements

Our thanks as ever to the incredible Vivienne Schuster and Jonny Geller for their guidance, feedback and support. Many thanks also to Carol 'The Married' Gambrill, Diana, Emma, Kate, Sarah and Gill. Thanks also to all at Random House, especially Susan Sandon and Andy McKillop for their advice and editorial expertise, Georgina, Richard, Mark, Ron, Justine, Cassie and Glenn (for being so patient!). And thanks as ever to our family and friends for their continued help and encouragement, particularly Tallulah for keeping us smiling throughout.

# *Chapter I*

**London, Present Day**

Laurie Vale had good intuition, but it still took her a while to admit to herself that this, her first private view in over a decade, might just be a success. Taking a moment to sip champagne in the corner of the small London gallery, Laurie surveyed her guests, who were milling around the brightly lit space, admiring the canvases she'd painstakingly mounted on the newly whitewashed brick walls. She felt too dizzy with exhaustion to be excited, but nevertheless, the rising hubbub of arty chit-chat, the clink of glasses, the steady movement of stilettos on the polished floorboards gave her a buzz of satisfaction. In the background the Cuban salsa CD she'd chosen tinkled merrily as a burst of laughter rose above the crowd.

Just in time for the party, as always, Roz, Laurie's agent, waved from the doorway, before swooping over to where Laurie was standing. She was wearing high boots and a floor-length sheepskin coat, neither of which showed any signs of having been subjected to the onslaught of dank February drizzle outside.

'Fantastic turnout,' Roz gushed, handing over a large bunch of pink roses. She towered above Laurie as she shrugged off her coat to reveal the shortest of black minidresses. 'The cabbie got completely lost. Does this really count as the East End?'

'It was all I could afford,' Laurie said apologetically,

kissing her and taking the roses and her huge coat. 'Brick Lane's up the road . . . honest.'

Roz swiped a glass of champagne from a waiter with a tray, not missing the opportunity to size him up. 'Oh well. It doesn't matter. There must be about fifty people. Good for you.'

'Thanks, but I feel like I'm on one of those *Faking It* TV programmes,' Laurie admitted. 'I keep thinking there's a hidden panel of people waiting to see whether I mess up.'

'Don't be ridiculous. You're the real thing, honey. Any sales so far?'

'A few maybes,' Laurie said, looking around her for a place to put the flowers and Roz's coat. 'You see the guy over there in the tweed jacket?' She pointed to the far corner of the room, to where a man was standing, his forefinger tapping his lips as he talked to another buyer Laurie hadn't seen before. 'He's interested in the big sunset for some swanky new private members club in Soho.' Laurie nodded to the huge canvas of red and orange paint dominating the far wall. 'Maybe I've overpriced it.'

'Don't discount,' Roz advised. 'Stick to your guns.' Roz's eyes sparkled as she scoped the room. She loved this kind of event. 'Where's the toy boy?'

Toy boy was hardly a fair description of James. 'He's twenty-eight. That's old by your standards,' Laurie pointed out.

'But young by yours,' Roz said, counting on her long fingers. 'Six years.'

'Five and a half.'

'But haven't I always told you that younger men are where it's at?' Roz gloated. 'And James is divine, you lucky girl. I bet he's got so much stamina . . .'

Laurie shook her head. She wasn't going to be drawn

2

into a discussion about her sex life, even though it was Roz's favourite subject.

'Anyway, he's *so* much better than you-know-who,' Roz added. '*Thank God* you've got him out of your system at long bloody last.'

Laurie didn't dignify Roz's remarks with a comment. She knew she was only trying to be encouraging in her own way. Perhaps Roz thought enough time had passed since their fateful holiday for her to be honest. After all, it was three years ago that their group holiday had ended in that disastrous romance for Laurie. But it had taken those three years for Laurie to even consider dating someone else and, whatever Roz thought, Laurie wasn't ready to hear it. And especially not tonight. Not when everything was going so well.

'Look, I really should go and put these in water and get back to it,' Laurie said. 'Thanks for sending all the invites out and everything. You've done so much. Everyone has – Janey with the venue, Toby with the wine, even Heather's agency has lent me the staff for free. Moral support and all that, it's much appreciated.'

'Friends, darling – we're the new family,' Roz said, putting an arm around Laurie's shoulder and giving it a squeeze, before waving across the room at Janey and Heather.

Upstairs in the small kitchenette, Laurie filled up a plastic cup with water and took a moment to catch her breath. What was wrong with her? Why did she feel so hemmed in by the crowd downstairs? Especially when so many of her friends had come to support her. Maybe it was the contrast between working on her own for so long and now suddenly being publicly exposed which made her feel so unsure of herself.

She wished now that she'd let her father come, instead of deliberately putting him off. Why had she? she wondered. Because she was selfish and hadn't wanted to babysit for him? Because she was embarrassed by how ordinary he was? Or was it simply because inviting him alone would have made it too painful that her mother wasn't with him and she wanted to protect him from well-meaning questions about his bereavement?

Laurie sipped the water, feeling guilty. She knew how much tonight would have meant to her mum. But she also knew, if she was being really honest, that her loss wasn't for Jean Vale, the woman who had finally slipped away nearly a year ago, having lived in a hazy world of her own. Laurie's loss was the ideal that she'd never had. The person she missed was her well-formed fantasy mother who would have been here tonight, graceful and elegant and making all her friends laugh. She missed the woman who would have publicly hugged Laurie, egged her on, given her confidence, bought one of her paintings and gently bullied other people into doing the same.

But Jean Vale hadn't been like that. Maybe she would have been if she hadn't been ill for years, slowly rotting from the inside, until it was almost unbearable to be near her. Laurie tipped the rest of the water away. She should have done more. She should have shouldered the burden instead of letting her father nurse and care for her mother, and, in the end, keep a bedside vigil beside her in the hospice.

She knew that his fierce determination that she should carry on with her life and not get involved in her mother's care arrangements had been a decision made out of love, but even so, Laurie still felt it as a rejection. It had made her feel as if she were being kept at arm's length, as if she

4

were being protected from something she didn't need protecting from. It was the same feeling she'd had since her parents had sent her away to school when she was eleven.

Laurie sighed. It would all be so much easier if she had brothers and sisters – anyone to share the burden of grief she felt, but she'd always been entirely alone. Yet there was no point in wallowing in self-pity or wishing for anything different. She had her friends and she had her independence. And maybe Roz was right. Maybe her friends were better than family.

Laurie stared down at Roz's pink roses in the sink. She mustn't let her friends down. She'd been saying for ages that she was going to have one last stab at making a living out of her art, and now here she was with a chance to show the world that she was an artist. She mustn't blow it.

Laurie had no idea what time it was that James woke her the next morning, but as she swam up into consciousness from exhausted, alcohol-fuelled sleep, she was aware of her thighs being caressed. She grinned, stretching luxuriously towards James's tongue beneath the duvet.

Laurie sighed to herself, feeling herself becoming aroused, despite her headache. She wondered how many women James Cadogan had practised this particular wake-up exercise on, but she didn't care. In the three months they'd been seeing each other, she deliberately hadn't enquired about his past love life. And, more importantly, he hadn't enquired about hers. She was determined that this was going to be a baggage-free relationship – and so far, it was working.

'Good morning,' he said, flinging back the duvet and gasping for air, ten minutes later, as Laurie slowly sank back in a post-orgasm sigh. He exhaled happily, his head thumping back on the pillow as he laid down next to her.

'Christ, I'm thirsty!' he said, sitting up immediately and scratching his mane of thick black hair, so that it stuck up at an even stranger angle. In a second, he'd thrown the duvet off and was standing up on the sheepskin rug by the side of his futon.

Laurie couldn't help snorting with laughter.

'What?' he asked, looking over his shoulder at her, a grin on his face.

She shook her head. There was no way she could explain to him why she found him so funny. Why she found his lack of seriousness so refreshing. She liked his attitude to sex, she realised, as she sat up and drew up her knees under the duvet. She liked the fact that he always treated it as yet another one of his – or in this case, her – physical cravings to be satisfied. Despite his trendy clothes and haircut and his blossoming career as a music producer, James, at heart, was as primitive as a caveman. Now that he'd scratched one particular itch, he was on to the next. The next being some form of liquid.

She watched his smooth buttocks, as he negotiated his way across the littered floor of his bedroom. He seemed completely happy within his own body, as if his naturally slim physique, with his long, lean legs and toned, svelte torso were the most obvious thing in the world. He probably didn't even consider for a second, she thought, how lucky he was to be so naturally good-looking and fit, and Laurie liked his lack of vanity.

She immediately checked herself. She'd vowed she wouldn't do this. She mustn't start overanalysing James or her feelings for him, or deconstructing the parts of his personality she liked and disliked, otherwise it was bound to go horribly wrong. Instead, she forced herself to concentrate on the present, piecing together the events that had led her to being in James's bed.

Now she remembered how he'd bundled her into a taxi at 4 a.m., after coffee and bagels in Brick Lane. She'd been too drunk and too tired after the exhibition to argue against staying at his, but she wished that she'd been more together. It wasn't that she didn't like sleeping with James, but she so much preferred doing it in her own bed.

She knew she was being a snob and that admittedly James had the largest room in his shared house, but even so, there was something steadfastly 'student' about the whole place, including its varying number of other inhabitants whom James had acquired without any sort of vetting process. Now she could hear the vague pitter-patter of someone playing bongos upstairs.

James's downstairs bedroom was large and draughty and entirely painted white, including the floorboards, but in a hurry, so that the whole effect was uneven and streaky, like a child's chalk scribble on a blackboard. At one end was a huge window, the curtains of which Laurie had never seen open. Beneath it was a jumble of wires and computers on a sagging desk, an electric guitar propped up against the wall. Piles of CDs and tapes teetered dangerously, while a hideous white wardrobe and chest of drawers took up the rest of the space, with clothes spilling out in every direction. There was also a life-size cut-out of Elvis in his Vegas heyday, which made phallic shadows on the ceiling at night.

The rest of the room was taken up with the large sprawling futon in which Laurie now sat, surrounded by piles of books and magazines, dirty socks and three lava lamps, their wax suspended into weird foetal-like sculptures.

James returned with a bottle of Evian he'd found by the stereo in the corner.

'Want some?' he asked, after taking a sip and waving it towards Laurie.

'How old is it?' she asked, amused that she found it perfectly acceptable to share bodily fluids with James, but not a stale bottle of water.

James swallowed another mouthful with a big gulp and looked at the label on the bottle, as if it would give him some clue as to the vintage. 'Dunno,' he said. 'Not older than a couple of months.'

He wiggled his thick eyebrows at her, challenging her to take the bottle, but she shook her head. James shrugged and got in under the duvet, holding her tight. His feet were freezing as he put them on Laurie's legs.

'So, Miss Arty-Pants. How's the hangover?' he asked, cuddling her.

'I wish you hadn't mentioned it,' she said, feeling it kick in. She reached over him and lunged for the water, after all. As she did, she glanced at the small travel alarm clock on the floor. 'Oh shit,' she said, collapsing on James's smooth chest.

'What?'

'I'm supposed to meet Tamsin for breakfast.'

'Tamsin . . . Tamsin?' James was clearly searching for a face to fit the name.

'My flatmate,' Laurie said, fixing him with a long-suffering smile. She remembered all of *his* friends.

'Oh yes . . . blonde.'

Laurie rolled her eyes at him. 'I promised I'd meet her this morning. I've got to head home and shower.'

'Don't go,' James moaned sleepily, pulling her back down under the duvet. 'You can shower here.'

'In your bathroom?'

'What's wrong with it?'

'Let's just say that I like my creature comforts more than you do. Call it an age thing. You know, you can get up and come too if you want. And then we could –'

But James had already closed his eyes and was pulling the duvet up around his chin. Laurie got out of bed pulling on her clothes from last night. They stank of stale smoke.

'I'll see you, sleepyhead,' she whispered, ruffling his hair, before kissing his forehead. 'Call me when you're conscious.'


Laurie admired Tamsin. She had done since they'd been friends at sixth-form college where they'd smoked, read poetry, painted their nails black and chased unsuitable boys. Since then, Tamsin had achieved a much more complete make-over than Laurie, holding down an impressive job as a law consultant, which involved her flying first class around the world. She even had a handsome airline captain as a boyfriend.

It was petite, blonde Tamsin, dressed in a blue cashmere jumper and gold jewellery, who sat down with Laurie for the post-mortem of the private view in their favourite café in Borough Market a couple of hours later. Laurie, meanwhile, was in paint-splattered jeans and no make-up, her wet hair pushed under a woolly hat.

'I mean, there were quite a few people interested, but no chequebooks flying about, apart from for the big sunset piece,' Laurie explained, 'but that was entirely thanks to Roz,' she added, as she slouched over the table and recounted the events of the night before.

'I wish I'd been there,' Tamsin muttered for the third time.

'Stop saying that,' said Laurie, stretching her arm across the table and touching Tamsin's arm. 'You couldn't help it that the flight was delayed. I know you would have been there if you could.'

'Can I at least buy a painting, to make it up to you?'

'Don't be ridiculous. My paintings are all over the flat as it is. There's no point in you buying one.' Laurie sat up as the waitress arrived with a large plate of banana pancakes with maple syrup. 'Talking of the flat, I think the shower is on the blink again. When I get some money from the exhibition – if I do – I think I'll decorate a bit, what do you say?'

Tamsin didn't reply. Instead, she sipped her latte from the glass. Then she wiped her finger along the edge of the table. Laurie caught her expression, as she loaded a fork-ful. Something in the delicate features of her friend's face made her put the fork down and wipe her mouth.

'OK, come on, spit it out,' Laurie tested, looking at Tamsin before sucking on the straw from her fresh-juice smoothie.

'What? Oh no. No, it's nothing, really.'

Laurie put the smoothie down. 'Is it something to do with Captain Mike?' Laurie said his name with a deep smooth voice and double chins. Usually, Tamsin shared the joke, but today she didn't laugh.

'We've decided to live together,' Tamsin blurted out.

'But . . . but I thought you'd only just . . .' Laurie stopped herself. She was about to say 'started seeing him', but who was she to be judgemental? If it was love, then of course Tamsin was going to move in straight away. She smiled and half stood and gestured for Tamsin to lean forward so that she could give her an awkward hug across the small table. 'Wow!' she said.

Tamsin squeezed her back. 'I know, isn't it great? I keep pinching myself.'

Laurie sat back down and smiled, but inside she felt sad. Another one bites the dust, she thought. She'd seen it happen with nearly all of her friends. In no time at all, there'd be an expensive wedding and then there'd be pregnancy and a baby and in less than a year Laurie would have nothing in common with her at all. Now, despite everything Laurie had said about the private view, she felt more in limbo than ever.

'So . . .' she said, looking at her plate, but her appetite had gone.

'I guess it's all change,' Tamsin said happily, with a shrug, launching forth on Mike's romantic proposal of cohabitation while she was in the cockpit of his 747 flying across the Alps.

But Laurie's mind was already racing ahead. She and Tamsin had bought their tiny flat together almost ten years ago. At the time, signing up for a joint mortgage with each other had seemed a lot safer than with any of the men either of them were dating. Besides, the flat was low risk and cheap and it was an arrangement that had suited them both over the years. And recently, with Tamsin spending more and more time away, Laurie had the flat mostly to herself. Now, the thought of trying to find a lodger filled her with dread.

'So what are you going to do?' Laurie asked, bringing her friend gently back down to earth.

'Well, the thing is . . . I know you're hard up for cash. And I thought . . . Mike and I thought we could move into the flat together. Or you could buy me out instead?' Tamsin hurried on. 'If you want. And Mike and I could buy somewhere else and you could keep the flat.'

Tamsin clearly felt guilty. She blushed furiously. Laurie stared at her, but she didn't meet her eye. They both knew that Laurie buying Tamsin out wasn't even a vague possibility.

'The point is, Laurie, that you've got your art underway now and well . . . I've been waiting for quite a while until you . . .'

'Until I what?'

'You know . . . felt more stable.'

Laurie was stunned. She felt as if she were being ditched by someone she considered to be her true friend. Even worse, she now felt embarrassed about all the times she'd confided in Tamsin. She'd thought that Tamsin was being supportive about her grief over her mother, her confusion over her love life and the direction of her career. Now Laurie realised she'd just been biding her time.

'I suppose it's best if you take the flat,' Laurie said. 'If that's what you want. I guess I'll move out.'

Tamsin smiled, clearly relieved. 'I knew you'd be brilliant about it. I've got it all sorted with a solicitor. It'll only take a month or so to swap over the paperwork, although I don't want to put you under any pressure.' When Laurie didn't say anything, she added, 'So what are you going to do? Where will you live?'

'I'll work something out.'

'That's you all over,' Tamsin laughed, drawing a line under the subject. 'You're so resourceful. You could always stay with James, couldn't you?'

Laurie could only manage a hollow smile. 'Er, no.'

There was a small pause.

'So. What are you doing next Sunday? Only, I've asked Mike's parents to come for lunch and I thought I'd cook it at home. You and James are very welcome to join us.'

'No. Thanks anyway, but I think I'll go over and see Dad.'

'How is he?' Tamsin asked, her voice full of sympathy.

'Oh, fine!' Bill Vale said, happily, when Laurie asked him the same question the following week. 'Never better,' he continued, then checked himself. 'Well, considering.'

Laurie wondered how many times her father had practised this answer. Now she couldn't tell whether her beloved, but slightly bemusing, father was putting this on for her benefit, or whether he genuinely meant it. There certainly seemed to be a grain of truth in his protestations. His cheeks were rosy and he'd put on weight, which he needed for his tall frame. His white hair was neatly combed and he was wearing a faun checked shirt and a red tie, along with an old cardigan and grey trousers. Laurie followed him into the small terraced cottage where he lived alone in Tunbridge Wells.

'How did it go?' her father asked, referring to the private view, as they walked into the small, cosy lounge.

'Exhausting. I felt bad you didn't come, Dad.'

'Well, I didn't want to cramp your style,' he joked, but she saw now that she'd hurt his feelings. 'Not to worry, you'll have plenty more.'

'I don't know about that,' Laurie replied, flopping down on to the beige velvet sofa.

'Drink?' asked her father, walking across the green carpet in his leather slippers to the small drinks cabinet, where his cut-glass tumblers gleamed in a row. He'd always had an air of formality about him, after years teaching maths in a school in Canterbury, and Laurie always more of a visitor, than his daughter.

She nodded, then rubbed her hat back off her head. She hadn't had a good week. The combination of Tamsin's bombshell about the flat and having to dismantle the exhibition had left her feeling deflated and miserable. Yet it was pointless asking her father for emotional support. He'd never understood that what she required was for him to listen, not to take each problem and try to fix it. She knew that if she really unburdened herself of her angst, including her imminent homelessness, her father would probably try to make a spreadsheet of her expenses on his new computer, get in a muddle and resort to getting out his chequebook. She hoped that he still had at least several healthy decades of retirement left and she wanted him to save his money for that, not for bailing her out.

'So did you make lots of money?' he asked.

Laurie hated lying and couldn't bring herself to tell him she was hideously in debt after the event. 'It was more about getting my name out there, rather than the money,' she said.

Her father made a grunt-like sigh as he sat down in the armchair, pulling the Sunday paper from under him. 'Yes, well, your mother knew you were talented from the moment you started scribbling. Dreams are worth pursuing, you know.'

'Yes, I know, but it would be good to start making even a meagre living out of it,' she said, before she'd had time to censor herself.

'It'll all come right in the end, you'll see. Something, or someone, will come along.'

Laurie bristled at his contrite advice. She knew he was only trying to help, but his confidence in her always had the odd effect of sapping Laurie's own belief in herself. Something about his blind trust made her flare with annoyance. He made it all sound as if it were fate. As if it were all so easy.

14

'So, what have you been up to?' Laurie asked, changing the subject and taking a sip of her gin and tonic.

'Well, there's been lots to do on the Residents' Association Committee. Trevor Sandler's resigned as chairman while he has a hip replacement, so we're now stuck for a stand-in . . .'

Later, as Laurie helped him prepare lunch in his small kitchen, she was amazed by how quickly and resourcefully Bill Vale had learnt to live by himself. Only once did he refer to her mother again, and when he did, he stopped talking and took a quick, sharp intake of breath and looked out of the steamy window.

'She would have been out in the garden, planting,' he said, wistfully. 'We would have had a garden full of daffodils in the old schoolhouse.'

'I know,' Laurie said, softly. She watched the lines around his eyes grow deeper. Then he rubbed his bushy white eyebrows.

'Come on,' he said, as if Laurie had been the one expressing her regrets. 'She wouldn't want us to sit here getting maudlin,' he said. 'No point in that, at all.'

Laurie nodded, sad that their conversation was over. That was probably the closest he would come to admitting that he missed his wife. That was all he was going to let out. But then, perhaps, Laurie thought – not for the first time – that that was all there was. Perhaps her father was lucky enough not to possess great depths of emotion at all.

She'd learnt long ago that her father considered all displays of emotion to be rather childish and silly. Even after her mother had died, Laurie hadn't seen him cry. Instead, he'd been stoical and brave, displaying the kind of stiff-upper-lipped attitude towards his misfortune that he'd always tried – and failed – to instil in Laurie.

And yet Laurie was sure that her father had loved her mother in his own way. It was just that their relationship seemed to be based on quiet companionship rather than any sort of passion. Whenever Laurie thought of them together, she always pictured them sitting down, showing their affection with a small touch of their hands, the making of a cup of tea for each other, or a thousand of their other traditional rituals. She'd never seen them do anything spontaneous, like dance together, and she'd never caught them kissing, like her friends claimed to have done with their own parents.

When she'd been away at school, Laurie had always wondered whether her parents had a secret private life. But as soon as she'd been home, she'd seen how ridiculous such a notion had been. And over the years, her mother's aloofness and seeming contentment with her marriage had always prevented Laurie from asking her anything personal about her feelings. And now it was too late. She would never know how her mother had truly felt about anything. And she wouldn't even know where to begin with her father.

After lunch, her father went to his neighbours to pick up the Residents' Association newsletters. Laurie offered to go with him, but he wouldn't hear of it. Left alone in the house, Laurie felt a familiar kind of guilty boredom which made her limbs ache. Outside, the branches of the straggly peach tree in her father's small garden slapped against the patio doors, like fingers drumming. The bird boxes attached to the small shed looked damp and empty.

Her father had moved to this house when her mother had gone into the hospice and Laurie never felt quite at home here, although the furniture was the same and there were familiar objects around: the silver-framed photograph of her parents on their wedding day, her mother looking self-conscious at nearly forty in a modest white suit, a picture of Laurie looking gappy and happy on her first bicycle, the set of her father's model cars he used to build and his collection of action-hero novels in a glass-fronted bookcase.

Laurie drained her glass and walked into the small kitchen to finish clearing up after lunch. The chicken carcass was on the carving board next to the sink, the plates and small bowls stacked neatly beside it.

On the wall next to the small table was a pinboard covered in postcards. Laurie looked at them – some old and battered, some new. And then she saw the corner of the postcard she'd sent herself and she froze.

'No,' she said out loud, recoiling at the thought. She mustn't think about it. She mustn't let him enter her head. But already her hand was moving towards the board, removing the postcard and turning it over.

*Dear Mum and Dad – having an amazing time. Here with Roz, Heather et al, but have met someone. I am in love! So, so happy. Will fill you in when I get back. If I come back. This is IT. Am in paradise. L x*

For a second, she was livid with her father for keeping the postcard. How dare he still keep reminders when she had destroyed all of hers? But then, she couldn't blame him. It must have made him so happy to have read Laurie's words to her mother, when she was so sick.

The thought of this – the realisation that she'd some-how let down her parents, as well as having been let down herself – made Laurie feel instantaneously furious. She tore up the postcard into tiny pieces and put it in the bin.

Then she dumped the chicken carcass on top of it and quickly shut the bin cupboard door.

Like an alcoholic, or a drug addict, reminders of another life had to be dealt with. Stamped out, not given in to. She would not let his memory back in. She brushed her hands together, mentally congratulating herself on dealing with the situation. It was over. Over and gone. For ever. She had James now. James and a new life. She may have been derailed once, but that was in the past. She was back on track and steaming towards her future.

Suddenly, the phone rang, startling her. She raced to the study door, to pick up the nearest handset, then lunged across the large wooden desk to pick up the phone, noticing that her father had installed a new computer table.

'Five-four-nine-oh,' she said, mimicking her father's telephone manner.

'Hello, is Bill there?' The woman's voice sounded tentative.

Laurie smiled silently as a shocking possibility occurred to her. What if her father had a new woman in his life? What if he was seeing someone else? What if that was the reason he looked so healthy and happy? No, it couldn't be! Not Bill Vale.

But maybe . . . just maybe there was life left in him after all . . .

Laurie stretched the curly cable of the phone and moved round the desk to sit in her father's leather swivel chair, pleased to have someone to talk to. 'He's popped out. Can I help? I'm his daughter.'

There was a long silence at the other end of the phone. So long in fact that Laurie looked at the receiver and then spoke again. 'Hello? Are you there?'

'Yes, I'm here.'

'Well, can I tell Dad who called?'

'Could you tell him . . . could you give him a message?'

'Of course. Go ahead,' Laurie said to the woman, turning over an empty envelope on the green leather blotter and plucking out a biro from the pot on the desk.

'Could you tell him . . . could you tell him that Tony . . . that Tony has passed away.'

'Tony?' Laurie repeated the unfamiliar name. 'I'm sorry, was Tony a friend of Dad's?'

'No, he wasn't,' the woman said. 'But I want Bill to know. The funeral is next week. If Bill wants to come, tell him . . .' The woman trailed off. Laurie was about to prompt her, when the woman started speaking again. Her voice sounded more businesslike, as if she'd composed herself. 'Tell him to call me.'

Laurie wrote down the message and the number the woman gave, trying to fathom out the strange tone in the woman's voice.

'OK,' she said, gently, 'I'll tell Dad. Would you mind leaving your name?'

'It's Rachel.'

'Rachel,' Laurie said, writing it down. 'And he'll know who you are?'

'Oh yes.'

'You're a friend then?' Laurie prompted.

'No,' said Rachel slowly. 'I'm not his friend.' There was a pause. 'I'm his sister.'

It was Laurie's turn to be speechless. She felt her blood racing to her cheeks, as her hand started to sweat around the receiver.

'His *what*?'

'He never mentioned me?' Rachel asked.

Laurie's voice cracked. 'Listen, I don't know who you

are,' she said, 'and I'm sorry for your loss, but I think you've got the wrong number. My father doesn't have a sister. I think you've made a mistake.'

'No, there's no mistake,' the woman said, wearily. 'I'm sorry to shock you. I know this must be hard. You're Laurel, aren't you?'

'I don't see . . .' Laurie trailed out. 'Yes, my name is Laurel Vale . . . Laurie.'

'He named you after our mum.'

Laurie swallowed hard. It was true that she'd been named after her grandmother, but how the hell could this woman, this Rachel person, possibly know –

'Laurie, could we meet?' Rachel asked. 'I don't think your father will come to Tony's funeral, but I would so love to talk to you. And you should meet your family. It's time.'

# Chapter II

**Stepmouth, March 1953**

It was nine in the morning and Stepmouth high street was wide awake. Cold blasts of air funnelled up from the harbour. Swallows and house martins darted between the chimneys and gables of the brightly coloured shopfronts. Cormorants and gulls shrieked and duelled in the ice-blue sky.

People stood huddled in groups: at the bus stop, thumping gloved hands together, smoking cigarettes, discussing shopping lists, all waiting for the motor coach to arrive; outside Vale Supplies, peddling gossip, cooing at pram-bound babies, trading recipes and ration-book coupons.

Over beneath the fishmonger's rippling white awning, Mark Piper, the bald and bearded fishmonger, and his wife, Eileen, stood haggling with rubber-booted Stephen Able, the captain of the *Mary Jane*, over a trolleyload of fish, lobsters and crabs, which he'd wheeled up from the quayside to sell.

Outside the Channel Arms, ruddy-faced brewery men in smudged flat caps and sweat-stained vests rolled beer barrels down the ramp of their spluttering diesel lorry. Sandy, brown soapsuds slid down the windows of Ackroyd & Partners Solicitors, as Nick Meades washed them clean. A waxed black Citroën purred up the high street and on towards Summerglade Hill – like something out of a Chicago gangster film, Tony Glover thought, as it passed him by.

Tony was standing a couple of feet back from the end of the queue at the bus stop, with his arm round the slim waist of Margo Mitchell, his girlfriend of the last two and a half weeks.

The aroma of oven-fresh pasties and bread drifted through the open bakery doors, driving Tony nuts, making his stomach grumble, and leaving him wishing he'd taken his mother up on her offer of a fry-up before he'd left home.

But he'd been running late and hadn't had the time to spare. Because Margo Mitchell wasn't the kind of girl you kept waiting. Especially when you'd promised to take her shopping for the day – which he had, to the cosmopolitan stores of nearby Barnstaple. And especially when you wanted to impress her enough to get her to finally unfasten her Bastille of a bra and take a tumble with you up in the meadows some time soon – which he most certainly hoped that she would.

To get here on time, Tony had raced his bicycle at breakneck speed down the steep, treacherous, zigzagging road, which led from his village three miles up the West Step Valley to here.

And the rush had been worth it, hadn't it? *Margo* was worth it, wasn't she? Tony breathed in her sweet lemony perfume and kissed her pouting rouged lips, before looking her over again.

She was cute, all right, dressed in a rich cream woollen cardigan and sky-blue Terylene dress, with her golden hair tied up in bunches, showing off the silver earrings which she'd borrowed from her mother. And even if her and Tony didn't exactly have much in common, there were still a whole stack of reasons to be with a girl who looked like her.

'Like her tits, which are as big as beach balls,' Tony's best friend, Pete, had pointed out only last week with a faraway look in his eyes.

'And her lips, which could suck a golf ball through a straw,' their good friend Arthur had added with a sigh.

Margo was a catch, then, and certainly the prettiest girl Tony had ever been out with. Not that he was without assets himself. He was tall, a little over six feet, and lithe, from time spent boxing for his school (before he'd got himself kicked out, that was). He had a sartorial streak and was dressed today in a black greatcoat, buttoned up to the neck (in the style favoured by Richard Burton), along with razor-creased grey trousers and a pair of polished black leather boots. His eyes were twinkling and blue, the colour of the sea when viewed from the top of a cliff on a bright sunny day. 'Right bobby-dazzlers,' his mother had always said. His eyelashes were dark and long.

But if he'd been born handsome, he'd done his best to disguise the fact since. His face was a history of the scrapes he'd got himself into. One of his front teeth was chipped from popping beer-bottle tops for bets. The summer before, while showing off to tourist girls down at the beach, he'd misjudged a dive into a tidal pool and had crooked his nose on a rock. Up on his left temple ran an inch-long scar, a memento from the fight he'd got into at grammar school last September on his seventeenth birthday – the very same altercation which had led to his expulsion and put paid to any hopes he'd had of taking his education any further.

He didn't lose much sleep over his bumps and bruises, though. (The expulsion, however, *that* still made him mad . . . Since then he'd been washing dishes over at the Sea Catch Café on East Street, rubbing off grease and shining up glass, leaving his arms as hard as steel.) It was important, the way he saw it, to look tough, tough enough to stop people from messing with you. That's why he kept his thick dark hair slicked back with Brylcreem, like in the photos he'd seen in the newspapers of the notorious cosh-boy gangs from London.

Girls liked a guy to look tough, Tony reckoned, the same as they did in the movies. He thought he knew a bit about women, did Tony. Like how you could make them smile by telling them their hair looked nice, or what a knockout their new dress was. He'd learnt from experience that first dates were for necking, second dates for fingers and tops, and anything further a matter of guesswork and luck.

What he didn't yet know for sure, but had certainly begun to suspect, was that Margo Mitchell – with whom he'd never got past necking in all the time he'd known her - was a grade A tease.

'Do you love me, Tony Glover?' she whispered into his ear now. 'Do you? Do you love me?'

Normally, this kind of question (the silly, gushy, girly kind) would have brought Tony out in a rash, but seeing as it was the tenth time Margo had asked him in the last five minutes, all he did was shrug.

'Why don't we talk about something else?' he answered, exactly the same as he had done the previous nine times. Stepping away from her, he threaded a Craven "A" cigarette between his lips and reached into his coat pocket for his lighter.

'Because –'

But Tony never heard whatever it was Margo said next, because at that exact moment, he looked up, distracted by a bright flash of colour directly above his head. There, on the mottled, weathered wooden balcony of the church hall – which protruded over the bus stop and which was halfway through being repainted – stood two girls. Their matching yellow scarves fluttered in the seaward breeze, as vivid as a butterfly's wings.

They'd been staring at him and he'd caught them out. And now they were frozen, guilty, staring back. He knew their faces well enough: Pearl Glaister and Rachel Vale. Both of them – one fair-haired, the other red – were lookers, dolls, known by all the guys Tony's age in the town.

Red-haired Rachel Vale was the little sister of Bill and the daughter of Edward and Laurel. Pretty as a *Picture Post* pin-up, she hated Tony's guts and hadn't spoken a single word to him since her father had died eight years ago.

All pretty, sharp-tongued Rachel Vale had ever done had been to speak *about* Tony, usually within earshot, usually to tell other people exactly what she thought about him and his. She'd refused so much as to look at him, and had even crossed streets to avoid him. So why, he wanted to know, was she staring at him now?

In the very same breath in which he asked himself this question, he found his answer. Because the moment his eyes wandered from Rachel's, he noticed the open can of paint she was holding out above his head, waiting to tip.

The can slowly slipped from her hands. Deliberate or accidental? He couldn't tell. Either way – upright and full – it now plummeted towards him.

Tony had no time to jump aside. Instead, he ducked down low and lashed out at the can in mid-air to protect himself, swatting it away with a backward sweep of the palm of his hand.

As he rolled on to his side, he watched it spin over in the air – once, twice – with white paint spraying outwards from its rim like sparks from a Catherine wheel. As he came to a halt – half in, half out of the gutter – he checked his smarting hand and coat: nothing; not so much as a drop of paint.

Talk about a piece of luck . . .

Only then he heard the scream.

He didn't need to look over at Margo to know that it was her. He'd taken her to the flicks to see Bogey and Hepburn in *The African Queen* a week ago, and had spent the entire second half of the matinee French kissing her for all he was worth while trying to cop a feel, only for her to break free every time the music got scary and shriek hysterically at whatever fresh jeopardy had arrived on the screen.

Yet this new scream – three seconds long already and rising like an air-raid siren – infinitely surpassed Margo's previous efforts in both duration and pitch. It was a scream of real, not cinematic, horror. And looking up at Margo as he regained his balance, it wasn't hard for Tony to see why.

Which is more than could be said for Margo Mitchell's face – which could hardly be seen at all.

Tony blinked, stupefied. His princess had vanished and a whey-faced phantom now stood in her place.

Finally, Margo's lungs ran out of air and silence gripped the street. The other people who'd been standing near her in the bus queue had shrunk away like water from wax. Eyes wide, Margo goggled through the clown-like mask of paint on her face. A solitary, pitiful white bubble of paint inflated and popped at the corner of her mouth. Then, with her arms hanging loosely by her sides, her chest heaved and she started to wail.

Tony glared up at the balcony of the church hall. But Rachel Vale and her accomplice had fled. He couldn't believe it. He couldn't believe what Rachel Vale had done to Margo. He couldn't believe what she'd tried to do to *him*.

'Right,' he shouted, jumping to his feet. They weren't going to get away with this. He'd find them and make them apologise. To Margo *and* to him. And pay for Margo's clothes. And –

'You're bloody dead,' was all he heard before the punch connected squarely with his jaw and he found himself lying flat on his back.

Forty-five-year-old, spud-faced, cauliflower-eared Bernie Cunningham was a pig farmer by trade and a bar-brawler by persuasion. He had the strength of a shire horse and the stamina of a mule.

'Get up,' Cunningham snapped, tearing his paint-splattered tweed jacket off and hurling it into the gutter. Towering over Tony, he planted each foot before him like a tree. 'Think you're funny, do you, Glover? Making a mug out of me . . . Covering me in paint . . . Come on, you bastard – up!'

Tony scrabbled backwards. 'It's not how you think,' he told Cunningham, his face now rigid with tension. 'I didn't throw it at you . . . or I did, but only because it was thrown at me first . . . I mean . . .'

But Cunningham wasn't listening.

'Margo!' Tony shouted across to her. She must have seen what had really happened, mustn't she? 'Tell him,' he implored her. 'Tell him it wasn't me.'

But Margo wasn't listening, either. In fact, Margo wasn't even waiting to see what happened next. Poor, traumatised Margo Mitchell was turning and running back home to her mum.

Tony searched for support among the faces in the small crowd of people now gathered around. But none of them would look him in the eye. Like he didn't matter, he thought. Like whatever was going to happen to him didn't matter either.

Tony struggled up again. 'Please, Mr Cunningham,' he said.

Cunningham hawked and spat at the ground between Tony's feet. 'Enough talk,' he said, edging in within striking distance, before beckoning Tony forward with his raised fists.

Tony stared, mesmerised, as the bigger man swayed gently from side to side like a caged orang-utan. People yelled encouragement from the crowd.

The first punch – a jab – glanced off Tony's temple, snapping back his head. Pain bit into him. But he'd been hit plenty before, by his brother and father, as well as in the boxing ring. Automatically, his posture realigned. He shielded his face with his fists. He drew his elbows in tight to his body, protecting his stomach and ribs. Jaw clenched, neck tightened, he swallowed down the blood that had surfaced on his tongue.

Just a jab, he told himself, now watching Cunningham like a hawk. Because if it had been an uppercut or a round-house at that range, he knew damn well it would have knocked him out cold. He caught the glint in Cunningham's eyes. He was testing him out, that's all. Having some fun, before coming in for the kill.

Tony's adrenalin was up now. He focused not only on Cunningham's face, but the rest of him, too, dividing his body into zones, like a butcher would a carcass, mentally carving him up into threats and weaknesses, fists and elbows, ribs and teeth and eyes.

The next jab Cunningham tried, Tony pulled back from. The follow-up, he sidestepped. The old man wasn't going to have things all his own way, then. Buoyed by the thought, Tony tried a trick he'd learnt in the sparring ring at school. He darted forward, feinted left and suckered Cunningham into an opportunistic uppercut, which left his whole right side exposed. Tony powered in, catching Cunningham hard around the ear.

The crowd gasped.

Cunningham's response was to laugh.

Tony could have run then. Logically, he should have. This was sport to Cunningham. So what if Tony had managed to slip one punch past him? Tony was nothing but a dumb kid who Cunningham was going to teach a lesson.

But Tony hadn't run from anything in his life. Not from his brother and not from every other kid who'd come looking for him these last eight years, seeking to carve themselves out a reputation from the remains of his. A thousand people lived in this town and if he ran now then every single one of them would know.

'Come on, then, you fat ugly bastard,' he jeered at Cunningham. 'Let's see what you've got.'

Cunningham duly obliged. And what he had was a combination move which had secured him a place in two regimental finals during his service years and one county championship after the war: a left uppercut, followed by a right roundhouse.

Both blows hit home. Tony tottered and fell. His cheek was on the pavement. He could hear a rushing sound, like a river in spate, only he knew the noise was inside, not outside, his head. Something wet trickled down his throat. He coughed and what he tasted was sweet. When he touched his nose with his fingers he saw that they were drenched in blood.

'Get up,' boomed Cunningham. 'I'm not finished with you yet.'

Tony tried to focus on the blurred image of Cunningham, which shuddered above him like a reflection on a wind-ruffled pond. He attempted to stand, but his legs bent like rubber the moment he put his weight on them. Cunningham grabbed at him, hauling him to his feet.

She came out of nowhere, then: Rachel Vale, wedging herself in between the two men like a human crowbar, before ripping them apart.

'Leave him alone,' Tony heard her telling Cunningham.

'You!' Cunningham replied in astonishment. 'You, of all people . . . You move yourself, kid, or I'll –'

'Or you'll what?' she demanded. 'Hit me, too? If you so much as lay a finger on me, I'll call for my brother Bill and he'll . . .'

The sound of gushing water filled Tony's ears again. Nausea rippled through his stomach. He slumped back down on to the pavement, aware now of the crowd closing in and looking down.

'He's telling you the truth,' he heard Rachel Vale insist. 'It wasn't his fault. It was mine. I . . .'

Tony rolled over into the gutter and retched.

The next thing he knew, she was helping him up. For the second time that day, that life, Tony Glover and Rachel Vale stared into one another's eyes. Then she was supporting him, walking him slowly away from Cunningham and everyone else.

'Don't worry,' she told him. 'You'll be fine. You're going to be just fine in a minute.'

She kept on saying it as she supported him down the high street, leading him on past the fish-and-chip shop, beneath the flapping pub signs and then left at the end of the street, away from the quayside and harbour, out across the car park, until they reached St Jude's Cemetery.

She sat him down on the low stone cemetery wall. Gradually, the fresh sea air began to clear Tony's mind and vision. Rachel pulled a tissue from her skirt pocket and pushed it into his hand.

'Don't stare,' she told him. 'It's rude.'

But he couldn't stop himself. He'd known she was pretty, but he'd never looked up close, not like now. He noticed that her skin was soft and that her hair wasn't really red at all, but a deep russet brown. Her nose, ears, mouth . . . everything about her looked sharp and angry. But beneath the mask – there in those pale moss-green eyes – he detected something softer, buried, deliberately concealed. Concealed from him. He'd have given anything right then just to see her smile.

'Hold your head up and pinch the bridge of your nose,' she ordered him, pushing the tissue into his hand. 'It'll stop the bleeding. I learnt it at school.'

Bunching up her long pleated skirt, so as not to rip it, she perched on the wall next to him, and stared across at the vast mass of Summerglade Hill, which loomed up behind the town, stretching high into the sky.

'You heard what I told Cunningham,' she then said. 'It was my fault what happened. Not yours. I'll pay for your girlfriend's clothes . . .'

'Since when did you have the money to pay for something like that?' he asked her groggily, glancing down at her clothes, which were pretty but cheap, the same as those of most kids in this town. 'Let me guess, your brother will lend it to you, because he's my biggest fan –'

'Don't you even talk about him,' she snapped, turning back to face him. 'And never you mind how I get the money.

31

If I say I will, I will. I owe you and I don't want to owe you. Do you understand?' Her eyes flashed with determination. 'I don't want to owe you a penny, Tony Glover.'

'And I don't want your money,' he told her. 'Not now that you've apologised.'

She turned puce. 'I never said I apologised. Only that I owe you. I don't regret what I did, only that it went too far.'

'Too far?'

She grimaced. 'Dropping the whole tin on you like that. It was an accident. All I meant to do was pour a few drops on your head. Just enough to make you look stupid.'

'Well, that's a relief . . .'

'Why?' she asked, peering at him through narrowed eyes as she tilted her head to one side.

He smiled at her ruefully. 'Because for a minute back there, I thought you didn't like me or something.'

She stared at him, stupefied. Then she realised he was making a joke at his own expense and the tension fell from her face. Suddenly, she snorted with laughter.

'You know what, Tony Glover?' she said. 'Maybe you're not such a nasty bastard after all.'

'Why today?' he asked suddenly.

'What?'

'How come you decided to cover me in paint today?'

She looked down at her pale bare bony knees. 'I don't know. Because Pearl's uncle keeps the keys for the church hall and we sometimes sneak up there to smoke. And we saw the paint there that the workmen had left. And I don't know, just because . . .' She shrugged, defensive again.

'Just because what?'

A car horn sounded then and they both looked across the car park to see Christopher Asbury, a kid who'd been in the same year as Tony at grammar school, a rich boy whose father loved him and trusted him enough let him drive his car at the weekend.

Sitting in the passenger seat, alongside another boy, was Anne, a girl Tony had seen Rachel hanging around with before. Leaning out of the back window was Rachel's erstwhile accomplice, Pearl Glaister.

'Rachel Vale, get in here now!' Pearl shouted over.

Rachel slid off the wall and smoothed down her dress.

'Just because what?' Tony asked her again.

Her eyes flashed with sudden fire. 'Just because when I saw you standing next to Margo Mitchell, all I wanted to do was to wipe that smug smile off your face . . .'

'Well, you certainly did that.'

'Yeah,' she said. And, finally, he saw the anger leave her and got a glimpse of that smile he'd so wanted to see. 'I certainly did, didn't I?'

Then she was gone, running over to the car, leaving him there on the wall in the cold.


Tony Glover cycled up the tortuously steep road which criss-crossed up Summerglade Hill, and then on another two miles past the turn-off which led across the moor, until finally, he reached the small village of Brookford.

He turned off the main road at the black-and-yellow AA telephone box which marked the beginning of his street. Brookford Cottages was a row of eight terraced houses, all of which were owned by the local council. In 1936, Tony had been born in number 8, the red-painted house which stood last in the row.

The old Vauxhall which belonged to Tony's stepfather was parked outside. He'd been teaching Tony how to drive in it these last few months. Tony had been looking at maps only the night before, planning out places to drive Margo to on a date. Not that there was much chance of that happening any more.

Tony ducked through the gap in the tall, whitewashed picket fence to the right of the property. His mother did the laundry for several of the guest houses down in the town and the garden was a billowing crop of bedsheets and pillowcases. The smell of washing powder clogged the air.

'Oh Christ,' Don exclaimed, looking up from an old radio he'd been tinkering with on the back doorstep, noticing the state of Tony's face.

Tony's stepfather was a big, slow-moving man, with a complexion like nettle rash. He looked like a drinker, but wasn't. An electrician by trade, he worked over at the Watersbind Hydroelectric Power Station. Tony liked him, trusted him, and had done ever since the moment five years ago when he'd told Tony he wanted to marry his mum and take good care of her.

Don raised a scarred forefinger to his lips. Putting down the glass valve he'd been cleaning, he stood and rearranged his cardigan and shirt where it had risen up over his fuzzy belly.

The four-year-old twins, Tony's half-brothers, who'd been playing marbles in the corner of the yard, now jumped up in unison. Physically, they were the opposite of their father, fast like Tony, but with an added refinement, lending them a birdlike quality, which had always reminded Tony of his mum. Both had jet-black hair and straight fringes which his mother trimmed with cloth shears along the line of a pudding bowl every Saturday after their weekly bath.

'What've you done?' Mikey called out. He was dressed in scuffed brown lace-up shoes, a blue V-neck jumper and a pair of hand-me-down grey flannel trousers. He ran over to get a closer look.

His identically dressed identical twin, Adam, chased after. The boys stood side by side and examined Tony's face in silent awe, through dark intelligent eyes.

'You've been hit,' Adam announced. 'He's been hit. Look, Dad. Look, Mikey.' Tears welled up in his eyes. 'Someone's hit our Tony.'

'Who?' Mikey demanded. He looked around the garden as if the perpetrator might still be at large. 'Who did it? Where's he now? Why'd he do it?'

Tony wanted to make them proud, the way his own elder brother Keith never had. What he didn't want was for them to see him like this. 'I'm fine,' he tried to reassure them.

'You sure as hell won't be if your mother sees you like that,' Don said. He softly tapped the twins on the shoulders. 'Back to your marbles now, lads, and leave me and Tony to talk.'

Reluctantly, the boys walked away, and slumped back down next to the gnarled old pear tree. They whispered to one another, then Adam set about gathering the steel ball bearings and twinkling glass marbles into a pile, while Mikey drew a line in the dust with his finger from where they would shoot.

'What are you smiling at?' Don asked Tony in surprise.

'Nothing,' Tony answered, 'just that me and Keith used to play marbles there, too, when we were kids.' His smile faded and he turned to face Don. Don didn't want to hear about Keith. No one did.

'We'd best get you cleaned up,' Don said.

They weaved through the pillowcases and sheets to the wooden shed at the back of the yard which housed the outdoor toilet. Don turned on the tap which rose up like a metal sapling out of the ground beside it.

'Here,' he said, taking the worn bar of carbolic antiseptic soap from the tin box nailed to the outside of the shed and handing it to Tony.

Tony ran his hands beneath the tap and lathered up the soap between his hands.

'Who did it?' asked Don.

'Cunningham.' The tap water thundered on to the mud.

'Bernie Cunningham?' Don hissed in disbelief. 'Jesus, Tony. What did you want to go messing with him for?'

'I didn't. It wasn't my fau –'

The sound of tuneless whistling cut him off. Don switched off the tap immediately and both men stared at each other uneasily. Through the billowing sheets, they watched Tony's mother walk towards them, dragging an empty wicker laundry basket behind her. She was wearing an old brown dress, patchy with perspiration. She was forty-seven, four years younger than Don, and wore her neat black hair tied up beneath a red-and-white-checked cotton scarf.

Reaching up to pluck the pegs from the line and drop another load of dried sheets into the basket, she suddenly spotted her husband and son standing there in silent conspiracy beside the tap.

She was on them in seconds.

'You promised me!' she shouted at Tony. 'You promised me you wouldn't. Not ever again.' She glared in disgust at the dried blood on his face.

Don repositioned himself between them. 'Now just hold on a minute, Sissy,' he cautioned Tony's mother. 'We don't know what happened yet. He says it wasn't his –'

'I can see what's bloody happened,' she shouted, barging Don aside and shoving her face up close to Tony's.

'He's been bloody fighting again, that's what. Go on!' She eyeballed Tony. 'Deny it!'

Adam and Mikey began to keen.

'Listen to them. See what you're doing to us,' hissed Tony's mother.

'I'm sor –' Tony attempted to apologise.

Violently, she shook her head. 'No! That's no good!'

He reached out to touch her shoulder. He wanted to comfort her, hated to see her like this, hated even more that it was him who'd made her feel this way. 'Please . . .' he implored.

She recoiled from him, like he'd stuck a needle into her flesh. It was hatred, not misery, which he saw in her eyes. Then she turned to Don. 'You know what I said the last time,' she snapped.

'You don't need to do this,' Don said. 'Six months' time and he'll be off with the army.'

'I don't care. I won't go through this again.' She spat the words out, like she'd been chewing them over for months. 'Not again. Not like I did with –'

She shut her mouth and looked away, but what she hadn't said, Tony had heard. *Not like I did with Keith.* That's what she'd wanted to tell him.

Tony's spine turned to ice. He pushed past her and ran towards the house.

'Go on then!' his mother screamed after him. 'Get out! Get out and don't come back!'

He didn't – wouldn't – look back. She was wrong, wrong about him having started the fight, wrong about him having broken his promise to her about not fighting. But most of all, she was wrong about him being anything like Keith. Keith? She didn't even know who Keith was any more.

Inside the house, Tony ran past the musty-smelling larder, through the steam-fogged kitchen and on up the rickety stairs.

His room was the one next to his mother's. He shared it with the twins. The faces of Roy Rogers and Dan Dare stared out at him from the posters on the walls. Tony tripped over a punctured leather football, before kicking it hard to one side, smashing a badly painted model of the *Golden Hind* which lay in the corner next to the bin.

He felt like Gulliver in here. This wasn't his room any more. He'd outgrown this place. He was surplus to requirement, the last reminder of a dead marriage. His mum, Don, the twins . . . they had their life to get on with and he needed to get out and begin his.

His mother was wrong about him, but right about one thing: the sooner he left, the better it would be, for all of them.

Footsteps drum-rolled up the stairs. His mother slammed her bedroom door and the thin wall shook. Still, he couldn't quite let go. Still, an impulse told him to go through and talk to her and stroke her hair and make it all better. Like he'd always done when he'd been a kid.

But it wasn't his dad she was hiding from in there any more. His dad had died of a fever on New Year's Day 1939, after having passed out drunk in the gutter the freezing night before. And nor was it Tony's brother she was turning the key on now, because Keith had been eight years in prison already now.

No, now it was Tony she'd gone in there to escape. And the only way to prove to her that he wasn't like his brother or his dad was to do what they'd never done, and that was to leave her in peace.

He pulled out his kitbag from under his bed, chucked

in his important stuff: the copy of *The Count of Monte Cristo* he was halfway through reading, his pot of Brylcreem, his comb, cut-neck razor, shaving soap and mirror. He shoved his clothes in on top.

He looked up to see Don standing in the doorway.

'She'll calm down,' he told Tony. 'Give her a few hours and she'll . . .' But his words ran out, because they both knew it wasn't true. Tony's mother was a woman who stood by her ultimatums. She'd succeeded in cutting Keith out of her life, and now she was washing her hands of Tony, too.

'Where will you go?' Don asked.

'Grandad's.'

'But it's –'

'It'll be OK.'

'Do you need to borrow any money?'

'No, thanks. The twins . . .' Tony said, hauling his bag up on his shoulder.

'I told them to stay in the garden.'

'Will you say goodbye to them for me? I'm going to leave by the front door.'

'But they'll –'

But Tony was firm. 'Mum won't want me to see them any more, so I won't. Not until I've proved her wrong. She won't believe what I tell her, so I'm going to show her, Don. I'll prove to her who I am. And who I'm not.'

The two men stared at each other.

'Good luck,' Don said, holding out his hand.

Tony shook it and then left.


Tony sat shivering on a broken rocking chair in the corner of his grandad's shed, wrapped in two sweaters, his coat and a heavy blanket. His head still ached from the fight.

Above him, rain strafed the corrugated-iron roof and the wind shrieked like ghosts.

His grandad had always called this building a shed, but it was much more substantial than that. A mile east of Brookford, it was on a slither of otherwise useless dirt on Farmer Dooley's land, which Farmer Dooley had given to Tony's grandad in return for having saved his life by pulling him out from under a tractor before Tony had been born. Tony's grandad had used it for rearing chickens and rabbits for the pot, and in the latter years of his life, hiding from his wife's nagging.

The old storm lamp hanging from a hook in the ceiling flickered erratically in the draught. Down to the last of its oil, it hissed at the damp, mouldy air and threatened to sputter out at any second.

Tony refused to let the situation depress him, though. A galaxy of dust shimmered in the lamplight. Life remained packed with possibilities. He knew that leaving had still been the right thing to do. This was a crossroads, not a dead end.

Of course, he'd need to insulate the shed properly, if it was going to be his home. Which he'd already decided it was. Because there was no point in wasting his pay from the café on renting a room down in town. Not when summer and all its fine weather would soon be here. There was running water and a potting sink outside. Once he got himself a gas stove and a mattress to sleep on, he'd be fine.

He wouldn't be here for ever, anyway. Six months. That was all. Don was right. In six months' time, he'd be facing a medical board which would duly pass him fit to do his national service. Then it would be off to Aldershot for him to do his basic army training. And after that, out there in the wide world, anything was possible, wasn't it? All he had to do was survive until then.

The lamp died and Tony shivered. Before he could stop himself, he found himself thinking of home. He pictured himself in the living room, watching the orange and green flames flicker on the coal fire, listening to the radio, while Don smoked his pipe and his mother's voice drifted downstairs from where she was putting the twins to bed.

But Tony wasn't there; he was here, cold, hungry and alone.

He searched for a good thought to lead him into sleep. He tried thinking of Margo, tried imagining lying with her on a warm beach, his fingers toying with a red silk ribbon in her golden hair, his lips pressed up against hers.

But it was a thought which slithered like an eel from his grasp. Margo Mitchell didn't want to see him any more. That's what her mother had told him – standing on their doorstep, pointing a broom at him like a bayoneted rifle – when Tony had gone round to Margo's house after the fight to apologise.

'She never wants to speak to you again,' he'd been firmly told.

He pulled the blanket tighter around his shoulders.

But then he remembered Rachel Vale, pretty, red-haired Rachel Vale.

'Just because what?' he'd asked her as they'd sat on the wall of St Jude's Cemetery.

'Just because when I saw you standing next to Margo Mitchell, all I wanted to do was to wipe that smug smile off your face . . .'

That smile was back now, only this time it wasn't smug at all, but puzzled. Because however much Tony Glover had previously thought he knew about women, this one

41

had him confused. Hatred was one reason to cover someone with paint, all right. But wasn't jealousy another? And yet surely, as she'd looked down at him from the church-hall balcony, jealousy had been the last thing on Rachel Vale's mind . . .

As, indeed, she was the last thing on Tony Glover's now, as he sank into a deep and dreamful sleep.

# *Chapter III*

Rachel Glover threw down the pile of letters and unopened cards and picked up the phone, cursing at the intrusion of yet another call. It was Anton Philippe.

'I've just heard the tragic news,' he said, his French-accented voice laden with sincerity. 'I can hardly believe it. Please accept my deepest condolences, Mrs Glover.'

'Tony liked doing business with you,' Rachel said, bluntly, taking off her glasses.

'He was one of my best customers. But more than that, he was an incredible man. A true friend –'

'I appreciate you calling, Anton.'

'If there's anything I can do –'

Why did people say that? Rachel wondered. It was a natural response, probably. A safe offer made with no probable outcome, because there was nothing Anton or anyone could do to bring Tony back. Nothing they could do to make this ordeal any better.

Of course, if she was being her normal charming self, she would have told Anton it was him alone who had nurtured her and Tony's love of art over the years and in return had gained her husband's undying respect and loyalty. She would have peppered the conversation with anecdotes and shared memories of their famous lunches in Paris, until, no doubt, Anton would have been forced to shed a tear. As it was, she was in no mood for flattery.

43

As Anton continued talking, Rachel looked across the room to the abstract painting above the white marble fireplace in the drawing room. Tony had bought it for this exact spot in Dreycott Manor, their country home in Somerset, when the artist was barely out of college. Now he was on display at Tate Modern and the painting was worth a fortune. It had been there for fifteen years, but now she could move it up to the apartment in London, where she supposed she would now spend most of her time. There was no point in festering in the countryside. Besides, if she stayed here, she'd be beset by visitors wanting to see the abandoned widow. And she didn't feel like a widow. Not yet.

The fact she'd thought about moving the painting, that she *could* and probably *would* move the painting, momentarily filled Rachel with an illicit thrill. This naughty schoolgirl reaction to her husband's death was baffling, even to herself. It was as if she'd regressed to her most rebellious self, doing things to defy Tony in revenge for him defying her and dying. And yet she'd never seriously defied him before, not in all the years of their marriage. It went against the very foundations of how she'd built the success of their partnership – on compromise and making Tony feel in control. But now she wanted to provoke him, as if by annoying him she could get him to react. She couldn't seem to connect with the fact that he would never react to anything she did, ever again. It didn't feel true.

Rachel shivered and sat down heavily on one of the wide window seats. As she pressed the red call-end button on the phone, she looked across at her son Christopher, who was pouring coffee from a china pot on the low ottoman by the fire. Benson, Tony's springer spaniel, lay dejectedly on the rug behind him.

Despite the fire roaring in the fireplace behind Christopher, the room – which had always been the cosiest and most friendly in the large house – gave Rachel no comfort today. In the corner, a shiny grand piano was laden with framed photographs of her family. Four low, comfortable sofas, upholstered in cream leather were dotted around the room. Thick drapes hung at each of the two large picture windows, which looked out over the lawns to the misty paddock beyond. And everywhere, in every vase, huge floral tributes from family and friends filled the air with the scent of lilies and roses.

'Anton,' she explained, noticing that her eldest son was going bald on top, as he bent over the tray. He'd inherited her natural red hair, although while hers was still a thick auburn mane, thanks to her monthly visits to her trusted colourist at the Knightsbridge salon, Christopher's hair had always been a weaker ginger version, which he'd kept in the same combed-over style since he'd been a chorister.

Her son, Rachel mused, as she opened another of the thick cream envelopes on the pile beside her, was not ageing particularly well. In her opinion he'd looked his best when he was seven. It didn't help that as an adult, he'd developed the pinched, poker face of his profession as a barrister. Now in his mid-forties, he still had a resemblance to his father, but had none of Tony's ruggedness, none of the scars, none of the charisma in his features that had made Tony so handsome.

'You got rid of him rather fast,' Christopher said, walking over and handing her a cup and saucer. 'Are you sure this isn't too much? I'd be happy to take phone calls for you, if only you'd let me?'

Rachel pretended not to hear him, reading another of the condolence cards. She accepted the coffee from him, without looking at him. 'From the Richards. Couldn't they have done better than a Hallmark card? I mean, these verses. Ugh! They make me want to die myself, they're so bad.' She threw the card down.

'At least they sent a card and flowers. If they hadn't you'd have –'

'I know, I know. I would have struck them off, despite thirty years of friendship.'

'I don't know what you want from everyone, Mother.'

'I don't want anything. I don't want anyone to mention it.'

'But –'

'Try and understand, Christopher. This is just the way it is. If they say something, it's wrong, if they don't say something, it's wrong. I'm being what your father would call *difficult*.'

Christopher was silent and Rachel felt a pang of guilt. The fire crackling in the grate seemed extraordinarily loud.

'I haven't seen Lucy today,' she said, eventually, referring to Christopher's wife.

Christopher cleared his throat. 'She's a bit upset, you know, with the baby not sleeping.'

Rachel took a sip of coffee and placed the cup down gently on the saucer. She'd been wrenched out of another Xanax-induced sleep by Thomas's screams last night. 'It's time Lucy got that child into a routine,' Rachel said. 'I told her as much.'

'I know,' Christopher said, his icy tone not hiding his disapproval.

'Don't look at me like that. I'm saying what needs to be said. She's creating a rod for her own back.'

'It's not that easy, Mother.'

'He's only a baby, for God's sake. He doesn't have to have

his every whim attended to. The sooner you get it under control, the easier he'll be and the happier you'll be.'

Christopher appeared to be biting his tongue and Rachel had to swallow her irritation. She could imagine him venting his frustration with Lucy upstairs, pacing back and forth and ranting about his mother. But Rachel didn't care. If only Christopher would have the balls to stand up to her, then everything would be OK. But he never had, and probably never would.

'Tell me you disagree and I won't mention it again.'

Christopher wouldn't look her in the eye.

'Exactly. Children need a firm hand,' Rachel said, the irony of her words not lost on either of them, as she picked up the pile of envelopes beside her and began to flick through them once more.

Left alone, Rachel sighed and took her glasses off again. She rubbed her fingertips over her eyebrows and under her eyes, which felt puffy. Even so, she knew she didn't look as bad as she felt. Most people, when they met her assumed that she was in her mid-fifties, never suspecting that she was a decade older.

'I know, I know,' she said aloud, talking to Tony. 'I'm being bad-tempered, but you've no idea how much there is to organise.'

Rachel shook her head and smiled, imagining the look Tony would have given her. It was almost as if she could sense his presence. As if this was all a joke and he was real and alive.

'This is all so bloody stressful and it's your fault!'

'Mum! Who are you talking to?'

Rachel was startled to see her youngest son was watching her from the doorway.

'Nick,' she said, standing up. 'I didn't hear you arrive.'

She went to greet him, reaching up to hold both his shoulders. He was tanned, his skiing trip cut short by his father's death. His fair hair had lightened in the sun. He was approaching forty, yet he still held on to the playboy good looks which matched his frivolous lifestyle. Rachel was about to ask him whether he had a companion in tow, but when she kissed his cheek, a sob escaped him and she drew back to see his handsome face crumple with grief.

Rachel inwardly groaned and held him, his weight heavy on her. She wasn't used to seeing men in tears. Tony had never wept – except with joy. He'd coped with everything life had thrown at him with courage and steely determination. Why couldn't his children be more like him and pull themselves together? And if Nick was like this, she dreaded to think how Claire would be when she arrived from Palma for the funeral. Every time Rachel had called in the past week, Claire had sounded as if she'd completely gone to pieces.

Eventually, Rachel managed to wriggle out from underneath her son and, taking his hand, she led him gently to the sofa by the fire. Benson, who had stirred when Nick had entered the room, circled his patch on the rug again and flopped down. He raised an unimpressed eyebrow at Nick and snorted.

'I'm sorry,' Nick said, as Rachel plucked a tissue from the silver holder on the mantelpiece and offered it to her son. 'It's just that I didn't say goodbye to him. I didn't see him one last time. He never knew –'

Why didn't this move her? Why didn't she feel anything but a vague sense of disconnection? She almost wanted to laugh and tell her son that this was all another hoax of Tony's.

'I can't believe it either.'

'But how will we . . . how will we live without him?'

'We'll get through this,' she reassured him, but she knew she sounded phoney even to herself. So instead, she asked Nick about the details of the skiing trip. But Nick's mind, which was usually so capricious, wouldn't be deviated today. Tony's departure had clearly sent him into a panic.

'But what about you? What about Ararat? Who's going to run it?'

'I don't see why things have to change too much,' Rachel said, bristling slightly. It seemed to have escaped Nick's notice that Ararat Holdings was a joint venture. That his parents had set up and continued to run the successful property company *together*. Forcing herself not to take offence, she moved away from him. 'There's no need to worry.'

'But wouldn't it be better if we sold it?'

So that you can get your hands on all the money, Rachel thought bitterly, noting the 'we' in Nick's question. 'No. *I* couldn't sell Ararat. That certainly wasn't in your father's and my plans.'

Rachel didn't want to have this conversation about business. Not now and certainly not with Nick. Ararat Holdings was hers and Tony's. It had nothing to do with Nick, or Christopher for that matter. She and Tony had made a decision long ago to educate them and let them go their own way.

Christopher, probably in reaction to seeing his elder sister Anna self-destruct, had followed a straight and narrow path into law. Nick, meanwhile, had changed his career like his cars and Rachel had lost count of the times Tony had bailed him out.

Now it occurred to Rachel that, with his father gone and

her saying that she wouldn't sell it, Nick thought that Rachel would involve him in Ararat. She loved Nick, but he was hardly the most reliable of her children and Ararat was too precious and too successful for her to let him make mistakes. No, Ararat's future would be decided by her and its current financial director and her grandson-in-law, Sam Delamere.

But she couldn't tell Nick any of this. Because Nick had always been so jealous of Claire and her husband Sam. He'd never been able to accept that Claire was Tony's little princess and that Tony had always treated Sam like his favourite son.

It was Tony who had taken Sam on as his protégé and had trained him up from the beginning, letting him manage a few villas, until he'd taken on the boutique hotels and had helped Tony expand the property portfolio. It was also Tony who had engineered it so that Sam would meet Claire. He'd encouraged their relationship right from the start and it had been a dream come true when they'd married the year before last.

Now Rachel thought about it, the most logical thing to do would be to ask Sam to run the company, now that Tony had gone. It was true that it was too much for her, and since Sam was virtually running Ararat's operations single-handedly from its central office on the Spanish island of Mallorca, it seemed the most natural thing that he should take over Tony's position. Yes, she thought, Sam was the only member of her family whose judgement she truly trusted. He was her rock and the sooner he got here the better.

'But don't you think –' Nick persisted.

'Nick, darling, do we have to discuss business now?' she stopped him. 'It's been a busy morning and I'm rather tired . . .'

She needed to reserve her strength for comforting Claire, not justifying herself to her son. Claire was the one who would need her the most.

'Of course. I'm being so selfish. Poor Mummy. You must feel so dreadful.'

Upstairs in her bedroom, Rachel kicked off her shoes and padded across the thick pile carpet to her walk-in cupboard. As she opened the door, the light came on automatically, illuminating rows of designer suits and shoes, and shelves stacked with the casual clothes she wore in the country.

She walked inside and started rifling through the rails, trying to select an outfit she could wear for the funeral. She knew she should dash up to London to get something special, but her thrifty nature had kicked in along with a sudden weariness at the thought of all the effort she was going to have to make over the next week. She knew that all eyes would be on her, but she also knew that Tony would be the first to tell her not to buy a new outfit on his behalf. Especially as he wouldn't be there to see it himself.

She pulled out a couple of suits and threw them on to the chair. Then she stopped, rubbed her face. She might as well admit to herself the reason that she was back in her cupboard. Steeling herself, she knelt down and pulled out the hatbox she'd deliberately unearthed nearly a week ago.

Maybe it was because in fifty years she'd never felt out of her depth, but her first reaction on Tony's death had been to turn to her brother Bill. As if on autopilot, she'd come to Somerset, walked into the house, gone upstairs and found the hatbox straight away. Inside had been a folder containing the papers she'd paid for from a private

51

detective, and had had constantly updated since, with the details of Bill's whereabouts.

It was the only secret that she'd ever kept from Tony. A secret she'd kept hidden in her closet for all this time. She'd felt giddy as she'd spread the papers out over the bed she'd shared with her husband. It had felt worse than if she'd been on the bed with a new lover.

For so long, Rachel had imagined that the day she'd contact her brother, the past would be magically erased. She'd acted on such a moment of impulse when she'd telephoned him that she'd honestly thought that Bill would answer the phone. She'd assumed that somehow he would have sensed this was her true hour of need and would have been waiting to come to the rescue.

What she hadn't expected was to speak to her niece, Laurel – or Laurie, as she liked to be known. She'd seen her name on the piece of paper the detective had given her, but she'd never imagined that she was a real person. Yet the sound of Laurie's voice, her suspicion and her obvious confusion, had jolted Rachel into reality. This wasn't a fantasy world where Bill would come running and forgive her. This was a messy, complicated situation and all at once she'd become aware of how much time had passed.

Rachel had appealed to Laurie, but she'd been able to tell, as the call had ended, that she'd made a fool of herself. For someone who had built a successful business by shrewdly playing the market and being an expert at negotiation, Rachel now felt as if she'd made a terribly bad move. She'd shown her hand and had opened herself up for rejection. What if Laurie hadn't mentioned her call to Bill? What if he didn't come to the funeral?

She knew that the likelihood was that her call would have stirred Bill's wrath, not his compassion. What if, on top of Tony's death, she now had proof that she'd lost Bill for ever, too. Because for so long she'd lived with a shred of hope. And what if that hope was gone? She shuddered at the thought. It was too much to even begin to contemplate.

Instead, she turned her attention to the papers in the box – the newspaper cuttings from the aftermath of the flood, fifty years old now and faded. They still managed to shock her – the images of the houses she'd known so well swept away by the sheer force of water, cars crushed, buried in mud and left upside down in the street. And worse, the tree way above the harbour bridge, where they'd found her mother's body after the waters had dropped, caught in the branches as if she'd been doing a cartwheel.

There were pictures, too, of the bedraggled survivors in the makeshift camp they'd set up after the flood. Even with the poor quality of the newspaper pictures, it was still possible to see the haunted look on the faces of the homeless and bereaved. She remembered it all as if it were yesterday.

She turned her attention to the stack of unopened letters addressed to Bill, dating back just as far, that were bound with plastic bands and marked RETURN TO SENDER. Behind them was the only surviving photograph of Bill and her with their parents. It had been sent to Rachel by a family friend after the flood, but was now sepia with age, a relic from a different era. It had been taken in the 1940s, sometime during the war – her father in his uniform, her mother smiling, holding on to her hat, her hair pinned up under it in a fashionable hairnet. Rachel had just been a kid, in brown sandals and a simple cotton dress. She stood next to Bill, holding his hand, and in the photograph, he was smiling down at her. They looked like the perfect family unit.

She'd felt so confused over the past few days, but one thought had remained constant: if anything good was to come out of Tony's death, then it had to be to reach some kind of reconciliation with her brother. With Tony gone, Bill was her only link to her past and there was so much that she hadn't resolved. So much that she still needed to understand.

Rachel closed her eyes for a second, feeling slightly dizzy. Everything about the future and the past seemed so fluid, as if everything she'd taken for granted could change at a moment's notice. Up until last week, she was with Tony, for ever. Fact.

Now she was starting to question every other fact about her life. The fact that for so long she'd only looked forward. The fact that she hadn't ever discussed her past or come to terms with what had happened in the Stepmouth flood. The fact that she'd promised Tony long ago never to mention Bill, as if by banning his name Rachel would stop thinking about him. But now, for the first time, she could admit the biggest fact of all – she hadn't stopped thinking about Bill, or needing him, or wanting his forgiveness and understanding. But now she was at his mercy. Until he called her back, or gave her some sign, she would just have to wait.

By the next morning, Rachel had slumped into a blank depression. The baby had kept her awake again, but she wouldn't have slept anyway. She dressed early and retreated to the office, slowly turning back and forth in Tony's large chair, her fingers clasped in front of her, as she stared at the aerial photograph which was mounted on the wall. It was of Sa Costa, the old *finca* in Mallorca that she and Tony had restored together. It was their family home, but today, rather than filling her with happy memories and the desire to go there immediately, she felt as if she'd somehow betrayed the life she'd built with Tony.

He filled her every thought. It was as if she could picture him right before her, telling her off for making such a rash decision to telephone her brother without once thinking of the consequences. In her mind, she tried to explain to him how she felt, but he bamboozled her with the force of his own feelings. They'd so rarely had a truly cross word between them, but now she could only picture him angry and stubborn. It brought back memories of the few times they'd argued, and this, in itself, made her feel ashamed and guilty.

It was almost lunchtime, when Brenda, the housekeeper, knocked at the door and interrupted her thoughts. Brenda was short with curly grey hair. For as long as Rachel could remember, she'd always worn a housecoat and today was no exception. She peered round the door, her unmade-up face comfortingly familiar.

'Call for you, Rachel,' she said. She'd never lost her Scottish lilt in all the years she'd been living in Somerset. 'Didn't you hear the phone?'

'Where is everyone?' Rachel asked.

'Christopher, Lucy and the baby are out, and I made Nick take poor old Benson for a walk. You need a cuppa?'

Rachel smiled wearily, years of happy communication between the two women meaning that Brenda instinctively understood her. She nodded, before picking up the phone.

'Yes?'

'Rachel? It's Laurie. Laurie Vale. We spoke the other day.'

Rachel jolted upright in the chair and clutched the phone with both hands.

'I don't know if I'm doing the right thing . . . I mean, I must be crazy . . .' Laurie's voice sounded agitated and Rachel tried to visualise her, but couldn't. All she kept seeing was a younger version of herself. 'I don't even know you. You're a complete stranger. I shouldn't be speaking to you at all, but I've decided to come to the funeral . . . if you want me to?' Laurie blurted out.

'Of course I want you to!' Rachel exclaimed. 'What . . . what about your father? Did you tell Bill I called?'

'I'll explain about Dad when I see you.'

'But . . . but you're coming? Oh . . .' Rachel said, smiling for the first time in a week. She couldn't believe she was having a conversation with her niece. She felt as if she'd been given a second chance.

When the short phone call was over, and Rachel had managed to persuade Laurie to agree to coming to stay the night before the funeral, she bowed her head and put her lips to the phone. 'Thank you,' she whispered.

Laurie's call gave Rachel just the boost of energy that she needed and helped to blast Tony's presence from the forefront of her mind. By the next morning, she'd bounced back to her natural state of hyperefficiency and had sorted out the best spare room for Laurie, organised all the flowers, taken a host of calls and had even spent several hours playing with Thomas so that Lucy could get some sleep.

A steady stream of respectful visitors descended on Dreycott Manor in the morning – family friends and well-wishers from the village. Rachel dealt with them all with a quiet grace, but their grief failed to touch her. She knew that everyone was eyeing her suspiciously, especially Christopher who seemed to be hovering in case she slipped into yesterday's 'difficult' mode and she offended someone.

Rachel was early to meet Laurie's train. She parked her Mercedes coupé in the small car park at the village station and turned off the engine. She pulled out the tiny silver compact from inside her handbag and checked her face, smoothing her dark red lipstick.

She'd tried to pretend to herself that Laurie coming here was no big deal. She was just another name on the ever expanding guest list for the funeral tomorrow, but as Rachel sat in the car, she knew that meeting Laurie was a huge step towards healing her past. Everything rested on being able to forge a relationship with this unknown young woman. If she could win over Laurie Vale, then perhaps she could eventually win over Bill. And if she could win over Bill – well, then everything might make sense.

She felt her pulse racing as she saw the train pull into the small platform and she got out of the car. And for the first time since Tony had died, Rachel felt truly alone. With each step she took towards the platform, she felt as if she were stepping along an unknown path, further and further away from everything she'd ever shared with Tony. For one second, she looked round towards her car. But it was too late to turn back. She had to go through with this, whatever the consequences might be.

And then she spotted Laurie, standing alone by the entrance to the car park. Her resemblance to Bill, even from a distance, made Rachel gasp. She was wearing a long, shapeless multicoloured wool coat, a long scarf twisted around her neck and big black lace-up boots. She had red hair, cropped very short, so that her high cheek-bones and huge almond-shaped eyes were striking, even from a distance. Rachel could feel her heart in her throat as she raised her arm to wave.

She'd been expecting Laurie to be tall, but Rachel stood

above her as they came face to face in the middle of the path.

'Hello, Laurie,' Rachel said, not sure whether to hug her, or to shake her hand. 'I'm Rachel. Your aunt . . .'

Rachel had been planning on covering her nervousness by launching into a friendly conversation and asking about Bill. But something about the way her niece was staring at her made her feel tongue-tied and exposed, and Rachel felt herself blushing for the first time in years.

And then, to Rachel's surprise, Laurie laughed, breaking the tension.

'I'm so sorry,' Laurie gushed, obviously flustered. 'I always laugh when I'm nervous. It's just that . . . you're so *not* like Dad! I mean, I don't mean to be rude, but I was expecting a little old lady with grey hair.'

Rachel laughed in return, mostly with relief. She now comprehended the huge risk she'd taken asking Laurie to her home. What if she'd been mousy, or insecure, or demanding? What if she'd been aggressive, or annoyed? Now she wanted to hug this strange young woman for being so normal.

'Believe me,' she said, 'there's a little old lady with grey hair inside.'

'Oh, I'm sorry. I'm being so insensitive. I'm sorry about –'

'Don't be,' Rachel interrupted quickly. 'You didn't know him, and besides, I'm so sick of everyone treading on eggshells around me. Listen, we've got a bit of time before we're due back at the house. Shall we go to the pub and not be sorry for a while?'

Rachel hadn't been to the village pub for several years, but it seemed to make sense to bring Laurie to the thatched-roofed old cider house. As much as she wanted to show off the picture-perfect village, she also wanted to get to know Laurie on neutral territory, to put her at her ease.

Tony used to come here to drink with his sons when they came home for Christmas, or to play a game of pool. As Rachel pushed up the latch and stepped down on to the worn old step, the smell of cigarette smoke, mixed with the wood fire and smell of beer, reminded her so strongly of the essence of Tony that, for a second, she couldn't breathe.

'So? Am I what you expected?' she asked Laurie, as they sat at the small table by the fireplace. They'd been chatting easily on the way to the pub and Rachel had learnt all about Laurie's life in London. Now she wanted to steer the conversation around to more urgent matters.

'I didn't know what to expect,' Laurie said. 'Up until a few days ago, I didn't even know that you existed.'

Rachel took a sip of her white wine. 'And how's Bill?' She tried to make it sound conversational, rather than desperate, but she failed at both. She'd been longing to ask Laurie about her father since the moment she'd seen her, but it was only now that she found the courage.

Laurie sighed. 'Very angry and upset. I've never argued with him before. He forbade me to see you. He said that you would ruin my life, like you ruined his. I'm sorry if that sounds harsh, but I might as well tell you the truth.'

Rachel nodded, feeling something crush inside her. But it was no more than she suspected, she reminded herself. She mustn't be too disappointed. After all, there was still hope. There was still Laurie, this brave young woman who Rachel found herself instantly drawn to.

'But you came anyway?' she asked.

'I was curious,' Laurie confessed. 'I always wanted a

family, you see. There was only ever me. No cousins, no siblings, no one. Not on my mother's side, either. I can't get over the fact that Dad kept you from me. That he kept you a secret. He made out you were some . . . I don't know. But clearly you're not what he thinks.'

Rachel smiled gently, feeling for Laurie and her obvious confusion. 'I guess Bill had his reasons for being angry with me.'

'What reasons, though? What did you argue about?'

'Mum mainly. He's got issues about our mother's death. And so many other things, I've lost count.'

'But your mother – my grandmother – she died in the village you both grew up in, didn't she? In the flood. Or is that a lie as well?'

'No, that's true. He told you that much at least.'

'He showed me the newspaper clippings. Grandma's name was down on the list of fatalities.' Laurie paused. 'Oh my God!' she said.

'What is it?'

'I remember now. The newspaper. It said my grandmother died, but her son and daughter survived. Dad told me it was a misprint. But it wasn't. It was you. I'll never forgive him for this.'

'Oh, Laurie, don't say that. We all have to keep hold of the ability to forgive.'

But Laurie wasn't listening.

'You're the only one, aren't you? There aren't any other brothers and sisters – I mean aunts and uncles – he hasn't told me about?'

'No, there's only me.'

'And what about my grandfather, Edward? Dad said he died in the war.'

'During the war, yes . . .'

60

'Dad said that he was shot. He never said any more about it.'

'No, neither of us ever did like to talk about it.' Rachel drew a full stop to the conversation then lightened up with a smile. 'Don't worry. Your father will come round, I'm sure,' she said.

'He won't. I know him. I saw his face. He'd kill me if he knew I was here.'

Rachel bowed her head. 'I didn't mean to cause you any heartache, Laurie. Believe me. And just for the record, I'm not going to ruin your life.'

And then the conversation moved on and Rachel began to fill Laurie in on the details of her family. She found it odd having to describe people she knew so well. She wanted to present everyone in the best possible light. She wanted Laurie to like her and her family as much as she found herself liking and admiring her niece.

'And Tony? I don't mean to pry, but how . . . how did he die?' Laurie asked, eventually.

'He had a heart attack. It was very quick.'

'I'm sorry.'

'We were on holiday.' Rachel hadn't told anyone this, not even Christopher and Nick. 'I thought he was joking. I thought he was fooling around at first. And then . . . then suddenly he was gone.'

Why could she tell Laurie this, when she couldn't even begin to express any of her emotions to her own children? Why was it easy to be honest with this stranger half her age? With Tony gone, she hardly had anyone to confide in, but somehow Laurie seemed distanced enough from her family for her to be able to tell her the truth. It felt like a huge relief just to be talking. Just to be herself for the first time since Tony had gone.

61

'Were you close?' Laurie asked.

Rachel stared at her, amazed that she could ask such a question.

'Oh, Laurie,' she said, feeling her chest contract with pain and tears unexpectedly swamping her eyes. 'You have no idea . . .'

# Chapter IV

**Stepmouth, March 1953**

Wiping the perspiration from his pale, freckled forehead on the back of his hand, Bill Vale angrily scratched his fingers through his shaggy dark auburn hair. He was a big, burly man and his shirt was stretched like a tarpaulin across his broad shoulders and back, glued there by a slick of sweat.

He drove the hoe hard into the heavy allotment ground, then went through the motion again and again, inching forward, slicing through bramble roots, decapitating nettles, churning over the lugubrious soil for planting, pausing only occasionally to bend down and pick out rocks and stones as they sparked off the hoe, before slinging them into the nearby hedgerow.

His face was kind and approachable, with sharply defined cheekbones, a short straight nose and a dependable square jaw. Only his eyes stopped him from being handsome. Light brown in colour, where they could have been doe-like and soft, instead they appeared hard and as tough as teak.

When he reached the end of the rectangle which he'd marked out with four rows of canes and a length of parcel string, he stood up straight. He stabbed the hoe into the ground and watched it quiver there like a spear. He was exhausted but, even so, there was a crease of a smile at the corner of his mouth. He liked being up here alone, away from the town and the shop, responsible for no one but himself.

The allotment was one of thirty council-owned plots of land into which this field on the brow of Summerglade Hill had been divided during the war. A few weeks ago, it had been nothing but a thatch of weeds and thorn. All Bill's own fault. He'd let it go to seed following his father's death. But now he'd cleared it and only the planting was left to do.

As a reward, he took a thin flat square of Nestlé's milk chocolate from his pocket, peeled off its foil wrapping and slipped it into his mouth, savouring every second of its luxurious sweetness as it melted on his tongue.

Bill's father had taken on the allotment when the army had sent him home to his family in time for Christmas of 1944, after a piece of German shrapnel had torn a four-inch gash in his face and melted his right eye like ice. He'd never made use of the glass eye he'd been given, electing instead to wear a brown leather eyepatch.

'Makes me look more like a pirate and less like a freak' was how he'd explained it to Bill as they'd sat up here talking one sunny Sunday, as the war had raged on across Europe. 'Stops people from staring so much.'

Bill had always worshipped his father. 'They stare because you're a hero, Dad,' he'd answered. 'Because it's thanks to you and other people like you that we're going to win the war.'

They'd been resting on a fallen tree, the two of them, after a long afternoon spent pulling up beetroots, potatoes and onions. Distorted snatches of conversations from the other townspeople tending to their allotments drifted towards them on the breeze, and gnats and flies buzzed lazily in the warm currents of air.

'When you consider how lucky I am, it's funny that I give a damn for what people think,' Bill's father continued, as if his son hadn't spoken, 'but I do.' He was dressed in scruffy brown cords and a worn red pullover ('The Pope's pullover', as he'd always called it, on account of how holey it had been).

'Why lucky, Dad?'

'Because the two lads I was with when that shell hit never made it out.'

Thinking of his dad lying bleeding and covered in rubble and dust in a bombed-out farmhouse was something Bill had never been able to get a grip on. Bill had never hurt anyone in his life, but he wanted to hurt the bastards who'd hurt his dad. He wanted to hurt them bad. He'd turn eighteen later the next year, but the war would be over by then, everyone said, and then there'd be no one left to fight.

'I wish I could have been with you, Dad,' Bill said. 'I wish I could have been there to help.'

'I don't, son.'

'Why not?'

'Because someone needed to be here to take care of your mother and sister.'

'But —'

His father looked up at him sharply. 'I mean it. And if it's help you want to give me, then that's the best there is. To always look after them. To watch over them when I'm not there. To be there when they need you. No matter what.'

'But you're back now, Dad —'

'I said no matter what.'

'All right, Dad,' Bill told him. 'I always will. No matter what.'

The smell of burning foliage reached them, along with

the crackle of twigs. A hundred yards away, a stick-thin figure was busy flapping a blanket over a bonfire, drawing the flames up high. Bill stared at the tiny grey clouds accelerating towards the sky, the gaps between them growing wider and wider as they went. Like smoke signals, he thought, from a Red Indian's fire.

'You're a good lad,' his father told him as he stood up.

Bill's mother was leaning over the raspberry canes, with her bare arms outstretched and her bright white apron strings glinting in the sun. Eight-year-old Rachel was sitting at her feet, with hair like the flames of the bonfire, licking all the way down to her waist. Bill watched his father walk towards them. At Rachel's side was a cloth-lined wicker basket from which she was sneaking handfuls of raspberries whenever their mother's back was turned. Mid-mouthful, Rachel spotted their father and squealed and leapt up and scampered away.

'Stop thief!' their father roared dramatically, before giving chase.

Their laughter was contagious, and Bill grinned at them darting between the raspberry canes and around the lettuce patch.

But now their laughter was gone.

Nine summers had past by since that day. The fallen tree on which Bill had been sitting had long since rotted into the ground. He stared across the desolate patch of ground where he'd once watched his family play.

'No matter what,' he said aloud.

He turned round and gazed into the distance.

The view from up here on top of Summerglade Hill was like an aerial photograph. Below and straight ahead – to the north – was Bill's home town of Stepmouth and, beyond that, the Bristol Channel. Watercolour green and watercolour brown, the moors rolled out along the coastline to the east and west.

Summerglade Hill itself was flanked by the two deep, steep, wooded valleys of the East and West Step Rivers. The sum of a myriad tributaries which had drained off the heights of Exmoor behind, these rivers had already dropped two miles in altitude by the time they'd got this far. Usually slow-running, they were temporarily heavy from the recent rainfall, and as their gradients grew steeper still, they began cascading from one short waterfall to the next, as if running down a flight of steps.

Some eight hundred feet below, near the foot of Summerglade Hill, the twin rivers converged at Watersbind, where the hydroelectric power station harnessed their power. A single river, the Step, emerged from this bubbling, frothing pool, flowing beneath the great stone arch of Watersbind Bridge, and over another hundred-foot stretch of rapids, before finally levelling out and rumbling through the Step Valley and into a deep-carved channel which ran clean through the centre of Stepmouth.

The estuary town spread out both east and west from here, contained to the north by a grey eyelid of rocky beach and the great green eye of the sea. Two bridges connected the two divided sides of Stepmouth: South Bridge crossed the river where it entered the town and Harbour Bridge where it fanned out into the sea.

A jumble of crooked houses and hotels crowded out over each side of the river channel, like beasts seeking to slake their thirst, and among them was Vale Supplies, the grocery store where Bill lived and worked. A two-storey, semi-detached brick building, it was one of the first shops you encountered on the main road into town. Bill had been born there twenty-six years before in 1927.

'But can't die there,' he said, surprising himself that he'd spoken the words aloud.

The thought of being anchored to this tiny corner of the world for the rest of his life filled him with horror. Yet in the same breath, he doubted his ability to leave. He'd tried before and he'd failed.

He'd made his break, going to Durham University in 1948 to study civil engineering after he'd done his national service in the army. But he'd only lasted six months, before returning home to run the shop. Exhaustion . . . it had been etched into his mother's brow and bagged beneath her eyes at the end of his second term at Durham. Although she hadn't complained once, he'd realised the moment he'd seen her that it had finally started proving too much for her, managing the shop and bringing up Rachel. And so he'd given his studies up.

And now he couldn't – *wouldn't* – leave, not while he was still needed here. He'd vowed that much to his dad.

Can't die here, then, but probably would.

Years ago, he used to imagine this view being covered with structures he'd engineered himself. He'd dreamt of fantastical bridges spanning the rivers, a great pier to rival Brighton's, funicular railways climbing the hills and the pinnacle of an opera house reaching for the sky.

He still had the drawings under his bed at home, along with his collapsed drawing board and the one photo he'd kept of Susan Castle, the girl he'd been engaged to at university, but who'd broken up with him after he'd dropped out, and not joined him here as he'd hoped.

But enough of dreams. And regrets. He checked his silver-plated wristwatch. Its glass face was cracked. His father had been wearing it the day he'd died. Bill had never got it fixed, preferring to be reminded of what had happened each time he looked at it. He never wanted to forget his dad.

Bill walked over to his old black Norton motorcycle, which he'd fixed up with the help of his best friend Richard Horner. Mounting the bike, he gunned it into life and pushed it across the rough ground to the road. It was half past seven already: time to get back to the shop and start the working day.

At the bottom of Summerglade Hill, Bill drove straight over the crossroads and on to the high street. Halfway down, outside the freshly painted church hall, a couple of schoolboys were play-fighting in front of the *Viva Zapata!* poster glued to the green metal bus stop. Several cars could be seen in the car park at the harbour end of the street.

Bill turned right almost immediately, driving beneath the lolling branches of a towering oak tree and into the alleyway which ran between Vale Supplies and Giles Weatherly's ironmongery store next door.

Cutting the engine, Bill propped the Norton up on its stand, behind Giles's delivery van and then rolled himself a smoke. It was a habit he'd taken up during his time he'd spent in the army. He'd hoped to see the world, even fight, but he'd ended up in a barracks in Yorkshire instead, learning how to shine boots and march in them.

An alley door led directly into his family's house, but Bill went through into the tiny backyard instead. He stripped off his shirt and washed the dirt from his hands and face with freezing water from the tap. As he towelled himself dry, he peered over the back fence which his father had erected to keep him and his sister safe as kids.

Several feet below, the River Step sparkled in its channel.

Boulders broke its surface every couple of yards, as grey and slick as seals. Bill loved the sound of the chattering water. He'd been brought up on it. Quite literally. Supported on struts, his bedroom had been built out over the yard, so that it now stretched out over his head, protruding over the river.

It was the same with all the terraced houses backing on to both sides of the river channel. With nowhere else to expand, they'd pushed out backwards, so that now the gap between the properties on the east side and west side of town was less than twenty feet.

Inside the kitchen, it smelt of polish and Drummer pine disinfectant. Dried bunches of lavender hung from the creosoted beam which cut the low white-plastered ceiling in two. The gas stove gleamed as good as it had done when they'd had it installed five years ago. Brass pots and pans and stainless-steel ladles and knives glinted on the wall.

Bill walked on through the parlour and into the gloomy hallway, only to find his mother, wrapped in a heavy blue dressing gown, sitting patiently at the bottom of the stairs. She was a pretty woman, aged forty-six, with dark hair and a generous smile which failed to conceal entirely a perpetual sadness in her eyes.

'Good morning, William.'

'Mum . . .' He leant down to kiss her, a puzzled frown agitating his brow. 'What are you –' *doing there*, he'd been about to ask. But he'd already guessed. He reared up. 'Rachel!' he bellowed up the stairs.

'Don't waste your breath,' said Mrs Vale. 'She can't hear.'

'Won't hear, more like,' Bill retorted, before demanding, 'How long have you been waiting here?'

'Well, not long . . . you see, I was going to try and see if I could . . .' Mrs Vale didn't look at him as she spoke and he guessed that she was trying not to get Rachel in trouble. The fact was, she'd probably been sitting here waiting for half an hour.

'She should have come down to help.'

'Well, you're here now,' his mother said hopefully, 'so why don't we just –'

'Just what, Mum? Pretend it didn't happen? Pretend she's not as selfish and lazy as she is? Rachel!' he shouted up the stairs again.

Still he got no response.

'You were exactly the same when you were her age,' Mrs Vale tried pointing out.

But Bill wasn't listening. He and his sister were nothing alike. He did; she did as little as she could: that was the plain fact of the matter.

'She knew I'd dropped your chair round at Giles's last night,' he said. 'I told her before you went to bed. And I told her I was going up to the allotment first thing this morning, so it would be up to her to help you out this morning.'

His mother's wheelchair. That was the chair he was talking about. One of its wheels had seized up and he'd taken it next door for Giles Weatherly to mend.

Ever since Mrs Vale had lost the use of her legs, she'd worked hard at making herself as independent as she could. She was a methodical woman, who still kept the store's accounts immaculate, and who'd also developed a system giving her almost full mobility around the house. She had two wheelchairs, one upstairs and one down, and could negotiate the stairs between herself. Apart from this morning, when – as Rachel had known – Mrs Vale would have to make do with just one.

'I'll fetch it down for you now,' Bill told her.

The moment his mother had wheeled herself into the kitchen to make breakfast, Bill ran back up the stairs and glared up at the ladder which led to his sister's attic room. The chipped, yellow-painted trapdoor at the top was shut and pinned to it was a notice in Rachel's erratic handwriting, which read:

Rachel's Place!
No Bill Stickers!
No Bill Vale either!

'Selfish little cow,' he growled.

He climbed up and unceremoniously punched the trapdoor open with the butt of his hand, listening with grim satisfaction as it keeled over and slammed down on the floor above.

That'll teach her, he thought. That'll make her sit up and listen.

Emerging through the opening into the crepuscular light of Rachel's pot-pourri-scented room, Bill saw that she hadn't, in fact, moved at all. On her face was a look of beatific peace. Everything about her, in fact – from the statuesque folds of the white sheet which covered her body, to the healthy blush of her cheeks – spoke of the serene, as if she were no mere mortal at all, but rather an angel drifted down from heaven during the night.

All of which pissed Bill off more than he could ever have expressed.

Bill tore down the thin green material which covered the skylight and let the sunlight flood in.

But still she didn't stir.

He reached forward to shake her. But then he froze midmotion as a better idea entered his mind. Bill wasn't a cruel man and, in spite of his present mood, he did love his too-big-for-her-boots little sister. But a short, sharp shock would do her good. He leant in closer. He'd get his mouth as close to her ear as possible . . . and then he'd fill his lungs . . . and then he'd –

It was a magnificent roar, an emperor of a roar, the roar of two half-starved, five-hundred-pound Bengal tigers fighting over lunch. It was the kind of roar which vibrated crockery off shelves, the kind of roar which could have torn down the walls of Jericho, and undoubtedly the right kind of roar to put the fear of God up a lazy, good-for-nothing, seventeen-year-old girl and show her who was boss.

Aside from one salient fact: it was Rachel who'd roared, not Bill.

Just as Bill's lungs had reached their maximum capacity, just as he'd opened his mouth to bellow into Rachel's ear with all his might and convert her into a quaking, gibbering, respectful wreck . . . her eyes had flashed open and she'd emitted an ear-piercing roar of her own.

Jumping back, Bill cracked his skull on the beam above and dust avalanched down.

'Get up!' he shouted, rubbing furiously at his eyes.

'I am,' she yelled back. And – he now saw – she was. She'd leapt up and, tearing the sheets from around her, she now strode towards him in her crumpled white night-shirt. 'Get out!'

'What?'

'Out!' she repeated. 'Now!'

'Now you listen to me –' he started.

'No, you listen to me. You know what it says on the door. You know you're not allowed.'

He tried to be calm, tried to remain the adult. 'I'm not going until you listen to what I've got to say.'

'Go ahead then, talk. Talk as much as you bloody well like and *then* get out.' She stood there, glowering at him.

'Do you know what I came back from the allotment to find?' he began.

'Let me guess,' she said, 'a nuclear bomb?'

'No, actually,' he said, electing to ignore the sarcasm. 'Mum: sitting at the bottom of the stairs.'

Rachel's lip curled. 'Gosh. Our own mother. In our own house. What do you want, a medal?'

'Do you know why she was sitting there?'

'Shock me.'

'Because you were too bloody lazy to get up and carry her chair down for her,' he snapped.

'Don't swear at me,' she said.

'Why not?'

'Because I'll just swear bloody right back at you.' But then her expression suddenly altered. 'What do you mean Mum needed help to get in her chair? Oh,' she then said, her expression suddenly altering again, 'you took the other chair over to Giles's house last night, didn't you? And I was meant to . . . shit . . .' Crestfallen, she clamped her hand over her mouth. 'I'm sorry,' she said. 'I'm sorry, I forgot.'

He was tempted to say more. To tell her that sorry wasn't good enough. And that they had to work as a team, because if they didn't, then the whole thing – their business, their family – would fall apart. And to tell her that it was his responsibility to look out for them all and to keep them safe. To remind her that that was what he'd come home to do.

'Tell it to Mum,' he told her instead.

Because there was no point in lecturing Rachel. Because

he already knew what she thought: that he was interfering, petty and dull. And that she didn't want him to act like a father towards her, because she was old enough now to look after herself.

And, looking at her now, he was beginning to see that she was probably right.

Bill had only a couple of deliveries to make that afternoon and, as he set out from the alley on the shop bicycle, he was clean-shaven, with his fingernails scrubbed, his starched white shirt sharply creased and his previously unruly hair now pacified with a wet brush. In every way, he was as orderly and well presented as the shop itself.

The high street was quiet with the morning's shopping mostly done and people now at lunch. A heady mix of beer, cider and smoke funnelled from the windows of the Channel Arms and the Smuggler's Rest, while the acrid vinegary whiff of battered cod and saveloys drifted through the doorway of the Captain Ahab fish-and-chip shop.

Bill cycled quickly past, waving to grey-haired John Mitchell, who was leaning out of his upstairs window, watering the hanging baskets of daffodils above his bright orange front door.

At the corner of Bay Street, liver-spotted, tittle-tattling Mrs Carver flagged Bill down and made him promise to remind his mother about the Women's Institute meeting that Saturday afternoon.

Then Bill was off again, turning right at the end of the high street, before juddering along the cobbled quayside, weaving around the lapping cats and slapdash vermilion splashes of spilt mackerel guts. The tide was out and fishing boats lay tilted on the chocolatey muddy harbour bottom to his left. The briny stink of drying fishing nets was all around.

Bill's stomach sprung like a jack-in-the-box as he rode over the stony hump of Harbour Bridge. He pumped the pedals round faster, charging like a knight on a steed through a fluttering explosion of indignant squawking seabirds.

His first delivery – tea, coffee, Cadbury's Fingers – was to the utilitarian and uninspiring red-brick town hall, which slunk beside St Hilda's Church. Bill, his mother and his sister had been members of the church's congregation for as long as Bill could remember. This last Sunday gone, he'd stood behind his mother's wheelchair for twenty minutes in the cool shade cast down by the church's clock tower, staring at the immaculate granite crucifix which marked his father's grave.

The second delivery was to another of Bill's regulars: the Sea Catch Café. It had been run by Mr and Mrs Alun Jones for the last thirty years, although recently there'd been rumours – largely spread by Mr Jones, who was keen to retire to his homeland of Wales – of them putting the place up for sale. Only his wife, Mavis, having no one to hand the business over to, was yet to be convinced. Their natural successor and only child, a disgraced daughter, had run off with an American during the war.

The Sea Catch Café was a three-storey building, double the width of Vale Supplies, backing on to the opposite river bank. Downstairs were the tearooms and restaurant. Mr and Mrs Jones lived upstairs and also kept a few rooms for bed and breakfast.

Bill leant his bike up against the wall of the side alley, next to the bins and their attendant stink of boiled pota-toes and fried onions. Tucking the packed brown paper grocery bag from the bike's basket under one arm, he reached out to knock at the door.

Before his knuckles connected with it, however, the door swung open, revealing Tony Glover, whose face promptly turned ashen.

'Still here, then?' Bill said. He looked Glover unwaveringly in the eye. 'Alun's not fired you yet, then? Not given you your notice?'

Glover scratched at his brow, not answering.

'He will.' Bill said. 'You'll mess up. Just you wait. You won't be able to help yourself. And when you do, no one else will give you a job. And then you'll know it's time to leave this town.'

Glover lowered his hand from his face. And that's when Bill saw it: the swelling on Glover's eye, the cut above, and the bruising on his nose.

'So who do I owe a drink to?' Bill asked.

'What?'

'For giving you the kicking you no doubt deserved,' Bill explained.

'I fell over.'

Bill wanted to hurt Glover, like whoever it was who had done this to him. He wanted it bad. But that would make him no better than Glover, he reasoned. That would make him an animal, too.

Bill thrust the bag roughly at Glover.

'Tell Alun everything's there,' he said. He glared at Glover, hard. 'And hurry up,' he told him. 'Or I'll be putting in another complaint to your boss.'

The doorbell rang with a brittle chime as Bill opened the front door of Vale Supplies and stepped inside. The white-and-black-tiled floor was spotless from when he'd mopped it that morning. Familiar products were stacked up high and in symmetrical order on the shelves: wide, cylindrical jars of sweets, canned soups and vegetables, bottled sauces and jars of instant coffee and cocoa, packets of suet and semolina, and boxes of scouring powders, soap flakes and oats.

Mrs Macgregor was wedged into the shop's public telephone booth, gripping the black Bakelite handset like a cosh, as she gave her weekly lecture on the perils of drink to her son Arthur, who'd moved to Bristol three years before. Behind the burnished counter, Rachel was up the old wooden shop ladder, reaching for a bottle of Camp Coffee and Chicory Essence from the top shelf. She brought it down and rang the sale up on the black till, before bagging the bottle and handing it over to Norman Miller with a smile.

'Bill,' Norman said civilly, tipping his trilby in acknowledgement. He had a son, Alan, who was Bill's age. He'd gone away to university at the same time as Bill and now lived in London with a good job at a bank and a pretty wife and a baby boy.

'Beware of Bristol,' Mrs Macgregor remarked cryptically as she followed Mr Miller outside. 'It's a crucible of sin . . .'

It was stifling inside and Bill wedged the door open after her, then turned to his sister, who'd picked up a magazine. She looked up and smiled at him like the morning's argument had never occurred. Capricious didn't come close. Teenage girls, he thought. He'd never understood them when he'd been a teenager himself, so what chance did he have now?

Rachel closed her magazine. It was a copy of *Illustrated*, with Marilyn Monroe on the cover, glistening with diamonds and wearing a low-cut red-and-black lace dress.

'What do you think?' she asked, holding Monroe's face up next to her own.

'About the diamonds?' he teased. 'Oh yes, they'd really suit you.'

She rolled her eyes. 'I mean the hair. Do you think I should change my colour to match hers?'

'Would it make you happy?'

'It might get me a new boyfriend.'

He chose to overlook the use of the word 'new', which implied that she already had one.

'You're too young for boyfriends,' he said.

'And you're too old not to have a girlfriend,' she countered.

'How about me? Am I the right age to get served?'

Bill turned round to see a woman standing behind him. There was something familiar about her face and, for a moment, he thought he'd seen her before, but then he decided he was mistaken.

Like Bill, she was in her mid-twenties. In her hand was a small black leather suitcase, plastered with shipping stickers. She looked impossibly modern. And . . . stylish? Was that the right word, Bill wondered, to describe a woman like this? Because her clothes – a distractingly short skirt with a matching shiny blue jacket, tapered in around her waist by a wide white belt – were cut in a way he'd never seen outside of magazines, and certainly not here in the shop, close enough to touch. Not, it occurred to him with a sudden blush, that he should be thinking about touching it at all.

'Hi,' she said, smiling brightly.

Bill opened his mouth to speak, but nothing came out.

She took a step closer to him. Then another. Then she peered into his eyes. 'Are you OK?' she asked. Her accent sounded American, only softer. Perhaps Canadian, he thought.

'Er . . .'

As she stared at him, *into* him, he suddenly felt that it was vital that he say something interesting in reply – that she was the kind of woman who *deserved* an interesting reply, *expected* one even – and that she'd be so, *so* disappointed if he let her down.

'Er . . .'

'Is he always like this?' the woman asked Rachel.

'Only on days with a Y in them,' Rachel answered.

The woman grinned. 'Very droll,' she said. 'I like that.'

Putting her suitcase down, the woman seemed to lose interest in Bill and, instead, started looking around the shop. Her hair was short, blonde and tightly curled, and she wore a bright red hat perched on top of it which matched her lipstick and nail polish. She had a beauty spot on her jaw to the left of her wide curved lips.

'Candy,' the woman then announced, stopping in front of the glass-topped section of the counter, beneath which the more expensive sweets were displayed. 'I mean sweets,' she corrected herself. 'I need to buy some. As a gift.'

'Allow me to –' Rachel began.

'– help you,' Bill said, completing his sister's sentence for her. He walked behind the counter and brushed firmly past Rachel, ignoring the indignant look she shot him. He stood opposite the woman, and as she stared down at the neatly aligned bars of chocolate laid out beneath the glass screen, he gazed at her reflection.

'I'm going for a break,' Rachel announced behind him.

'Take your time,' Bill answered without looking round.

'How about that big bar of Rowntree's York chocolate?' the woman decided, tapping the glass with her fingernail.

'Of course.' Bill smiled at her. The woman smiled back. Gosh, he thought. Having her smile at him felt pretty good. 'You'll need to register first,' he then said, remembering himself.

'Register?'

'Your ration book. Before making a purchase.'

'You're kidding, right?' she said.

'Er, no . . .'

'You mean I can't just give you cash?'

'No,' he said. 'Rationing still applies to sweets.'

'Well, Jesus H. Christ,' she declared, 'if that doesn't take the biscuit – not that I imagine even *he* could actually take the biscuit,' she reflected, 'not unless he had his ration book too, right?'

'Right,' Bill said, trying not to smile.

'Well, shit, shit, shit to that. Oh, God,' she said, 'and sorry . . .' She waved her arm apologetically. 'Sorry for swearing. And for blaspheming. They're both habits I guess I should kick now that I've come back home.'

He shrugged. He didn't know what to say. The truth was he rather liked the way she swore. 'Home?' he enquired.

'Yep.' Her grey eyes scanned the shelves behind him. 'Don't suppose a tin of pilchards would make much of a present, now, would it?'

'No.'

Her gaze switched back to him, suddenly serious. 'I'm at a loss. All the way from New York without a gift. God, I'm such a jerk.' She took a final lingering look at the Rowntree's bar, then sighed, turning to go.

A thought occurred to him. 'No, wait.'

'What?'

'I've got an idea.'

She looked at him expectantly. 'So shoot.'

'I could let you choose some chocolate and take it off my rations for next week.'

'No.' She was adamant. 'I couldn't possibly.'

But this was suddenly something he really wanted to do for her. 'I insist.' He took out the red-and-white Rowntree's bar and held it out to her.

She stared at the chocolate. 'Well, I've got to admit,' she said, 'you would be getting me out of a scrape. But what about you?' she asked.

'I'll survive without. I haven't got much of a sweet tooth, to tell the truth,' he lied.

'Yeah? Well, OK then,' she said, beaming at him. She took the chocolate bar and slipped it into her jacket pocket. 'But only if you let me pay you back.'

'I'm not allowed to take money for –' he started to explain.

'No, I mean when I register here. You know, after I get my ration book all worked out.'

'Oh. How long are you staying?'

'A while.' She laughed nervously. 'Maybe even a long while, who knows?'

He walked round the counter to join her. 'How far is it you're going?'

'Not far.'

'Let me take your bag,' he offered.

'Thanks, but no thanks.'

He lowered his eyes, embarrassed.

'Sorry.' She touched his arm. 'I didn't mean it to sound like that. I mean, I'd be happy to walk with you any other time, only, like I say, I've been away a long time and, well, I'd rather arrive by myself.'

'It's all right. I understand.'

She smiled at him sweetly, then patted her pocket. 'Thanks for the loan of the chocolate.' She reached out her hand. 'I'm Emily, by the way.'

He shook her hand. Her skin was cold to the touch, but he could have held it longer. 'Bill.'

She looked him straight in the eye, before adding, 'Emily Jones.'

He shrugged, acting like it meant nothing, even though it did. Emily Jones. The daughter of Alun and Mavis, the owners of the Sea Catch Café. Emily Jones, who'd briefly scandalised the town by defying her parents and running off with an American navigator near the end of the war when she'd just turned eighteen.

So he had recognised her, after all. Even though she'd changed so much in the eight years she'd been away. He'd never spoken to her while she'd been living here, but he remembered all right, how people had gossiped at the time and how her mother had acted like she'd been in mourning ever since. He wondered if Emily knew about him, and his father, and the far greater scandal which had taken place here at the shop barely a month after she'd left. But the brightness of her smile said no.

It was a smile he'd be thinking about for the rest of the day. 'Well, welcome home, Emily Jones,' he said.

'Assuming that my mother agrees that I do still have a home to come back to,' she said. 'So knock on wood, hey? For luck.' She did just that, rapping her knuckles hard against the counter.

'Good luck,' he said, meaning it. 'Hopefully I'll see you around,' he added, meaning that, too.

'Thanks,' she answered. 'You will.'

He followed her to the open doorway and watched her as she walked away.

Behind him, he heard Rachel coming back into the shop. 'So who was she?' she called out.

'Just someone new,' Bill answered, not taking his eyes off Emily Jones until she rounded the corner at the end of the street.

# Chapter V

**Somerset, Present Day**

Peering through the rain-drenched windscreen, Sam Delamere could smell the cigarette smoke on Claire from when she'd chain-smoked two Marlboros between the airport arrivals hall and the car park.

'What do you think this is, National Village Idiot Day? Pull over! Get out of the fucking way!' Claire yelled at the oblivious driver of the rusty red Mini which was trundling along the potholed road in front of them. 'Do you know why I hate the stupid English countryside?' she demanded of Sam, who was driving. 'Because it's full of stupid English cu—'

'Please stop,' Sam said.

'Stop what?'

'You know what.'

'Well, obviously I don't. Because if I did, then I wouldn't be fucking well asking you, would I?'

'That,' said Sam. 'Swearing. Saying fuck. Whatever. In front of Archie. Just don't, OK?'

'But you just said it yourself,' she scoffed.

'Only to illustrate what I was talking about.'

'You still said it.'

He sighed, pushing his straight sandy-brown hair back from his tanned brow. Here it was: the same old thing: her trying to reduce their conversation to the level of childish bickering the moment she was put on the defensive. She was twenty-eight, only seven years younger than Sam, but sometimes she made him feel more like the father she'd never known, than the husband he was.

His instinct, of course, was to fight his corner, but he bit it down. Claire thrived on conflict and, given half a chance, would only use his reaction to escalate their argument into a full-blown row. And he wasn't going to let that happen, not today, not when what she really needed was his support.

Instead, he tried to see the situation for what it was: her just picking a fight; him just happening to be in her firing line. She was angry and upset about the death of her grandfather, Tony, and lashing out at Sam was her way of dealing with it. He understood. He was upset, too.

'Fine,' he said. 'So I swore. So I was wrong.' He knew that the easiest way to bring this conversation to a close was to make her think she'd won.

'Wrong,' Claire chimed in confirmation.

Sam's pale blue eyes darkened. 'So I won't say it again. And I'd appreciate it if you didn't either.'

Claire twisted round and stared at Archie, who was strapped into a black baby seat in the back of the rented MPV, which they'd picked up from Luton airport two hours ago.

'Little Archie doesn't understand, anyway. Do you, babe?' She addressed their son in the awkward, sing-song baby-talk voice she always used with him. Reaching out, she smoothed down the two-and-a-half-year-old's wiry brown hair, and watched as it promptly sprung back up again, like bracken after a storm. 'Clucking, chucking,' she said, 'mucking, fucking . . . they're all the same to you, aren't they, sweetie? Just silly grown-up words . . .'

'I got yo-yo,' Archie announced, holding up the fluorescent-yellow plastic toy which Sam had picked up at a store in Palma airport. 'I want Gramps and Nanna,' he added.

These were the names Archie had given Sam's parents.

'Not today. We're going to see Grandma Rachel today,' Claire said.

'Gramps and Nanna,' Archie repeated.

Claire's voice grew terse. 'I said not today.'

'Gramps and –'

'That's enough, Archie,' she snapped. 'Now be quiet.'

Archie started to wail.

'What Mummy means,' Sam soothed, 'is you can go and see them another time. Soon. Daddy will take you soon. OK?'

'They spoil him, you know,' Claire said. 'That's why he's always whinging about going to see them.'

'How would you know?' Sam was referring to the fact that Claire had only visited his parents once since Archie had been born. Sam brought Archie to see them every few months, but Claire always managed to find somewhere else she needed to be.

Claire groaned. 'Please let's not get into this now,' she said.

Sam accelerated past the Mini and into the winding country lanes.

'I love you, Mummy,' Archie said.

Claire reached back and squeezed Archie's knee. 'I love you, too, sweetie.'

Sam glanced in the rear-view mirror to see Archie beaming him a crooked smile, which melted Sam's heart.

'Still,' Claire continued, 'at least your parents have the decency to live in a town. Why Grandma and Pops insisted on buying this dreary old pile out here in the middle of nowhere is something I'll never understand.'

So they could send you to the expensive Catholic girls' school down the road, was the answer Sam knew but didn't say. Because you got yourself expelled from the International School in Mallorca for dealing grass to your friends. Because your grandparents were terrified that you'd turn out like your mum, who walked out on you right after you were born and OD'd in a Parisian squat a year later.

Not that either the relocation or the expensive school had done Claire any good, Sam reflected. She'd been expelled from her new English school, too, after having been caught wrapped around a handsome guitar teacher in the photography darkroom. She'd moved back to Mallorca, then. Instead of punishing her, the ever-indulgent Rachel and Tony had set her up in a back-street apartment in Palma old town, overlooking the flying buttresses and sandstone pinnacles of La Seu Cathedral. Which was where she and Sam had met.

Sam turned off the country lane and on to the long, straight, frost-pocked driveway which led to Dreycott Manor. Gravel crunched beneath the tyres. He turned to Claire and saw tears streaming down her face. Pulling over, he took her hand and gently squeezed it. Rain rattled on the roof.

'I never thought he'd die. I never thought about it once,' Claire said, rubbing at her eyes, smearing mascara across her cheeks. 'I thought Pops was indestructible.'

'I know.' Sam had worked for Tony for almost a decade. And just as Tony had treated Claire like his own daughter, so he'd come to treat Sam like one of his own sons. Or even better than his sons, Sam remembered Claire having once remarked.

Sam kept hold of Claire's hand. They stared up the avenue of emaciated, wintering chestnut trees to Dreycott Manor's wide and symmetrical Georgian façade. Only the beat-up blue Ford, belonging to Brenda, the housekeeper, was parked out front, which meant the other family members – Rachel, Nick, Christopher and Lucy, in their Aston Martins and Mercs – had probably already left for the church, to be there in time to greet their fellow mourners as they arrived.

'Do I look awful?' Claire asked.

'No.' Her long black hair was piled luxuriantly on top of her head, but her sallow complexion worried Sam. As did the ash-grey bags beneath her eyes. She was skinny from too many cigarettes and late nights. He squeezed her hand tighter. 'You look beautiful, the same as you always do,' he reassured her. 'You're as beautiful as the day I met you.'

Sam and Claire's relationship had started with a bang. Literally. They'd jumped into bed within five minutes of meeting each other on a warm afternoon in September 1994.

Looking down at her in the cool tiled hallway of her Palma apartment, as she'd set about unbuttoning his Levi's, the last thing Sam had imagined was that they'd still be together nearly a decade later.

He'd thought it was just casual sex. It had happened to him a couple of times before, after evenings spent kissing smoky, often drunk strangers in noisy London nightclubs after he'd left university. But it had never happened to him sober, never this quick, and never in the broad light of day. Not like now.

As she swept her long dark hair back from her face –

'she', because he hadn't yet learnt her name – and he let out a low groan, he thought how pretty she was and about how her brown eyes and tanned skin made her seem impossibly exotic compared with the quiet, pale-skinned girl he'd broken up with in London a month before.

He glimpsed the tiny tattooed ☺ on her bare ankle and wondered if it had hurt, and who she'd been with when she'd had it done. He wondered, too, if the new aftershave he was wearing possessed an aphrodisiac quality which might explain this otherwise totally inexplicable, yet fortuitous, turn of events. He also thought about her age.

'When was the last time you had sex with someone fit, foxy and nineteen?' she'd coyly asked him only a minute before.

He hadn't slept with anyone aged nineteen since he'd been nineteen himself, seven years earlier. He'd always imagined that girls aged nineteen wouldn't have much to say that would be of interest to him, and vice versa. Nearly all of his friends were older than him, a lot older. He'd always cultivated the friendships of people already at the top.

Only now, as this nineteen-year-old stranger stood up and told him how much she wanted to go to bed with him, and led him down the hallway and into her bedroom and pushed him down on the crumpled white sheets and switched on the overhead fan, and told him he looked incredible, and told him that she wanted him to take her right here right now, he discovered that he was actually very much interested in hearing every single husky nineteen-year-old syllable she had to say.

'Claire,' she answered, as they lay toe to toe in the bath two hours later.

'Sam,' he introduced himself back (although she hadn't asked). He'd only come over to her apartment to get the phone number for the gas company, who hadn't yet connected up the apartment below into which he'd just moved. That the remainder of his afternoon had segued into a barely credible plot line from a soft-porn film was something he was still attempting to fathom. He stared at Claire through the steam and breathed in the scent of aloe. 'Do you, er, normally –' he started to ask.

She finished his question for him. '– sleep with guys before I've even told them my name? No. But it's always been something I wanted to try.'

The tap dripped, sending rippling rainbows out across the oily surface of the water. Maybe she was lying, he thought. Maybe she did do this kind of thing all the time. Maybe she was a nymph and this was how she got her kicks. Or then again, maybe she was telling the truth. Maybe she was just nineteen and curious about whether the racy romances she'd seen enacted on TV could be replicated in reality. He knew three things: she had a winning smile; it was still directed at him; and he was curious, too.

'I'd like to see you again,' he said.

'What?' she teased. 'All of me?'

'I was thinking dinner. I was thinking I'd like to take you out. I'm new to the island. You could show me around, if you wanted. I was thinking we could talk and get to know each other a little. You know, do some of that stuff other people do *before* sharing a bath . . .' Immediately, he wondered if he'd sounded too keen, whether he might have scared her off.

She studied his face in the same way a jeweller might study a gem, searching for signs of authenticity. Her toes wriggled against his. 'Perhaps,' she finally answered, standing up and stepping out of the bath.

Water chased itself in runnels down her golden skin, splashing on to the terracotta floor.

'Is that a perhaps yes, or a perhaps no?' he asked.

'A perhaps sooner than you think . . .'

She was right. He left her apartment half an hour later and three hours after that he found himself sitting beside her in an exclusive harbourside restaurant, topping up her glass with Chianti and discreetly whispering in her ear, 'You knew all along, didn't you, you crazy girl?' to which she only laughed in reply.

Because of course she really *had* known all along who he was. Because she'd guessed the moment he'd told her he'd moved into the apartment beneath hers. Because she'd already known that her grandfather had earmarked that apartment for his new star employee. Sam's seduction had all been part of a risqué game to her, a game she was still playing now at dinner, as she slipped her hand under the tablecloth and along his thigh.

On the other side of the table was Tony Glover, chairman of Ararat Holdings, Sam's new boss and Claire's grandfather, or 'Pops,' as Sam had already discovered that she liked to call him. In between Tony and Morgan Cole, Ararat's financial director, was Tony's wife and business partner, Rachel.

As Sam looked up from whispering to Claire, he saw Tony smiling at him. It was a smile which Sam recognised, a smile of approval. It was the same smile Tony had given him when Sam had accepted the position of marketing director six weeks earlier, after no less than five rounds of weeding-out interviews. There was confidence in the smile, too, the same confidence that had told Sam then that Tony had already known that Sam wasn't going to turn the job down.

At the end of the meal, it was Tony who asked Sam if he'd make sure Claire got safely home, making Sam suddenly wonder whether it wasn't only the job which Tony had been vetting him for.

'She's my princess, Sam, so you make sure you take good care of her, OK?' Tony said.

Back at Claire's apartment, Sam and Claire drank champagne and laughed about what she'd done till four and then fucked till five. By six he'd fallen in love, in love with her voice, with the Mediterranean heat, with the contours of her breasts, the touch of her tongue, the smell of her sheets and with the oil painting of the monastery of Santo Bartholomew on her bedroom wall. He'd fallen head over heels in love with her life, thinking that perhaps it could one day be his.

By the time he woke at noon and saw the sunlight filtering in through the window's muslin drapes, he was already fantasising about building a long future for himself on this beautiful island off the coast of Spain. Because if things were to work out with his job and between himself and this crazy, intriguing, boozy-breathed, beautiful, game-playing girl, then who knew how different and amazing his life might become in a few years' time?

And wasn't that why he'd quit his job in the City and decided to move out here? Because he'd wanted to differentiate his life from those of his broker colleagues, who'd all been set on following the same uninspired, if well-remunerated, blueprint through life. And wasn't that also why he'd recently broken up with his girlfriend of the last three years? Because hers had been a creature-comfort-driven suburban dream and it had made him want to scream.

He reached over and kissed Claire gently on the lips as she slept: because she'd shaken his world up in less than a day and had given him exactly the fresh start he'd wanted. But much more than that, because he hoped that, with this girl, each day would feel like a fresh start in a freshly shaken world.

Nearly a decade later and Sam still desired her. It was one of the few things in their relationship which hadn't changed. He sat on the unfamiliar bed in the unfamiliar bedroom in Dreycott Manor, fastening his black silk tie over his crisp white shirt, and watching Claire as she finished dressing for Tony's funeral. He smoothed down his hair with the palms of his hands.

Claire sat down beside him and pulled on her leather boots, then stood up and turned her back on him. 'Be an angel, darling,' she said.

He could feel her shaking as he zipped up her simple black dress. She'd wept again since Brenda had shown them up to this rarely used and rather shabby guest room in the old servants' quarters at the back of the house. The room had an air of hopelessness to it and neglect. It reminded Sam of his parents' room in the modern estate house he'd grown up in. It felt like being trapped inside a sigh.

Sam knew his wife's predilection for drama and emotional dishonesty only too well, but he'd never seen her genuinely knocked like this. Nor had he seen her so uncertain of herself. It was as if, with Tony gone, her world had lurched suddenly sideways and she'd yet to find her feet.

Sam kissed her lightly on the nape of her neck. She held his head there a moment for reassurance, before releasing him and walking to the tarnished, full-length mirror on the wall.

'She'd better be pretty damned special, whoever she is,' she said, starting on her make-up. She flicked Sam a glance. 'I still can't get over it. Bloody cuckoo.'

The 'new cousin'. That's how Brenda had described the interloper whose belongings were currently ensconced in the largest and most impressive of the guest rooms at the front of the house, the same room which had been Claire's room while she'd been at school near here, and in which Sam and Claire had stayed on every single one of their previous visits.

'I don't want a new cousin,' Claire grumbled.

'Well, technically, she's not your cousin,' Sam pointed out. 'She's your great-uncle Bill's daughter, which makes her your –'

'I don't care if it makes her my fairy fucking godmother,' Claire snapped. 'She still shouldn't be here. In my old room. With all my old things.' Claire sighed. 'Pops would've been appalled, you know. He wouldn't even allow Bill's name to be mentioned. There's no way he would have wanted his daughter here.'

Sam knew the story of Tony and Rachel's falling-out with her brother Bill as well as anyone. Not very well at all, in other words, seeing as Rachel and Tony had always remained remarkably unforthcoming about the details. It all revolved around some crazy quarrel from fifty years ago surrounding their mother's death. Which had been a tragic accident anyway, so Sam understood, so what exactly all the subsequent fuss was about he didn't know. All he did know was that Rachel had now obviously made overtures to heal the family rift. Hence their own relegation to the back of the house.

'But Rachel obviously does,' he pointed out to Claire. 'Otherwise she wouldn't have invited her.'

'She's probably so upset she doesn't know what she's doing.'

'Somehow I doubt that.' Rachel was one of the most clear-headed people Sam had ever met. He'd flown out to see her in Biarritz the day Tony had died, taking his lawyer with him. He'd wanted to be there to comfort her, but also to help her with the mass of bureaucracy and paperwork which would have arisen. But he needn't have worried on either count. Armed with only a phone, Rachel had dealt with everything, up to and including the transportation of Tony's body back to the UK, by the time Sam had arrived. Her resilience and reserves of strength had left him in awe.

'What was it Brenda said she was called?' Claire mused aloud. 'Laura? Louise?'

Sam didn't know either. He'd been too preoccupied with carrying a wriggling, giggling Archie up the stairs at the time and had only caught snatches of Claire and Brenda's conversation.

'Something beginning with L, anyway,' Claire concluded.

'She might be nice,' Sam suggested. 'And Brenda says she's only a few years older than you, so – who knows? – you two might even end up friends.'

'Sure, and pigs might fly.' Claire lit a cigarette. 'She's probably just after some cash, you know. I bet that's what it is. She's probably worked out how much Pops was worth and figures we can spare a bit.'

'You don't know that.' He pulled on his suit jacket.

'And I don't not know it, either. I can't think of another

reason why some long-lost relative would crawl out of the woodwork at a funeral. Can you?'

'Even if that were the reason,' Sam equivocated, 'she's not going to get any.'

'How do you know?'

'Because she'll have to get past Rachel first. And me.'

Sam hadn't meant to say this last bit aloud. But it was out now and Claire was far from lacking intuition. Her eyes flashed with interest.

'She's spoken to you, hasn't she?' she demanded, spinning round to face him, all thoughts of her mysterious 'new cousin' instantly brushed aside. Stubbing out her cigarette on the ornamental commemorative plate she'd been using as an ashtray, she hurried over to him. She gripped his suit collar in her fists and pulled him towards her, staring deep into his eyes.

'She's asked *you* to run Ararat with her and not Uncle Chris and Uncle Nick, hasn't she?'

Claire had guessed right. Rachel had called Sam that morning, offering him a 5 per cent shareholding in the company and the position of managing director. From now on, in conjunction with the board – which would include the other family members – and under the chairmanship of Rachel herself, Ararat's destiny lay in Sam's hands.

He'd been half expecting it, knowing that, of all the family members, he was the one best placed to take over. He knew, of course, that Rachel was more than capable of running the company, but it seemed she no longer had the will. As it was, she'd already started withdrawing herself from her management role these last two years. The same had been true of Tony. Rachel had wanted them both to enjoy their money before they'd got too old.

97

As a result, in the last couple of years, Sam's job had been injected with a new lease of life, as he'd been given an increasingly free reign in strategising Ararat's future. He'd concentrated on centralising the company's administration in Palma, while aggressively expanding its interests around the Mediterranean. Sam had always loved the variety of his work, and he'd immediately set about broadening his knowledge, taking a personal interest in learning even the smallest details of every aspect of the business, from the accounts of each hotel and villa, to the names of each and every one of Ararat's four hundred employees.

His hands-on approach had worked. He'd increased the company's operating profits by nearly 30 per cent. Tony and Rachel had been delighted, but unsurprised. And Sam had loved every minute of it.

Which was why, that morning, he'd had no hesitation in accepting Rachel's offer. As he'd listened to the favourable terms she'd outlined, he'd silently sworn to repay the trust she'd placed in him with interest. Rachel had then told him that she was planning to break the news to the rest of the family after the funeral and that she'd want him by her side when she did. She'd asked Sam to tell no one until then and also to prepare a few remarks of his own to make.

'I knew it,' Claire squealed. She wrapped her arms around Sam's waist and pressed her forehead against his chest. 'You've worked so hard. I'm so proud of you. Of us.' She looked tearfully up at him. 'Pops would have handed it over to you when he retired anyway, you know. He told me. I just wish he'd lived long enough to tell you himself.'

Sam pulled her in tight, enveloping her with his arms,

hugging her as she quivered against him, the same as he had done when he'd come back from France three years before to tell her that he'd fallen in love with someone else and was leaving.

X. His Ex. That's how he thought of her now, the other woman, the woman he'd fallen in love with – *thought* he'd fallen in love with – in less than three weeks in southern France in the summer of 2000. X, like he'd tried to cross her out in his mind, which he had. X, like she no longer existed, which in his world she no longer did. X. He'd burnt the only photographs of her he'd ever possessed.

Even though he'd been with Claire for several years then, they hadn't been married. Not that he saw that as any kind of an excuse for what he'd done. He knew that infidelity had nothing to do with marriage and everything to do with love. Either he hadn't loved Claire enough to stay faithful, or he'd loved or desired X more.

Immediately after he'd finished the affair, he'd tried thinking of X as a Siren, who'd entered his life and whose call he'd been unable to resist. But he'd soon come to recognise this for the lame excuse it was. He'd been the one to blame. Like an adolescent, he'd bought into the fantasy of love making anything possible, that was all. For a while, he'd cut loose and let his emotions carry him away. But only for a while. Because then he'd grown up and reality had staked its claim in his life once more.

In the run-up to the affair, Sam had been living with Claire in a small *finca* in the mountain town of Deià in the north-west of Mallorca, while their new penthouse in Portals Nous – infinitely more fashionable than Palma, in Claire's opinion – had undergone the lengthy process of being restyled to suit Claire's taste.

Six years had passed since Sam had first met Claire, and their afternoons of lying toe to toe in her aloe-scented bath had long since been squeezed out to make room for business commitments on his behalf and social engagements on hers.

In the week, he worked and she didn't. In the evenings, after suppers with her family and friends (whom they often chatted to more than each other), Sam went home and Claire stayed out. On the rare weekends when he wasn't working, he clambered through the mountain olive groves on his own, while she drove down to sea level and lazed on the beaches and lounged in the bars.

He knew, of course, that something was wrong. His problem was that he couldn't see what. Not enough to do something about it anyway. He and Claire had different interests, and he couldn't see how to bring them closer. He wasn't ecstatic about being with her, but he wasn't unhappy about it either. They got along most of the time, like friends. Sometimes they had fun. Occasionally he adored her. And there was always the sex, which was always good. All of which, when combined with a job he loved, and a boss who actively condoned his match with Claire, made for an attractive status quo.

Then in 2000 he met X, at the bottom of a swimming pool in southern France. It was like discovering he could breathe underwater, like his life could become a place of miracles.

He'd been overseeing the final phases of the construction of one of Ararat's boutique hotels near Cannes at the time and had taken the opportunity to tour the three villas owned by the company in the surrounding vicinity. He hadn't seen Claire for over two weeks and hadn't spoken to her for four days.

X had been staying at one of the villas with a group of friends. The water in the villa's swimming pool had drained away overnight. As Ararat's mortified rep, who'd been driving Sam around, attempted to sort out this unforeseen problem by phone, Sam climbed down the pool steps and on to the dry pool bottom to take a look for himself.

She was already standing there with a sarong wrapped round her tanned hips. She had one foot either side of the rip in the pool lining and was peering down at the crack in the concrete beneath. As she looked up at Sam, they both smiled. (Within a week, he'd have convinced them it was because they were destined to be together; within a month he'd have attempted to convince himself it had been nothing more than a case of infatuation, brought about by the heat of the noonday sun.)

'What do you think happened?' she asked. 'An earthquake?'

'If it was,' he wanted to tell her, 'then it's still going on,' because looking into her eyes, that's exactly how he felt.

And he wanted an earthquake. That's what he suddenly realised, after having chatted with her for an hour. He wanted his precious status quo to be shaken and rocked. He wanted to feel this alive and to remember what it felt like to flirt. He wanted to take his emotional life off hold and run forward and see what was round the corner.

He came back the next day, ostensibly to check on the pool. And the day after that, openly to check on this woman. All the time he was gone, he missed the smile she put on his face. He missed her voice, telling him more about her life. He asked her out for a drink and then dinner, and then, while her friends were packing their bags, he asked her to stay for another week. He recognised the moment she agreed as the happiest of his life.

Before they slept together, he told her about Claire. And he told her about Ararat. He explained how he could no longer tell where his work life ended and his home life began. He told her he'd got lost somewhere in the middle, stretched between the two. He'd compromised his passion to fuel his ambition, he now realised. He was living a half-life, a lie. It was like being slowly suffocated, he said. X was like oxygen to him, he told her. She was extraordinary and with her he could be extraordinary, too. He told her she'd made him remember himself.

If she wanted him to, he'd give it all up for her. He promised her this. He'd go back and tell Claire that he'd fallen in love with someone else and was leaving. He'd tell Tony and Rachel and then he'd resign. He wanted to be with X because of who she was, not because of who she knew, or where she lived. He'd return to the UK to see her. If she wanted to, they could make a fresh start then, together. All she had to do was say yes . . .

She did.


The church was already packed with mourners by the time Sam and Rachel arrived. Sam didn't stop to look at the mostly middle-aged, mostly leathery, tanned faces of the affluent men and women who sat silently and respectfully in the crowded rows of seats, waiting for the service to begin. Instead, he hurried Claire down the aisle and ushered her in beside Rachel on the long oak pew reserved for close family at the front.

Claire kissed her grandmother, whispering into her ear, and Sam reached across and touched Rachel's hand. Static raindrops glistened like sequins on her drying hat and coat.

102

Sam sat and stared at Tony's unadorned wooden coffin. Elaborate flower arrangements were stacked all around and at its side was the cast-iron lectern, from behind which Sam would soon be doing his reading.

On a parallel pew across the aisle from Sam sat two identical male twins, in their early fifties. Both of them stared fixedly ahead. Sam assumed they were Tony's half-brothers, who lived in Canada, and with whom Sam wasn't acquainted, since Tony had lost touch with them over the years.

In all the time Sam had known him, Tony had point-edly never spoken about his youth. Like it was something he'd wanted buried and forgotten.

The organ swelled with the sound of Bach and Sam stared back at the coffin. Outside, the thunder rolled.

This was the first funeral Sam had attended which had really meant anything to him, the others having been for distant relatives whom he'd barely known. Sam was lucky, in that both of his parents were still alive and well, play-ing their golf, watching their TV soaps and eating their microwaved TV dinners. The same went for his brother, Tom, who'd moved to be with his boyfriend in Australia six years before. His grandparents, too, were happy and well.

The cloying scent of lilies reached Sam's nostrils. He shivered. He could hardly stomach the thought that Tony – a true friend who'd trusted him and taught him so much – was simply no longer here. For the first time since he'd heard the news of Tony's death, Sam felt like he was going to cry.

He thought of Archie, of how readily he'd give his life to protect him. The bond between them was like iron, forged a second after Claire had told Sam she was pregnant, and a second before he'd been about to tell her that their relationship was at an end.

As Claire had wrapped her arms around him and pressed her belly up against his, he'd found himself consumed with thoughts of the child inside. How could he start a new life somewhere else with X, when a new life, created by him and reliant on him, had already begun to grow here?

With each passing second, he'd felt his will deserting him. Until, finally, he'd said nothing at all.

And he'd been right, hadn't he? Hadn't he been right to cease all contact with X? To give up the other life they might have shared together so that he could be a father to his son? Anything else was an impossible dream, a fantasy constructed away from the currents and tides of the real world.

That's what he'd told himself as he'd moved with Claire into their new Portals Nous home. And that's what he'd continued telling himself. Day after day. Week after week. Month after month. Until, eventually, he'd come to believe it as truth.

He glanced across at Claire now. This was his reality, this woman who'd borne him his child, this woman to whom he'd tried to be a better husband, and to whom, he'd vowed to himself, he'd stay faithful from now on.

Things weren't perfect between them, he knew. He thought she'd been unfaithful to him as well, just over a year ago, although he had no proof. He'd seen her with another, younger, handsome man, lunching in the La Boveda bar in Palma. When he'd got home from work that night, Claire had lied to him and told him she'd been out on her best friend Sadie's boat all day. On another occasion, Sam had come home early and seen the same man leaving their apartment building and flagging down a taxi. But Sam had never challenged Claire. After what he'd done himself, he'd felt he hadn't the right.

The organ wheezed to a stop and the vicar took his place at the lectern. Rain beat against the stained-glass windows and the service began.

When Sam's turn came to speak, he walked to the lectern and faced the congregation. He took a piece of paper from his inside pocket and unfolded it. Printed on it in his own meticulous handwriting was a poem by Christina Rossetti, which Tony had known off by heart.

Sam read it through in his mind, memorising it as he did:

> My heart is like a singing bird
> Whose nest is in a watered shoot;
> My heart is like an apple-tree
> Whose boughs are bent with thickset fruit;
> My heart is like a rainbow shell
> That paddles in a halcyon sea;
> My heart is gladder than all these
> Because my love is come to me.

He then returned the piece of paper to his jacket pocket, cleared his throat and looked up at the pew he'd just left. He'd meant to look at Rachel Glover as he started to recite the poem, to look at her as if she were the only woman in the universe, to make the poem truly hers as he read it out loud.

Instead, he found himself looking at X. His Ex. The other woman, the woman he'd fallen in love with – *thought* he'd fallen in love with – in less than three weeks in southern France in the summer of 2000.

Only now – seeing her here in the flesh, sitting between Nick and Christopher, almost close enough to reach out and touch – he no longer thought of her as X at all. But as Laurie, Laurie Vale, the woman he'd once promised his life to, but had then betrayed.

# *Chapter VI*

'Ouch!' said Rachel, as the pin pricked the back of her knee.

'Hold still,' mumbled Laurel Vale, removing the last pin from between her lips.

Rachel was standing on a chair in the back parlour behind the shop. It was dark outside, the yellow glass lampshade hanging on gold chains from the ceiling casting a warm light over the small room. A coal hissed and slipped in the small grate as the announcement of the evening concert from the BBC crackled from the radio on the brown sideboard.

From where Rachel was standing, she could see the cobwebs blowing in the draught towards the two old gas masks on top of the cupboard. A layer of dust peppered the top of the portrait of the deceased King on the wall and the top of the oval wooden mirror. Rachel supposed that she really ought to step up her cleaning efforts, before Bill noticed the dust, too. Still, she thought, she wouldn't have seen it unless she'd been standing on a chair and she could probably get away with it until her mother instigated the annual spring clean, which was bound to happen at the start of April.

Rachel glanced down. Laurel Vale sat below her in her wheelchair wearing her grey housecoat over her usual black day dress. Her hair was tied up in a pink-and-purple silk scarf and she bent over, peering intently through her

107

horn-rimmed glasses, as she carefully pinned up the hem of Rachel's new dress. Next to her, the leaf was pulled out on the table to accommodate the new electric Singer sewing machine and several empty Oxo tins which were stuffed with bobbins, cottons, brightly coloured ribbons, buttons and bits of lace. Offcuts of the red material of Rachel's new dress had scattered on to the brown lino, like fallen blossom.

Rachel lifted her wrist to her nose to see if she could still smell the dab of rosewater scent she'd borrowed from Anne earlier, but it had faded. Instead, she got a whiff of the suet pudding and boiled cabbage supper that she and her mother had pretended to enjoy. She looked down at the paper pattern sleeve on the table and the picture of the model on the front, standing with her arms akimbo to accentuate her tiny waist. She looked as if she didn't have a care in the world and Rachel tried to replicate the pose, practising a sunny smile in the top of the mirror opposite.

Her mother's firm, warm hands were on her legs in an instant, pivoting her on the chair, so that she turned and faced the other wall, as the sonorous tones of a Beethoven symphony started on the radio. On the shelf above the door to the hall was a row of brass monkeys, which had once been her grandfather's. On the other wall was an oversized dresser stacked with the best china plates, and her mother's collection of Dickens novels, none of which Rachel had read herself, in spite of her mother's encouragement. She dreaded to think what her mother would say if she knew that under Rachel's pillow was *Forever Amber*, the racy novel that was doing the rounds in school.

Her mother sat back. 'There.'

Freed at last, Rachel jumped down from the chair and

wriggled her hips, so that the dress swished about her knees.

'What do you think?' she asked, plunging her hands into the front pockets on the skirt and jiving around on the tiny rag rug.

Her mother pulled the tape measure from around her neck and laughed. She took off her glasses and laid them on the table. She looked years younger without them on. Even so, her curly black hair peeping out from under the scarf was flecked with grey at her temples and there were deep lines around her soft brown eyes. Only her neck showed that she was still a woman in her prime. It was long, smooth and proud and always housed a simple silver cross, which she often held in her fingers like a talisman.

Rachel looked down at her pitifully flat chest. She tutted. 'I wish I was curvy.'

'You're fine as you are,' said Rachel's mother curling up the tape measure with her deft fingers.

'I look like a boy.'

Laurel Vale closed her eyes and shook her head in a familiar gesture of exasperation. She had a thick line between her eyebrows, which deepened now as she fixed Rachel with one of her knowing looks.

'We're given what we're given,' she said. 'Don't you go wishing for anything different. You've got your grand-mother's beautiful legs. What more do you want?'

Rachel looked down at her own legs and then couldn't help glance at her mother's legs, motionless beneath the tartan shawl over her knees. She too had once had fine legs – still did, only they didn't work.

It baffled Rachel that her mother's legs looked so normal and yet she couldn't move them at all. At first, Rachel had secretly hoped that her mother was faking. That she'd given up the will to move deliberately. To make some kind of statement.

But that had just been childish fantasy. Her mother had a will of iron and the pride of a lioness. There was nothing false in her silent anguish when Rachel supported her up the stairs every night to her bed. She knew that her mother hated relying on her daughter. But her mother coped with such strength and dignity that sometimes Rachel forgot that she was disabled at all. Compared to most people, her mother seemed astonishingly abled.

'Pearl's got new stockings,' Rachel said.

'I can't afford new stockings this month.'

'Then will you paint lines down the back on them for me?' Rachel begged, looking over her shoulder at her mother, sticking out a freckly white calf towards her. 'Anne's mother did for her.'

'I don't care what Anne's mother did. You're not going out looking like a . . .' Rachel looked at her mother, daring her to swear, or say a bad word. But she knew she couldn't. '. . . you-know-what,' she continued. 'Now hop it. Out of that dress so that I can stitch it while you're in the bath.'

Rachel peered through the crack in the doorway to where the tin bath was set up by the range in the kitchen. She knew that as soon as she went in there, she'd be able to see her breath.

'Can't we put the bath in here? It's so much warmer.'

'No.'

It was one of her mother's special 'no's'. The no of the boss of the household. The no that meant no without an explanation needed, or given.

In one deft move, her mother had turned round her chair and had pushed open the door and slipped down the ramp into the kitchen. A blast of cold air hit Rachel's legs. She watched her mother lift down the heavy kettle from the range and expertly pour it into the tin bath.

'Come on. And look lively about it,' she said from inside a cloud of steam, as Rachel slipped out of the dress and laid it carefully over the back of the chair. 'Before your brother comes in and wants his turn.'

There was no arguing with her mother. Friday night was bath night and Laurel Vale insisted on hygiene in her household. Rachel wondered, if just once, her mother could drop the routine she lived by.

Rachel reluctantly followed her into the kitchen, shivering.

'Shall I wash your hair?' her mother asked.

'I'll do it myself,' Rachel said, feeling self-conscious. She didn't like her mother hovering over her as if she were still a child.

Her mother nodded as she wheeled away. 'I'll leave you to it, then.'

'Mum,' Rachel called out after her. 'Thanks for my dress. It's lovely.'

Her mother turned in the half-light, her face sad. 'I wish your father could see you all grown up,' she said.

Considering that the absence of her father was such a big issue in their household, Rachel found it ironic that she couldn't remember his presence at all. She would never tell Bill or her mother, but over the years since Thomas Vale's departure, the more Rachel studied the photograph on the lace tablecloth by her mother's tall mahogany bed, the further away he seemed. In the end, she accepted that this stiff black-and-white image of her father was almost the sum total of her memory.

She had no doubt (her mother had told her often enough)

that her father had loved her, but she had no evidence to prove it – no keepsake, or note, no lock of hair or trinket that she could claim for herself. She knew she ought to miss him more and that it was a terrible thing to lose a parent, but her mother did enough missing for both of them. Rachel had decided long ago that she might as well leave all the grieving to her mother and concentrate on living. After all, there was enough retrospection in her life and, for Rachel, the future was much more intriguing.

She wasn't going to tell anyone – not even her best friends, Anne and Pearl, about her plans, but Rachel had already mapped out her future: long-distance travel (Africa particularly appealed), an extremely exciting love affair with someone exotic and unusual (a lavish marriage would follow), unlimited wealth (at the very least she would need a big town house and a chauffeur-driven car) and, most importantly, Rachel would be distinguished in her own right.

She'd read enough about Florence Nightingale and Emily Pankhurst to know that she had more in common with these types of women, than with the stoical domestic types her mother knew in the local WI. No, she thought, interlacing her fingers and stretching her lean arms away from her, a life of cooking three meals a day and scrubbing the front porch was not for her. If she had her way, people would cook and clean for her.

Rachel wallowed in the bathwater, letting the Lifebuoy soap dissolve in her hands. She knew that it would annoy Bill to find the water cloudy and the soap a slimy mess, but she was far too busy daydreaming to care. One day she would live in a house with a bathroom of her own, with big gold taps and mirrors all around. She had no idea how she would achieve it, but Rachel knew that she would.

She had to. Bill may be cut out for running the shop and being a good Stepmouth boy, but Rachel certainly knew she wasn't.

And she knew that nothing was ever going to change around here. She'd assumed after her father's death, even before the trial, that they would all move away and start afresh. She'd assumed that people would treat them as outcasts. That every time they came into the shop, they'd be reminded of what had happened there. That the Vales would be for ever tainted.

But instead her mother had used the pittance that her father had left them all to refurbish, repaint and secure the shop. That's when her obsession with the locks had started. Three on the front door, three on the back, two on each window. She'd made the shop into a fortress safer than the Bank of England. And once she was satisfied that they'd never be broken into again, with the keys sounding like warning bells on the iron loop on her belt, she'd declared that it would be business as usual. She'd defied anyone to baulk at her will, or to give her sympathy, as if her spirit and sheer force of will could wipe away what had happened.

And she'd succeeded. After a while, Laurel Vale's determination that things should carry on as if nothing had happened, meant that they did. If people thought they were coming into the scene of a crime when they entered the shop at first, over time, they'd seemed to forget. With the sheer repetition of the daily routine, of the shop opening and closing, of the same customers coming and going, it was as if a thin layer of the tissue paper her mother used to wrap up the best china was laid again and again upon the shop, until, over time, the tragedy was dampened down, was muffled by the weight of normality.

They never talked about it at home. It was there, of course, the aftermath of what had happened, but it was all under the surface. By day, her mother was cheerful and polite in the shop, by night, once the supper was over and the dishes cleared, she went to her room.

And that was when Rachel felt the weight of her mother's private grief. There, in the sound of muffled crying and fervent prayers behind her mother's locked bedroom door. There in the row of black dresses that hung on the washing line. It was there in the heavy, suffocating silence on the anniversary of her father's death, or his birthday, or their wedding anniversary. There, in the row of her mother's religious tapestries framed in the dark upstairs hallway all dedicated to the loving memory of Thomas Vale.

Sometimes Rachel longed to find a way to purge all the grief out of her mother and the anger out of Bill. She wished that they could be set free, that just for once they could be truly happy. But it would never happen. In her darker moods, Rachel thought that Bill and her mother deserved each other. Her mother *wanted* to hold on to her grief and Bill *wanted* to stay impudently angry. It made them who they were. Well, one thing was for certain: she was different from them both.

Rachel heard the back door banging, then she heard Bill call out: 'I'm home.'

'Ah, there you are,' she heard her mother say, her voice lightening up. Rachel scowled, picturing Bill leaning down for her to kiss him. Sometimes her mother's devotion to him made her sick. She heard her mother turn off the radio.

'I'm starving,' Bill said.

'I've saved your supper. It's in the oven.'

Rachel crossed her arms over herself and slunk down into the bath.

'Do you mind,' she snapped, as her brother barged in through the door.

'But –'

'Get out!'

'Well, hurry up.'

As Bill retreated, Rachel lifted one of her lean legs out of the bath, pointing her toes, inspecting her shin as if she were a ballerina. Then with a smile, she took Bill's cut-throat razor which she'd liberated from the outside lavatory and started shaving her legs. She had no intention of hurrying up. He wasn't her father. He had no right bossing her about. For once, Bill Vale could bend to her wishes.

The rag-and-bone men were around early on Saturday morning. Rachel could hear the horse and the bell out in the high street before she heard Bill shouting for her to get up and help him take an old mattress out. She ignored him and put her pillow over her head. But then she remembered that she was going to the dance tonight. There was no point in winding up Bill, because if she pushed him too far, he might just scupper her plans.

Outside, there wasn't a cloud in the sky and the birds were chirruping and chasing each other across the river. Bill was at the front of the shop, by the entrance to the lane, standing next to a slumped mattress, his shirtsleeves rolled up.

'Oh,' Bill said. 'You're awake.'

'Sorry I didn't come sooner, I thought I'd find half a carrot for the horse,' Rachel said, brandishing the limp vegetable she'd taken from the compost bucket by the back door.

Bill didn't have time to comment before Rachel was laughing and pointing across the lane to where James Peters was speeding out of his cottage, pulling on his braces, before racing out to scoop up the horse manure into a coal bucket for his rose garden.

'Morning, James,' Bill shouted, but he was too busy to reply.

'We should sell that stuff in the shop,' Rachel remarked to Bill, as she patted the giant shire horse and fed him the carrot. 'We'd make a fortune.'

Bill laughed, holding up the mattress. 'I can't see Mum approving. Give me a hand with this, would you?'

Back inside, Rachel helped her mother get up, rubbing the small of her back for her where she'd seized up in the night. Then she helped her down the stairs and into the kitchen, where Bill had prepared fried eggs and bacon. Rachel flicked through the paper while they ate, and when Bill opened the shop shutters at ten to nine, everyone seemed to be in a good mood.

It was busy straight away, with the locals keen to stock up on weekend essentials before the tourist buses would inevitably start arriving. It was ten o'clock before there was a lull.

'I'm going to do the deliveries,' Bill announced, untying the apron he often wore in the shop. 'There's only a couple in town and one over at the Jones's. I won't be long. If Ralph comes with the dairy order, tell him to wait.'

'I'll go,' Rachel said, racing from behind the counter and barring Bill's way at the door. 'Let me do it.'

'You can't. I need you to stay and help Mum. And when I say stay, I mean stay. No running off to the beach with Anne and Pearl.'

'But if you're waiting for a delivery, wouldn't it be better if I went out on the bike?' Rachel argued pleasantly. 'Here,' she said, going to pull the packages from Bill's hand. 'Let me.'

'No,' Bill began, pulling the packages back away from her.

Rachel turned towards their mother. 'It's not fair. He's always saying I should do more and here I am offering to help and he won't let me.'

'Let her go, Bill,' said Laurel Vale, polishing the counter. 'It'll be better if you're here.'

'Fine!' he said, finally pushing the packages to Rachel so that she jerked backward. 'But I want you back straight away. It's all hands on deck today.'

'You know, you really should stop being so distrustful.'

'Then give me a reason to trust you,' Bill hissed.

'You two, stop it,' their mother said. 'Bill, that's enough.'

Rachel felt stupid for being so intrigued by Emily Jones, but all the girls she knew were her own age and all their mothers were just that: mothers. Apart from the odd eccentrics in Stepmouth, there was nobody even vaguely out of the ordinary. Certainly no one modern, and Emily was like a breath of fresh air, a breath of hope from the outside world. The world to which Rachel felt she would one day belong.

'Hey there,' said Emily, her accent sounding fabulously exotic, as she greeted Rachel by the front door of the Sea Catch Café a few minutes later. 'Where's your brother?'

'He's busy today in the shop. You know, the weather. I came instead.' Rachel dismounted and leant the bike against the wall.

Emily breathed in and sighed. 'I don't blame you for getting out. There's a real taste of springtime, isn't there?'

Emily was even more glamorous than she remembered. She was wearing a white fitted jumper and a blue skirt, but the way her clothes fitted her curvy body made her look like the model Rachel had been admiring on her pattern yesterday. Her blonde hair was curled up and she wore a pretty blue clip in the side at the front. Her lips were painted a deep pinky red and she was smoking a long cigarette with a gold tip – a brand that Rachel had never seen. Rachel had never wanted to look like anyone before, except, of course, Marilyn Monroe, but she was in the movies. Now she found herself longing to be like Emily.

Rachel handed the small bundle of groceries from the front basket of the bike to Emily.

'I guess everyone will be busy today,' Emily said, after she'd thanked her. 'You should come with your family and eat here one time. I know we're only a tearoom at the moment, but I'm going to turn it into a diner, or a restaurant.' She pointed behind her to the interior. 'I was thinking we could get a jazz band at nights. Make it a party place. What do you think?'

Rachel didn't know what to say. She didn't know what a diner was and she'd never been to a restaurant with her family. She never went anywhere with her mother, except to visit friends and to church. The only time they ever went on day trips on the bus, they took bloater paste and spam sandwiches with them. Eating in a restaurant with a jazz band seemed to Rachel to be the last word in extravagance. From her in-depth knowledge of the residents of Stepmouth, she knew for a fact that the town would be scandalised by such an establishment.

'I think it sounds wonderful.'

'The diner, or the restaurant?'

'What's a diner?'

Emily laughed, but not in a patronising way. 'A diner? Well, it's a sort of milk bar. There's a fabulous one in New York I used to go to all the time. They have small booths where you sit and drink milkshakes and eat burgers. They even have little juke boxes for each table.'

'I'm going to go to New York one day.' Rachel had only meant to think it, not say it.

'You'll love it there,' Emily said, as if Rachel's admission had been the most natural thing in the world and entirely realistic. 'You've got to go up the Empire State building. Oh, and to Macy's. You won't believe the shops. I can tell you exactly where to go.'

There was a pause. She could tell Emily was looking at her, but she was too embarrassed to meet her eye. She didn't dare elaborate on her plans. Emily stubbed out her cigarette on the doorstep.

'So, what are you doing later?' she asked, conversationally, changing the subject. 'I mean, what does one do on a Saturday night in this place? I still haven't worked it out.'

'I'm going to the dance. It's only a local thing.'

'Anything is better than nothing,' Emily said. 'What are you wearing?'

'My mum's made me a dress.'

'Come on in for a second,' Emily said, with a smile, as if she'd just had an idea. 'I might have something for you.'

Rachel hadn't been inside the café before, it being strictly the preserve of tourists. It was bigger than she'd imagined with red checked tablecloths adorning all the tables. One side was all windows which looked out over the river far below. Yellow and purple pansies flourished in all the window boxes. It looked vaguely Alpine, like a picture of a skiing lodge Rachel had seen in a magazine.

'Ah, there's my main man,' Emily said, and Rachel followed her gaze, as a door opened in the back wall next to the service hatch. Rachel's heart lurched. Because Tony Glover was standing in the doorway, wiping his hands on a cloth. He froze when he saw her.

'Tony's my saviour in the kitchen,' Emily continued. 'Honestly, I don't know how I'd manage without him. I think one day he'll be a fine chef. Do you two know each other?'

*Emily didn't know.*

It struck Rachel now with such a force, that she stared at Emily, dumbfounded. *Emily didn't know.* She didn't know the history between the Vales and the Glovers. She had no idea of the millions of reasons why she and Tony must never be left alone together.

Should she say something? Should she shatter Emily's illusions? Needing an answer, Rachel glanced at Tony. A shaft of sunlight beamed from the window between them, particles of dust shimmering in the air. When he met her eyes, she could see the question in them and she couldn't breathe.

Once again, her preconceptions fell away and Rachel had the feeling back that she'd had after the fight, that something was being stripped away and she was looking at the truth. Because she couldn't deny the fact that Tony Glover looked so normal, standing there. He looked like a real person. He didn't look at all like a good-for-nothing scoundrel she knew him to be. He didn't look like the town's bogeyman. He looked like someone being employed by Emily. Someone who Emily liked, respected and trusted. And he also looked undeniably handsome as he stood by the window, the bright sunlight catching the side of his face.

'Well? Do you, or don't you?' Emily asked again. She was looking between Rachel and Tony, clearly confused.

'Sort of,' Tony said. He rubbed the side of his face.

Emily nodded. 'Good. Then you two can amuse yourselves. I'll be back in a sec,' she said, opening the hall doorway.

As Emily left the room, the air between Rachel and Tony seemed to be so charged that she could hardly speak. She tried to imagine that they really had been elevated to some Alpine resort, far away from Stepmouth and everyone they knew. It wasn't difficult. Even without any words being spoken it already felt as if they were floating in their own bubble where all the rules they'd always lived by didn't exist.

'How's your face?' she asked. The bruises seemed to have cleared up.

'Much better.'

'Yes, well, like I said, sorry.' She tried to make herself sound hard, harsh even, but instead, her voice had turned husky.

'Don't be. I got thrown out of home. But it was time I left anyway . . . time I set up on my own. So I guess you did me a favour. Mum, you know, she doesn't approve of fighting.'

Rachel stared at him, as this revelation struck her. Tony's mother, the harridan, the scandalous, shameless mother, had morals? She'd thrown her son out of home for fighting?

'So where are you living?' she asked.

'In a shed up on old Dooley's land. He gave it to my grandfather for saving his life.'

Another thunderbolt struck Rachel. There was a Glover who had *saved* lives?

121

'He did?'

Emily burst back through the door and Rachel jumped.

'There,' she said, out of breath as she handed Rachel a small, square package.

Rachel ripped her eyes away from Tony's, as she took the package from Emily. The square packet had black-and-white checks on it and a cartoon of a woman bending over. A clear cellophane window at the top revealed that inside were a pair of sheer ribbed nylons.

'There. The best you can get,' Emily said, smiling at Rachel.

'I can't,' Rachel stumbled for words, astounded by the generosity of Emily's gift.

'Oh, go on. Your brother did me a big favour, the other day. He gave me chocolate to give to my mum. So I owe him a favour back, only I know he hates chocolate –'

'What? He loves chocolate,' Rachel interrupted. 'It's his favourite thing in the whole world. Did he tell you he didn't?'

An enigmatic smile settled on Emily's face. 'It doesn't matter,' she said. 'But thanks. I will get him some chocolate to pay him back. And in the meantime, these are for you. Every girl always needs new nylons. All the ones I've ever met, anyway.'

Rachel couldn't find the words. They were the most beautiful nylons she'd ever seen. They would turn Anne green with envy.

'Take them for your dance tonight. A girl's got to have something a little special now and then to impress the boys.' Emily winked at Rachel and glanced deliberately over her shoulder at the kitchen door. But Tony had gone.

'Well? Say something,' Emily said, excited at giving her gift.

'Thank you,' Rachel gushed.

\*     \*     \*

Outside the café, Rachel took the bike and turned down the side alley. Once she was sure she was out of sight, she took the packet of cigarettes she'd been saving from her pocket. In the distance, she could hear the chink of the fishing-boat masts in the harbour and the distant sound of a car changing gear on Harbour Bridge. Close to, she could almost hear her own heartbeat.

She took a deep drag on the cigarette, thinking of how glamorous Emily had looked today. And then, despite herself, her mind was filled with the image of Tony, the sunlight on his face, his dark blue eyes boring into her. Tony Glover. She wished now more than ever that he was standing right here. She wanted to challenge him, to fight with him, to make him explain why seeing him just now had left her so jangled and confused.

Rachel closed her eyes briefly, exhaling the cigarette smoke, feeling the dizzy buzz in her head. But there was something else too: a softening feeling, a warm flush that spread through her stomach as she thought about Tony's face.

She opened her eyes abruptly, feeling caught out. This couldn't be. She couldn't feel desire for Tony Glover. She simply couldn't. She threw her cigarette away, shivering as she marched the bike back on to the road. She couldn't admire his flesh and blood. She wasn't allowed to.

Because Tony's flesh and blood was bad. Bad through and through. It was Tony's flesh and blood that had destroyed her family. Because it had been his brother Keith Glover who, with a balaclava over his face and a shotgun in his hand, had broken into Vale Stores in the dead of night and broken open the till looking for money. It had been Keith Glover who had turned upon the shocked appearance of her father in his pyjamas and had shot him at point-blank range. It had been Keith Glover who had coldly watched him fall dead to the floor, to reveal his terrified wife behind him. And it had been Keith Glover who'd then fired again before running, shattering Laurel Vale's pelvis and paralysing her for life.

# Chapter VII

**Mallorca, Present Day**

Laurie got out of the cab by the gates of Sa Costa and sighed happily at the balmy onslaught of noonday heat. The pretty young woman who'd been waiting for her on the dusty cypress tree-lined road, leant down and spoke through the window to the driver in rapid Spanish, before turning to Laurie.

'Mrs Glover telephoned me. I'm Maria,' she introduced herself, shaking Laurie's hand. She had dark ringlets, a flowery patterned dress and fashionable sunglasses and Laurie felt every inch the Englishwoman abroad, blinking like a vole who'd emerged from a long winter of London drizzle.

'I work in the Ararat office in Palma,' Maria continued, as the cab driver popped open the boot and, sucking on a cigarette, walked around the car to heave Laurie's bags out. 'I keep an eye on the place. I'm afraid the drive has just been resurfaced, so we can't take the taxi up to the house.'

Maria must work with Sam, Laurie thought immediately, feeling an illicit thrill at this chink of knowledge into Sam's world – a world that was so terrifyingly near, she could almost feel it. Perhaps Maria might even mention that Laurie had arrived in Mallorca . . .

Laurie checked herself, turning her attention to gathering up her bags. Was she crazy? Why was she even thinking this? She wasn't going to give Sam bloody Delamere any of her brain space. That wasn't why she was here. She wanted absolutely nothing to do with him. She was here at the invitation of her wonderful new aunt and nothing – especially not Sam – was going to spoil her new relationship with her family.

'We'll walk from here,' Maria said, withdrawing one of the five-euro notes that Laurie was about to hand over to the driver. 'Local prices,' she explained. 'For the family.'

Laurie put the money back in her purse, thinking yet again that Rachel's influence seemed to have a tinge of the Mafia about it. She could only imagine what Tony must have been like, but Rachel was like the Godfather herself, getting her own way with such ease and grace that it was virtually impossible to contradict her wishes.

Not that Laurie had wanted to refuse her generous offer: the exclusive use of Rachel's Mallorca villa for a couple of months in order to work. The timing of it simply seemed too fatalistic to resist.

And certainly, now that she was here, all her doubts seem to vanish into the hazy, Mallorcan air. As the cab drove away, leaving a cloud of dust, Laurie became aware of how quiet it was, the silence only broken by the twitter of birds in the trees above and the metronomic trill of the cicadas.

'Mrs Glover, she is very kind to my family. We are very sad about Mr Glover. We are all very, very sorry,' said Maria, as she unlocked a small ornate cast-iron gate, next to the big electronic ones. 'It was a tragic loss for you.'

Laurie hardly heard her. She was more intrigued by the villa. Bougainvillea, the colour of raspberry blancmange, covered the wall along the small road, and beyond the gates she could see flowering cactuses and small palm trees lining the drive which twisted away, as if into a jungle. She was so awed that she realised too late that Maria was offering her condolences and giving her a look of unbridled sympathy.

'Oh, yes,' she stumbled, feeling like a fraud. 'It was a terrible shock.' Laurie covered her embarrassment by yanking the handle on the large suitcase, so that she could pull it on its wheels. She also had a large bag, full of canvases, brushes and paints, which she now heaved on to her shoulder. She'd even brought a hammer with her to knock together the canvas frames.

Laurie followed Maria up the edge of the new drive. As soon as the side gate clanked behind them, Laurie's head filled with the scent of flowers battling with the aroma of the fresh, sparkling tarmac. She could hear the lazy pulse of discreetly hidden water sprinklers and it felt if she'd been transported to a secret garden, a million miles away from the stress of her own life.

'We all miss Mr Glover,' Maria was saying. 'He always made a big fuss of us all. It won't be the same without him. He loved this house. When he bought it, it was a ruin. My father said it had been empty for over fifty years. But of course you know this.'

They'd turned around the bend in the driveway and Maria's voice trailed away, as Laurie couldn't help stopping, awed by the view before her. The house, originally an old farmhouse was magnificent. Its pale rustic bricks were covered in a swathe of red flowers which crept up and around the arched wooden doorway. Three huge palm trees with criss-crossed trunks and towering fronds stood at its front. Behind them, through the manicured shrubs, Laurie could see a vine-covered eating area with an enormous barbecue. It was the kind of place only seen in the very glossiest pages of the most expensive, exclusive holiday brochures. And it was hers. All hers.

'You're so lucky. Your family . . . they are wonderful people,' Maria said, waiting for Laurie to catch up with her.

'I've not been close to them, until recently,' Laurie mumbled, but Maria didn't pick up on her hint at the literal truth. Instead, she unlocked the front door and glanced at her small gold watch.

'I'm so sorry, I have to leave you now. I have to get back to the office. My cousin, Fabio, he will clean the pool and also bring you fresh deliveries, if you want. When the family is here, he brings fish and fruit from the market.'

This was paradise, Laurie thought. She wouldn't even have to leave to go shopping. It was just as Rachel had promised. She would be all alone with no one to disturb her.

Maria handed over the keys to Laurie and then pulled a card from her small handbag. 'Dante, the gardener, comes every day, but he doesn't speak much English. If you have any problems, or want to ask anything, please call me.'

'Thank you, I appreciate it.'

Maria smiled and waved, trotting off down the drive. 'Enjoy,' she said.

Left alone, Laurie pushed open the heavy front door, and sighed, as the coolness hit her. Inside the entrance hall, the decor was simple, with terracotta tiles on the floor and plain white walls dotted with tastefully framed abstract pictures. She paused to look at a black-and-white photograph on the stand in the hall, smiling as she recognised Christopher and Nick as small boys, regretting, as she had done when they'd shown her similar pictures in Dreycott Manor on the night before Tony's funeral, that she hadn't been in the happy family photographs herself. Still, it was possible to make up for lost time, she thought, replacing the photograph.

An antique wooden grandfather clock ticked in time with her footsteps as she made her way towards the foot of the marble staircase and a set of heavy oak doors. Laurie pushed one of them tentatively and it swung back to reveal a vast open-plan living area, with comfortable rattan sofas and chairs dotted around and a huge rustic farmhouse table with seating for eighteen. Large wooden fans hung from the high ceilings and, through an archway, she could see a massive kitchen with an old-fashioned range and modern cooker and sleek breakfast bar, complete with a table-top jukebox.

But it was the wall of sliding glass doors that was the most impressive feature of the room. Tiptoeing over the bright rug, Laurie turned the lock on one of the doors and stepped out on to the terrace. It was only then that she realised the true magnificence of Sa Costa. It simply had the most stunning view: down over the infinity pool, past the manicured lawns, and through a canopy of olive, euca-lyptus and citrus trees to the expanse of blue sea twinkling beyond. Laurie remembered that Rachel had mentioned a path leading through the grove to the beach, but she'd assumed that her aunt had meant a public path. She hadn't for one second suspected that Rachel had meant that the villa had a private beach.

Now she felt torn between whooping with glee and shrivelling with guilt. Rachel had made it all sound so simple and so obvious that Laurie should come here to work, but now Laurie felt as if she'd casually accepted a present without opening it and had taken it home and found something ludicrously expensive inside. How was she to know that Rachel's villa was going to be like this?

'Oh my God!' she exclaimed, aloud, breathing in the warm air and watching the butterflies dance near her face. She jumped as a kingfisher darted past her ear and dipped its beak into the surface of the pool and flew off over the white diving board.

Then, suddenly, her phone rang, breaking the silence. It was Roz. She was clearly as excited as Laurie at the prospect of Laurie working abroad for a few months and was intrigued about the villa. She'd managed to pin down a few commissions after Laurie's exhibition and was anxious that Laurie get on with them. She was also entirely seduced by the thought of Laurie's new family and had wanted to know every detail of Tony's funeral. And Laurie had willingly obliged, except for one huge omission.

Somehow, she hadn't been able to bring herself to tell Roz about seeing Sam again. She hadn't been able to trust herself to sound blasé about it and she knew that once Roz got a sniff of her confused feelings, she wouldn't hear the end of it. She also knew that if Roz knew about Sam, there was no way she would have supported Laurie's decision to come to Mallorca where she would potentially be so close to him.

'So when's James coming out?' Roz gushed, after Laurie had described the view.

'Give me a chance! I've literally only just arrived. Besides, James is busy. He's recording an album for the next month.'

'Poor you. Won't you get bored? I don't want you running off with the pool boy.'

Laurie laughed. 'No chance. I've got work to do, remember?'

'Well, if you do need company, I'm always free to jump on a plane. Now don't forget to call me. I miss you already.'

Laurie rang off. Despite her good-humoured banter with Roz, she couldn't help feeling guilty for not telling the whole truth. It was the same sickly feeling she had had since she'd told her father she was going away to stay in 'a friend's' villa to work. Laurie hugged her arms around her, feeling rattled. How had she managed to turn from being the most honest person she knew, to being the kind of person who could easily tell a barrage of white lies to the two people she trusted most in the world?

But she had no choice. Things had been uncomfortably strained between her and her father since Laurie had admitted that she'd been to Tony's funeral and Laurie couldn't bear to make them any worse.

'I told you, don't mention that woman's name to me,' her father had said, after an audible intake of breath on the other end of the phone when Laurie had rung him on her return from Somerset.

'But, Dad, Rachel's not as bad as –'

'I can't stop you doing what you have to do in your life, Laurel,' he'd interrupted. 'I can't stop you making choices that I disagree with. But you know how I feel about this. You have expressly gone against my wishes and, in doing so, have hurt me deeply and deliberately. I suggest that if you wish for us to remain civil to one another, you no longer discuss this matter with me.'

It had been a direct threat and his meaning had been as clear as the water below her in the pool. The choice had been – and remained – Rachel or her father.

'You're being so unreasonable,' Laurie had objected on the telephone.

'And you're being deliberately provocative. I don't want to fall out with you. Nothing would make me sadder, but we will if you keep on about this. If you continue to consort with that woman . . .'

'So you don't want to know anything? You don't want to know how she was? Or how I felt? Or about the rest of your family? *My* family.'

'No, I don't.'

'But –'

'I have to go now,' he'd said abruptly, and had put down the phone.

Well, it was his loss, Laurie decided, turning back towards the house. If he couldn't see that Rachel was kind and generous and sweet, then that was his problem. Laurie wasn't going to let him ruin her new relationship with Rachel because of some ludicrous grudge he refused to explain. She, for one, was going to make up for lost time and enjoy her new-found status as part of a wealthy family.

After she'd devoured one of the fresh cartons of peach juice in the well-stocked American-style fridge, Laurie explored the villa. Her overwhelming impression as she dawdled from room to room was one of taste and cleanliness. It was like being in a stylish hotel, rather than a lived-in home.

It wasn't until she reached the very top of the house that she found her favourite room. She back-dived on to the bed, with its pretty green-and-white quilt, bouncing gently on the soft mattress beneath the high exposed wooden rafters. Then, she turned her head and looked out of the small window, framed by the red flowers that ran over the white window sill. She could see the rocky peaks of the Tramuntana mountains in the distance.

It felt tranquil and serene up here and she decided to get her case and start unpacking her hopelessly shabby clothes into the simple antique wardrobe and tallboy right away. Once she got settled, she was bound to stop feeling so intimidated by the place.

It was only then that she saw it. She couldn't believe that she hadn't spotted it straight away. It was as glaringly obvious as a head in a jar, sitting on the small wooden table, and just as shocking. She jumped off the bed, backing away from the picture of Sam and Claire smiling on their wedding day.

Laurie caught her breath and forced herself to walk around the bed and pick up the picture. Her eyes blurred as she looked into those pale blue eyes she knew so well, remembering the funeral. Then, even worse, as she stared at Sam's face, she thought back to the last time she'd seen him before that dreadful moment.

It had been three years ago. Three long, miserable, difficult years erased in a second, as her memory defied her and proved that she'd just been kidding herself. Sam had been lurking in the shadows of her mind all along in full Technicolor, just waiting for this very moment to step out and reclaim her.

It had been a hot September. A perfect September, but now it was at an end. In the departures terminal at Nice airport, Sam Delamere held Laurie like a lovesick teenager, as the final call for her flight back to England was announced. Desperately, he kissed her eyelids, her nose, her chin, her earlobes, until she laughed through her tears. She'd been so close to him, had spent so much time inside his personal zone, that his skin felt like her own, as if, over the three weeks they'd been together, they'd become the same

133

person. The thought of now being apart, of breathing different air, was more painful than anything she'd ever experienced.

'I love you, Laurie Vale,' he said. 'You and I are meant to be. I promise you that we'll be together for the rest of our lives. I promise, you hear me? Say you hear me.'

'I hear you, darling. Oh, Sam, I can't bear this.'

He rested his forehead against hers.

'I can't say goodbye,' he said. 'It's ridiculous, but I can't.'

She shook her head and he wiped away a tear from her cheek.

'I'm going to sort everything out,' he said, gently. 'It'll be a week at the most, then I'll come and find you.'

As well as the pain of parting, Laurie felt a sudden wave of pity – or was it guilt? – for the other woman, Claire, who Sam was returning home to break up with. Laurie had been dumped before. She knew how tough it was going to be for both of them. Even when, like now, the relationship was practically over anyway.

'Be kind to her, Sam,' she said. 'Don't hurt her any more than you have to.'

He nodded. He understood. Above them, the tannoy system blurted out an urgent call for all remaining passengers on her flight.

Laurie clung on to Sam.

'Just go. Just go quickly. The sooner you do, the sooner we'll be together again,' he said and the pain in his voice had broken her heart.

At first, after she'd returned to England from her time with Sam, she'd been euphoric, unable to help telling everyone she knew that she'd found the love of her life. She threw herself into planning their future. They'd spent ages together talking about the places they wanted to visit, and Laurie started obsessing about a round-the-world trip to kick off their time together.

In a few days her flat was piled high with brochures and *Lonely Planet* guidebooks, as well as details of new properties in five different postcodes, just in case Sam thought it best to move first. As she waited for Sam to call with the good news that he was on his way to her, she rearranged her and Tamsin's flat, assessing everything in terms of how Sam would see it. She even organised a party in Sam's honour, so that he could meet everyone she knew.

Then, two days after she'd been expecting to start her new life with him, a postcard arrived. It showed the bay of Palma on the front. It was a cheap card, with no particular meaning. On the back it said: *I'm sorry. I can't explain, but it would never have worked out. Please don't try to contact me. We can never see each other again. Best just to forget. Take care of yourself, Sam.*

Laurie felt physically winded, as she read and reread the card. Distraught, she turned the card over and over, trying to fathom its meaning. Best just to forget? *Forget?* How could she forget?

It didn't make sense. He'd been her perfect man. He'd made her laugh, he'd made her feel effervescent, as if every moment she'd been with him she'd been the best she could possibly be. He'd made her shine. He'd inspired her. She'd had her best ideas ever when they'd been together. Sure, it had been a whirlwind romance, but he'd fallen in love with her . . . hadn't he? He'd told her often enough.

Unable to believe it, she convinced herself that something terrible had happened and that Sam needed her help. She tried all his numbers, but there was no answer on any of them, not even an answer machine. Then his mobile phone was disconnected. She rang the international operator who said that the number was no longer in use.

And then, finally, the truth hit her. The postcard wasn't a mistake, or somehow a coded plea for help. The truth was that he hadn't been maimed in a terrible accident and was lying in a coma, unable to call her to explain. The truth was that he'd gone home to Claire and had written to Laurie straight away. And he meant what he'd said. Sam really didn't want her to contact him. Whatever they'd had together, it was over. For ever.

A hollow pain ripped through her. Everything she'd ever known, her whole judgement, the very foundation of her personality, seemed to sink away from her like a capsized boat. Roz and Tamsin, Heather and Janey rallied round, reassuring her that it was normal for holiday flings to end badly, but Laurie couldn't be comforted.

How could she have got it so wrong? He'd been lying all along. The profound conversations they'd had about the meaning of life until dawn had been all for show. The emotionally, physically amazing sex had been a sham. She'd been in love with a liar and she only had herself to blame.

Laurie left the bedroom and shut the door. They had been dark days. Dark days that she'd fought to leave behind her. And they *were* behind her. Laurie thought back to the person she'd once been sobbing over at Nice airport and she felt as if she were looking back on a stranger.

She was over Sam, she reminded herself, sternly. These feelings she'd been having were no more than were to be expected as the result of hideous coincidence. Seeing Sam was bound to make her remember the past. But the past was just that: the past. There was nothing to be gained from even thinking about it.

Everything was different now, she reminded herself, as she put on her sarong in the hallway, leaving her suitcase exploded on the floor. It took some mental effort to leave it like that, but she made herself do it. She wasn't going to creep around Rachel's house for weeks on end, like a guilty servant, she was going to enjoy herself. And right now, all she needed was to swim. It would clear her head and stop these feelings, these painful memories she had no intention of reliving.

It was only halfway down the steep bumpy slope through the trees that she looked up and got her first glimpse of the sandy cove below. And what she saw made her momentarily forget her experience in the room upstairs. The beach was completely deserted, apart from a dilapidated boathouse which nestled against the far rocks, up from the shoreline. What if the boathouse could be used as a studio? she wondered. It would be absolutely perfect!

Gasping with delight, she ran down the rest of the way, ripping off her sarong and flinging it on the sand. Then she strode into the warm water, diving under the small rippling waves. As she stood up, her toes grasped the sand on the bottom and her skin tingled all over at the touch of the water.

What the hell, she thought, looking around her, before slipping out of her bikini, scrunching it up in a ball and flinging it, so that it landed with a splat on the sand. It was time to live a little. Lying back in the water, she let her ears fill with the sound of the sea, feeling the sun on her skin, as she floated.

But her thoughts weren't so easily calmed. All this – this villa, this private beach, this new family of hers – was all too strange. Why had she gone to Tony's funeral? she wondered. What quirk of fate had driven her to pay her respects to a man she'd never met? She still couldn't fathom it. She thought about Tony, about her lost uncle as she looked up at the view that must have once given him so much pleasure. And then she thought about his coffin in the small Somerset church.

At first, she felt as if time were warping. She told herself that it was an hallucination, that it simply couldn't be Sam, but someone else connected to Rachel, her family, Tony, this place, the coffin in front of her. But she knew from the helter-skelter ride her insides were taking that this was real. That the man who had come in late, the man who was speaking, was the only man who'd ever broken her heart.

Laurie's whole body adrenalised as she listened to him read a love poem, looking all the time at Rachel. She glanced along the pew to where her aunt was clutching the hand of a young woman. Were she and Sam . . . ?

Laurie couldn't watch. She felt sickened by the irony of the words coming out of Sam's mouth. How dare he speak of love? How dare he sound like he meant every word? How dare he be connected to Rachel? Rachel was her new aunt and here he was spoiling everything.

Laurie couldn't help herself watching him finish the reading and come and sit back in the pew, as if he were the head of the family. She watched Rachel lean over and kiss him. Then, as she watched the woman next to him smile sadly and stroke his cheek, a part of her withered inside.

Then the service was over and she was on her feet moving towards the end of the pew where Rachel was waiting. She looked so serene in her black dress and hat, and her eyes had a misty quality to them that was almost beyond tears.

'Laurie,' she said, stretching out both her hands. 'This is Claire.'

Laurie forced her head to turn robotically to the pretty woman next to Rachel. Claire. Of course it was Claire. When Rachel had mentioned her the previous evening, it hadn't even crossed her mind that it might be *the* Claire. But how *could* she have known? Sam had never told Laurie his girlfriend's surname. And now, here she was, in the flesh.

'Ah, *you're* Laurie,' Claire said.

She'd been crying during the service and her eyes were puffy and her nose blotchy, but even so, Laurie could tell that she had flawless skin and the kind of swishy long dark hair that could only be achieved with extremely regular visits to a salon. In fact, the more Laurie studied her new relation, the more she could tell that Claire was a different breed of woman from her entirely. She was the type that Sam had once claimed he despised: the manicured type, the type whose outside mattered more than the inside. Nevertheless, Laurie immediately felt old and unfashionable next to her.

A hundred questions filled Laurie's head. What if Sam had told her? What if Claire knew all about their affair? What if she made a scene? Laurie felt desperate. She didn't want her credibility blown with Rachel, especially not here.

'I'm sorry about Tony,' Laurie said, her voice croaking unattractively as she shook Claire's hand. She could tell Claire was scrutinising her, but she couldn't tell how much she knew about her. 'It must be terrible for you . . .'

She mumbled herself into silence, but Claire didn't seem to mind. Instead, she tugged enthusiastically at Sam's arm.

'This is my husband, Sam,' she said, pulling Sam forward. 'And you'll meet Archie, our son, later. He's at the house. We didn't think we should bring him . . . Sam, this is her, this is Laurie, the mystery cousin.'

Sam Delamere. After all this time, in the most unexpected place imaginable, Laurie was face to face with her ex-lover. And he was married. To her. To Claire. The girl he'd claimed he didn't love, but clearly did. And they had a child.

In all the times Laurie had imagined seeing Sam again, she had never once considered that he would be a father. The knowledge filled her with such a surge of foolish jealousy that she had to clamp her hand shut to overcome her desire to slap his face.

'How nice to meet you, Laurie,' he said. The familiarity of the way he said her name filled her with anger, her sense of betrayal threatening to engulf her. For one moment, she was tempted to say something facetious, to blow his cover and expose him. She could feel Rachel watching her and time seemed to stop. She imagined turning to Rachel and telling her that she knew all about Sam. That he was a liar. A cheat. A breaker of promises.

Instead, she found herself scooped up into his net of lies. Dismayed and powerless, she fell in with his face-saving strategy, hardly betraying any of the tension she felt. She forced herself to meet his outstretched hand with her own sweating palm. As they touched, the surface of her skin flushed with goose pimples.

'Hi,' she said. She only managed to look at his chest.

'We're going to the crematorium,' Rachel said.

'Just the close family,' Claire added. 'But obviously you're welcome . . .'

Laurie shook her head.

'There's at least two cars,' Rachel said, appealing to her, but her usual clear-headedness seemed to have vanished, as if she'd let go and Claire was now in charge.

'I think it's better if I see you back at the house,' Laurie mumbled, as Claire linked arms with Rachel to gently chaperone her down the aisle.

'Are you sure, Laurie?' Claire asked, her look concerned. Laurie smiled feebly and nodded. 'Then we'll chat later,' Claire said over her shoulder, as she passed. 'We won't be long.'

Then, as Sam stepped in behind them, he looked at Laurie. Just for one second. The merest glance, but still it hit her as if he'd fired a shot from a pistol straight into her chest at point-blank range. She watched in slow motion as he blinked and walked away from her.

Of course she'd run away. There'd been no other choice. She'd been too dismayed by the cruel coincidence, too baffled and shaken up by the twist of fate that had thrown Sam in her path again. There had been no way she'd have been able to face Rachel or to have made small talk with Claire.

As soon as she'd returned to the safety of her life in London, she'd decided to cut Rachel out of her life for good. Her father had been right. She'd lived for long enough without Rachel to know that she could do it perfectly well. What good could possibly come out of being connected to a family of which Sam was such a central part? Instead, she'd forced herself to focus instead on James and on moving out of the flat before Mike and Tamsin took it over as their own.

But still Laurie had been angry. She hadn't told anyone about her meeting with Sam, but his presence in her life again festered inside her, refusing to go away. And then she'd told her father about going to the funeral and his stubbornness had just made her more confused.

And then right in the middle of it all, Rachel had called and had offered her the use of her villa in Mallorca for a couple of months. Laurie had been dismayed by the timing of her aunt's call. She hadn't given her a decision straight away, but as she put the phone down, a sadistic, nasty, but nevertheless delicious thought struck Laurie. Taking Rachel up on her offer was the perfect way to get at Sam. The perfect punishment for everything he'd done.

The fact that she was Rachel's newly favoured niece, the fact that she would be right under Sam's nose – not that she had any intention of seeing him – would mean that he'd be reminded every day of his deceit. Her presence in Mallorca would make him squirm, and for once, he'd be the one plagued by questions. Yes, she thought, she would give Sam Delamere a taste of his own medicine.

Which is why she'd called Rachel back and gratefully accepted her offer. The very next day, with James's help, she'd moved her stuff out of the flat into storage and she'd felt immediately better. She had a house for the summer and James promised that he'd be out to see her as soon as he could find a break in his schedule.

But now, as she lay in the sea, Laurie's cold-hearted need to get at Sam didn't equate to the reality of being in Rachel's home. It had already wrong-footed her and she'd only been here for an hour.

Laurie put her feet down in the water and swept her hair back from her face and stood up. She shouldn't get sunburnt on her first day, but she felt better for floating for ages. She walked slowly out of the water, feeling resolute. She'd made her choice to accept Rachel's offer;

whether through desperation, revenge or greed, or a mixture of all three, she was here now. And she was here to work.

It was only when she went to pick up her sarong that she saw that somebody was on their way down the path from the house. As Laurie snatched up the sarong to cover her body, she recognised the swishy-haired designer-clad figure, waving excitedly. And, with a sinking sense of dread, she suddenly realised the hidden cost of staying at Sa Costa: Claire Delamere had come to pay her a visit.

# Chapter VIII

**Stepmouth, April 1953**

Most of the men Tony knew – from school, the pub and snooker halls – only talked about practical matters: where to go, how to get there and what to do when they did. They were always busy breaking things, or making things, or grunting at each other over diagrams and illustrations of things. Either that or getting so drunk that they didn't have to think or talk about anything at all.

Girls, though, girls seemed to be able to talk about anything. Even stuff that wasn't there to touch. Like moods and dreams and gossip. Give a girl an hour and she could fill it with words. And Tony loved that most of all: the listening. It was what he missed most about school. He'd been a good student and would easily have passed his exams, if he hadn't been kicked out. Even now, he read a couple of books – novels, histories, travel journals – each week. He loved learning new things and hearing about places he'd never been.

And that was why he loved being around his new boss, Emily Jones, who could talk faster than a horse-race commentator, and who'd seen more than Tony Glover could even imagine.

'Not that Jones is strictly my name any more, you understand.'

It was mid-morning and Tony and Emily were sitting on the back doorstep of the Sea Catch Café. Potato peelings were piled up like wood shavings at their booted feet, next to a dented metal bucket full of peeled spuds. River water chuckled by at the end of the yard and the sun beat down from a clear sky.

'Not in the eyes of God,' Emily continued. She was wearing loose-fitting jeans and a white short-sleeved shirt, which she'd tied in a knot at her waist. 'Not the way Mum sees it. According to her, you marry a man and you take his name and you do it for life. Even if that man is one she thoroughly disapproves of. And even if that man turns out to be a total prick.'

Tony gagged on the swig of hot sweet tea he'd just taken. Emily was talking about her ex-husband, Buck, the American soldier she'd married and moved to America to be with after the war (and whom she'd subsequently divorced and returned home to escape).

'I said that last bit, of course, not her,' Emily added. 'And not to her face, of course, because that would only have made her cry. Not that Mum would probably even know what a prick was,' she reflected. 'Not if it came up and shook her by the hand. Not that it would.'

Tony snorted with laughter.

'What's so funny?' she asked, taking a long contemplative drag on her cigarette.

But she was smirking, too, because she already knew exactly what it was: the swearing, the lavatory humour. She'd picked it up from cooking in Buck's uncle's New Jersey restaurant six nights a week, fifty-two weeks a year. And now there wasn't a damn thing she could do about it. The same as the accent, it had stuck.

'Nope, Mum says God doesn't recognise divorce, and so neither does she. According to her, my name's still Emily Drane. And will stay that way till the day I die. Drane,' she said sourly. 'I ask you. With a surname like that, you'd have thought I'd have guessed that Buck would turn out to be full of shit.'

Tony smiled. 'Would you ever marry again?' he asked, accepting the lipstick-stained Pall Mall cigarette she passed to him.

'Maybe. If the right guy came along. But it's not something I'm planning on rushing into.' A blackbird burst from the cherry tree in the centre of the yard. Blossom exploded like flak into the air. 'Nope, once bitten, twice shy, that's me.'

Tony brushed a fleck of ash off his baggy blue kitchen trousers. 'What about dates?'

'Why?' she asked coyly. 'Do you know someone who's going to ask me out on one?'

Tony blushed. Talking to his new boss about this kind of thing was taking some getting used to. All her parents had ever really done was order him around. 'No,' he said, 'but someone's sure to. They'd be crazy not to,' he added truthfully. If he'd been a few years older, and not so preoccupied with someone else right now, he might even have tried his luck himself.

'If someone did and I liked them well enough, I'd probably go. Only I wouldn't go mistaking fun for love this time, you know? Not like with Buck. How about you? Have you asked Rachel Vale out yet?'

The question caught Tony off guard. His heart punched his ribcage. He stared at her, baffled.

This time, it was her who was grinning. 'Because it's only a matter of time before you do,' she went on. 'Or she asks you . . .' She nudged him teasingly. 'Come on, don't be so uptight. I saw the way you two were looking at each other when she called round. Or *not* looking at each other, which is even more obvious . . .'

Tony's mind spun back, remembering how excruciatingly awkward it had been, the two of them, him and Rachel, alone in the café, while Emily had gone to fetch the nylons. He remembered the nylons, too, and how he'd felt lying awake in his grandad's shack that night, picturing Rachel in the arms of someone else at the dance he hadn't gone to, because he'd had no money to spend. He'd imagined how the nylons might have felt to touch . . . and how her warm skin might have felt beneath . . .

'I bet she'd say yes,' Emily declared. 'I bet she's sitting at home right now, hoping you're going to call round and ask. And you should, you know. Because she won't wait around for ever, a pretty girl like that. Before you know it, there'll be someone else knocking on her door and you'll have missed your chance.'

'How do you know they haven't already?' It was the first time he'd admitted to anyone that he'd given Rachel a second thought. It felt like walking on rotten floorboards that could give at any second.

'I don't. And neither do you.'

'Forget it,' he said, as much to himself as her. 'It would never work.'

'Why not?'

'Because there are things about me and the Vale family that you don't understand.'

'Like what your brother did to Mr Vale? Like Mrs Vale ending up in that wheelchair? Or Bill Vale blaming you because your brother's no longer here to hate?'

'So you've heard.' Of course she would have. This town was too small for secrets. Just because he'd never discussed it with her didn't mean she wouldn't have already found out.

'Dad told me,' she admitted.

147

'Then you'll also know why nothing's ever going to happen between me and Rachel.'

'Dad also said you were a good kid. A hard worker. And I happen to agree.'

'Some people don't see it that way.'

'Like Bill Vale?'

'And his mother.'

'But not Rachel?'

'I don't know.' He remembered sitting with Rachel on the wall of St Jude's Cemetery after he'd fought with Cunningham. Could it really have been jealousy that had made her throw that paint? Or was he kidding himself even to hope that? 'Maybe,' he said.

'So find out.'

He flicked the cigarette away. He didn't want to find out, in case he found out he was wrong.

'You've got to think positive,' she said, as if reading his thoughts.

He wished she was right: that enthusiasm would be enough to make it happen. Because he did want to see Rachel again, just to talk to her, even if only to see her smile one more time.

'Bill would kill me if I even went near her,' he said.

'Not if you had a good enough reason, he wouldn't . . .'

'What's that supposed to mean?'

But Emily was already standing and stretching, smoothing her jeans down. 'Time we got back to work,' she said.

An armoury of pans hung from the kitchen rafters. Bunches of basil, rosemary, parsley and thyme were laid out on the worktop, making the air smell soupy and dense. Emily inspected the thin strips of linguine which she'd supervised Tony painstakingly rolling out on the stained wooden chopping board before they'd gone out for their break. He'd only ever seen pasta in a can before.

Without being asked, he pulled down a deep pan and half filled it with cold water. Guy Mitchell was singing 'Look at that Girl' on the crackling radio and Tony hummed along as he set about quartering the potatoes so they'd cook quicker, dropping them one by one into the pan. They lay there submerged, like scoops of vanilla ice cream.

'Cattle food on,' he announced, setting the pan on the stove.

Cattle. That's what Emily called the tourists who came to eat in the Sea Catch Café. Cattle, because they acted like a herd. And cattle, because all they wanted to do was eat the same old food day in, year out.

The sepia menu in the café's window hadn't changed in the eight years that Emily had spent in America. All the dreary British staples were present and correct: tea and biscuits, jam and toast, and not forgetting, of course, potatoes. Potatoes with everything: fried potatoes with liver and onion; boiled potatoes with cabbage and tripe; chipped potatoes with fish on a Friday; mashed potatoes with chicken on Sunday.

'We're going to change all that,' Emily had informed Tony the first day her mother had agreed to let her take over the kitchen. 'Little by little. You and me, Tony, working as a team, we're going to teach these people how to eat.'

Previously, all his chores had been menial: floor scrubbing, vegetable prepping, washing up. The cooking had been done by Emily's mother, while Emily's father had managed the café.

'I don't want us to work like that, though,' Emily had told him. 'I want to train you up as a chef. I want to be able to rely on you when I'm not here and know that either one of us is more than capable of making meals fit for kings.'

Not that there'd been too many kings knocking on their door just yet, she'd acknowledged. Not with it looking as tacky and lacklustre as it did. But that would all change, too. Mr and Mrs Jones were now actively planning on retiring to Wales and Emily was going to buy the place from them with the divorce money left over from Buck. Then she'd be able to do it up as she saw fit.

'*Marinara*,' she announced now, beckoning Tony over. 'Your basic Italian tomato sauce.' She set a cast-iron kettle to boil and tipped several tomatoes from a rustling brown paper bag on to the worktop and proceeded to cut crosses in their tops and bases. 'So the skins will split easily when we *blanch* them,' she explained.

Tony had loved working for her these last few weeks. She'd made him use his brain as well as his hands, teaching him different cooking techniques and recipes each day. But there was something he'd been meaning to tell her, something that he was worried might affect her plans. He liked her too much to keep on deceiving her.

'You know I'm going to have to leave when I turn eighteen, don't you?' he said. 'In September. You know I'm going to have to do my national service in the army.'

Now that he'd finally spat it out, he was relieved. And if she fired him now, well, at least he'd been honest, at least it would be her letting him down and not the other way round.

'Uh-huh.' She handed him a knife and pointed at three cloves of garlic.

'So why are you still teaching me all this?' he asked, starting to chop.

'Because there'll still be a job here for you when you get back.'

She said it so simply, but it hadn't even occurred to him. 'Are you serious?' he asked.

'Why wouldn't I be?'

'I don't know.' He did; it was because he hadn't imagined she'd consider he was worth it.

'You learn quick, Tony. You'll make a good chef. Of course I'm going to want you back.'

She pulled a notebook from her jeans pocket and started scribbling on it with a blunt pencil.

Tony picked up a leaf of basil and held it up to his nose to hide his smile. A chef. He liked the sound of that. So long as the army didn't send him off to Korea or somewhere to get killed first, he considered, then maybe she was right. Maybe he could come back here and pick up where he'd left off. And then . . . well, who knew, one day he might even end up with a restaurant of his own.

Ripping the sheet from the notebook, Emily took an envelope from the dresser drawer. 'I need you to run an errand,' she said. 'But you reek of garlic, so first go wash your hands. Rub them with a stainless-steel spoon. It'll get the smell off.'


'Is this some kind of a joke?' snapped Rachel Vale. Her cheeks were puce, like they'd been slapped.

Her hair was straggly and wet from when she'd been washing it in the kitchen sink, before Bill had asked her to mind the shop while he helped supervise the coal delivery in the yard. An artery throbbed angrily in her neck, visible above the collar of her creased robin-red checked shirt. With her arms hanging down low and her fingers furled into fists, she reminded Tony of a comic-book story he'd once read about Calamity Jane, in which she'd beaten the crap out of two cowboys for trying to steal her horse.

'What?' Tony asked.

She thrust the letter across the counter at him. 'What do you think?'

On the counter, next to the letter, was the envelope in which Tony had delivered it. Rachel's name was scrawled across it in Emily's slanting handwriting. He picked up the letter and read whatever it was that Emily had written which had caused such offence.

Dear Rachel,
I'd like to take you out on a date.
Please meet me beneath the tower of St Hilda's Church
at seven o'clock, so we can arrange when and where.
Hopefully yours,
Tony Glover

He swallowed. He blinked. He gawped. He reread the words and stared in disbelief, too stupefied to speak. *A date?* Emily had told him it was a shopping list. *At the church at seven?* Emily had told him to deliver the envelope to Rachel as quickly as possible. ('Not Bill,' she'd specified, and Tony now saw why.) *Hopefully yours?* Had Emily lost her mind? He was going to kill her. Who the hell did she think she was, messing with his life like this? Her, with her divorced husband on the other side of the Atlantic ... since when did she become an expert on matters of the heart? He felt sick with embarrassment. Oh, Christ, what had she done?

'Well?' The way Rachel stabbed her finger at the letter, it might as well have been his eye.

Tony could smell the shampoo on her which she hadn't had time to wash out. It was Silvikrin, the same as his mother used, but its familiarity brought no comfort now. 'I can explain,' he started to say.

Only it then occurred to him that he couldn't. Or rather he could. He could confirm Rachel's suspicion that it was all a joke. He could tell her that it was Emily's joke and Emily's handwriting. But chances were Rachel wouldn't believe him, or think Emily capable of such a prank. She'd think the opposite: that it was *his* joke, *his* handwriting, and that he'd done it to be cruel.

'What's the matter? Cat got your tongue?'

Tony's mouth opened, closed, opened again. His guts clenched. Even if he stuck to the truth and Rachel did believe him about Emily having written the letter, she'd still end up hurt, thinking herself the butt of a joke. And Tony didn't want that.

Especially as he knew that none of this had anything to do with cruelty. It was all Emily's crazy way of trying to help. 'Not if you had a good enough reason.' That's what she'd said in the yard. And that's what she'd given him now.

'Because if you think you can just walk in here and make a fool out of me, Tony Glover, you've got another think coming,' Rachel said, tearing the letter in two. 'What?' she scoffed. 'You didn't think I'd actually fall for this, did you? Don't tell me you were dumb enough to think I'd actually turn up at the church for you and your mates to laugh at?'

'I –'

'Because that would never happen. And do you want to know why? Because I don't like you, Tony Glover. Not one little bit. You're arrogant. Stupid. And about as good-looking as a pig's arse. There!' she declared triumphantly. 'So what do you think about that?'

What Tony thought was that she was amazing. Even with what she was saying. Even with the way she was saying it. Even though she obviously wanted him dead. He felt the full power of her personality focused entirely on him, like the sun through a magnifying glass. And it felt wonderful. So wonderful, in fact, that he suddenly wished he *had* written the letter himself. Suddenly he wanted to be every bit as crazy as Emily Drane, because suddenly she didn't seem crazy at all.

'It's not a joke,' he said. And it wasn't. Not any more. He took the two torn pieces of paper and matched them up and turned them round to face her. 'I'm asking you out.' He said it slowly, so there could be no mistake.

Bill Vale strode through from the back of the shop.

'What are you doing here?' he asked Tony, his expression turned to lead.

Tony knew then that he'd blown it. He'd never get a chance to persuade Rachel that he meant what he'd just said. She'd end up thinking it was all part of the joke. Then he remembered – and glanced at – the torn letter in the middle of the counter. He tried not to look at it, as if not seeing it himself might somehow make it invisible to Bill. But it was too late.

Simultaneously, Bill and Tony grabbed for it. But it was Rachel who got there first.

'It's Emily's,' she told her brother, stepping away from him, shielding the letter with her shoulder. 'Her grocery list. She telephoned earlier to say that she'd be sending her' – she looked Tony over with obvious distaste – '*boy* over with it. He somehow managed to rip it on the way . . .'

Tony couldn't believe what he was hearing. Why was

she covering for him like this? All she had to do was hand over the letter to her brother and sit back and watch the fireworks begin.

'Two pounds of cornflour,' Rachel recited, pretending to read off the pieces of paper in her hand, 'and two tins of condensed milk . . .'

'Wait outside,' Bill told Tony. 'I don't care who you're running your errands for, you don't ever come in here. Now get out. I'll bring Emily's order to you in a minute.'

'Tony Glover,' Rachel called after Tony.

She was packing groceries into a cardboard box. She held up the torn pieces of paper, so that both him and Bill could see. Tony knew it. She'd been toying with him. Now she was going to tell Bill everything.

'The answer's yes,' she said.

'To what?' Bill asked.

'To the query on the list.'

'What query?' Bill asked.

'It's not important,' Rachel answered, reaching up for a packet of flour.

But as what she meant sunk in, as far as Tony was concerned, she'd never been more wrong in her life.


Tony stared across the graveyard and up at the clock tower for what must have been the tenth time. Above it, soundlessly, bats snatched insects from the air, darting across the pearly circle of moon like minnows across the surface of a well. The leaves of the sycamore trees hung motionless on the branches, black as tar. The clock read one minute past seven: Rachel Vale was late.

Or not coming at all. Because that was more likely, wasn't it? That she'd changed her mind, or had never planned on meeting him in the first place? Because who was to say that she wasn't playing a joke of her own, leaving him out here, feeling stupid and small, the same way he'd initially made her feel in the shop?

Tony tried clinging to Emily's advice about thinking positive, but he couldn't manage it. Instead, he feared the worst, because, suddenly, Rachel was too important to lose.

But why? he asked himself in the same breath. Why her? Why this desperate need to see her? Was he doing it for him? Because he'd thought he could never have her? Because having her meant he could have anything? Or was he doing it for her? Because by doing his best to make her happy, he'd be wiping away the sadness his brother had brought her? Was that what this was all about? Forgiveness? Restitution? Even redemption?

Or was he doing it for them both? Because by being together he hoped they'd uncover a happiness within themselves which would always elude them apart?

He shivered. The truth was he didn't know. And now it didn't matter. His ears strained through the night a final time, attempting to filter out any sound which might indicate her approach. But all he got was confirmation of what he already knew: he was alone.

He was next to a cracked and mildewed wooden bench on the opposite side of the graveyard to where Edward Vale had been buried eight years before. On the day of the funeral, Tony's mother had kept him from school, behind closed curtains at home. He'd wanted to go. He'd told her he had nothing to hide. But she'd told him it didn't work that way, and never would. And now it looked like she'd been right and Emily was wrong.

The long cycle ride back through the dark to his grandfather's shack now stretched depressingly ahead of him. These last few nights, Tony had been putting off going back there for as long as possible. Like last night, when he'd stayed out at the Bay Road Snooker Club, with Pete and Arthur, until it had shut at eleven.

It was the loneliness he couldn't bear, though he'd told Don the opposite when he'd called round last week to see how Tony was getting on. 'She's feeling guilty,' Don had told him, meaning his mother. 'She hasn't actually said as much, but I know her well enough to know that it's eating her up.' Everything which Tony had gone on to show Don – the stove he'd rigged up, the insulation and the tin bath outside – had seemed pointless from then on, like components of a childish game. If his mother had wanted him back, then why couldn't she just tell him? Why couldn't they just talk about it and work out their differences?

But at the same time, he knew why not: because what had driven them apart wasn't words, but actions, *his* actions.

And that was why he had to stick it out. He had to show her that he could make it on his own. As an adult. To be allowed back, he knew he had to prove to her that he could stand on his own two feet.

He set off along the mossy path which meandered through the gravestones towards the churchyard gate. Suddenly his body went rigid. He'd heard something.

Snap.

There it was again: the crack of a branch. Then came a hiss. Then another. Until, finally, he realised it was somebody whispering his name.

'Tony? Tony, are you there?'

As soon as he saw her – standing in the shadow of a marble tomb – he wanted to jump up and punch the sky. But he wouldn't let himself, not until he knew she was here for the same reason as him. He stepped out of the shadows so that she could see him.

'Here,' he answered.

There were other things he'd planned to say: 'You're beautiful', and 'I haven't stopped thinking about you since we talked after the fight'; things that were true. And yet 'Here' was all he said, because her being here was all that actually mattered.

They walked towards each other, then stopped. Their breath mingled in the cold night air. Her hair was combed back and pinned down by a white Alice band. She was wearing a thick, dark V-neck sweater and scarf. Her skin seemed to glow, the colour of the moon. She looked ethereal, as if she came from another, more beautiful world. He knew he'd remember her this way until the day he died.

'You managed to get away, then?'

'I told Mum and Bill that I was popping round to Pearl's to borrow a school book . . .' She was breathless, excited, or scared . . .

'You think I'm crazy, don't you?' he asked.

Her eyes danced with excitement. 'Isn't that why I'm here?'

'What? Because you like crazy people?'

'Or because I want to be crazy, too . . .'

Bill . . . Keith . . . Everything Tony had planned on saying about them, about how they'd affected his and Rachel's lives, he no longer wanted to discuss. He didn't want their brothers hijacking this moment. He wanted to keep it theirs.

She stepped in close to him and looked him over so intently that for an insane instant he became convinced she was going to kiss him.

158

'You look weird' was what she actually said, flipping his tie up over his jacket.

He laughed. And as he did, some of the tension eased from his shoulders and the frown flattened on his face.

'I don't mean you look bad,' she said. 'You don't. You look older, that's all. It's probably the tie.'

She said older, but he guessed she meant boring. He knew it had been a mistake to wear the tie, but he'd had no choice. 'It's a present,' he explained. 'From Emily.'

Emily had had it waiting for him when he'd got back from seeing Rachel at Vale Supplies that afternoon. So he didn't look like he'd been sweating in a kitchen all day, she'd said. She'd told him to go and use the bath upstairs and had lent him an ironed blue shirt to wear, too. He'd clipped his nails, combed his hair and polished his shoes till they'd gleamed like quartz. He'd made Emily promise to tell no one that he was hoping to see Rachel Vale. And never – no matter what came of it – to tell Bill Vale a thing.

'Are you two friends?' Rachel asked.

Were they? He hoped so. 'As much as we can be, seeing as how I work for her,' he said.

'I wish I had a job,' she said.

'One day you will.'

She shrugged, grinning. 'Not necessarily. I might marry someone rich. Or, better still, end up rich myself and retire by the time I'm thirty.'

'You might.' He knew she was only teasing, but he remembered now how she'd stood up to him in the shop that afternoon. He thought she could probably do anything she put her mind to.

'Do you like your job?' she asked. 'Do you prefer it to school?'

He'd never thought to compare the two. 'There's not

159

much difference, I suppose,' he said. 'It's all about learning and getting enough knowledge to get you to the next place.'

'And where's your next place?'

'I'm not sure.' He smiled. 'You ask a lot of questions, you know.'

'I'm just trying to work you out.'

'Is that why you came?' he asked.

'I don't know. I shouldn't have. I shouldn't be here at all.'

'Neither of us should be.'

Her expression turned serious. 'We can talk about why not,' she said, 'until we're blue in the face. I thought about that on the way over here.'

'What else did you think about?'

'That it took a lot of guts to do what you did this afternoon. To walk in there and ask me out.'

With a little help, Tony thought.

'And we wouldn't be here, either of us, unless we wanted to be,' she continued.

They stared at each other in silence. He could feel the moment slipping away, but couldn't think of what he might say to stop it.

Rachel shivered. 'I'm going to have to get going soon,' she said. 'Or Mum and Bill will start asking questions . . .'

Tony felt crushed, miserable. He avoided her eyes. 'So, I'll see you around, then, I suppose . . .'

Suddenly, she tugged at the lapel of his jacket. 'Kiss me,' she whispered urgently.

Before he knew it, before he'd even consciously moved his head towards hers, their lips were touching and they'd started to kiss. He closed his eyes and it was like soaring through space.

She broke away from him with a start, like she'd been jolted, or shocked. Stepping back, the heel of her shoe clipped a cracked flower vase, half hidden in a clump of wilted daffodils. From its perch on a nearby gravestone, a white owl watched them unblinkingly.

Tony had kissed plenty of girls before, but never like this. He couldn't explain how connected to her, how mixed with her, he'd felt. He hadn't wanted it to end.

Rachel reached out and unfastened his tie, sliding the knot down, then pulling, letting it slither from around his neck like a snake.

'That's better,' she said. 'That's more like the you I know. Not that I know you at all.'

The comment brought him back down to earth.

'Can I keep it?' she asked, scrunching the tie in her hand.

'I didn't think you liked it.'

'I don't.' She held it up to her face, and inhaled the night through it. 'But it will remind me of you.'

She kissed him hard on the lips.

'I've got to go,' she told him.

The finality of it threw him into a panic. 'When can I see you again?' he blurted out, forgetting everything he'd ever learnt about playing it cool with girls, instead wanting there to be no mistake about just how keen on her he was. He'd lived in this town with her for his whole life; they'd wasted enough time already.

'You decide. Write me another letter.'

'But what about Bill?' he asked, remembering how close he'd come to intercepting the last one, nervous that he might somehow find the next.

Rachel looked around. Her gaze stopped at the vase by their feet. 'Write to me here,' she said, kneeling down and setting the vase upright and placing a flat stone on top.

'And I can do the same to you. This is our place now.'

She kissed him then, a last time, before squeezing his hands so tight that they hurt. 'Always be this romantic,' she whispered into his ear.

Then she was gone, swallowed up by the dark.

# Chapter IX

**Mallorca, Present Day**

The sunlight poured in through the skylight and the cold shower switched off automatically as Sam stepped out from beneath its jets. Foamy water gurgled down the drain and the smell of camomile body wash lingered in the air. Dripping on to the wet room's white-tiled floor, Sam peered up close at his reflection in the backlit shaving mirror, noticing for the first time the tiny wrinkles at the corners of his eyes.

Crow's feet. That's what his mother had called hers when he'd naively pointed them out as a child. He remembered how ancient he'd considered her at the time. Calculating their respective ages, he smiled. She'd probably only been in her thirties, the same as he was now. He thought about how much of her life had still stretched ahead of her then and wondered if she'd realised it herself. Or guessed how quickly it could pass.

Laughter lines, not crow's feet, he decided, noticing how his smile had served to accentuate them. Either that or not enough sunscreen. But nothing to do with age, he reassured himself. Nor stress. He pushed back his hair and started to rub his temples with the balls of his thumbs, the way the doctor had shown him. Stress, he told himself, was all in the mind.

He walked through to check on Archie. Even though barely ten minutes had past since Sam had put him to bed and read him some stories, he was already asleep. Sam stood there, listening to him breathe, watching him curled up in the tiny bed with his toy panda. No matter how little sense the rest of Sam's life sometimes made, Archie was there to remind him that there would always be a purpose to it all.

He thought back to that morning, to when Archie had sneaked into his and Claire's bedroom and tugged at his fingers, whispering over and over, 'Up, Daddy, up, up, up,' until Sam had finally rolled out of bed. In the kitchen, they'd cut slices of bread into fish shapes, and then Sam had toasted them and covered them with scrambled eggs. He'd discovered Archie no longer liked his cereal in a plastic bowl, but in a china one. 'Like a *gwone* up, Daddy.' Sam smiled. But it was a sad kind of smile, because here, before his very eyes, with each new word Archie mastered, he knew his life was slipping by, hour by day by year.

'Sweet dreams, my beautiful boy,' he said softly, closing the door on his way out.

He towelled down as he walked through to his and Claire's bedroom. The night was so humid, it was like wading through sweat. He picked up the remote and flicked the A/C up to max. Already, any benefit he'd derived from the cold shower had been lost. The air-conditioning unit clicked on in the wall behind him and started to hum.

Letting the towel fall around his ankles, he stood naked beneath the ceiling fan and stared through the damask curtain at the illuminated silhouettes of the yachts lined up stern to dock in the harbour of Puerto Portals below the village.

One of them, *The Ark Angel*, was Claire's, a thirty-five-metre Benetti steel-hulled motor yacht, which had been left to her by Tony (in spirit; in law, it was still held as a company asset).

It was the *Angel* Tony had been staying on when he'd died off Biarritz. But tonight it was to be a place of celebration. Its two decks were already decorated with red (Claire's favourite colour) balloons in anticipation of the drinks party which Sam and Claire were to host. It was their wedding anniversary, put back a few weeks because of Tony's funeral.

Claire was big on anniversaries, big on anything, in fact, which gave her an excuse to party. But this was to be a smaller gathering than intended, since – at Sam's suggestion – they'd cut family from the original guest list. To avoid diluting the effect of Tony's funeral, he'd said.

Claire was sitting on the edge of the bed, wearing the red lace suspender belt and matching bra Sam had picked up from her favourite Westbourne Grove boutique the last time he'd been in London on business. The cream silk dressing gown she'd been wearing when he'd got back from playing squash after work lay in a ruffled heap on the rough-flecked sisal carpet. Bass throbbed out from discreetly hidden speakers. On the off-white wall opposite her, *MTV Dance* played on a flatscreen TV, one of three which Claire had had installed in their five-bedroom penthouse apartment. Claire watched it unblinkingly. She looked vampire-like without her make-up in the flickering light.

The room, styled with grey and beige furnishings, had an oddly impersonal feel to it. That was down to Claire, who'd always been keen on interior design. Ever since Sam had known her, she'd talked of one day making a business out if it. He wished she would. From her general delegation of the role to their nanny, Isabel Salvador, it was obvious that motherhood provided her with little satis-faction. So why *not* try something else? It would certainly have given them something else to talk about other than domestic issues and island gossip . . . Ambition, industry . . . Sam believed everyone could cultivate such qualities in themselves. They were qualities he respected, qualities he could have respected in *her*. Yet each time he'd offered to help turn her business idea into reality, she'd demurred. The timing had never been right, she'd always claimed. From the way she'd always said it, he'd come to suspect it never would be.

'What do you think?' she asked him now. She was waggling her toes at him; she'd painted her toenails gold.

A misty childhood memory surfaced in Sam's mind of eating Cadbury's chocolate, while watching the new colour TV his dad had bought the family one rainy afternoon just before Christmas. 'You look like a Bond girl,' he replied.

Claire grinned. Flattered? Amused? He couldn't tell which.

'Gold-toe-girl,' she artfully sang to the tune of *Goldfinger*, as she slowly uncrossed her legs to reveal that she wasn't wearing any knickers. 'Or Pussy Galore,' she joked, giggling, as she watched him running his eyes over her tanned legs. 'So tell me, husband,' she asked, 'after all these years of marriage, do I still look good enough to eat?'

They made love – *love*, that's what he told himself, because that's what he wanted to believe – in the air-conditioned atmosphere with the fan spiralling above them.

Towards the end, Sam felt Claire's nails digging deeper into his shoulders. Her eyes were closed, her teeth gritted. Passion could still captivate, he'd learnt. With or without love. With more of it, or with less.

'Harder,' she was telling him now. He watched her eyes flash open. 'Look at me, Sam. Look me in the eyes.'

His heart pounded. He did as he was told. Because he had to show her that he wanted her. Because he had to prove it to himself as well. It was like with each thrust he was trying to bring them closer, to cement them together. He wanted to make them one, not two. He wanted to fuse them like two separate chemicals into an unbreakable compound.

They rolled over, her clinging to him. She leant forward, her jade necklace hanging down between her pointed breasts, trailing across his face and chest. As she pressed down on him, he kissed her face feverishly. He thrust faster, harder, until finally he came.

She flopped down sweating beside him. 'Happy anniversary,' she gasped.

He lay there panting, remembering how her eyes had flashed open and stared into his, as she'd told him to look at her. A bead of sweat chased down his jawline and neck.

It hit him then, as she slid her hand into his and gripped it tight. In that moment of potentially perfect unity, his heartbeat stuttered, then raced. Air leapt like flames from his lungs. He felt trapped, like he was underwater. His brow ran wet with sweat. He turned from Claire to stop her seeing.

Instinct told him to crawl under the bed, to curl up on the floor in a ball. Get away from her, it seemed to shout. But he fought it. He knew what this was. It was the same debilitation which had possessed him as he'd stood at the church lectern and stared at Laurie Vale. It was fear and he mustn't give in to it. Do that, he knew, and he'd find himself in the grip of a full-blown anxiety attack: breathless, dizzy, panicked and cramped.

He knew it, because that's what had happened to him after the funeral, when Rachel had announced the news about Sam taking over Ararat to the rest of the family at Dreycott Manor. When she'd asked Sam to say a few words, he'd started stuttering like he hadn't done since he'd been a child. As the family had stared at him in confusion, he'd managed to excuse himself and leave. That's when he'd locked himself in the bathroom. That's when the real panic had set in.

'Are you OK, Sam?' Claire was asking him now.

The throb of the bass boomed. Slowly – one, two, three, four – Sam started to count to ten. He focused on the light clock on the wall, telling himself that the pain was psychosomatic. It would pass. He'd been assured of that. In time. The same as the nervousness. And the sense of impending discovery, which had dogged his every step since Tony's funeral. In time, he'd been told, it would all go away.

He'd had himself checked out the day he'd got back to Mallorca after the funeral. The biggies: cancer, heart disease; the tests (ECG, blood) for those had turned up negative. Stress, the company doctor had put his little episode down to. Unsurprising, considering what had happened to Tony, she'd opined. She'd asked Sam about his dreams then, about whether he felt he was losing control of his life. More relaxation, she'd then prescribed when he'd replied in the negative. Less alcohol (not that he drank much, anyway) and plenty of sleep. And, of course, time. Because time was the greatest healer of all.

'Sam?' He registered the note of urgency now present in Claire's voice. (He'd told her nothing about his consultation with the doctor.)

Eight, he continued to count. Nine . . . The clock's second hand flickered forward. As quick as it had come, the pain vanished from his chest, like a giant hand had released him from its grip. His shoulders slumped. His heartbeat slowed. He breathed in deep and closed his eyes.

With a supreme effort, he managed to speak. 'I'm fine,' he replied, forcing a smile as he rolled over to face Claire. Then the smile became genuine as he realised that, for now, he'd beaten it – the worry, the fear – just like the doctor had told him he could. Then came anger, anger that he could have been so weak.

'What happened?' she asked.

'Nothing.'

'You went all quiet on me.' She studied his face. 'And you've turned a very peculiar colour.'

Getting up, he took his towel from the floor and wiped the sweat from his brow. He sat on the edge of the bed. 'I must be dehydrated.' The croak in his voice abetted the lie.

She peered round at him, eyeing him sceptically. 'You're sure that's all?'

'Yes.'

She fetched a bottle of Evian from her dressing table.

'Drink,' she told him.

He drained it in one, a whole litre.

'You're getting some colour back now,' she said. 'Serves you right.'

'Why?'

'Playing squash in this weather and then fucking . . . what did you expect?'

He breathed out. There. He had an excuse and he hadn't even used it. He had played squash, with his colleague and friend, Günther, after work. He'd lost five games in a row (the only five Günther had ever won). Sam shrugged at Claire, grinned, happy now to make a joke of it. Because he could now; now that he felt normal; now that his heartbeat was metronome-steady and it was like nothing had ever happened.

'It was a bit stupid, wasn't it?' he agreed.

She nodded, smiled. Finally, her expression relaxed. 'Though it does keep you in good shape,' she remarked, kneeling on the bed behind him and stroking her hands over his well-defined arms. She began kneading his shoulders. 'You're still terribly tense. You're not worried about tonight, are you?'

'No.'

'Sure?'

'Positive. Why would I be?'

She ignored the question. They both knew why. Because of his uncharacteristic behaviour after the funeral when Rachel had asked him to give a speech. When he'd unlocked the bathroom door, he'd told everyone he hadn't been stuttering at all, but choking, because he'd half swallowed some chewing gum. But he hadn't thought that anyone had believed him then, and here was the proof of it now. 'Only if you are,' Claire continued, 'there's no need for you to give a speech.'

'Didn't I just tell you I wasn't worried?' he snapped. No one had mentioned the incident until now. He'd assumed it had been forgotten in the wider misery of the day. But of course it had been noted. Of course it had been noted by Claire.

'No need to be like that,' she chided, before musing, 'But if it's not the party that's stressing you out, then what could it be, I wonder?' He didn't like the mockery in her voice, but he liked even less what she asked him next: 'Don't tell me you've still got a bee in your bonnet about Laurie Vale?'

He felt the tension heighten in her fingers. He had to be careful how he answered. Claire was bright. That was one of the traits which had drawn him to her in the first place. But he was bright, too, bright enough to know that he couldn't simply dismiss her questions as idle curiosity, much less wifely concern.

Was she suspicious already? That was his greatest fear. Had his body language betrayed him when he'd introduced himself to Laurie at the funeral as if to a stranger? Had it led Claire to wonder why he'd then studiously avoided so much as looking at their beautiful new relation? Or had Claire spotted the fear in his eyes when she'd told him last night about Laurie's arrival on the island? Could it be that Claire had intuitively diagnosed what the doctor had failed to: namely that the cause of his anxiety was a woman who'd reappeared in his life with the power to destroy it?

He didn't need to fake his disgust about this latest turn of events when he answered, 'I can't believe she didn't consult me.'

'Who?'

'Rachel. I can't believe she's moved that woman into the villa without running it by me first.' Laurie Vale was to be staying at Sa Costa for the summer, last night's email from Rachel had said.

'But why should she?' Claire asked, working her fingers around Sam's neck.

Because I don't want Laurie Vale anywhere near us, was the truth he couldn't say.

'Because I might have already arranged for someone else to stay there,' he replied instead. Which was also true. Plenty of Ararat's business associates had stayed at Sa Costa in the past. As well as being their home from home, Tony and Rachel had always looked on the property as a business asset, one which could be used to seal and sweeten any deal. 'Someone important,' Sam added.

'Rachel obviously thinks that Laurie *is* important.'

'Rachel hardly knows her.' Fifty years. That's how long Laurie's side of the family had been cut off from Claire's. It was just Sam's luck that Rachel had decided that now was the time to start rebuilding bridges. And just his luck that Laurie Vale had been the first person who'd volunteered to walk across.

'You've changed your tune, haven't you?' Claire asked.

'About what?'

'"You two might even end up friends",' Claire quoted. 'Isn't that what you told me before Pops's funeral?'

'And "pigs might fly", you told me,' he replied, remembering the conversation. 'And you were right: she probably is just a little gold-digger, coming over here to see what she can get.'

'My, my, well, it's certainly true what they say about a little power . . .' Claire's fingers pushed roughly at a knot of muscle in Sam's neck.

He twitched in pain, then turned on her. 'My job's to protect this company.'

She smirked, delighted at having baited him so easily. She started to say something, then stopped. Rolling away from him to the opposite side of the bed, she lit a cigarette and looked across at him with amusement.

'What?' he asked.

The fan's vortex obliterated the thin vapour trail of smoke which she blew out. 'What you said just now . . . about Laurie Vale . . . about her being a gold-digger . . .'

'What about it?'

Claire's smile broadened. 'Well, I forgot to mention it earlier . . .'

172

He didn't like the sound of this. 'Mention what?'

'That you'll be able to tell her yourself . . .'

Sam turned cold. 'I'm not following.'

'When she comes to the party tonight. And before you say she can't, it's too late: I've already asked and she's already said yes.'

At nine thirty Sam was standing on the *Angel*'s fly bridge. A citronella candle burned in a windproof holder at his side, making the air smell like the lemon groves he'd used to walk through near Deià. He nodded his head, feigning interest in a discussion taking place between Ararat's Parisian property lawyer, Luc Laporte, and the island's biggest yacht broker, Jamie Dodd, about the relative merits of two competing motor-yacht designers.

Sam sailed himself but, unlike Jamie and Luc, was no diesel-head. He had a schooner named *Flight*. It was small enough for him to crew on his own, to rig out and tack across the bay. Doing that on a clear day, with the sun on his skin, the wind pressed tight to the sails and the muscular flex of the sea on the tiller in his hand, he sometimes found himself overwhelmed by the simple harmony of it all.

Happiness, he thought at such times, was not thinking at all. Happiness was being. Being in the right place. Or with the right person. But not needing to question it all. Which is what he'd caught himself doing daily – even hourly – of late.

The last time Sam had been here on the *Angel*, he'd been with Tony. It had been lunchtime and they'd been planning ways of getting themselves a decent foothold in the burgeoning Croatian tourist industry. Everything had seemed so much simpler then. Certainty had seemed so attainable. Now, as Sam sipped desultorily at his champagne, he thought of Tony and wished him well.

Tony had loved this boat. Or being seen on it at any rate. Sam smiled, remembering how his father-in-law would happily burn up a thousand bucks of fuel to hop between Palma and Ibiza old town, where he'd have the *Angel* moor up alongside Rachel's favourite seafood restaurant, and wait there until he and Rachel had dined, before bringing them back home.

Sam was the opposite. Whenever he could dissuade Claire from the city lights, he'd drive her to one of the island's less fashionable hilltop restaurants, where they could sit and eat without being disturbed. He and Claire talked then, he felt, about themselves in a way which they never did otherwise. It was like the only way they could catch glimpses of the people they'd been when they'd first met, was by sweeping aside the clutter of the life they'd built together since.

'The point being, Jamie, now is *exactly* the right time to invest,' Luc was saying, 'because that's what no one else will be doing.' Ash crumbled from Luc's cigar on to the deck. 'What do you think, Sam?'

Both Luc and Jamie looked to him for support. Sam guessed the conversation had moved on to something other than boats, but was clueless as to what.

'I think it's a tricky one,' he equivocated. 'But go on,' he said to them both, 'I'm interested in hearing what the two of you think.'

Nodding to the boat's stewardess for more champagne, Jamie picked up the conversational baton. 'It's too big a risk,' he declared. 'I think it's much safer to . . .'

With a look, Sam warded off the stewardess from topping up his own glass. He didn't want to drink. He felt no cause to celebrate. And he needed to remain alert. Looking back down the stairwell which led to the aft deck, he saw that Laurie was still there, being busily interviewed by a gaggle of Claire's chattering friends. Where they, like Claire, were dressed in uniform black, Laurie wore a simple white dress. He'd watched her kick off her flat white Birkenstocks as she'd stepped aboard. He found her more beautiful than any of them, more beautiful than Claire, and hated himself for thinking it.

She glanced up at him, before returning to her conversation as if he'd been no more than a shadow.

Revenge? Malice? Entertainment even? Sam ticked off the boxes. Because it could have been any of them, Laurie's motivation for being here. He didn't believe for a second that she'd come to Mallorca to work. Not like Rachel did. And Claire now claimed to as well.

'She is family, after all,' Claire had told him as she'd swatted aside his protest over having invited Laurie to the party. 'And it'll also mean I can keep a close eye on her,' she'd added, more realistically. 'And, besides, Rachel asked me to.'

No, Sam didn't know why Laurie was here. What he did know, however, was that he wasn't going to allow her to cause a scene. Not in front of all these people. Nor plant herself on this island – *his* island – like some rumbling epicentre threatening to rip his world apart. The circle of women around her opened up as Claire pointed to the bow of the boat. Laurie walked that way, out of Sam's line of sight. He waited for Claire's back to turn.

'You'll have to excuse me, gentlemen,' he then said.

He hurried down the stairwell and then towards the bow. The chattering voices from the party faded behind him. Then, suddenly, he stopped.

175

There she was, standing alone on the vessel's prow, looking out to the harbour entrance, silhouetted against the shimmering Mediterranean night sky. Popular cultural references flew at him – *Titanic, The French Lieutenant's Woman* – all of them romantic, and all of them doomed.

He wanted to go to her, to get this over with as soon as possible. But there was too great a chance of being discovered there together, bathing in the moonlight like the lovers they'd once been.

He ducked out of sight and sank into the shadows cast by the empty wheelhouse to wait.

Alongside the *Angel*, another party was taking place on a boat called *Moondance*. Sam watched its immaculately attired skipper, resplendent in peaked cap and glistening epaulettes, standing by the *passerelle* and welcoming guests aboard. The two boats' music mingled between them in a heady fusion, salsa from the *Moondance* and Parisian loungecore from the *Angel*, as chosen by Claire.

Everywhere Sam looked – on the *Moondance* and back towards the *Angel*'s aft deck – he saw people smiling, crystal champagne flutes being raised, canapés being eaten and cigarettes burning like fireflies against the still dark sea.

When finally he did hear Laurie's footsteps padding softly towards him across the teak deck, he stepped from the shadows and into her path.

Startled, she held up her hand to her chest. As she recognised him, her expression turned to bitterness.

'We need to talk,' he said.

'Do we?'

'You know we do.'

'What about?'

Even now as he spoke, Claire could be walking up behind him unseen. 'Us,' he hissed.

'There's an us?'

'Yes. No.' He didn't know what to say. 'There was,' he answered, 'once.'

Her expression gave nothing away. 'Only from the way you acted at my uncle's funeral, I was assuming that you and I had never met before.'

A sense of unreality reigned over the situation. Just as he'd initially refused to believe what he'd seen with his own eyes as he'd stood at the lectern at Tony's funeral, so a part of him persisted in refusing to believe it was possible that Laurie could genuinely be related to Claire. Or even be standing before him now. But it *was* true. And nothing was going to change it. Like it or not, this was the hand that fate had thrown him, and now it was up to him to deal with it.

'I'm sorry,' he said. Even to him, the words sounded hopelessly inadequate.

'Sorry?'

'Yes.'

'About pretending you didn't know me?'

'Yes.'

'Anything else?'

'What?'

'You heard.' For the first time, she'd raised her voice.

'Listen . . . can we –' He indicated the open wheelhouse door at his side.

She completed his sentence for him: '– finish this discussion inside?'

'Yes.'

'Why should I? You finished whatever we had a long time ago, Sam. What on earth makes you think I've got anything more to say to you?'

'There are still things I need you to hear.'

'So that you can feel better about yourself? Forget it.'

She tried to push past him, but he stood his ground.

'Get out of my way,' she said.

Without thinking, he gripped her wrist. 'Please . . . just for a minute.'

'Let go,' she warned him, 'or I'll scream.' He recognised in her eyes a hardness he was only used to seeing in business rivals. He worried that it was him who'd put it there. Maybe he'd been crazy to think he could simply persuade her to go home quietly and walk back out of his life. But maybe crazy was how he'd always acted around her.

'That's what you're here for anyway, isn't it?' he said, determined not to give up, determined at least to make her see what it was that she was about to do. 'To scream: to get your own back on me: to let everyone know what a shit I am: to ruin me.'

'Would you blame me if it was?'

'No.' He said it without hesitating. He said it because he knew that after the way he'd treated her she had every right. 'But I wish you wouldn't.'

'I'll give you two minutes,' she told him, brushing past him as she stepped into the wheelhouse.

Inside, an orange safety light glowed alongside the luminous green and yellow dials, but otherwise the room was a chamber of shadows. Sam was glad he couldn't see her face. It made what he had to say easier. She stood with her back to the wheel.

'Well?' she asked.

'Why are you here, Laurie?'

'Because Claire – your *wife*,' she pointedly corrected herself, 'invited me.'

'No, I mean here on the island.'

'Because Rachel – a member of your family and mine – invited me.'

Frustration rose up inside him. 'I mean why are you really here?' he demanded.

'To work.' A harsh burst of laughter escaped from her. 'Or did you think it was because of you?'

'I didn't know.'

'Makes you feel stupid, doesn't it?'

'What?'

'Not knowing what's going on. Not knowing why some-one's doing something. Why someone's doing something to you.'

'This isn't a game,' he said.

'Isn't it?'

'No.'

'I suppose you're right.' Here in the darkness, listening to her breathing so close, he could have been lying in bed beside her, wakeful in the middle of the night. 'But I was, wasn't I?' she said. 'To you.'

'No.'

'That's what it felt like, Sam. Afterwards. After you wrote to me. Or don't you remember? Because that's the thing about games, isn't it, Sam? They're not important once they're over. You can just walk away from them and get on with real life.'

But he did remember. It felt like it had happened today. 'The reason I wrote was because I couldn't bring myself to speak to you.'

'You couldn't bring yourself to speak to me,' she slowly repeated. 'To come on to me, yes. You managed that OK. And to fuck me. And even to tell me you'd fallen in love with me.' Disbelief, bitterness, rose up in her voice. 'But

179

to call me on the phone. A big grown-up businessman like you. You couldn't bring yourself to do that?'

But that was where she was wrong. One call . . . He'd known at the time it would have been enough to make him leave Claire all over again. One call was something he hadn't been able to risk, because one call would have made him the bad man he'd been trying so hard not to be.

'Do you know what it felt like, Sam? Have you any idea what it felt like to be me after you did what you did?'

He remembered how it had been when he'd first noticed her at Tony's funeral. The sight of her – that initial glimpse – had filled him with such happiness that he'd wanted to call out to her, to run and hug her there and then. But then – just as fast – he'd remembered how he'd hurt her and he'd burned with shame. 'I had no choice.'

'We always have a choice.'

He felt sickened by himself, by what he'd done. He suddenly no longer knew who the worse man was, the one who'd betrayed Claire, or the one who'd betrayed the woman he'd loved.

'You've got to leave,' he told her. 'You've got to leave this boat and you've got to leave this island.'

Silence, then: 'What I do is my business. You've got no right to tell me to do anything.'

They stared at each other.

'Were you already engaged when you were with me?' she then asked. 'Had you already decided you were going to spend your life with Claire?'

'No,' he answered, and then, before he could prevent himself, out of some desperate need for exoneration, he added, 'and I wasn't a father either. I didn't even know I was going to be. That had already happened, you see, before I met you. But Claire only told me she was pregnant when I got back.'

'Laurie!' a muffled voice called from outside.

'I did what I thought was right,' he told Laurie, before opening the door and calling outside, 'In here, Claire.'

'Well, will you look at you two,' Claire said, lurching into the doorway and squinting into the darkness, 'huddled in there together like a couple of old flames.'

'I was just explaining to Laurie here –' Sam started to say.

'– about navigation,' Laurie interrupted. 'He was just explaining to me how you move from one place to the next. And about how easy it all is these days.'

But somehow Claire missed the underlying anger.

'How terribly dull of you, Sam,' admonished Claire, slipping her arms around him and kissing him on the cheek. 'Well, you've both hogged each other long enough. Now it's time to come back and help me get this party really started.'

# *Chapter X*

'Boo!'

Rachel jumped, as Tony leapt out from behind the wall and pinched her waist.

'You scared me!' she said, pretending to be cross, but she could feel her cheeks flushing as she spun round and smiled at him.

Silently, she slipped the two-day-old note that she'd been clutching into her pocket, amazed that she'd ever doubted that its contents would come to pass. But they had. Tony was here. Outside the Baptist chapel at ten sharp on Saturday, just as he'd instructed in his secret note. He was as good as his word. She hadn't had to use her alibi of waiting here for Pearl. She hadn't had to answer any awkward questions. Instead, everything was going to plan.

Tony had dressed up for the occasion and she was touched that he'd made the effort for her, just as she'd done for him. She was wearing her favourite red skirt and white blouse with a band in her hair. He was wearing a blue short-sleeved shirt, open at the neck and she could see where the wispy hair on his chest started.

She bit her lip, amazed and ashamed at the level of her desire for him. Would he guess, she wondered, how much she'd been thinking about him, in the agonising three days since their last meeting? Would he know that as she'd

182

spring-cleaned the parlour at home, she'd been doodling his name in the dust?

Rachel knew that she'd die of shame if Tony knew the extent of her girlish fantasies. Convinced that they must show on her face, she tried to compose herself to look demure, but she couldn't dampen down the excitement she felt, just seeing him. As if reading her mind, his eyes connected with hers, like magnets too powerful to be drawn apart.

'Come on,' he said, breaking the moment, 'before anyone sees us.'

He took her hand, helping her jump over the wall and then up towards the steep hillside footpath, which cut up through the fir trees behind the Baptist chapel. Rachel hurried to keep up with him, glad that she'd changed into her pumps at the last minute and had left her shoes behind.

Tony was carrying a heavy grey army knapsack on his back, but he was still fast, hurrying up the hill and over the stone wall at the top. He stopped, waiting for Rachel to catch up and smiling at her, as she bent double, all pride gone, her hands on her knees, as she caught her breath. Then they were off again, down the rutted lane, across the paddock and onwards up again towards the copse at the top of the hill.

Rachel hadn't been up here before, mainly because it had never occurred to her to take a short cut vertically uphill. But that was what it was like being with Tony. Only a few weeks ago, Stepmouth had seemed like the most dull, suffocating place she could imagine, but with Tony as her guide, Rachel had discovered new places in the town of her birth that she'd never dreamt existed.

At first Rachel had been worried that they'd never get to see each other in private, but Tony had laughed at her, taking her to all his old haunts where they were sure to be alone: the disused gypsy caravan by the viewing gate on Summerglade Hill, the concealed suntrap on the roof of the lifeboat station, the shelter in the cinema car park, the garage behind the bakery and, once, to Tony's shed.

Rachel loved every minute of it. While her friends twittered about petty town gossip, Rachel carried herself aloft, aware that in one sentence she could silence them with the biggest bit of gossip of all time. She knew that she'd never let slip, though. Not to anyone. She was bursting to tell someone, especially Pearl, but somehow something stopped her. She knew that if she spoke about it and tried to describe how special what she had with Tony was, it might break the spell.

She stopped, smoothing out her hair, noticing how the birds were singing all around them, the vividness of the shiny new grass and the scent of blossom in the air. Tony stopped for her, holding out his hand, and she laughed at his enthusiasm, running to catch up with him and place her hand in his.

It must have taken forty minutes, but it felt like no time before they were at the top of the hill. They were totally alone, apart from the rabbits scurrying for cover behind the birch trees. Rachel glanced at the roof of the Baptist chapel far down below and the town that now looked like a model. With this perspective on it, it felt much easier to have escaped than she would ever have imagined and she couldn't believe she'd been so worried. She'd told Bill and her mother she was going to Barnstaple with Pearl for the afternoon, which had got her off the hook. Now she said a silent prayer that Bill wouldn't run into Pearl or her parents and discover Rachel's lie. She couldn't bear for anything to spoil today.

'Nearly there,' said Tony, hardly pausing and heading off through the trees, to where a long hedgerow separated the land from the road.

'Where are we going?' she panted, as he pulled her onwards, beating a gap with a stick through the thicket.

'I told you. It's a surprise,' he said, as she squeezed through past him and down into the dry ditch on the side of the road. She helped pull Tony up the other side and they lay exhausted on the far slope of the ditch, staring up at the fluffy clouds against the blue sky.

Rachel looked over her shoulder down the open road, surprised to see that they were a few yards away from the bus stop. It was risky catching a bus, but she figured, as Tony already had, that it was better waiting for it here, than down in the town.

She watched Tony as he took a small pair of binoculars from his knapsack. He gave her a knowing look, then, before she could question him, he was back off across the ditch and scrambling nimbly up to the fork in the trunk of an oak tree.

'What are you doing?' Rachel called up after him, shading her eyes against the sun.

'I borrowed them off Arthur. If I wait up here, I can see when the bus comes round the bend. I'll be able to see who's on it. Whether it's safe.'

'You've thought of everything,' she said, laughing.

'I just want to get us out of here.'

Towards the top of the hill, the bus, in a noisy first gear, was slower than walking speed. The tradition with the town's children was to make an expectantly rising collective whoop, as the bus neared the brow of the hill. It always felt as if, any second, it might roll back downhill but, miraculously, it never did.

Rachel thought about all the stories she'd heard about women in the Resistance in France during the war. She liked the dangerous feeling she had when she was with Tony. As if the world was their enemy and they were freedom fighters all on their own. In a way, she supposed, they were.

'Get down!' Tony shouted, and she ducked back down into the ditch, as she heard the bottle-green bus shuddering up the last part of the steep hill. Rachel peeked through the long grass.

She crossed her fingers, hoping that none of the regulars from the shop were on board, or anyone from school who would be bound to make a fuss if they saw Rachel and Tony together.

'All clear,' Tony called, and in a moment he was by her side, as she flagged down the bus. He winked at her, as they walked aboard.

Tony bought two tickets to Wolcombe.

'You do want to go, don't you?' he checked.

'Of course I do!'

'It's just that you look all worried.'

'Then let me pay half the fare,' Rachel insisted, digging in her pocket for her purse. She'd seen Tony's shed and how sparsely equipped it was and she knew that he didn't have much money. Two return fares seemed too much for him to pay.

Tony stopped her. 'No. It's my treat.'

The bus driver looked between them.

'But –'

'No buts, we're going to enjoy ourselves and you're not going to worry about a thing.'

Tony seemed so calm about it, but Rachel buzzed all over with excitement as he led her up the aisle of the lumbering bus to the long seat at the back. It felt like the most daring thing she'd ever done. The thought of being alone together, away from Stepmouth and all its hazards for a whole day, made her shake with anticipation.

'I thought we'd take a picnic,' Tony said, patting his knapsack, as he swung in to sit next to her.

Rachel grinned at him and was about to speak, when a huge man in his late twenties slapped the metal bar above the seat back in front of them, and leered over the top at them both. He had an ugly tattoo stretching down his fore-arm and a ginger crew cut which made his ruddy, freck-led face look huge.

'Well, if it isn't Anthony Glover,' the man said in a sneer-ing, slow drawl. A foamy reservoir of saliva bobbed in the crease of his lips. His breath stank of stale beer.

'You seen your brother Keith? Only if you do, tell him I want a word.'

Tony looked perfectly calm as he faced the man. 'I'm minding my own business, Douglas, why don't you mind yours.'

It wasn't a question. Rachel could sense from the men-acing threat in Tony's voice that one move from Douglas and there'd be a fight.

She put her hand on Tony's arm, feeling his tense muscles beneath her fingertips. Fear crept around her like a cold draught. Douglas looked at Tony and then glanced down his nose at Rachel, as if she were nothing. For a second she thought he was working on an insult, or threat, but his brain cells didn't seem up to it and he decided against it. Instead, he hawked loudly and spat out of the open top part of the window, before retreating back up to the front of the bus.

'Just tell him you saw me,' he snarled as he went. 'He owes me.'

187

'Who was he?' Rachel asked, when Douglas had gone. Tony looked tense, as if his good mood had been crushed out of him. He sat rigidly in the seat.

'No one. He used to hang out with my brother. That's all.'

'Oh.'

Rachel was silent, following Tony's gaze to where he was focused intently on the roll of flesh on the back of Douglas's head. Even though she now had a flash of what it was like to be Tony and to have his life blighted by Keith everywhere he went, she still wasn't sure she was the person to comfort him.

She crept her fingers along the pitted red leather seat of the bus and put her hand over Tony's, but he didn't move. She longed to say something to make it better, to bring Tony's guard down again, so that he was her Tony once more, not the hard, anxious Tony that everyone else saw, ready to defend himself at any moment.

She stared out of the window, feeling her hand over his, forcing herself to leave it there, even though she felt as if she were burning him. She could see a faint reflection of her own worried expression in the glass. Even though they were touching, Rachel could feel all her closeness with Tony draining away. And it was all Douglas's fault. He'd ruined everything.

But then, perhaps there would always be Douglases, always somebody who would mention Keith to them. What if it was always like this when they did? she panicked. What if they never overcame the past? What if it was always going to slap them back down into the people they were before they got together?

Rachel turned to face Tony. She wasn't going to let that happen. She'd taken too many risks to let everything fall apart now. Besides, as she saw it, the whole point of being together was that there were no barriers between them.

'Tony? I was wondering. I know we haven't spoken about it before, but now that it's come up, I was wondering . . .' She lost her nerve. What was she doing? Of course they hadn't spoken about it before, because she'd deliberately chosen not to. Because they both had. Because they'd both known, as she did now, that it was a subject that, once broached, might tear them apart.

But Rachel knew she couldn't ignore it any longer. Even if Douglas hadn't ruined everything, they'd still have had to face talking about Keith, sooner or later. The subject couldn't be swept away. It was the scariest thing she'd ever had to ask anyone, but the longer she didn't ask Tony, the bigger the question became.

She took a deep breath. 'I was wondering . . . well, how you *do* feel about your brother?'

'Keith? You want to talk about Keith? Right now? Here?'

Tony sounded so gruff and annoyed that she recoiled away from him. He looked down at where her hand had left his, seeming only to notice it now that it had gone. He stared at the space between their fingers.

'What do you want to know?' he asked, more gently.

'I don't know. Anything. Anything you want to tell me.'

For a long time, his face was sombre, almost as if he were too scared to talk. She waited for ages and was about to give in and change the subject, when Tony spoke.

'He used to write to Mum, after . . . you know. Anyway, Mum always threw the letters in the bin, but he never stopped writing. Month after month. For nearly a year. They never stopped coming. One day, I read one of them.'

Rachel held her breath. She'd never imagined anything other than that Keith had been locked away, written off and forgotten. The fact that he had the power to communicate with the outside world, or at least with his family filled her with a morbid fascination.

'What did it say?'

'The words themselves . . . the sentences on their own . . . didn't matter. They were just daily stuff about the prison routine, food and stuff. It was more his attitude that struck me. He sounded so unlike the Keith I knew.'

'In what way?'

Tony glanced past her, out of the window. 'I don't know. Just changed. Wiser. Older. Not denying who he was or what he did.'

Tony's eyes switched anxiously back towards Rachel, but she forced herself to continue listening. She'd asked for this after all.

'Go on.'

'Well, after I read that first letter, I wrote back to him.'

'You did what?' She'd almost shouted the words.

'We've been corresponding ever since.'

She'd been expecting Tony to tell her that he hated his brother. After all, that was what she'd assumed. How else could he have asked her out? Now this unthinkable revelation completely threw her and she was unable to understand what it meant. How could Tony communicate with his brother and see her at the same time? It didn't make sense.

Now it was as if she were seeing herself from the top corner of the bus. She'd been pretending that she was safe with Tony, but now she thought of all the reasons why she shouldn't be here, speeding away from everything that she knew. She could hear the bus changing up a gear as they hit the straight stretch of coast road, and behind Tony's head, the high hedgerows seemed to whizz past the window at a dizzying speed.

She wanted to fight. She wanted to shout at Tony. To scream. How could he? How could he want to have anything to do with that murderer, that animal who'd killed her dad and crippled her mum? But she couldn't, not here on the bus. And not before she'd heard everything Tony had to say. She owed him that much.

'So . . . have you seen him?' She sounded formal and pinched, as if it were her mother speaking.

'No, the first thing he wrote to me was that he never wanted me to visit him. He's got this thing that he never wants me to set foot inside the prison.'

Tony's eyes seemed to be imploring her to understand, but Rachel felt as if she no longer knew anything about him. As if she'd assumed far too much.

'Please don't look at me like that. Like you hate me.'

'It's him I hate.'

'I know. And you should. I hate him too for what he did. For what he was, but not who he is now. You see, that's just it: he's changed.'

'He can't have. People don't change.'

'But Keith has. It might be too late for him, but you see, he's got this notion that I'm good. That I'm the one who'll make it. He thinks there's certain images and things I mustn't have in my head. Like the war, like the pills he used to take, like the inside of a prison. He's always telling me to keep on the straight and narrow.'

The memory of Tony fighting came to Rachel like a film clip. And as Tony peered over the seat and glanced anxiously towards Douglas, who had risen from his seat to get off the bus at the farm stop, she knew she should stand up and get off as well. She should walk away from Tony and never turn back. She should go back home, to her mother, to Bill, to the people she loved.

191

But already another part of her was jumping to Tony's – *her* Tony's – defence. Keith Glover had no right to be concerned about his brother, because of course Tony was good, of course he was on the straight and narrow. He didn't need lecturing. *And* he was going to make it. Wherever *it* was. He didn't need a killer to tell him that.

'I don't understand how you can bear to communicate with him,' she said, as the bus sped up once more. Tony didn't look at Douglas who peered into the bus from the side of the road.

'He's my brother.'

'So you're saying that you forgive him? Is that it? Just because he's family?' She felt a tightness in the top of her chest. For a second, she was tempted to stop the bus and get off at the stop they'd just passed and run all the way home. Even braving Douglas might be better than the fear she now felt.

'Him being family has nothing to do with it. What he did was terrible, evil and he deserves all the punishment that's been given to him. He'd be the first to admit that.'

'You mean . . . you mean . . . he's sorry?'

'Of course he's sorry,' Tony said. 'Can you imagine living with what he did?'

'Yes,' she said, bitterly.

Tony wiped his hands over his face. 'I'm sorry, I didn't mean it like that.'

Rachel picked at a loose thread in the hem of her skirt. She felt so confused. 'Are you suggesting that somehow I should feel sorry for him?'

'All I've learnt is that my life has been a lot easier to live since I forgave him. If you forgive the person you most hate, you set yourself free.'

There was a long pause.

'Will you see him again, when he's out?' she asked, eventually.

'That won't be for years.'

She glanced over at Tony, wanting to cry. He looked so sad, so ashamed, as he sat looking at his hands in his lap. Rachel yearned for the closeness that they'd had before this conversation, wishing that it had never happened. It felt as if everything was different.

Then, as her eyes met his, she saw in them the tenderness that only she knew existed. He was Tony, her Tony. No one else's. She simply couldn't walk away from him. If she did, that would mean that Keith had won again.

'I'm sorry,' Rachel said, reaching out to touch him. 'I'm not angry with you. It's not your fault.'

'You don't hate me?'

'No. This is us, remember?'

He leant over and kissed her then, his lips lingering softly on hers. Rachel squeezed her eyes tightly shut, sealing some kind of unspoken pact with Tony, as much as with herself. It felt as if she were freefalling, as if they'd stepped off a cliff together. Whatever she'd believed before had just been wiped away. In its place was only Tony. She had no idea where her faith in him would lead, but she knew now that it was all she had.

Wolcombe was hardly as crowded as Stepmouth, but it boasted a pier with a small funfair that had been open since the end of the war. As she and Tony whizzed around the helter-skelter on old rope mats, and bobbed high above the sea on the merry-go-round, leaning back on the gold twirling poles, their laughter obliterated the seriousness of their conversation on the bus. A few hours later, it was as if it had never happened.

193

They'd walked right to the end of the pier, before Tony was satisfied that they'd found the right spot to eat their lunch. He rolled his trouser legs up and set out a blanket from the knapsack on the rough planks. Rachel sat down in the sunshine, dangling her legs over the edge of the pier. They were so high up, it felt as if they were sitting on the edge of a cloud.

Far below them the seagulls shrieked as they dipped into the waves and skirted through the criss-crossed iron structure underneath the pier. Behind, the plinkity-plonk music from the fair drifted towards them on the salty breeze, while below came the crescendo and diminuendo of the sea gently breaking along the long stretch of sandy beach either side of the pier, the water spurting in dramatic white plumes as it hit each wooden breakwater.

Rachel shuffled forward and leant on the iron bar, resting her head on her arms, so that she felt the wind on her face. Her skirt rippled up her thighs. She closed one eye against the glare of the sun and stared along to the far end of the beach to where the faded red-and-white-striped bathing huts stretched into the distance like an abandoned production line of Punch and Judy tents.

'I haven't been here since I was a kid,' Rachel said, the waves bringing back a distant memory of her father holding a bucket and spade on the beach. She remembered laughing at his feet, as the water buried them in the sand and he pretended to fall over in the shallow surf. It was the first happy memory of her father she'd ever had and she breathed in the salty air, willing more details to come, but nothing did.

'What's the matter?' Tony asked, touching her shoulder.

'Oh, nothing.'

'No, go on. Tell me what you were thinking about?'

She remembered telling Tony on the bus that he could tell her anything. Now, she turned to face him.

'Daddy,' she said. Saying it that way made her feel vulnerable.

'What was he like?' Tony asked.

'That's just it,' Rachel admitted. 'I can't remember. But looking at the beach made me think of him when I was little. He was always clowning around to make me laugh. He used to carry me up on his shoulders. I remember holding on to his ears and twisting them. And every time I did, he stuck his tongue out.' She laughed and then they were silent.

'I wish I could have met him.'

'So do I,' Rachel said, meaning it. 'I think he would have liked you.'

They stared at each other and she felt her eyes blurring with tears, but they didn't fall.

'You must be hungry,' Tony said, wiping away their bittersweet moment. He turned to unload his knapsack. 'Only I bought a few things to eat.'

Rachel later laughed at Tony for his modesty. The few things to eat turned out to be a feast fit for a queen. And best of all, Tony had prepared it all for her himself. She felt truly exotic as he assaulted her taste buds with new sensations: home-made pasta salad and ham quiche. And the dishes kept on coming. By the time he revealed his home-made coffee cake from the bag, she was laughing. She'd never eaten so much delicious food in her life.

'You really made all this?' He must have been up all night preparing it all.

'Emily showed me how. She's a good teacher. She says I should be a chef.'

'I don't know who would eat your food,' Rachel teased,

adding quickly when she saw his crestfallen face, 'only that it's way too good for anyone around here.'

Tony looked satisfied with her answer. He was stretched out on the rug, leaning up on one elbow. 'Maybe I'll go to London one day and set up a restaurant of my own.'

Rachel smiled at him. She'd never imagined that she would find somebody her own age in Stepmouth who also had ambitions. She was tempted to tell Tony about her own plans for her future, but they seemed so airy-fairy compared to his. The tangibility of his idea and the proof of his talent resting in her stomach made her much more excited than any of her own ideas. Unlike hers, his future seemed fabulously achievable.

'I'll come with you and be the manageress,' she said, sitting up on her knees.

'You want to be the boss, do you?'

'Why not? Emily's the boss of her place. Why shouldn't I be in charge of something? I could make us a fortune!'

Tony slowly smiled. Then he raised his bottle of ginger beer to clink with hers. 'Why not indeed, Rachel Vale. Here's to being the boss,' he said.

As Rachel smiled at him over the top of the bottle, she felt closer to being the person she wanted to be than ever before.

# Chapter XI

**Mallorca, Present Day**

'Look at you. Aren't you just like your daddy?' Rachel tick-led Archie under the chin and laughed as he smiled and wriggled away from her.

'Granny, look . . . ball!' he replied, throwing his red ball away from them both, with a surprisingly strong overarm, so that it bounced down the terrace steps and on to the flint-and-marble-paved patio.

'Go and get it, then.'

Rachel waved to him, glad to have something to smile about at long last, glad she'd plucked up the courage to come to Mallorca. Glad, too, that she was still capable of doing something helpful, like babysitting for a morning for Claire while the nanny was on holiday and Claire had her fortnightly pedicure. It made Rachel feel normal again, as if she were a functional member of her own family, not somebody everyone was avoiding in case they acciden-tally upset her.

It had been four months since Tony had gone and time seemed to be doing funny things to her. Maybe her sense of unreality was due to the fact that she was so drained and weary, exhausted with the process of grieving, but she felt as if she hadn't been to Sa Costa for ten years. Now she wished she'd come before. Instead, she'd endured day after day of cold, grey drizzle, the wind whistling eerily around Dreycott House in the dark nights as she failed to sleep. She'd meant to go up to the apartment in London, but somehow she hadn't been able to face it.

But this morning, when she'd been woken up by the bright sunshine pouring in through the window, Rachel had heard the birds chirruping as they nested in the eves of the house and she'd felt vaguely normal once more. And as she'd opened the window and breathed in the scent of the flowers trailing across the sill and heard the distant whisper of the sea it had felt as if she'd woken up after months in a coma.

Now, sitting here in the gentle mid-morning breeze, the heat warming her bones, it felt as if everything had changed in her absence. She couldn't remember when the row of spiky orange flowers which looked so neat against the trimmed box hedges had been chosen and planted, she didn't recall the lawns ever looking so densely green, or the striped blue-and-white canvas canopy over the terrace so faded. She'd never noticed so many geckos darting up the walls to where they rested in the shade of the thick trunk of the vine, or known the vine itself to bloom so abundantly.

And not only did she feel that her home had changed, but Archie had changed too. She hadn't paid much attention to him at Tony's funeral, but since she'd last seen him, he'd learnt to talk properly and seemed to be growing phenomenally fast.

If only she could freeze time and keep him just as he was, she mused, watching him as he hurried away in his little blue checked shorts towards where his toys were laid out on the wooden sunlounger, chattering away in a monologue about his ball and train.

She knew she was being indulgent, but she'd spent too many years feeling guilty about favouritism towards her own children, so what harm was there in admitting that she loved Archie so much more than Christopher's son Thomas? Thomas was always crying and was so molly-coddled, but Archie had that same fragile quality that Claire had had as a child and it made her feel more protective towards him than ever. He was her legacy. The reminder of all the good things that she and Tony had done together.

Rachel turned as the terrace door slid open behind her and Laurie appeared, carrying a tray, laden with a cafetière and cups. She could smell the aroma of freshly ground coffee beans and the sweet, fresh pastries Fabio had delivered this morning. Rachel cleared the papers she'd been reading to make room on the slatted wooden table for the tray.

Laurie had insisted when Rachel had arrived late last night that Rachel's weekend visit wouldn't disturb her, but now that she was here Rachel wondered whether Laurie wasn't just being polite. But even if she was, Rachel thought selfishly, she was pleased that they were having this opportunity to talk properly together. Her curiosity about her niece had only increased since they'd last met, and she'd been thinking about Laurie working out here over the past three weeks.

'Honestly, that child melts my heart,' Rachel said, nodding towards Archie who was throwing his ball towards the flower bed and making for the brand new bike on the lawn. 'He's so clever.'

Laurie didn't say anything, but Rachel couldn't help noticing that she glanced rather sternly at Archie as she bent over the table to put the tray down.

'I'm not very good with children.'

'Nonsense. I think Archie likes you. Anyway, it's different when you have children of your own. You'll see.'

'To be honest, I can't see it happening for quite some time.'

Laurie was wearing a wide-brimmed straw hat and a tatty green sundress, which emphasised her sun-kissed freckled skin. As she poured the coffee into the cups, Rachel wanted to tell her not to leave it too late to settle down and start a family. She'd never been so aware, as she had been since Tony's death, that time was so precious. But despite their candid conversation so far this morning, she knew she couldn't be so personal with Laurie. Still, she was amazed that someone as attractive as her wasn't at least engaged to some handsome arty type. Or maybe that wasn't what young women wanted these days. Laurie had certainly made it clear that her career was her priority.

Rachel applauded Archie, as he called out to her to watch him pedalling over the grass.

'Grandchildren are wonderful. It's wonderful seeing them and then even more wonderful handing them back when they get too much. Although, in my case, sometimes that doesn't happen,' she added, accepting the coffee Laurie handed to her.

Rachel was determined to come clean about a few family facts. But now she found herself struggling to find the right words, and her oblique hint at the truth hadn't captured Laurie's attention.

It had been years since she'd had to mention Anna. In that time, Claire had become so much like her own daughter that Rachel almost managed to forget sometimes that she wasn't. Would Laurie judge her for what had happened? Would she think that Rachel had been a bad parent to Anna? But she would only judge her if she were to know the whole story and there was no need for her to know anything other than the bare details.

'I was just thinking that I feel so old sometimes, especially when I see how quickly Archie is growing,' she said with a sigh. 'You know, of course, that he's actually my great-grandson. That's why he's so special. Claire's my granddaughter, you see. Although Tony and I brought her up as our own.' She took a sip of coffee, aware that she had Laurie's full attention now. 'Claire's mother, Anna, died when she was barely twenty. Claire was just a baby. We adopted her as our daughter. That's why she's so much younger than Christopher and Nick.'

Rachel managed to make it sound as if they'd done the most natural thing in the world. It amazed her how a lifetime's career as a businesswoman had taught her the skill of glossing over unpleasant facts, so that she could dress up even the most horrible trauma as a happily-ever-after fairy tale. But one look at Laurie and Rachel could see instantly that she hadn't fooled her with her flippant tone.

'I had no idea. What happened?'

'With Anna?'

Rachel thought about telling her the details. 'It's so long ago . . . It's just . . . well, everything has turned out for the best as far as Claire is concerned. Anna was very ill and depressed.' Rachel heard her voice crack. 'You know what? Can we talk about it another time? I can't think about Anna. It's too much. It reminds me of Tony and –'

'Oh, Rachel, I'm so sorry. We've been so busy chatting and I haven't even asked you how you're coping?'

Rachel took off her sunglasses and laid them on the table. She knew that without them she looked tired and haggard. She felt vulnerable, as if she were revealing two black eyes.

'Most days I seem to be able to function, but it all seems unreal. I seem to yo-yo all the time between perfectly fine

201

and being a wreck a moment later. Like now,' she said, exasperated with herself as she fought back yet more unexpected tears. 'I've been feeling so angry with Tony in these last few weeks. Everything has been making me furious. Poor Tony. I keep blaming him for everything.'

'I suppose it's natural.'

Rachel shook her head in denial. How could she explain how frustrating this was? She hated being this fragile and out of control. Why wasn't she coping better? She was amazed that she was admitting her feelings again to this young woman. And yet it felt right to trust Laurie.

'Sorry,' she said, glancing at her niece who was sitting calmly, her arms folded on the table.

Laurie batted away Rachel's apology and smiled gently. 'It doesn't matter.'

'You know, coming here was so hard,' Rachel admitted. 'Tony and I had so many good times here. I thought it would be too painful. It *is* too painful in a way. I'm so glad you're here, Laurie.'

'Maybe you should be on your own, though. I can make myself scarce if it'd be easier for you.'

'Please don't.'

'You know, I wouldn't feel guilty. I think it's perfectly normal to feel angry. I think Dad did when Mum died, but it was different, I suppose. She was ill for such a long time, that by the time she went, he was ready to say goodbye. I think that's why he recovered so quickly.'

Rachel looked away at the horizon. She wanted to tell Laurie that Bill was lucky. He'd said goodbye to his wife, but she hadn't had the chance with Tony. But how could she expect Laurie to understand that having someone you love the most unexpectedly torn away from you was the most cruel thing that could ever happen to a person?

She didn't want to turn bitter, not like her mother had, but Rachel couldn't help feeling recently that she was being punished. The way in which Tony had gone seemed too calculated. Too cruel. Which is why she'd started to bargain with herself. If she made herself do the one thing that had been impossible to do all her adult life and to reach a reconciliation with her brother, then she could prove that the impossible was possible. And if she did that, then Tony would come back and everything would be normal again. Or at the very least, she'd come to terms with him being gone.

'How is Bill? Did you tell him about the funeral, about coming here?' she asked, pulling herself together.

Laurie shook her head and sat back in her chair and clasped her hands across her flat stomach. As she talked about her father, Rachel felt as if she were looking at herself fifty years ago, lamenting the same problem. Bill clearly hadn't changed. He was as stubborn as ever. And now here he was hurting another generation in the same way he'd hurt her. Rachel placed her coffee cup on the table.

'I need to see him, Laurie. The thing is . . . I want you to ask him to visit you here. Not right away, but soon. We could plan it together.'

'He wouldn't come.'

'But he wouldn't have to know I was here. In fact, in some ways it's perfect that he doesn't know the truth. If you could only get him out here, then I'd be able to do the rest –'

Rachel stopped herself. She could tell she'd pushed it too far. She'd wanted to wait a while, until she'd really got to know Laurie, before she voiced her plan, not blurt it out straight away. It felt as if she were asking Laurie to take sides. And she knew only too well how that felt.

But something in Laurie's expression told Rachel that she wasn't listening anyway. Almost at the same instant, she heard a loud splash from the direction of the swimming pool.

Laurie pushed back her chair so fiercely as she stood up that it fell over. Her coffee cup smashed on to the terrace. But Laurie didn't stop. She was running towards the pool.

As if in slow motion, Rachel felt herself rising to her feet, her scream coming out with such a force that the crows in the trees on the other side of the pool flapped, squawking into the air. Archie had fallen in.

Laurie's sprint turned seamlessly into a dive as she flung herself into the water. Rachel saw her shoes and her hat fly off in mid-air. For a terrifying moment, she vanished. And then a second later, Laurie's head appeared, followed by Archie's. She hauled him on to the side of the pool holding him upright by the stomach, while she flipped out on to the side beside him. By the time Rachel reached them both, Laurie had gently lifted Archie on to her knee and was patting his back as he coughed.

'Oh God!' Rachel panicked. 'I should have been watching. Oh God! Oh Archie . . .'

'It was an accident.'

'If anything happened to him –'

'It didn't.' Laurie sounded decisive. How could she be so calm? Rachel stared down at her, her dress flattened to her body, her hair dripping down her face, but she seemed completely unruffled. 'He's fine. Aren't you, Archie?'

Archie nodded and looked so forlorn that Laurie laughed gently, before squeezing him in a tight hug. 'There. It's all over now. Look at us. We're all wet. What will your mummy say?'

'He could have drowned,' Rachel said. 'He could have

drowned and it would have been my fault. I wasn't watching him. And now Claire . . . Claire will think –'

The next thing she knew, Laurie was supporting her to her feet. She felt her arm around her shoulders.

'It's over,' she was saying, firmly. Then she leant in close to her. 'You're frightening Archie, Rachel. Just try and calm down. Now, I'm going to get us both dried off. I want you to go inside and lie down. Everything's fine. Let's not make a big deal of it. OK?'

Rachel jolted awake. She could see through the open double doors to where Claire was talking to Laurie in the hall. She scrambled to her feet, a hollow feeling of embarrassment covering her like a slick of sweat. She didn't know which was more shameful: that she'd allowed Archie to fall into the pool, or that she'd overreacted the way she had, or that, inexplicably, she'd fallen asleep and left Laurie to deal with Archie. Brenda, who'd been looking after her in Dreycott House had been right after all. She should consult the doctor and get something to level her out.

Rachel smoothed down her white linen trousers. She'd never been a hysterical type of woman. She'd never lost her head in front of her family. Thank God for Laurie, she thought, hurrying out into the hall.

'Oh, Claire –' Rachel began, but Laurie silenced her with a look.

She'd changed into a paint-splattered white vest and a pair of frayed denim shorts which showed off her toned legs and dirty bare feet. She looked like a tomboy next to Claire, who was dressed in raw-silk silver trousers and a satin halter-neck silver top, the sun catching the bronze highlights in her long hair as she stood in the open doorway. Her newly varnished toenails glittered in her open-toed stiletto sandals.

'As I said,' Laurie's tone was deliberately pointed for Rachel's benefit, as she handed over a bag to Claire. 'I'm sorry his clothes are a bit wet. It was my fault. We were playing around . . .'

Rachel was astonished at the ease with which Laurie could tell such a white lie.

'Oh, don't worry,' said Claire, looking disinterestedly into the dripping carrier bag and then down at Archie who was wearing a pair of dungarees which were way too small. Rachel wondered where on earth Laurie had found them.

'We went swimming,' Archie explained, looking at Laurie, who winked at him and ruffled his hair with her fingertips.

'Yes we did. You're quite a daredevil, aren't you, young man?'

But Claire ignored them both, turning her attention to Rachel. 'There you are. I'm taking you out for lunch. We'll drop Archie off at the crèche and then I've booked a table for two at Reed's.'

Rachel glanced at Laurie.

'No, no, I mean, two o'clock, not necessarily *for* two,' Claire explained quickly, realising her faux pas.

'Thanks, but I've got work to do,' Laurie said, ducking past Rachel and disappearing up the marble staircase. 'Bye-bye, Archie. Keep out of trouble.'

There was a small pause as she left. Then Claire smiled at Rachel and Rachel realised how much she'd missed her.

'Please, darling, can't we stay here?' Rachel pleaded. 'I feel like I've only just arrived. And, well, Reed's is so showy.'

'We don't have to if you really don't want to. I wanted to spoil you, that's all,' Claire said, but Rachel could tell how disappointed she was. 'We haven't been out together for ages. I thought it would be nice –'

'OK, OK, I'll come, but I want you to promise to come for dinner tomorrow. I want us to spend some family time here.'

'I'm not sure about Sam. I'll have to check.'

Rachel could tell by her tone that she didn't mean that he'd be busy with work. She watched Claire watching Archie, who was playing with the umbrellas in the stand by the door.

'What do you mean, darling?'

'Oh, nothing. He's just not being his usual self.' Rachel knew Claire wouldn't have mentioned it unless it was a real problem. 'He seems a bit panicky, that's all. It's probably just stress.'

Rachel thought back to the funeral, remembering how Sam had stuttered and been so strange when she'd announced he was taking over the business. At the time, she'd been more concerned with Christopher's and Nick's reactions to her announcement. She'd seen immediately that they'd been jealous and annoyed and she'd had to take them both aside and remind them that Sam, as a trusted member of their family, had done more for her and Tony than either of them could possibly have ever imagined. She was still annoyed that she'd had to shame them into being supportive.

But now, looking back, Rachel felt guilty for not paying more attention to Sam, for not having checked if he was OK at the time.

'He's not annoyed I asked him to take over, is he? I mean, I thought he would have wanted it. It's what Tony would have wanted. I thought he was pleased. I thought it was the right thing –'

'Oh God,' Claire groaned, shaking her head. 'I should never have said anything. Listen, forget I mentioned it.

Sam's thrilled with the promotion, as am I. He's not taking enough time off, that's all. I tell him all the time to chill out, but you know what he's like. He's stopped sailing and going to the gym. It's just work, work, work. I hardly see him any more.'

Rachel could sense how upset Claire was. She loved Sam desperately.

'I'll talk to him,' Rachel assured her.

'Please don't,' Claire begged, but only half-heartedly. Then she picked up Archie. 'I didn't come here to talk about my problems. Come on, let's go out and cheer ourselves up.'

It wasn't until late the following afternoon that Rachel had the chance to talk to Laurie again alone. She was surprised to learn from Dante, the gardener, that Laurie was using the old boathouse as her studio down on the beach. How strange that Laurie should choose such a secluded, inaccessible spot to work when the house had such wonderful light.

As she made her way down the path, Rachel realised that it had been ages since she'd been to the beach. There was so many wonderful aspects to Sa Costa, but she seemed to have forgotten how to enjoy them. But then, she'd hardly had the time. She'd been swamped with visits from friends on the island, Maria's mother, who wanted every detail of the funeral, a delivery from Fabio who brought his new baby (on the moped). She'd also made a short trip into the Ararat offices to catch up with the staff.

She'd been in constant contact with the office via fax, but going there herself had been a total shock. The plush offices, which Rachel had chosen herself for their secluded courtyard location in Palma's old town, had been completely rearranged. Sam had installed a new secretary, receptionist and a whole new team of marketing staff. Rachel had tried not to show how dismayed she'd felt, but as Maria showed her into the boardroom, with its new utilitarian furniture, Rachel had felt close to tears. She wasn't in charge any more. The whole atmosphere of the company seemed to have changed.

Still, everyone she'd met seemed to be pleased to see her, although she'd found the baffled glances she'd received from the new people quite disconcerting. Feeling as if she were in the way, she'd decided not to stay long, but the discreet enquiries she'd managed to make about Sam had revealed nothing untoward. The opposite, in fact. All the staff members she'd spoken to seemed happy and business was booming.

If anything, though, this had made Rachel more anxious. Because if it wasn't work that was getting Sam stressed, then what on earth was it? Tony. That was the only answer. Like her, Sam must be grieving. And also, like her, he probably needed some time to relax.

Down on the beach, Rachel approached Laurie's new work space from the side entrance. With the front and the back doors wide open, the old shed was filled with light and the sound of the water gently lapping on the shore.

Laurie was at the far end, working on a canvas. She had her back turned and Rachel couldn't see the look of concentration on her face, but she could sense Laurie's intensity, even from several metres away. An upturned rusty oil drum was next to her. On top of it were several mixing boards of paint, a jug of water and a small radio, which was playing a crackly Spanish guitar piece. The weathered concrete floor was covered in sand and a few lumps of gnarled driftwood. In the middle, an ancient peeling rowing boat was filled with cushions, a towel and a swimming costume were drying over its side.

Dotted around the walls, several canvases were propped up, some of them supported by old pieces of rope hanging from the ceiling. They were all similarly themed – large abstract sunsets and seascapes – the colours perfectly blended and merged, the light in each one captured perfectly.

But as Rachel stepped inside the shed to get a better look, Laurie made a small yelp and raced towards her, the colour high in her cheeks.

'Half of these aren't finished,' she said, barring Rachel's view. 'I'd rather show you when they're done.'

Rachel took a step back outside the shed. She hadn't come across anyone as stubborn as Laurie for as long as she could remember. Well, probably not since she'd last seen Bill.

'Listen, I'm sorry about yesterday,' Rachel said, as Laurie came out to join her. 'I guess I overreacted.'

Laurie pulled a dirty rag from the waistband of her shorts and wiped her hands. 'Why upset her when she doesn't need to know?'

'Well, thank you. For everything. For doing that for me.'

'I'd better get used to it, hadn't I? If I'm to persuade Dad to come out here.'

She said it flippantly, as if it were no big deal, but Rachel could tell that she meant it. She stared at Laurie, tongue-tied.

'Anything else?' Laurie asked, obviously keen to get on.

'No,' Rachel answered.

'OK, well, I'll be up to the house when the light fades,' Laurie said, turning away.

Rachel remembered another reason for her visit: to tell

210

Laurie about Sam and Claire coming for dinner. But Laurie was already walking back to her canvas and Rachel didn't want to disturb her again. She hesitated and then turned up back towards the path.

Rachel was used to people in her life being transparent, or if not transparent, then at least clear in their motives. But as she prepared dinner later on, she realised that it was different with Laurie. She sensed a private, passionate side to Laurie which intrigued her. Just seeing how she'd transformed the old boat shed had shown Rachel how sensual she was, and she was even more intrigued by the glimpse she'd had of Laurie's secretiveness.

Which was why she didn't hesitate when Laurie's mobile phone rang just before suppertime. Laurie had left it on the small table by the door and it was only after Rachel had pressed the green button to answer it that she realised how stupid she'd been. What if it had been Bill?

But a second later, as James Cadogan introduced himself, all thoughts of Bill vanished. Here he was, Rachel thought, marvelling at her good fortune as she grilled red peppers and the impressive young man at the same time. Here was the chink in Laurie's armour. Laurie had a new lover! And in no time Rachel was already concocting a plan.

By the end of the short call, Rachel was smiling. Not only had she conspired with James on a sure-fire plan to cheer Laurie up and get her to relax, but in a few minutes she'd found out more about Laurie than from a whole morning of chatting. Why on earth hadn't she mentioned James? He was wonderful. Rachel was so excited about her secret with him, she was itching to run down to the beach and tell Laurie.

But then, she started to get nervous. What if Laurie

hadn't mentioned James for a reason? She'd had plenty of opportunity during their conversations to bring up her love life and to talk about her feelings. Now Rachel started to panic, cursing herself for being so rash. What if she'd assumed too much? What if she'd accidentally put her foot in it?

But her thoughts didn't get any further before she heard the screech of tyres on the driveway. Rachel turned down the grill and went to open the front door. As she got there, she saw Claire and Sam getting out of Claire's light blue Audi convertible. There was a faint whiff of rubber from where Claire had braked. Claire slammed her car door and stormed towards the house, tottering purposefully in her high heels and skimpy jeans.

'Tell him to stop being so bad-tempered,' she snapped, storming past Rachel into the house.

Sam, who'd shut his passenger door more carefully, walked towards Rachel who was holding the front door open. He slung the jacket of his cream linen suit over his shoulder, holding it by the hook. He looked as if he'd just come from work.

'Hi.' Sam stooped wearily to kiss Rachel's cheek. Even if Claire hadn't mentioned Sam being anxious to her, she would've been able to tell. He looked as if the new burden of responsibility she'd given him had made him suddenly older. His tanned face was less boyish, with more lines around his eyes than she remembered. It suited him. Rachel knew that Sam was one of those men who would only become more attractive with age. Even with a shadow of stubble around his chin, he looked undeniably handsome.

Rachel wished she could hug him and tell him that whatever his row with Claire was about, she was proud of him. Just being around Archie and Claire, not to mention Laurie, these past few days had been such a tonic. And now that Sam was here, the Mallorcan branch of her family was complete.

'Sam, darling, I've missed you so much,' she said, honestly, as she drew him into the house and shut the door. 'You've hardly been around.'

Sam smiled wearily and she saw the hint of the charm she knew so well. 'You can't have it all,' he said. 'If you will give me a company to run, what do you expect?'

Rachel smiled back. She wanted to mention her trip into the office today, but she was worried that he would think she was interfering. She'd handed over the reins to him, after all; she had to trust him. If she mentioned Ararat, he might think she was snooping behind his back. No, this was family time and she would have to start learning to separate the two.

'Do you want me to give you two a moment?' she asked, looking through the open double doors into the living room towards where Claire had disappeared out on to the terrace. A trail of her cigarette smoke lingered with her perfume in the air.

'No,' Sam said. 'It's nothing. It's just a silly argument about Archie,' he added, unconvincingly. 'You know what Claire's like – she'll have forgotten all about it in a minute. Why don't I fix us some drinks?'

'That would be lovely.'

But Rachel's plans for a relaxing dinner failed to materialise. Laurie, on her return from the beach, seemed unduly annoyed that Rachel had failed to tell her that she was expected to join them for dinner, or indeed that people were over for dinner at all. Huddled in a towel, her hair in rat's tails from where she'd been for an evening swim

213

in the sea, she greeted Sam and Claire with a slightly aloof air that irked Rachel.

Rachel tried to smooth things over and play it down, but after Laurie had showered and joined them outside, she seemed withdrawn and contemplative. It was too late for Rachel to apologise for her social blunder and she kicked herself for not having warned Laurie. Instead, she had no choice but to carry on as if nothing had happened. Yet the more she tried to inject some fun into the evening, the more tension she could sense around the dinner table. Only Claire seemed to be making an effort, trying to draw Laurie into conversation – and failing every time.

Meanwhile, Sam glowered in silence, taking no interest in the conversation, as he busied himself with the barbecue on the terrace. Rachel watched him, as he turned over the chicken kebabs and steaks, the aromatic smell from the marinade she'd made from the garden herbs and local wine filling the night air. He was obviously still fuming over the spat he'd had with Claire in the car.

It wasn't until dinner was over and the night had turned chilly and Claire had taken the dirty plates inside, giving an 'I told you so' look to Rachel as she passed, that Rachel decided that the time had come to tackle Sam.

'Sam, I was thinking: you must take Laurie out on *Flight*,' Rachel said, watching Sam's face in the soft glow of the candles on the table.

'I'm sure Laurie has better things to do than come sailing –'

'Nonsense. You'd love it, wouldn't you, Laurie?'

'Well, I . . .' Laurie raised her eyebrows, clearly embarrassed, Rachel deduced, by Sam's reticence, but Rachel wasn't going to be put off. She stretched across the table and poured more red wine into Laurie's glass and into her own.

'The boat's Sam's pride and joy. He sails so well.'

'I've hardly had the time, recently,' Sam mumbled, putting his hand over the top of his glass to bar Rachel from pouring him any more wine. She put the bottle back, disappointed. She knew that Sam would relax if he had a few more drinks. How often had they all sat here on the red-cushioned chairs, the scent of jasmine from the trellis around the dining area, making it an oasis of calm? Rachel loved sitting out here at night surrounded by her family. It was one of her favourite places. Sam had once said it was one of his, too.

'All the more reason that you should go, then. Take Laurie out for a spin. Show her the bay. I bet you've never seen the whole bay of Palma from the sea.'

'Only on a postcard,' Laurie said, quietly.

Sam held the stem of his empty glass and stared at it. Rachel knew him well enough to know that he was angry, but couldn't fathom out why he was being so deliberately obstructive. Why wasn't he making more of an effort to be friendly towards Laurie? It was so unlike him. One of the qualities Rachel had always admired so much about Sam was his ability to make people feel special. Where had his charm disappeared to? she wondered. Well, she wasn't going to stand for it.

'Sam, I don't know why you're being difficult, but I think you should make a date, right now. Otherwise you won't do it. You'll get too busy –'

'Rachel, it's a nice thought, but I really want to get on with my painting,' Laurie pleaded. 'Can't we –'

What was wrong with everyone today? They were all behaving like spoilt children. Well, fine, she'd treat them like that, too, and force them into going whether they liked it or not. Why shouldn't she? After all, it was for their own good.

'Next Tuesday,' she said, throwing her blue linen napkin on the table. 'Sam, you're obviously working far too hard. I want you to take the whole day off and enjoy yourself. And, Laurie, you need a break, too. I'm not having any arguments. It's next Tuesday. It's a public holiday, so there won't be a problem with work.'

'Next Tuesday what?' asked Claire, coming back with a cardigan for Rachel.

'Sam's taking Laurie sailing on his boat.' Rachel put the cardigan on.

'Is he now? Well, I'd rather you than me,' Claire laughed. 'I can't stand it. It's so . . . splashy. And I warn you, he'll squash you when he's changing tack.'

Laurie took a small sip of wine. She didn't say anything. She didn't even smile.

'Well, I think it'll do you both the world of good,' Rachel said, hoping that Claire would be pleased that she'd kept up her end of the bargain and had forced Sam into some leisure time. She hadn't expected it to be such hard work.

'Absolutely. That's what I've been telling him,' Claire said, walking behind Sam and planting a kiss on the top of his head. 'I try to exercise him as best I can, but it's not the same as fresh air, I suppose.'

Sam shirked away from her, clearly irritated and embarrassed by such an obvious innuendo.

'What!' Claire laughed at him.

Sam suddenly shifted back in his chair, forcing Claire to move out of the way. 'You know what?' he said. 'I'm getting cold too. I think it's time we headed back home.'

'You can't go yet.' Rachel thought he was joking.

'I've got an early meeting,' Sam explained, rising from his chair. 'Thank you for dinner, Rachel.'

In spite of Claire's protests, Sam couldn't be swayed and it wasn't long before he kissed both Rachel's cheeks and nodded towards Laurie. 'I'll see you next week, then,' he said.

Less than five minutes after Claire's car had sped up the driveway, Laurie made her excuses and retired to her room.

Left alone, Rachel pulled the cardigan tighter around her and buried her nose into the soft fibres, smelling the faint aroma of cigar smoke. It reminded her so strongly of Tony that she felt weak sadness and self-pity.

Tonight had been a disaster. Everything was crumbling around her and her lack of control made her feel more lonely than ever. If only Tony had been there, then Sam and Claire would have been happy and Laurie would –

Laurie wouldn't have been there, she reminded herself. No wonder it was so difficult playing happy families when she'd changed all the rules.

# Chapter XII

Bill's friend, Richard Horner, was humming softly to himself as he continued his slow tour of inspection of the Jowett Jupiter, lovingly trailing his fingers across the car's sleek waxed black bodywork that he and Bill had been busy polishing all morning.

'It's not a woman, you know, Richard,' Bill laughed.

'No,' Richard agreed, 'but there's plenty of them who'll want to ride in it with you and it'll probably turn out to be a hell of a lot more reliable than any of them.' He winked at Bill. 'Though if the girls turn out to be faster than the car,' he joked, 'then I bet you'll not be disappointed, either.'

Richard was Bill's closest friend in the town. Nearly a foot shorter than Bill, he was a hard, straightforward man with a wiry figure and an angular face.

Bill and Richard's friendship stretched back to playing football together at school and after-school clubs. Richard had trained up as a mechanic in the army and Bill had been best man when Richard had married his childhood sweetheart, Rosie, four years before.

Rosie had since given birth to two little girls, the eldest of whom was Bill's three-year-old goddaughter, Joan. Whenever Bill went to Richard's cottage for Sunday lunch, or accompanied them on a trip to the beach, he'd find himself seized by a sudden and all-encompassing sense

218

of loss. He'd stare in astonishment at this family which had miraculously come from Richard. How, he'd wonder, was it possible? And would he ever be blessed with the same?

Bill and Richard were now in the garage on Lydgate Lane which they'd rented for the purpose of restoring the Jowett Jupiter. Both men wore grease-streaked blue overalls which Richard had borrowed from the coachbuilders in nearby Tarnworth where he worked. The room was muggy and rich with the stink of oil and varnish and sweat.

The Jupiter had been Richard's idea. He'd telephoned Bill from the coachbuilders the day it had arrived on the back of a tow truck, following the collision it had had with a lorry. Richard's boss had informed the Jupiter's rich young owner that he'd be better off selling it for scrap than paying for its repair. 'That'd take a real labour of love,' he'd announced, looking over the battered, buckled wreck of a car. 'More man hours and trouble than it's worth.'

And that's what had sent Richard's mind racing.

Bill had needed no persuading. A buried part of him had loved the romance of the challenge. He'd imagined himself at the Jupiter's wheel, racing through the countryside. He'd thought of the feeling of freedom it might bring.

He and Richard had combined what little savings they'd had and had set about scavenging and purchasing the necessary parts to restore the Jupiter to its current pristine condition.

Six months it had taken them. Six months of mechanical education for Bill. Six months of honing his teaching skills for Richard. Six months of hours snatched from evenings and weekends for them both.

But now they were here and it had all been worth it. The Jupiter, *their* Jupiter, was a thing of beauty, a magnificent piece of machinery, which they'd never have been able to afford to buy new or even second-hand. Now, though, thanks to their ambition and toil, it was theirs. Now, Bill hoped, it was finally ready to drive.

Richard stooped over the shining engine, which was visible beneath the hinged-up bonnet. Pensively, he stroked his black moustache.

'What's the verdict?' Bill asked.

Richard lowered the bonnet and clicked it shut. He stood up and rested his hand paternally on the car's soft top, as Bill had seen him do so many times before on his daughters' heads.

'You go first,' Richard said, tossing him the keys.

Bill snatched them from the air. 'We should go together.'

Richard began to roll a cigarette. 'I've had my fun fixing her up,' he said. 'Just go. I know you're itching to show her off.'

He wasn't kidding. In too much of a hurry to remove his battered work boots first, Bill hopped awkwardly from one foot to the other as he stripped off his overalls. He was wearing an old pair of slacks and a blue cotton shirt and braces beneath. He got into the car and started her up. The 1486cc flat-four pushrod engine purred like a cat.

Richard tapped at the glass and Bill opened the window.

'Are you going to go and see her?' Richard asked.

'Who?'

'Take a guess.'

'My mother?'

'Another guess,' Richard said in an appalling approximation of an American accent.

220

'Oh.' Bill scratched at his face in an effort to conceal his blush.

Emily. Emily Jones, that's who Richard meant. Bill talked about her too much, Richard had told him, too much for someone who was nothing more than a customer, as Bill had insisted she was.

Bill had to admit, he *had* been thinking about her a lot recently. He'd started looking forward to her calling into the shop. Whenever the bell rang, it was her he hoped to see when he looked up. Even though their brief conversations had always been centred around her placing her orders, he'd learnt little bits about her life: how her parents were moving away; how she was painting a new sign for the shop; how exciting it was to find herself being the boss for the first time in her life. In turn, he'd found himself talking up the town – even though he was hardly in love with it himself – wanting her to like it enough to stay.

'If I were you,' suggested Richard, 'looking so splendid in there, I'd certainly drive past the Sea Catch Café. At least a couple of times,' he added. 'Maybe even three.' He grinned. 'You never know: that way she might even take some notice of you.'

'Yeah, well, I'm not you,' Bill answered shortly. 'Which is why you wouldn't catch me doing anything quite so ridiculous as that.'

And it *was* ridiculous. Utterly ridiculous. Bill certainly thought so, anyway, as he found himself driving past the Sea Catch Café for the fifth time in as many minutes.

But it was exciting, too, feeling this sick with apprehension, breaking out from his daily routine and frittering away his time, without knowing what might happen next.

221

It felt like liberation. It felt like fun. And wasn't he owed a little of both? Hadn't he lost enough of his youth already? Hadn't he watched it gathering like dust on the window sills and shelves of Vale Supplies? Wasn't it about time he sent some ripples out across the rockpool-still waters of his life?

He smiled uneasily through the windscreen at his mother's gossipy friend, Mrs Carver, who was leaning on her umbrella outside the butcher's, and who'd been observing his comings and goings through her half-moon spectacles with increasing suspicion over the past five minutes.

But Bill didn't care. Any remarked peculiarity was by the by. His being here, acting the way he was, well, the Jupiter gave him all the excuse he needed. Why would anybody disbelieve him if he told them he was simply out testing it?

He rounded the corner on to Winstanton Parade, out of Mrs Carver's sight, and pulled over to the side of the road. Ridiculous, he told himself again. Ridiculous for a grown man like himself to be mooning over a grown woman like Emily Jones.

He wished he was more the man of the world which the Jupiter made him out to be. He wished he had more experience to draw on. But he didn't.

The truth was he'd never been much good with women. Like Susan Castle, the girl he'd got engaged to at university. He'd messed that up good and proper. She'd been the first girl he'd slept with (the only girl he'd slept with, in fact) and he'd wanted her to be the last. He'd thought they'd be happy together for life. He'd wanted them to be like his mother and father. But when it had come to the crunch, when he'd returned home to help his mother run the shop and Susan had broken off with him in a letter, he hadn't even left Stepmouth and tried to change her mind. He'd let her go, and what kind of love was that, that you didn't even fight for? Surely that was no kind of love at all.

And if he'd got it so wrong with Susan Castle, how would he know when he'd got it right with someone else? He'd only been out with three girls since he'd moved back to Stepmouth. And none of these Sunday teacake flirtations had blossomed into anything more substantial than stilted conversations and the occasional awkward fumbling in the dark.

He'd been to blame. In each case, it had been him who'd called it off. It wasn't that he'd found the girls in question unattractive, but that he'd found them naive. Or normal, as he'd also come to think of them. Because naive *was* the norm round here, wasn't it, for people his age? Aside from the airbase up the road, even the war had kept its distance. No bombs had been dropped on top of them. They'd seen no bodies stuffed into bags. Death, if it had come at all, had drifted down softly on to their doormats in feather-light telegrams, or reached them as whispers from the cushioning lips of a living parent.

Never immediate, then. Not like the night when Keith Glover had torn like a cyclone through the house in which Bill had grown up. When death's name had been screamed down the army barracks telephone to eighteen-year-old Bill by his hysterical nine-year-old sister.

Emily Jones, though . . . in Emily Jones, Bill suspected something different. Not only because she'd left this town and travelled. But because she'd married and divorced. Because she'd seen and experienced more than the rest of the girls in this town had done put together.

223

And that's where he saw his and Emily's common ground: in their difference from everyone else.

Ridiculous, then? Yes. But irresistible, too.

'One last time,' he said, prayer-like under his breath – wilful in forgetting that this was what he'd said the last time. (Not to mention the time before that.)

As he turned into East Street, he saw her: Emily Jones, strolling into the road as carelessly as if she were strolling into a meadow. He slammed on the brakes. The car slewed to a halt with precious inches to spare. He could have killed her, he thought, as she wandered round to the side of the car and peered in.

'Well, well, well,' she said, 'if it isn't Bill Vale.'

She was wearing what he guessed were her work clothes: loose brown trousers stuffed into old brown leather boots, a khaki shirt and white canvas apron. Scruffy like a land girl, he thought, remembering the pretty women from London who'd come down to help harvest the fields of the town's outlying farms during the war. As teenagers, Bill and his schoolmates had used to walk up through the country lanes, and clamber over ditches and stiles just to catch glimpses of the older girls' bare sunburnt shoulders and legs.

'Hello,' he said rather stiffly. He'd meant to compliment her, but already it was too late.

She smiled to herself as she looked the car over. 'You really are quite the dark horse, aren't you?'

It was the first time he'd seen her up close without her make-up on. Her skin was as pale as Rachel's and, without eyeshadow to draw out their sparkle, her grey eyes seemed as sly and as wise as a cat's.

'I mean, there I was thinking you were just a grocer,' she continued. 'And then just the other day your sister tells me that you were going to be an engineer. And that you've got boxes full of drawings at home . . . of concert halls . . . and bridges . . . and things you wanted to build . . .'

'She told you that?'

'Sure,' Emily continued. 'She seemed really proud. She said you would have been famous by now if you hadn't had to come home to take care of her and your mum.'

He stared back, embarrassed by his sister's unexpected boasting, but getting a buzz out of hearing that she'd said those things about him, too. Especially to Emily.

'She's not always so complimentary,' he said.

'You should dig those drawings out, you know. It's a terrible thing to let ambition go to waste. And look around . . .' She pointed to the end of East Street, to where you could see the wrecked old Bathers' Pavilion which over-looked the beach. 'We could do with your talents round here to give this place a little sparkle.'

For the first time in years Bill found himself looking at the neglected old eyesore of a building – really *looking* at it – as something other than background, something more than a decaying white landmark. The roof was mostly gone, but those walls, he thought, they were still standing in spite of the fact that the building hadn't been used for nearly twenty years. It could be really something, he thought, with a bit of work.

'I'd assumed you were a holidaymaker,' Emily said.

'What?'

'A holidaymaker,' she repeated.

Because of the Jupiter, he guessed. Because you didn't see cars like this around these parts too often.

'I'm giving it a test drive,' he explained, sticking to his original plan of acting like this meeting was all one great big coincidence.

'And the same goes for the other four times, right?'

'I'm sorry?'

'The other four times you've driven past the café in the past five minutes,' she elaborated.

*Oh, God.* He felt like he was sinking.

'They were all just part of the test, too, right?' she went on.

He stared at the walnut-veneered dashboard with its complex array of chrome instruments, wanting to groan. She'd been watching him . . . all this time . . . He felt like he was seven again, like his mother had caught him sneaking into the larder to steal biscuits from the tin, after having quietly observed every single step he'd taken across the creaky floorboards on the way.

'Exactly,' he said.

Smiling, she watched him as he shifted uncomfortably on the car's upholstered leather bench seat, and waited for him to settle, before peering innocently into his eyes. Only then did she deliver the *coup de grâce*: 'None of it had anything to do with trying to get my attention, then?' she asked.

'No,' he said automatically.

Why was he lying? Wasn't this what he'd wanted, to be talking to her about them – about the *possibility* of them – instead of how many pounds of flour and tins of baked beans she needed sent round? But his embarrassment over having been caught out was too strong to fight.

'That's a shame,' she said

His brow furrowed. 'It is?'

'Well, it would certainly have been very flattering. If you *had* been trying to get my attention. But never mind,' she said breezily, 'I'm sure my vanity will survive.'

*Say something!* a voice inside him screamed. *Say some-*

*thing! Say something! Say something! This could be your one and only chance!* But before he could obey, she said something first.

'You know what?' She leant in close.

'What?'

'I've never been out for a ride in a car like this.'

'Really?'

'Truly. Not once. Not even in the States.' She rattled her fingernails against the door. 'And there's so much room.'

'Yes.' He'd never noticed before how long her eyelashes were.

'Especially for one person,' she said.

'Yes.' Or how her nostrils flared ever so slightly as she breathed.

'And I bet it's so much fun and a real smooth ride, too,' she added.

'Oh, yes.' He was watching her mouth now, the way her bright white teeth were visible through the slight parting of her lips.

Now, he told himself. It's now or never.

'Would you . . .' he heard himself starting to say.

'Yes . . .' She smiled at him encouragingly.

He swallowed, his whole body tensing, braced for rejection. 'Would you like to come out for a drive with me sometime?'

'I thought you'd never ask,' she replied.

He didn't even think to hide his grin. 'I nearly never did.'

'I'd love to,' she said.

'Shall we say –'

'– next Saturday night?' she suggested.

Then he noticed Mrs Carver standing by the door to the Sea Catch Café, staring at them.

'A friend of yours?' Emily asked, following his line of sight.

'Of my mother's,' Bill explained. 'She's a bit of a gossip.'

'Is that a fact?'

'I'm afraid so.'

'In that case,' Emily said, 'how about we give her something to gossip about?'

He opened his mouth to answer, but before he'd uttered a single syllable, she'd rested her hands on the window frame, leant forward into the car and kissed him softly on the lips. As she pulled back, she ran her fingers slowly through her hair. Her cheeks had turned pink.

'Time for me to get back to work,' she said. As she walked backwards towards the café door, she stumbled, nearly fell. 'Next Saturday,' she called, waving to him. 'Seven. And don't you be late!' She turned then to Mrs Carver, who was standing slack-jawed with wonder. 'Handsome, isn't he?' she said deliberately loud enough for Bill to hear.

Bill sat immobilised in the car. The memory of her kiss lingered on his lips as if a butterfly had just alighted there. When he finally breathed in, he could smell rosemary and thyme. The whole world smelt wild and fresh.

Even though it had been Rachel's turn to do the duties, it had been their mother who'd cooked. She'd insisted on it, the same as she'd insisted that Bill and Rachel sit down for a family meal at a quarter to seven, when normally their Saturday supper would have started at six and been over with by now. And why? Well, it hadn't taken a genius to work that one out. Because Bill's mother had learnt from Edith Carver that her son was expected elsewhere – an elsewhere of which she completely disapproved.

'Very forward *indeed*,' she was pointedly saying.

Bill ignored Rachel, who was grinning at him cross-eyed, relishing every second of his discomfort. Mechanically, he continued to chew his way through the greasy grey mixture of liver, bacon and potatoes which his mother had ladled into his bowl only seconds before.

'And as for her and that American man . . . when she was still no more than a girl . . .'

Bill tore a strip of bread off the crusty round cob at the centre of the table. He swiped it across the brown gravy in his china bowl, momentarily revealing the existence of a blue-and-white floral pattern beneath, before the gravy seeped back across, burying the splash of colour like an artefact in mud.

'I call it impetuous,' his mother said. 'Leaving the country like that. Evidence of a flighty nature. At the very least.'

'She moved there to marry,' Bill pointed out.

'And later to divorce.'

'I hardly imagine that was part of her plan when she set out. After all, she did stay with him for seven years first.'

His mother stared at him fixedly. 'I stayed with your father till the day he died.'

Bill glared back, angry at her for using his dad's death against him like this. 'That still doesn't mean you can write off her relationship with her husband as some impetuous schoolgirl infatuation,' he snapped.

'Which is all the more reason for you not to go getting involved with her.'

'What?' he asked. 'You think she's somehow tainted just because she's lived with another man.'

Her eyes blazed defiantly.

'I think she's lovely,' Rachel suddenly said.

She wasn't laughing, or pulling faces any more. 'What?' Bill asked, assuming he must have misheard.

'Emily: I think she's lovely. And not flighty. Or tainted. Or anything else that Mum says she is.'

Bill could barely believe his sister was openly backing him up like this.

'And what would you know?' snapped their mother. 'A girl of your age.'

It was a question which Bill had lately been tempted to ask Rachel himself. What *did* she know? About love? About relationships? More than she once had and that was for sure. More than someone her age perhaps *should* know. Because he'd noticed the change that had come over her lately. A dreaminess had crept into her eyes and lent a lustre to her cheeks. He'd catch her sometimes, staring at the most mundane of objects around the house or shop – like a box of soap flakes on a shelf, or a cracked tile on the floor – with an inexplicable smile on her face. It was a look he recognised well enough. He'd seen it on Richard Horner's face when he'd first met Rosie. And in his own reflection as he'd shaved half an hour before in preparation for his date with Emily Jones.

He wondered who it was who'd sent his sister like this. He'd find out soon enough, he supposed. Secrets in Stepmouth never lasted long.

'You keep your nose out of it and eat your tea,' Mrs Vale told her.

Rachel opened her mouth to answer back, then thought better of it and instead took a forkful of food.

'What about me, then, Mum?' Bill demanded. 'I was engaged once, too, remember? Does that mean I shouldn't get a second chance either?'

'That no-good slut broke it off with you, not the other way round.'

*No-good slut.* There: she hadn't been able to resist saying it, had she? That's how she'd always think of Susan Castle, and probably Emily, too. Because they'd changed their minds.

'Because I left her, Mum. Because I moved back here.'

His chair scraped loudly across the floor as he stood. He pulled his suit jacket – the black one with the silk lining, his one good suit, which he'd bought for his father's funeral – from the back of his chair. He walked round the table and stood by his mother. As he leant down to kiss her, she reached up and touched his face. Her fingers smelt of the bitter layers of onions she'd peeled to make their supper.

'I only want what's best for you,' she said.

'I know.' He knew, too, how much she'd lost, and how much she wanted to protect what was left of her family. But he didn't need protecting. Not from Emily Jones. And that was something that his mother would have to learn.

He felt the corridor closing in around him as he walked to the alley door. He took the bunch of wild flowers – violets and bluebells – from the vase next to the hatstand. He'd picked them that morning from the hedgerow up by the allotment, binding them together with a length of parcel string.

'Wait,' Rachel said, appearing behind him.

She selected a bluebell from the bunch and slipped it into his buttonhole. She stepped back and smiled.

'You look wonderful,' she told him.

He smiled. 'Thanks,' he said. 'And thanks for sticking up for me back there. I won't forget it.'

As he stepped out into the alleyway, he pulled the bunch of keys from his trouser pocket and looked up at the window above, which was barred like all the shop's windows. Locks,

231

locks, locks: at least three on each door. This building had as many as a bank. Or a jail. And that's what occurred to him now, as he locked the door behind him: that sometimes locks worked both ways; that not only did they keep people out, but sometimes they kept them locked in, too.

Outside the Sea Catch Café, the Jupiter's engine idled as Bill waited for Emily to join him. A moment before, he'd handed her the bunch of wild flowers.

She'd wanted to put them in water, she'd told him, so that they wouldn't get spoilt. She'd run back inside so quickly that she'd left him wondering whether he'd inadvertently upset her, and whether the flowers, because they'd cost him nothing, had made him look cheap.

He stared at the small square red leather handbag she'd left on the tan seat beside him. It looked out of place, nothing to do with him, like a piece of lost property he should hand in.

All of a sudden, he felt out of his depth, terrified that he'd made a mistake in asking her out to begin with. Or being asked out by her? (He still wasn't sure which.) The same went for that kiss. Had it been real, meant for him? Or for Mrs Carver to see? Nothing but scandal for its own sake?

He watched now, as a curvy silhouette appeared in the brightly lit café doorway. There, in the shadowy enigma of Emily Jones, he'd find his answers.

A shouted goodbye, the door banging shut, and she was hurrying over, her daringly knee-length grey skirt flapping against her legs. He started to get out, so that he could walk round and open the passenger door for her. But she was too quick, already gesturing at him to stay put, then she climbed in, pulling the passenger door closed after her with a thump.

'So where are you going to take me on this drive?' she asked breathlessly, adjusting her red shawl around her neck, before twisting round to face him.

He had the tickets to the Barnstaple Plaza Dance already in his hand. He held them up, hoping she'd approve. Buying them had been Rosie's idea. She'd told Bill they'd be just perfect. Emily plucked them from his fingertips.

'*The Barnstaple Plaza Dance Committee proudly presents Dick Grewcock and his Travelling Trumpeters*,' she read aloud with an amused smile.

It suddenly occurred to Bill how different Emily and Rosie were. 'We don't have to go,' he said. 'Not if you don't want to.'

'No, it sounds great . . .'

He noticed how she'd managed to tame her curly blonde hair, tying it up on her head in a doughnut shape with a single white clip. She flicked the tickets absent-mindedly across the silver necklace which she wore on the outside of her blouse collar.

'You must be good on your feet, Bill,' she said, 'to take a girl out dancing on a first date . . . Do you go dancing a lot?'

Not since university in 1948. Not since he'd danced with Susan Castle, he nearly answered. He'd been dreading it, really, from the moment he'd picked up the tickets from the venue and had seen the photographs on the wall of the men and women twirling one another around like acrobats. All he'd been able to do was imagine what a mess his two left feet would make of Emily's shoes. He remembered how embarrassing his last attempt at lying to Emily had been and decided instead to risk the truth.

'No,' he answered, 'I'm terrible.'

'That makes two of us.'

They stared at each other for a second, before bursting out laughing.

'We could just go and listen to the band,' he then suggested.

'Think they're any good?'

'I doubt it.'

'What about Dick Grewcock? He certainly sounds *swell* . . .'

'I don't know anything about –' Bill started to answer, before her snort of laughter cut him short. 'Oh,' he said, suddenly laughing too, 'his name . . .'

She threaded a cigarette between her lips. He lit it for her with a match. Smoke and sulphur drifted between them.

'I know,' she suggested. 'Let's do exactly what we planned to in the first place: go for that drive. You know, out of town. Some place else.'

'But where? It's dark.'

'And clear. And bright. And beautiful. I know a place that'll suit us just fine.'

He took the tickets from her and tore them neatly in half, letting the pieces flutter like leaves on to his lap. It was strange, but now that all his preparations had come to nothing they no longer seemed important. Not with her smiling at him the way she was now.

'You're on,' he said, reaching down and letting the hand-brake go.

As they drove beneath the street lamps of the town, and over South Bridge, and up the steep and inky corridor of the Barnstaple Road, they talked. Or rather, Bill asked questions and Emily answered. It was an arrangement

234

which suited him fine; he had a million questions to ask her, about the millions of moments in her life which he'd already missed.

She told him about her relationship with Buck. About what a wild kid she'd been when she'd met him at a dance during the war.

'I thought you said you couldn't dance,' Bill reminded her.

'When you find out how much trouble it led to you'll know why I don't any more,' she replied.

She told him how seriously she'd taken herself, too. 'Honestly, Bill, the way I acted around Buck, you'd have thought we were the first people to have ever fallen in love. We put so much pressure on ourselves. Whatever happens to me from now on and whoever it happens with, I want it to happen at its own pace. Not because it's been forced. You know, I want the fun to last and not get squeezed out so soon.'

Whatever, whoever . . . Bill wondered if she could possibly mean him.

He asked her about what had happened next and how she came to leave Stepmouth. She relived her mother's disapproval.

'"I don't care how many restaurants his family own, Emily,"' she said, making Bill laugh with her perfect impersonation of her mother. '"You're too young to be seeing him and that's final."'

And she told him about how Buck called her 'hon' and 'doll' and how he got shot at by a couple of Messerschmitts while flying over Germany.

'So I ran away to be with him. In the military hospital in Kent. For months I kept writing to Mum and Dad to tell them I was fine but not where I was. In case they came after me to bring me home. Which I know damn well they would have.'

She and Buck had sailed to America after the war. 'We'd already got married in the hospital in Kent before he'd been invalided out. His CO had arranged it, no questions asked.'

Emily had fallen in love with the States, but out of love with Buck. She listed all the separate reasons – his nights out on the drink, his casual infidelities – which had balled into a big enough reason for her finally to leave.

They were up above the town now, branching off to the west, out across the moor along the old coast road.

'I would have stayed out there, you know, as well,' she confided in Bill. 'Only the collapse of my marriage with Buck . . . the disappearance of the family I'd always thought I'd have with him . . . it made me want to be with my own family. It made me want to come back home. To start over.'

'No kids then?'

'No, we were lucky there, although we didn't think it at the time.'

He didn't feel so much as a twinge of jealousy over everything she'd gone through with Buck, not like he'd expected. The way she'd spoken about it made it sound like it had happened to someone else entirely.

'And would you go back? To America, I mean.'

'Maybe one day. It's a great country, you know. Full of possibilities. I'd love to go there with the right man.'

They hadn't seen a single other vehicle since they'd set out, like they'd become the only people on the planet.

'How did you manage to convince your parents to let you move back in?' Bill asked. 'All that anger your mother had . . . all that resentment you must have caused . . .

236

where did it all go? It can't have just vanished . . .'

She laughed. 'Having a little money put aside from a divorce didn't hurt much. Especially when Dad was looking for someone to sell the family business to . . .' She sighed. 'Seriously, though,' she said. 'Time passes. People forgive. It's what happens. And that's a good thing, you know? It's what keeps the world turning round.'

'I'm glad you and your parents worked things out,' he said. 'I remember how nervous you looked that day you first called into the shop. Knock on wood, you said. For luck . . .'

'You remember?' She sounded surprised.

'A beautiful girl like you walking into the shop,' he said, 'it's not something you forget in a hurry.'

'You're a sweet man, Bill Vale,' she told him, gently kissing him on the cheek. 'And a good listener, too. I like that in a man.'

They drove another mile, rising now, higher even than Summerglade Hill.

'Next left,' she said. 'There, by that tree.'

The great shadow of a huge horse chestnut loomed up out of the darkness. Bill turned off on to the uneven track, slowing down, wary of getting a puncture. As they drove beneath the tree, the tips of the horse chestnut's branches scratched like cats' claws across the Jupiter's windscreen and roof. Another five yards and Bill turned off the engine. Silence engulfed them. In the distance, they could see the sea, shimmering beneath the half-moon and flicker of the stars.

'Welcome to Desolation,' Emily said.

'What?'

'That's what it's called. The name of this place. I once saw it on a map.'

Desolation . . . It didn't feel like that, not to Bill. It was the most beautiful place he'd ever been to.

'Look at the sky,' she said, peering up through the windscreen.

'Want a better view?'

'Always.' She started to get out.

'No,' he said, 'wait.'

He stepped out of the car and unfastened the folding roof, pulling it back and down, out of sight behind the seat. He got back in and sat beside her.

'It's amazing,' she said, staring up. He felt her sliding along the bench towards him, resting her head on his shoulder.

'All those stars,' Bill said. 'When I was a little boy, my dad used to tell me they were angels. He used to point up there' – Bill demonstrated now as he raised his arm – 'and say stuff like, "There's my Auntie Ada, and that's Ivor, your grandfather's brother, who had a real eye for the ladies . . ."' Bill cleared his throat and slowly lowered his arm. 'Only then you go to school, of course, and they tell you they're just stars, nothing more, and you never look on them the same way again . . .'

'I'm sorry,' she said, 'about your father. I've been meaning to tell you since I got back. Only I never got a chance. Or I did, but there were always other people around . . .'

Bill's body began to tighten like a spring. He hated talking about his father, about what had happened to him.

'My dad wrote to me about it after I'd moved to the States,' she continued. 'I'd moved to Kent by the time it happened, you see, to where Buck was recuperating in hospital.' She rested her hand on Bill's wrist. 'I remember your dad from when I was little. He was a lovely, kind man. A lot like you. You must miss him a lot.'

238

'I do.'

That tightening again . . . like a weight pressing down on him . . . suddenly, he needed to get it off his chest. 'I wish you wouldn't employ him, Keith Glover's brother,' he said.

'You mean Tony.'

Her face was shadowy, hard to read. 'He's dangerous,' Bill stated. 'You know that's why he got kicked out of school . . . because he fights . . .'

*'Fought.* He doesn't do it any more.'

'Only because the last time he did, he got beaten up by Bernie Cunningham.'

'Who's twice his size and a drunk and a bully. Sometimes,' she told him, 'people deserve a second chance.'

'And sometimes they don't.'

They stared at each other.

'Is that why you drove me up here?' she then asked. 'To argue?'

He was thrown by the question. 'No.'

'So let's close this conversation and remember why you did.'

'But –'

'I'll run the café how I want, Bill. And I'll employ who I want. But believe me: if Tony ever does step out of line,' she added, 'then I'll send him packing the same as I would do anyone else.' Her eyes were steady, uncompromising.

'Do you swear it?'

'Yes.'

He knew then that this was as much reassurance as he was ever going to get. 'We won't talk about it again,' he said.

He didn't know if he was doing the right thing by not trying harder to bring her round to his point of view. What would his mother say? That was easy. That he was wrong. And his father? His father would have liked Emily, he knew, would have respected her the same way Bill did, for her strength. But his father wasn't around, which left Bill with only his own instinct. And his own instinct told him that he should trust Emily's judgement. Keith Glover had cost him one girl already. There was no way he was going to let an argument over his younger brother cost him any chance he had with Emily as well.

'We'll find plenty of other things to talk about,' Emily said.

'I suppose so.'

'Happy things,' she said. 'And life's so much better when you spend it concentrating on those. I've got a good feeling about this,' she told him. She leant in closer. Then she smiled at him so warmly that it melted all the coldness he felt inside. 'Or we could just not talk at all,' she said.

It was the second time she'd kissed him on the lips, but to him it felt like the first. Where before, there in front of Mrs Carver, it had been over with almost before it had begun, now there was no abrupt ending. Now he had time to savour it: the softness of her lips, their gentle separation and the warm, electric flicker of her tongue against his. Warm breath funnelled from her nostrils on to his face. His arms were around her waist, her hands stroking through his hair.

Then a different kind of urgency possessed them, not of breaking apart, but of wanting to be closer still. Her fingers clawed at his hair, pulling him towards her. As she shuffled back along the bench towards the passenger door, he scrambled clumsily after her, first snagging, then ripping his trouser pocket on the handbrake along the way.

Visions flashed through his mind. Of being in church

tomorrow morning. Of his mother and Mrs Carver seeing the rip. But then they were gone. Because he didn't care. Because he wanted this more.

His body was squeezed up tight against Emily's now. Her skirt had ridden up high, right to the top of her black nylon stockings, but she made no attempt to readjust it. He caught a brief glimpse of white knickers beneath. Then they were kissing again.

The leather seat beneath them groaned each time they moved. She pulled his hand to her breast and pressed it down. He could feel the yield of her warm flesh beneath the thin material of her blouse. Then she was leaning forward, her palms momentarily pressed hard against his chest, as her fingers splayed outwards, before delving inside his jacket sleeves, forcing them back over his arms.

She shivered as he finished unbuttoning her blouse. Underneath, she was wearing a slip so smooth he guessed it must have been made of silk. He raised it up over her breasts as he kissed his way softly down her neck. She sighed, thrusting her pelvis hard against his. He hardened against her.

Then she was up, holding on to the windscreen with one arm for support. Balancing first on one foot and then the other, she kicked off her shoes, before tugging her skirt and knickers down to her ankles and stepping out of them. Impatient now, she set to work on him, feverishly tossing his tie to one side and unbuttoning his shirt. Another two seconds work and she'd unfastened his trouser buttons and had slid her hand inside.

He gasped, rising now, pulling his trousers and shorts down to his knees. She took him in her hand, straddling him as she did. As he entered her, she gasped. Her breasts quivered, the colour of milk in the moonlight. She pushed

241

down on top of him. Clamping her thighs tightly around his waist, they started rocking together, moving as one.

They could have been in a boat. There in the great wide black sea of the moor, with the Jupiter's roof down and the limitless sky stretching far and wide above, they could have travelled anywhere, the two of them together. Anywhere they'd wanted at all.

# *Chapter XIII*

**Mallorca, Present Day**

Laurie watched the cab that had dropped her off in the road leading down to the tiny harbour, until it had disappeared around the bend, back up towards the main road. It was the Tuesday morning after the hideous meal at Sa Costa. The day that Rachel had ordered Sam and Laurie to spend together on *Flight*. It was supposed to be a day of – how had Rachel put it? – 'rest and relaxation' for the two of them. How ironic, she thought, feeling tenser than ever.

She'd been expecting the harbour to be full of chic restaurants and women clad in designer clothes shopping in little boutiques, so she was amazed to discover that it was so rustic. On the street corner, three old women sat in a line beneath the overhanging shade of a rickety building which housed a small café. They chatted while they crocheted with fine white cotton. As Laurie passed them, the aroma of paella cooking wafted out of the open door, a TV on the wall inside blasting out the sound of a man talking in rapid Spanish, followed by a TV audience laughing.

Laurie slowed down and stopped on the corner, feeling her nerve deserting her. She shouldn't be here. She shouldn't have come. By simply being here, she was going against every vow she'd made to herself. Now she wished she'd tried harder to wriggle out of today's arrangement.

Surely there were a million excuses she could have used, so why hadn't she thought of one of them? She should have just called Sam and backed out of it days ago, hours ago even . . . but she hadn't.

Laurie felt her legs carrying her forward towards the harbour, a slick of sweat was breaking out all over her skin in the heat. Her heart was pounding. Her stomach clenched with what could only be a sickness induced by guilt. After all, she was an imposter. Feeling as she did, she knew she was deliberately betraying her new family and all the trust they'd placed in her. And not only her family. Wasn't it true that she was betraying her friends, James, herself? She should turn and get the hell away from here as fast as possible.

But something inside her was stronger than her common sense. The morbid fascination with all-things Sam which had first led her to accept Rachel's invitation to Mallorca, and then Claire's invitation to the anniversary party on the boat and now, ultimately, to be walking towards a date with her ex-lover, was just too powerful to resist.

She told herself that she'd had no choice. She'd had to accept Rachel's offer of the villa, because it had been too good to turn down. She'd had to accept Claire's invitation to the party or risk sounding incredibly rude. And she'd had no choice but to bow yet again to Rachel's wishes and agree to spend the day with Sam today.

She felt caught up in the relentless Glover procession of events and had no way of extricating herself without raising suspicion. Being at Rachel's villa was like being caught in the centre of a giant spider's web. On the one hand she wanted to know her aunt, but the pay-off was that Rachel wanted her to be part of the family. But that family included Sam and his wife and child. The only thing she could do was to play along and pretend that everything was normal.

But maybe having to behave normally, having to play this game in which Sam was a mere acquaintance, having to keep her feelings hidden all the time was the reason that her feelings were so powerful. And she'd spent too many sleepless nights in the last month to continue pretending that she didn't care for Sam, or secretly crave to be with him.

She knew deep down it was very, very wrong even to be thinking about him. In the same way that she knew that from the first moment that she'd seen Claire at the beach on her first day on the island that she should have packed her bags and left. But she'd hoped, foolishly, that seeing Sam and giving him the cold shoulder at his own party, of proving herself in front of him, of flaunting her independence, her indifference would have given her the satisfaction she craved. She'd told herself that it would have cured her need for revenge and that she'd be able to leave Sam in the past once and for all.

But her plan had failed spectacularly. Sam's apology, his hasty explanation, his obvious terror at her being back in his life had sunk into her heart like a knife and reopened an old wound that had refused to heal ever since. Instead of feeling vindicated, she'd once more become obsessed by the man that she'd once thought would be her future. As if she'd been drugged, Sam had seeped into her subconscious, his face had been in every stroke of paint, his voice in every murmur of the sea.

But the facts, she reminded herself, remained the same. Sam had made his choice and it hadn't been her. And now he was married, with a child, and they were inextricably bound by a family which would be destroyed if they ever found out their secret. Which is why running away would be the actions of a child. It wouldn't solve anything. It would only leave a trail of unanswered questions which Rachel was bound to pick at until she uncovered the truth. Which is why she had to go through with today's plan.

Down at the water's edge, the waves slapped gently against the concrete front. Several brightly coloured fishing boats bobbed in the water and a fisherman hosed down a small trawler, a cigarette hanging from his lip. She could see small black fish darting in the emerald-green shallows, and along the path, a gaggle of small local boys were fishing with a plastic bucket on a piece of string.

At the end of the path, where the cottages gave way to a jumble of old sheds, a jetty stretched out into the water, with small white yachts and power boats moored either side. High above, the sky was a brilliant blue, only a thin haze of cloud stretching like a veil above the seaweed-encrusted harbour wall.

Laurie walked slowly along the water's edge and stopped at the start of the jetty, looking down the vessels, wondering which one was *Flight*. She'd only heard the vaguest of instructions from Sam on Rachel's answering machine at the villa. Wouldn't it be ironic, she thought, after all her worrying, if Sam was the one who had bailed out? Could it be possible, she wondered, if he was feeling as nervous and uneasy about today as she was?

Then, suddenly, she saw him. He was at the far end of the jetty, hauling a heavy bag on to a boat. He was balancing with one foot on the bow of the boat and one foot on the concrete jetty. He was wearing khaki shorts and his chest and his feet were bare. His dark blond hair fell across

246

his tanned face. There was something so unexpectedly boyish about him, as he worked, and she could tell immediately that he was alone.

And then it happened. Just as she'd dreaded. She stopped to watch him, feeling something inside her flip over, her knees weakening beneath her and her throat going dry. Damn it! Why was he so goddamned attractive? She cursed the chemistry that made her physically react to him in this way.

*Oh God*, she panicked. She shouldn't go through with this. Sam hadn't seen her, it wasn't too late to run. This was too dangerous. She wasn't strong enough to be alone with him.

Laurie forced herself to think about Claire. Her cousin. Her *relative*. OK, so Laurie might find her a bit shallow and materialistic, she might be secretly jealous because Claire was beautiful, but Claire had shown nothing but faith in Laurie from the moment they'd met. She'd done everything to be friendly towards her new cousin. What would Claire think if she knew Laurie was standing here, feeling like she did about her husband? She would be horrified. Horrified and betrayed. Sam was the father of her child, for God's sake. Laurie closed her eyes for a moment, forcing herself to picture Archie's face, thinking about the cute little boy whose whole future she could so easily ruin. But still her heart pounded, knowing that she was about to spend the day with Sam.

She must focus on Archie and Claire and Sam's present situation, she told herself. She would have to be strong and keep her feelings well and truly hidden. She'd got herself into this mess and she would simply have to find her way through it. She would have to do everything in her power to guard her secret, so that no one, especially not Sam, would even suspect that she felt anything other than platonic friendship.

Yes, she decided, nearing the boat. She would take a leaf out of Sam's book. She would just have to be adult about the whole thing. She would have to make out that she believed, as Rachel and Claire did, that this was the most normal thing in the world. Two newly acquainted people out for a spot of sailing. Nothing more, nothing less.

Either side of her, the small yachts and powerboats were empty. Where was everyone, she wondered, stepping over a black cat which was stretched out on the concrete in the sun. Sam's yacht loomed ahead of her.

Rachel had told her that *Flight* was a thirty-four-foot classic schooner, as if that should mean something. Laurie hadn't taken much notice at the time, but now she could see why Sam was reportedly so proud of it.

As it was moored bow-to, she could see that the sleek sides were painted a glistening midnight blue. Beyond, on the beautiful varnished teak deck, she could see the proud wooden mast and boom, and the old-fashioned wooden wheel.

Then Sam emerged from the cockpit and jumped on deck. She cleared her throat to get his attention.

'You're here already?' he said, sounding flustered, as he glanced at the chunky silver watch on his wrist. He clambered forward to the bow of the boat, past the cleats and over the front deck, grabbing his short-sleeved linen shirt from the rail. He hastily put it on and did up two buttons, covering his tanned chest and the curls of dark blond hair. The same dark blond hair she'd once touched . . .

'Come aboard,' he said.

Laurie slipped off her shoes and held them in her hand. Then she grabbed Sam's outstretched hand and lunged her foot towards the pointed bow. It wasn't exactly the most dignified way of climbing aboard, but she was damned if she was going to make a fuss.

Sam steadied her for a moment as she found her footing on board and then let her hand go. He didn't look at her, or say hello. Nothing in fact. No 'Hi, Laurie, how are you?' with two Continental cheek kisses. Nothing.

Well, good. She didn't want him to kiss her. Formal was better. And him helping her on board had been a handshake in its own way.

'You don't mind if we get going straight away, do you?' he asked, hurrying away from her. She followed, watching as he jumped down into the cockpit and then swung down through the small open hatch into the cabin below. He pulled the large bag in the cockpit towards him. 'I'm not sure how much wind we're going to get,' he said. 'So if you want to get out into the bay and back, we'll have to hurry.'

Laurie felt a flash of irritation. She didn't *want* to go into the bay and back at all. She hadn't forced him into taking her sailing. It hadn't been *her* idea.

Laurie crossed her arms, feeling peeved. She'd spent so long thinking about how Sam would behave with her, but it hadn't occurred to her that he might continue to behave in private the same way that he had in public when they'd had dinner a few days ago. Now she felt thrown.

Back on deck, Sam set about issuing orders, calmly explaining the anatomy of the boat. She learnt that the two sails were called a mainsail and a headsail and that she would be in charge of winching in the headsail when they tacked. She forced herself not to make a facetious comment when he ran through the boat's safety drill. But she knew better than to point out the obvious emergency exits. Sam clearly wasn't in any mood for humour.

And then, without further ado, she was helping him pull up the anchor lines and, in no time at all, they were unfurling the sails. As the boat cut effortlessly through the waves, she watched Sam at the wheel, seemingly absorbed with the course of the boat, as they sailed out into a vast expanse of sea, a hundred white sails littering their path to the horizon. She couldn't begin to tell what he was thinking as his eyes were hidden behind the dark lenses of his glasses. He certainly didn't appear to be thinking about her. So far, he hadn't looked at her once.

'Right. There's the Barcelona ferry coming up, so we're going to tack, if that's OK,' he said, turning the wooden wheel, so that they would cut across the wake of the huge steel boat which loomed up ahead of them at an alarming speed. 'If you could unhook that rope, please.'

Laurie did as she was told, feeling her irritation swelling. Please! If he said please one more time! He was being so polite that she wanted to swear at him. But then the headsail caught the wind and the rope sped through her hands, burning them.

'Ouch!' she yelped, letting go.

'Winch in! Winch in!' Sam yelled, as the sail flapped angrily in the wind.

Laurie fell across the cockpit to the other side of the boat, pulling in the rope as the boat turned and the mainsail filled with wind from the other side.

She wound in the winch handle, but it was stiff and awkward to manoeuvre from where she was crouching in the cockpit.

'That's it. Little bit faster, please,' Sam called.

'I'm going as fast as I can,' Laurie protested, but Sam gently nudged her out of the way.

'Sorry, can I . . . ?' he asked, expertly winching the rest of the rope.

Laurie sat back, her hands and her feelings smarting, as the boat righted and they passed behind the ferry.

'It's OK,' Sam said. 'You did very well for your first time.'

How dare he be so condescending! Above her, Laurie could see the holidaymakers on the top deck of the ferry. She watched the steel propellers churning up the water. While the vast ship sped away from them, she'd never been so aware of her own pitifully small existence. And as they passed in its wake, Laurie squinted as the waves slopped into the boat and splashed her face.

Another fifteen minutes passed, then thirty, as they tacked once or twice more towards an unknown destination. But still Sam didn't say anything, other than the odd polite request for her to do something minor. And eventually even those fizzled out. He seemed to have run out of things to say. She could see from his face that he was pretending to concentrate on the sailing, keeping his fixed grin, as if this were the most pleasant, natural thing in the world for them to be doing.

Was this it, then? Sam was going to play at being polite strangers all day? Well, fine, she thought, she could be a polite stranger too. That was what she'd been intending to do all along, wasn't it? She was damned if she was going to break the ice.

But as time crawled by, the silence between them seemed to inflate, until it was as impenetrable as a balloon. It was so tangible that Laurie was afraid of puncturing it, in case it would explode. She busied herself staring at the water over the side of the boat, wondering about the depth of the blue green sea.

She trailed her hand over the edge of the boat, reaching her fingertips towards the water, studying the translucent reflection of the small waves on the shiny blue paint on the boat's side. So, he really wasn't going to say anything, she concluded. His apology in the wheelhouse had been it. That was all he had to say on the matter of their affair. He was content, now, to pretend that it had never happened.

She'd been such an idiot, she thought, feeling baffled disappointment course through her. She'd wasted so much mental energy thinking about Sam over the past few weeks. She hadn't even slept last night wondering how today was going to be, and all along Sam didn't give a shit. He had nothing left to say to her. She clearly meant nothing to him.

But, then, suddenly, Sam slapped the wheel. She'd been so absorbed in her thoughts that she jumped, ricocheting back to reality.

'What's happened? What's wrong?' she asked.

'We're becalmed.'

'What?'

'The wind's gone.' Sam looked up at the sails, obviously annoyed.

The mainsail was rapidly deflating, as if someone were blowing increasingly feeble breaths at it. A minute later, it was flapping limply. Sam hauled in the headsail, so that it wrapped neatly around the mast. Then he pulled in the mainsail, too.

'So what do we do now?' she asked.

'Sit it out. It'll pick up in a while. There's no point in motoring. This happens occasionally.'

Laurie stared at her feet. As the boat bobbed slowly. Only the gentle lapping of the waves against the boat's hull broke the silence.

Now she wished that Sam was still absorbed in sailing. At least then they had an excuse not to talk. But this? This was intolerable. She longed for an escape, but there was only sea around them and she didn't fancy making a swim for it.

'So?' Sam said, eventually. 'Fancy a picnic? Isabel, our nanny, packed us one. We might as well have it now.'

He stretched, jumping down the three steps into the cabin. A moment later, he slid the picnic hamper into the cockpit. Then he was back up the steps, crouching to unfasten the wicker basket's leather straps.

'Christ. Champagne,' Sam said, before rooting through the rest of the hamper. Laurie slid forward towards the edge of the cockpit. She could see that, apart from the bottle, there was a loaf of bread, a saucisson, Manchego cheese, some tortilla wrapped in greaseproof paper, crisps, home-made almond cakes, cutlery, plates and glasses. 'Looks like there's nothing else, so I guess it's champagne,' Sam said, unwrapping the foil, before glancing at the label on the perspiring bottle. 'It's a good one, too. Sorry.'

'You don't have to apologise.'

'When there's nothing to celebrate, it seems a waste.'

It was the nearest either of them had come to speaking the truth. Laurie braced herself, wondering whether Sam would be brave – or stupid – enough to say more.

'We should toast our new lives.' She'd meant to sound enthusiastic, as if she were making an effort, but maybe Sam thought she was being bitchy. She watched him pop the cork, twisting it into his hand with a muted hiss. He poured a glass for her and handed it over.

He filled his own glass and stared at it, clearly unwilling to make the toast she'd proposed. 'Well, I'm glad you're happy,' he said, eventually.

'Yes, I am.' She'd said it more brightly than she intended.

And it was right then, at that very moment, as Sam hunched down and put his elbows on his knees, that she realised that she'd inadvertently punctured whatever pretence was between them.

She swallowed hard, as he took off his sunglasses and rubbed his eyes. She could tell that she'd hurt his feelings, but she had to keep things on track. She had to back her words up . . . and fast. Surely she had so many new things in her life to celebrate, so many things she should be able to brag to Sam about: James, her career, she even had Rachel and a new family to be pleased about.

But sitting here now, faced with Sam's beaten and defeated expression, she couldn't help feeling beaten and defeated, too. She searched for something to say, but there seemed to be nothing she could cling on to, to hold up as a mascot to prove her happiness. She felt as at sea as they were. She forced herself to remember her strategy on the jetty. She must concentrate on the present. She must concentrate on Sam's wife and child.

'We're different people,' she said, trying to sound philosophical. 'Life moves on, doesn't it? There's a lot to celebrate. I mean . . . there's Archie . . . you're a father now, which must bring you so much . . . I don't know . . . fulfilment. And I've got things going with my paintings, which was what I always wanted . . . and . . . well . . .'

The champagne remained in her glass. There was a long silence as they both stared at the bottom of the cockpit, her words having fallen like invisible drops of acid between them. If she said any more, she'd sink them both.

Eventually, Sam raised his glass and looked at her directly for the first time. Laurie felt a flurry of butterflies in her stomach. The sadness in his eyes made her want to cry.

'I think we should toast the past. To who we were. Now that we've really left those people behind, I can't see any harm.'

'To who we were.' She dared herself to say it and then took a hasty sip of champagne, holding the bubbles in her mouth. She knew that she could so easily betray herself by crying, but she willed herself to be strong. She wouldn't show him how confused she was. She wouldn't let him see inside her, or let him think that she was vulnerable in any way. But she could feel her resolve slipping, she could feel her emotions beginning to slide away from her control.

Sam turned his head and looked inland. In the distance, the city of Palma rose out of the heat haze like a proud Spanish dancer, the cathedral with its balustrades like a majestic proud face, the white boats in the harbour below like the ruffle of a skirt. She followed his gaze to the view, the sight they'd come to see together. There was no need to mention the postcard he'd sent her, or her jibe at dinner about it. She knew they were both thinking of it.

'Telling you I was sorry wasn't good enough.' He said it as a bald statement of fact, not a question. He didn't look at her. 'You're still angry, aren't you?'

'Not angry. I'm over it,' she lied, forcing her voice to stay level. 'I think I understand a bit better why you did what you did. But you still broke . . . you still ended it. Anyway, it's a long time ago now.'

Sam nodded. Immediately that she'd said it, she'd wanted more than ever to reach out and touch his face. Having experienced the power of Sam's family for herself, she knew that however hard it had been for her, perhaps, just perhaps, it had been worse for him.

'So . . .' she said, desperately trying to brighten up. They mustn't discuss the past. If they did, then she would become completely unstuck. 'Sailing . . . this boat is wonderful, isn't it? I had no idea that it would be this, um –'

'Shit, that would cover it, wouldn't you say? Embarrassing, excruciating, awful.'

He was holding his champagne glass in his hand, his face so open and honest that she felt completely rumbled. He was batting away her attempts at social graces, like false serves.

'We should never have done this,' he said, with a sigh.

Laurie could feel her pulse as she stared at him. 'So why did you?' she asked.

'Because I wanted to see you.'

Again, his honesty floored her. His statement hung in the air, like the echo from the chime of a church bell. This was too real. Too painful. Too dangerous. She stayed silent, but Sam wasn't put off.

'I think it was the same for you, Laurie. You came because we need to do this. And this is pretty much as neutral a territory as we're going to get.' He gestured to the expanse of sea around them. He had a point.

She still couldn't look at him. 'We can't –'

'Talk. That's all we need to do.'

She flared for a second, annoyed that he was being the adult and she was being such a coward.

'What exactly do you want to talk about, Sam?' she snapped, her surliness a warning shot. He'd asked her to talk once before and it hadn't worked out. Why should she do it again? Why should he have it his way?

But when she looked up at him, his eyes seemed to bore right through her.

'You don't want to talk to me?'

Laurie felt herself deflating inside. She couldn't fight

him. She couldn't fight whatever it was that was still between them. The temptation was just too great.

She could feel him looking at her.

'So. How have you been?' he asked. His voice was soft as he asked her the most simple, yet most complicated question in the world.

Now she remembered that the one thing that had set Sam apart from everyone she'd ever known in her life was exactly this. It was this feeling that she was the only person that mattered in the whole world.

For a second Laurie thought about lying, about saying something glib, to revert back to her earlier tactics, but despite being virtually stationary in the water, they seemed to have travelled vast oceans in the last few minutes. They were in another country altogether.

'Honestly?' she asked, although there wasn't any other choice. 'Not great.'

'Me neither.'

Laurie laughed, tipping her head up to hold back such an overwhelming flood of relief that her eyes had filled with tears. At the same time, she wanted to hit him for so effortlessly prising her open like an oyster. It felt insanely intimate. More shocking than if he'd reached out and touched her skin. 'Oh God, Sam,' she said, finally letting go. 'Oh God. All right. Let's do this.'

And then, it was as if the last three years had never happened. The floodgates opened and she told him every-thing – about her mother dying, about her recent quarrel with her father, about her friends, the private view at the gallery, about Rachel and being in Mallorca.

'I'd love to see some of your new stuff,' Sam said, after she'd told him how much she'd loved working in the boat-house. 'I remember the sketchbook you kept when we were in France. I thought your drawings were beautiful. Have you still got it?'

She paused. 'We're being honest, aren't we?'

'I hope so.'

'I threw it away. I couldn't keep it. It was too . . . hard.' She remembered now with regret that the book had contained some of her best ever sketches and some of her best ideas. They'd all been inspired by Sam and the places she'd been with him. Now she realised that she'd spent the last three years trying to get back to that standard and to that feeling of spontaneous creativity.

Sam nodded and she felt relieved to have told him the truth, even though she knew it was hurtful for both of them. And buoyed up by her honesty, she took a deep breath and before she knew it, she was telling him the details of what had happened to her when she'd received his postcard.

And she told him without holding back. She told him about her confusion and her anger and her eventual acceptance. And Sam listened, taking none of it as a recrimination. And as she told him, she realised that it didn't matter any more. That it was all in the past. That she didn't feel bitter about it. And then they were on to her life now, about how she felt about this last attempt at making a go of her art, about her homelessness.

The only thing she held back was her new relationship with James. Why? she wondered, as soon as the opportunity had passed and Sam had started talking. Why? She wasn't sure. Because she was enjoying this? Because talking to Sam felt good? Because she wanted to keep her and Sam separate from the real world and all its waiting complications for a precious while longer? But why worry about it? It didn't matter. All that mattered was right here, right now.

Instead, she listened as Sam told her about Tony dying, about Ararat. He told her about Claire's pregnancy and his hasty marriage. He told her about how he felt when Archie was born. He told her about his guilt, his terror at seeing Laurie at Tony's funeral, his shock that they'd been reunited.

And gradually they drank the champagne and picked at the picnic. It was then that Laurie brought up the subject of her father's visit. She explained to Sam about Rachel wanting to meet him again and their plan to surprise him.

'I feel a bit hoodwinked,' she admitted, relieved to have someone to confide in at last. 'I'm really not sure I'm doing the right thing. Rachel wants to see Dad again so badly, and now I feel like I've agreed to something I can't get out of.'

Sam laughed and shook his head. 'That's Rachel for you. She tends to get what she wants.'

'I know she means well, but I feel like I'm about to betray Dad. And he feels betrayed enough by me already. He'll freak out when he finds out I've been staying at Rachel's all this time.'

'You're a good person, Laurie. Your dad must know that. He'll know that you have the right motives at heart.'

Laurie wasn't sure what her motives were any more, but she felt reassured to voice her fears.

'Will he?'

Sam smiled at her, his face kind. 'Whatever it is between Rachel and your dad, you have to let them sort it out. You can't live other people's lives for them, or protect them from pain. Same goes for children, same for parents.'

Later, they were still bobbing about with no wind, but rather than feeling cursed, Laurie felt blessed. She'd been hiding out in Rachel's villa avoiding this very situation, but now that it had happened, she wished she'd saved herself the heartache. Lying side by side on their backs in the cockpit, looking up at the bottomless blue expanse of sky, Laurie felt happier than she had done in years.

'What do we do if the wind never picks up?' she asked. 'If you're still determined not to use the engine . . .'

'I am. It's cheating. Well, unless we get run down by a ferry, tanker or powerboat, we could drift for days, until we bump into dry land.'

'You mean like a deserted island?'

'It's possible. I'm sure there are a few around.'

'What would we do?'

'We'd have to sit it out until we got rescued.'

Laurie smiled. 'Sounds like fun.'

Sam raised himself on his elbow, so that he was looking down at her. 'We could use the boat for shelter and I've got some matches, so we could make a fire and keep warm.'

'Wouldn't we get bored?'

'I could think of ways we could amuse ourselves. Dozens of ways, as a matter of fact.'

She turned her head to face Sam, her hair scrunching underneath her. His eyes were dancing, as he smiled at her. His face was just a few inches away. She remembered now the row of freckles above his left eyebrow, wondering, now that she saw them, how she'd ever forgotten such an important detail.

'You mean, we could sing songs?'

'Sing songs, yeah. Or practise tying knots.'

'Knots? That's what sailors do, is it? Tie knots?'

His lips were so close. She could feel herself being encompassed by him, as if she were sinking into him, like osmosis. But then, in less than a breath, something in their eyes connected and the world tilted. He was silent. His smile fading from his face.

'The problem is, some of us sailors tie such huge knots, we don't know how to get them undone.'

Her eyes didn't leave his. It would only take a tiny movement to move her head enough to kiss him. It would take less than a second to change their lives for ever.

But then Laurie saw her face reflected in Sam's eyes. She saw who she was and remembered where she was, and with whom. And no matter what kind of a knot Sam had tied himself in, she wasn't the solution. Sam was married. He had a son. He and Laurie were bound by a family that would be destroyed if she acted on the easiest impulse in the world.

This, she realised, feeling leaden with the responsibility of it, was her biggest test yet. She stayed very still, holding his gaze. Then she forced herself to take a deep breath.

'I guess the problem is that big knots can get even more complicated over time. And then you just have to leave them, or you make them worse.'

'You can't undo them at all?' he asked.

'Nope.'

For a second she pressed her cheek into his palm, as he touched her face. It felt like the softest pillow in the world. She closed her eyes.

'Don't say anything,' she whispered.

She felt Sam touch her hair lightly. 'We blew it, didn't we, Laurie Vale?'

She nodded mutely. He held her hair at the front, twisting a strand of it around his finger. 'For what it's worth, I'll always regret it.'

And then, above them, the courtesy flag fluttered and then the mainsail started to fill with wind.

\*    \*    \*

261

Much later, after Sam had made her sail the boat back to Palma, jibbing all the way, Laurie was exhausted and yet strangely calmed. As Sam gave her a lift back to the villa in his Porsche, she felt as if she'd undergone some sort of catharsis.

Having cleared the air, they chatted easily and freely about Archie and how Claire wouldn't probably be home until much later, Sam making Laurie laugh with his impressions of Claire's friends. He talked, too, about Ararat and the challenges he faced at work.

It was only as they drove towards the village and up the hill to the gates of the villa that Sam slowed down.

'Thank you for today,' he said. 'I didn't realise how much I've missed you. I mean . . . talking to you . . .'

Laurie turned to face him. She wanted to tell him that she'd realised the same thing. But it wasn't just the talking that she'd missed. It was being together that had refilled her like a cup that had been dry for a very long time. For one crazy second, she thought about telling him precisely that, but she'd never be able to tell him how today had made her feel.

'But that's good, isn't it, that we can still talk? That after everything we're still friends.'

She thought he was going to say something, but instead, he leant across her and took a small electronic key out of the glove compartment and pointed it at the gates of Sa Costa. The gates swung open automatically and they drove in silence up the drive. A minute later, they came to a stop and Laurie busied herself with her bag, nervous about how they were going to say goodbye. But when she sat up, Sam was staring at the villa.

'The front door's open. You didn't leave it open, did you?'

'No, I've got keys. Rachel's gone back to London.'

Sam's hand was on the car door, opening it. 'Christ, I've been dreading this,' he muttered. 'Rachel's so lax about security. I hope it's not a burglar. There've been so many around here. Stay here, I'll go and check it out.'

Laurie watched Sam run towards the front door. She breathed in, letting the scent, the atmosphere of him soak into her.

Then she came to her senses. What if there really was a burglar? What if he got hurt? And she was sitting here like a sentimental fool, wishing the day wasn't over.

She sprang out of the car and raced after Sam. It wasn't until she was near the open terrace doors that she heard shouting.

'Who the hell are you?' Sam was brandishing an umbrella, held aloft as a weapon.

'Hey!' James clambered off the sunlounger, holding up both hands, a beer in one of them.

Laurie ran to Sam's side. Her cheeks were burning. 'James! What the hell are you doing here?'

'You know each other?' Sam's face was incredulous. The umbrella fell to his side.

James glanced warily between Sam and Laurie. 'James Cadogan. Pleased to meet you.'

He dropped his stance of surrender and tentatively stepped forward to shake Sam's hand. Laurie watched the two men side by side: Sam, towering above, with his blond hair ruffled and salty from the day's sailing, James's dark hair wet from the swim in the pool, his trendy glasses perched on his head, his body honed and toned in his swimming shorts. Next to Sam, he looked like a boy.

'We thought you were a burglar. I'm Sam Delamere,' Sam explained curtly, shaking his hand as briefly as was polite. 'Laurie and I have been sailing.'

'Sam, of course! I know all about you. I talked to Rachel,' James said. 'She thought it would be great if I came and just sort of turned up! She organised Maria to come and let me in,' James laughed and moved to put his arm around Laurie's shoulder. 'Looks like the surprise worked. Hey, gorgeous,' he said, as he kissed the top of her head.

There was a brief pause.

'I was just dropping Laurie off,' Sam said, his tone curt and businesslike. 'I'm sure you have a lot to catch up on.'

Every word felt like a slap to Laurie. She watched him look James up and down and then his eyes flicked towards Laurie's. 'Thanks for a lovely day, Laurie,' he said.

'Sam?' Laurie called after him, but he pretended not to hear her. And in a moment he had gone.

# Chapter XIV

'Bastard,' Arthur said.

Pete sniggered and Tony glanced across. Arthur was addressing a willow tree behind them. He'd got his fishing line snagged in among its leaves on his last cast and was now trying to yank it free.

Ferret-faced and skinny, stocky and chiselled, Pete and Arthur couldn't have looked less similar. Standing here side by side in their shiny rainproof jackets and wellington boots, they looked like a vaudeville act in search of a stage. Not that Tony was in any kind of mood to laugh.

It was Sunday afternoon and the three of them were out for a day's fishing, loaded up with bottles of beer and sandwiches to take them through till teatime.

Summerglade Hill rose up behind them to where the murky sky stirred and shifted like a great grey soup coming to the boil. They'd seen lightning a few minutes before and had counted three seconds till the thunder had rumbled across the valley. The storm was three miles away then, but hopefully it might still pass them by.

Tony glanced up. It had grown darker since then. That's when he saw them, two white shapes, fast as bullets, darting across the sky.

'What the hell –' he said, pointing them out.

'Jesus Christ,' Arthur gasped. 'They look like bloody space rockets . . .'

265

Pete laughed. 'You read too many comic books, you great lump. They're jet planes, from over at the airbase.'

The planes disappeared, leaving Tony wondering what it would be like, flying up there, speeding away from the town, watching it disappear behind you like a speck of dust. He whipped the tip of his grandad's brown cane fishing rod over his shoulder and sent the line hissing out like a snake across the swollen River Step.

'Nice cast,' Pete commented, as Tony started to wind the slick dripping line steadily back in, monitoring its tension with his fingertips, patiently waiting for the tremble, or sudden jerk, that would indicate a fish biting down and starting its run.

'Thanks.'

Tony's answer came out as a kind of bark, the same as his comments had done all day. Because he didn't want to be talking to Pete. He wanted to be talking to Rachel instead. Only he couldn't. Because she was under strict curfew, busy revising for her summer-term exams which started in less than two weeks' time.

Tony hadn't spoken to her for two days now, not since they'd grabbed five precious minutes together after she'd run an errand for Bill to the Sea Catch Café. A delivery which had been accompanied by a sealed letter to Emily from Bill, Tony had noted. One which had made his boss blush as she'd read it.

'Dating,' Emily had described the situation with uncharacteristic brevity when he'd asked her about it. 'We're just having some fun . . .'

Which was what Tony wanted, too. But instead he had to subsist on stolen moments. And, of course, the weekly letters which Rachel had been leaving in the vase in the churchyard for him, every Sunday of the two months they'd been going out.

He'd learnt a lot about her from what she'd written. Small aspects of her life now loomed large in his mind: how her favourite poet was Christina Rossetti; what verb tables she'd learnt in French at school; that she loved the radio, but secretly longed for a television set; and how each night when she went to bed she stared up through the skylight and wished he'd appear . . .

But it was a different letter which he could feel in his trouser pocket now, digging into his thigh, fuelling his bad mood. It was one from his brother Keith which Pete had given him. (Keith always wrote care of Pete Booth, because if he'd written to Tony direct, his mother would only have torn up the letter.)

Up until now, Tony had always dealt with Keith by not thinking about what he'd actually done. He'd kept the murder just that: a word. He'd stopped himself ever attempting to imagine what it was that had actually happened at Vale Supplies that night. Instead, he'd separated the Keith who'd committed the murder, from the Keith who was his brother and who now lived in prison – in much the same way that, as a child, he'd always separated the drunk Keith who'd hit him at night, from the sober Keith who'd been his friend during the day.

Only, lately, Tony had started worrying himself sick about Keith getting out. In the letter in Tony's pocket, Keith had told Tony his lawyer was working on grounds for a new appeal.

And if he did get out, what then? How would Keith fit into the new life Tony was building with Rachel? How could Tony then pretend that Keith hadn't done the things he had?

The answer was he wouldn't and he couldn't. Tony loved his brother, but he had feelings now for Rachel, too. And he'd protect her. Not from the violent Keith, who Tony genuinely believed no longer existed. But from the memories of her past, which he knew Keith embodied.

He knew he should write to Keith to explain all of this – to tell him that their lives would have to diverge – but also knew that he didn't know how.

'What's she like, then, this mystery girl of yours?' Pete now asked him.

Tony sat on the upturned wooden beer crate. As he continued to wind in the reel, he stared poker-faced across the deep wooded gorge.

Pete scratched his sandy hair and cleared his throat. 'I said –'

'I heard you well enough the first time,' Tony interrupted. 'It just didn't make enough sense to warrant a reply.'

The truth was, Pete's question had thrown Tony. Apart from Emily, he'd spoken to no one about Rachel Vale.

'Well, you've certainly been spending all your time with someone,' Pete persisted. 'And it's certainly not us.'

'I work for a living, in case you hadn't noticed,' Tony replied. 'Which is more than can be said for you two –'

Tony managed to stop himself before he said *schoolkids*. But it didn't stop him from thinking it. Because they *were* different to him now. They learnt; he grafted. They lived with their parents; he fended for himself. They wanted to feel girls up; he wanted to know how Rachel felt about him.

'And I've known you long enough to know there's more to it than that,' Pete chided him.

Too long, Tony thought. The days they'd spent shooting milk bottles off walls with catapults now felt like they'd happened to someone else. Like the river before him, their lives had moved on.

'Pretty, is she?' Pete teased. 'Goes like the clappers, does she?'

A few months ago and Tony would have been happy enough to dish the dirt. He'd been the first of his friends to lose his virginity, a year and a half ago now, to a sour-faced Australian tourist twice his age. Other girls had followed, and he'd kissed and told on every one.

But Rachel Vale was different. Telling Pete and Arthur about having sex with her had been inconceivable, right from the start. Not only because, like every other aspect of his and Rachel's relationship, it was imperative that it remained a secret, but also because Pete and Arthur simply wouldn't have understood.

Four weeks ago, it had happened, his and Rachel's first time. They'd been fooling around on the dusty box bed he'd rigged up in his grandad's shed, when she'd presented him with a French letter that she'd pinched from Pearl's father's surgery the last time she'd been round at their house.

It was strange, thinking of it even now, but of the physical sex – the stripping off of their clothes, the awkward entwining of limbs and sliding and adjusting and eventual fitting together of their bodies – he now had almost no memory. It had been brief, uncomfortable, even painful for her, he knew. So much so that halfway through they'd had to stop.

It was what they'd gone on to feel as they'd lain beside one another on the crumpled blankets that he remembered most. A cool breeze had drifted through the window and stroked across his bare, sweating skin. As he'd moved his hand towards her, she'd reached for him. When their fingertips had touched, he'd felt peace flowing through him in a way he'd never experienced before. It was like the sensation he'd once undergone as he'd stood alone in St Hilda's Church as a child and stared up at the vaulted ceiling. Like that, but magnified a thousand times more. It had been like dying, feeling that much alive, being so aware of everything around him, as if he'd only had seconds left to live.

'Do you feel it, too?' she'd asked.

'Yes.'

Her hand had squeezed down on his.

He stared now at the river sliding past beneath him, as deceptively sluggish and solid as a flow of setting lava.

'Or maybe this one's not pretty at all,' Pete continued to muse aloud. 'Not like Margo Mitchell.' He winked across at Arthur who immediately picked up on the cue.

'The girl who puts the tit into titanic,' they simultaneously said.

Tony smiled at the old joke, but it was a weak smile. He stood up and cast the spinner out over the waters again.

'And not like Alice Banks with her luscious lips and yo-yo knickers,' Pete went on. 'In fact, I wouldn't mind betting that Tony's new lucky lady is a bit of a horse-frightener, and that's the real reason why he's keeping her to himself.' He sniggered. 'Aye, face like a pig, arse like a pig, I shouldn't wonder.'

Arthur snorted with laughter.

'Is that what you make her do, Tony?' Pete enquired. 'Wear a bag on her head when you're slipping it in?'

'You know what?' Tony answered.

'What?'

'If you're gonna fish, then why not fish for something you've got a hope in hell of catching?' He shoved the rod

270

into Pete's hand. 'And until then, why don't you just change the record or shut up?'

'You're a bad-tempered bastard, Tony Glover,' Pete told him. 'And whoever she is, she sure as hell isn't making you happy.'

Tony drained the last of his Guinness from the bottle and tossed it into the river. It disappeared beneath the surface, before bobbing back up again, several yards further down.

Tony was sick of the secrecy. Sick of bottling up everything he felt. Rachel didn't make him ashamed. She filled him with pride. And that's what really got to him the most. He didn't want to lie to his friends about her. Or act as though she didn't exist. He wanted to shout about her from the rooftops and tell the world that she was his.

He felt washed through all of a sudden with weariness. And longing, too. Because the one person who'd understand how he felt right now was Rachel, and she was the one person he couldn't talk to.

'I'm sorry,' he said to Pete.

If Pete answered, Tony never heard, because at that exact moment the clouds burst open and rain battered down, so hard you could scarcely believe it was liquid.

Then they were running, dragging their bags and rods behind them, tripping over each other, stumbling and slipping and scrabbling up the steep side of the valley to the shelter of the beech trees at the top.

As they stood there laughing, gasping for breath, all of them with their backs against the same tree, Tony felt himself relaxing for the first time in days. He took the beer which Arthur had opened for him and drank, tipping back his head and staring up, following the line of the trunk to the top of the tree.

Then his smile switched to a grin as he thought of a way to make himself feel happier still.

By ten o'clock on Monday night, the streets of Stepmouth were empty and quiet. Five minutes had passed now, since Tony had been leaning up against the broad shadowy trunk of the old oak tree which stood next to Vale Supplies.

Bunting left over from Coronation Day the week before hung from the branches. There'd been a street party here, which Tony had avoided. Rachel had spent it with her family and he hadn't wanted to be out celebrating with anyone else. He took a final pull on his Double Ace cigarette, before flicking it towards the gutter where it expired with a hiss on the slick wet pavement.

The rain had been drumming down steadily all day. In fact, the last time Tony could remember it *not* raining in the last week was in the few hours prior to the cloudburst he, Arthur and Pete had been caught out in the day before.

It all added up to bad news for the Sea Catch Café. The deluge of out-of-town customers which Emily had been banking on to sample her new evening menu had entirely dried up. Each afternoon Emily had covered the word *Café* on the sign above the door with a smaller, hand-painted sign which read *Bistro*, in an effort to woo more adventurous trade. But each night she'd taken it back down, with little or no results. Their consommés and sauces and puddings, on which they'd worked so hard, had all ended up in the bin.

Tony felt for her. Truly, he did. She'd been good to him and he wanted her to succeed. He'd invested enough of his own time in the café to make it personal. Now that her parents had finally moved to Pembrokeshire, the café's future was down to Tony and Emily alone. That said, he'd been glad that no one had showed up tonight, hungry and wanting to be fed, because he'd been let off work early as a result.

'No point in both of us hanging around waiting for no one to arrive,' Emily had declared. She'd offered him a lift home in her father's van, back to his grandad's shed near Brookford, but he'd declined. The cycle ride would do him good, he'd told her, as he'd taken his black oilskin jacket from the hook on the door.

She hadn't tried to change his mind. A few weeks ago, she'd offered to help find him a room to rent, but he'd turned that down, too. He'd told her he was fine taking care of himself, and she'd accepted it without prying any further. Self-reliance. She had it by the truckload. It had now taken root in him, too.

He stepped out from under the oak tree's shadows and stared up once more at the long, canopied branches which stretched out over the edge of the roof of Vale Supplies like a giant umbrella. Once more, he calculated the drop from the high branch to the roof, while once more wondering if it really would be strong enough to hold his weight.

It was risky, dangerous and stupid, he told himself, checking his jacket pocket for the folded piece of paper. He remembered the words he'd written there that lunchtime on his break, copied from the anthology he'd found in the town library.

'Always be this romantic.'

That's what Rachel had told him that first time they'd kissed in the graveyard. And that was why he was here now: to prove to her that he always would be.

The thought pushed him on. Ducking back under the tree, he reached up and gripped a branch. Then his arms snapped into motion. A swing of his legs, a twist of his abdomen and chest, and he was up, spreadeagled between the tree's limbs, like a fly in a web.

He moved quickly then, negotiating his way up through the thick foliage. Branches swished and hissed. Water showered down. He pictured the whole tree shaking. His heart pounded. Just one look, he thought, from Bill or his mother from that near first-floor window and he'd be rumbled. Just one person hurrying homewards down the street and the same . . .

Quick then. Faster, faster, as fast as he could. He was sweating, burning up, in the treetop now, drawing level with the roof. Now moving sideways, edging inch by inch, away from the trunk, towards the building. Under his feet, the branches grew thinner. The branch he clung to above started to bow. Still he kept working his hands along it, spreading his weight, tightrope-walking, balancing, trying not to slip.

As he looked down, he saw it: the overflowing guttering, the edge of the roof, the greasy black Welsh slate and the yellow rectangle of the skylight in Rachel's room.

It was all there, all within his reach . . .

When he jumped, he didn't consider the possibility of failure. If he had done, he would have faltered and fallen. They'd have found him tomorrow with his back broken and his neck snapped on the hard stone pavement below.

Instead, his jump became a leap of faith. He let go of the branch above and as the branch below wilted, he sprang upwards and outwards like a cat. Conviction carried him, stretching him, pushing him, taking him to Rachel.

He hit the roof hard, landing flat and slithering down its slope. The noise was horrific. An almighty creak. It sounded like the whole structure would cave in. He lunged at the

274

skylight's slight wooden frame, reached it, got a grip. With a final effort, he hauled himself up and stared down through the glass at Rachel who was staring back up at him with burning, unflinching eyes. A slate cracked by his foot. It rattled thunderously over the guttering. A moment's silence – then smash! – it shattered on the pavement below.

Rachel had the window open in seconds. He scrambled inside. Intoxication, elation . . . he felt like he'd jumped from sobriety to drunkenness in the blink of an eye.

He'd made it.

In the weak light thrown off by her desk lamp, her skin looked translucent, as if it had been drained of blood. The long white nightdress she wore only added to her ghostliness.

'You're crazy,' she whispered in disbelief.

He reached out to take her in his arms.

'Rachel!' A man's voice was calling from downstairs: Bill's; it could only be his. Tony's stomach lurched. Rachel jerked back from him like she'd been shot. She reached for the skylight and pulled it closed.

'Shit!' she gasped. 'Shit, shit, shit!' She stared around the room.

'Rachel!' Bill called again, nearer.

Footsteps hurried towards them up the stairs.

Tony looked at the tiny wardrobe in the corner of the room. It wasn't big enough to hide a mouse.

'I'm fine!' Rachel shouted down. 'It's nothing to –'

The footsteps didn't stop.

There, Tony saw the open trapdoor which led down to the rest of the house. Bill would burst through it any second now.

Rachel saw it, too. She reached out to slam it shut. Tony grabbed her wrist, shook his head.

'He'll break through,' he mouthed.

Because he would. Tony knew it. After hearing all that noise, Bill would find a way. And then it would be over. Bill would find him here. Then work it out. Then tell his mother. Together, they'd explode. Together, they'd tear him and Rachel apart.

'What's going on?' A woman's voice now: Rachel's mother.

Then Bill's, risen to a bellow: 'I'm coming up!'

The creak of the ladder: fourteen stones of muscle and bone coming at them. The terror in Rachel's eyes. Tony groaned. He shouldn't have come. He should have been patient. He wished himself invisible . . . And then he saw a way to make it so . . .

'The storm,' he hissed into Rachel's ear, diving now, past her, sliding smoothly, silently across the bare wooden boards.

Then there he was: in the darkness, under the bed, with his face pressed up against the wall. He held his breath and prayed.

A rush of breath and footsteps and Bill was in the room.

'Are you all right? What happened? What was that noise?'

'The storm. Outside.' It was Rachel speaking. She'd understood what Tony had meant. 'The storm,' she repeated. 'The roof. It must have been the wind.'

All around him, Tony felt the dust clinging to him, covering him, drifting into his nostrils, making him want to sneeze. He squeezed his eyes shut, willing himself into silence.

'Some wind to sound like that . . .' Bill was saying, '. . . like the whole house was falling down . . .'

Something was moving on Tony's neck now, slowly and

276

softly . . . a spider? He shivered involuntarily, forced himself still.

The floorboards started creaking. Bill was prowling now, circling. Tony imagined him looking up, down, around, searching the room, trying to make sense of what he'd heard. Could he see him? Could he see Tony hiding here? Had he already seen? Had this become about Tony's humiliation now?

'Look, there's water,' Bill said. 'There.'

Tony shut his eyes, tried to control his breathing. In: one, two. Out: three, four. What water? Where? Was Bill pointing at the floorboards. Had Tony left wet footprints? Was there a trail which led to the bed? Tony's feet seemed to buzz. Were they shaking? Could Bill see his boots? Were they sticking out, shining wet with rain? He waited for the grip of damning fingers on his ankles, the sudden yank as he was dragged out into the light. In: one, two. Out: three, four.

Rachel: 'I opened the window. Because of the noise. The water ran in. It could have been a branch,' she hurriedly added, 'falling on to the roof. Or a loose slate . . . or . . .'

Tony heard the click of the skylight being opened, the hiss of the wind outside . . . then came Bill's aftershave . . . Tony could smell it, the same as he could whenever Bill had been round to see Emily. In the broad light of day. That's how Bill courted Emily. Like a normal man. Not like Tony. Not like this, like a thief in the night, a frightened animal skulking in the dark.

Then another click and the wind dropped back to a moan. Suddenly, Tony wanted to be caught. Suddenly, he wanted the confrontation. He wasn't a child any more. He shouldn't have to live like this.

'So long as you're OK,' Bill said.

'Yes,' Rachel agreed.

'I won't be able to check until morning.'

'No.'

'Much too dangerous to go out there now.'

'Yes. The morning. It'll have cleared up by then.'

'What's happening?' Their mother again, calling from downstairs . . .

'Go back to bed, Mum,' Bill shouted down. 'There's nothing to worry about. You should think about turning in, too,' he added to Rachel.

'Yes, I should. Goodnight.'

'Goodnight.'

Tony listened to Bill's creaking withdrawal from the room and back down the ladder. Only then did he risk turning his head away from the wall to face the room. He flicked the spider from his jaw and watched it scuttle across the floorboards into the shadows. He listened to Rachel gently closing and bolting the trapdoor shut. Then he rolled out from under the bed and got to his feet.

The first thing she did after she'd turned round to face him was try to slap him across the face. With his adrenalin still rushing, he was too fast for her, though, and caught her wrist with inches to spare.

'What?' He didn't understand.

'You shouldn't have come,' she hissed.

'But I wanted to surprise you,' he started to explain. 'I wanted to be romantic . . . I thought you –'

'You could have died.'

'But it wasn't that dangerous,' he whispered back. 'In fact, once I got to the top of the tree, it was –'

'No, idiot,' she told him. 'I mean Bill could have killed you. If he'd found you. He had a knife.'

'A knife? But why?'

Her eyes narrowed to slits. 'How could you be so fucking stupid?'

He'd never heard her say that word before. He watched her sink down on to the bed. She covered her face with her hands, but not in time to hide the tears.

'Oh, God,' he then said, as it dawned on him what she was talking about.

It hadn't even occurred to him. How *could* he have been so stupid? Thief in the night: he'd been more right than he'd known. He'd tried to break into her house. Rachel's house. Bill's house. *This* house. In the middle of the night. After what had happened here. After what his brother had done . . .

He knelt down before her, forcing her hands from her face. She was shaking. She couldn't bring herself to look at him. Her eyes stayed shut as tight as mussels. Over and over, he kissed her hands.

'I'm sorry,' he told her. 'I didn't think . . . I didn't think . . . I'm so sorry . . .'

'God,' she moaned, 'this is all turning into such a mess.'

As he continued to hold her, slowly, her sobbing subsided. She leant forward and softly kissed him. Her face was wet with tears. She took his cap off and smoothed her hands over his Brylcreemed hair.

He knew then that she'd forgiven him, but the guilt he felt over what he'd just done wouldn't go. 'Look at us,' he said. 'We can't carry on like this. It's been driving me mad. And you're right – now I've started acting it too . . .'

'It's OK,' she whispered. 'We're OK. Everything's going to be OK.'

'No,' he said, 'it's not. And it's not going to go away, either. We've got to tell them. We've got to make them understand.'

'They won't ever understand.' He felt the sudden tension in her hands. 'Oh, Tony, what are we going to do?'

*I don't know,* he almost answered. Then he remembered it, the piece of paper in his jacket pocket, and his belief in them returned. 'Keep believing in each other,' he told her instead.

Delving deep into his jacket pocket, he removed the piece of paper.

'What is it?' she asked.

'A poem. By Christina Rossetti. Listen. It's about you. It's about you and how you make me feel.'

The first four lines read:

> My heart is like a singing bird
> Whose nest is in a watered shoot;
> My heart is like an apple-tree
> Whose boughs are bent with thickset fruit;

He lowered the paper, because he found he no longer needed it. It was like the words had become his and, by speaking them to her now, he was making them hers as well. He recited the next four lines:

> My heart is like a rainbow shell
> That paddles in a halcyon sea;
> My heart is gladder than all these
> Because my love is come to me.

But then he saw she wasn't smiling, which is what he'd so desperately wanted. Because that's what it had been all about for him, the whole madness of this evening, about showing her that he loved her, about proving it to her with action and then telling it to her in words. That's why he'd chosen this poem. Because that's what he thought it showed.

'What is it?' he asked. 'Did I do something wrong?' There'd been a time when he'd thought he knew all about women. Now he felt he suddenly knew nothing about the woman he wanted to know everything about.

'No,' she said, pulling him close, holding him tighter than he'd ever been held in his life. 'You got it exactly right.'

'I love you,' he told her.

She seemed to deflate in his arms. 'And I love you,' she whispered.

When she looked at him again, all the anguish had gone from her face. In its place burned fierce hope. She spoke quickly, like everything she was saying was fact, not speculation.

'Once I've finished school, and left home, none of this will matter.'

'But what about today? What about tonight? What about tomorrow?'

'We'll have to wait,' she told him. 'Will you? Can you do that? Can you keep believing until then.'

'You know I can.'

'Then we will.'

He smiled then. Both of them did. At the same time. Like they were one.

'And when you've left home?' He could barely credit himself for asking this. They stared unblinking into each other's eyes. She knew exactly what he'd just asked.

'We'll marry,' she said.

'We'll marry,' he repeated.

'And move away,' she said, kissing him now. 'To a big city somewhere. And you'll be an even better chef . . . and

281

I can work as a waitress or something while you do your bit in the army . . . and in the evenings I can study book-keeping . . . and then after you've left the army, if we want to, we can start a hotel or a restaurant . . . and . . . and we can go places and meet people and do things we haven't even dreamt of . . .'

She was grinning now, staring wide-eyed around her, like she was seeing it all, like the words she was speaking were altering the very fabric of their world. Climbing off the bed, she pulled her nightdress up over her head and stood there naked before him.

He stood and she helped him undress, slowly circling him as she did, until they were standing face to face. He cupped her small breasts in his hands, stroking his thumbs across them. As she reached in between his legs, he slid his hand in between hers, slowly stroking his fingers over her soft downy hair. She touched her nose against his, pulling him back with her on to the bed. He pressed his slim hips against hers, and moaned. They'd never done it in a real bed like this before. He wanted it so much. It would be like a taste of things to come, a snapshot of the future they'd one day inhabit together, when they'd have a place of their own.

'Have you got one?' she asked. 'A letter?'

A French letter, she meant. The same as the first time they'd done it, she'd made him wear one every time since. A girl at Rachel's school had got in the family way the year before and had had to leave. She'd been sent to live with relatives and no one had seen her since. Tony had bought some from the barber's shop on East Street, but stupidly, he hadn't any with him now.

'No,' he admitted.

He was desperate to carry on. His fingers snaked insistently across the soft smooth skin at the tops of her thighs.

'Please,' he said. 'It'll be all right.'

His whole body pressed against hers, imploring her. He wanted this too much to stop. Already, he knew it was going to be different – gentle, slow and sensuous – because already that's how their bodies were moving. He couldn't lose this moment now.

Then she nodded her head and, kissing him deeply, pulled him closer.

# Chapter XV

**Mallorca, Present Day**

Sam was sitting next to Archie near the top of the great flight of sandstone steps which led up to the worn embattlements of Sant Bartholomew Monastery. Cicadas scratched in the myrtle groves below. The sun blazed down, leaving Sam's brow glistening with sweat. At the bottom of the steep-sided mountain on which the Benedictine monks had long ago built their retreat, the island of Mallorca stretched away to where it slid into the shimmering sapphire expanse of the Mediterranean sea.

Tugging his baseball cap down to shield his eyes, Sam breathed in the scent of lavender and wild garlic which rose up from the cracked and dusty ground like the aroma of soup from a pot. He adored being here with Archie, just the two of them. He didn't spend enough time with his son, he knew, but at least he did whenever he could. Like today – a Sunday – when he'd got up early and left Claire snoring softly in bed.

It hadn't been difficult not to disturb her. They'd been lying on opposite sides of the mattress, like magnets which had driven one another apart during the night. She'd still been asleep when Archie and Sam had left an hour later.

'And if you look all the way over there,' Sam was telling Archie now, 'you can see Palma.' He was pointing east, ten kilometres away, to where the city's whitewashed apartment blocks rose up like ramparts from the rusty earth. 'And who lives in Palma?' he asked.

'Mummy and Daddy?'

'That's right. And can you think of anyone else?'

Archie frowned. He stared pensively at his T-shirt, a gift from Rachel, which read, *I* ♥ *My Grandma Best*. 'Don't know,' he finally said.

'*Archie*. Archie does.'

'Archie!' Archie exclaimed, grinning up at Sam as if he'd known the answer all along and had only been teasing. 'Archie and Mummy and Daddy. Family,' he then added brightly.

Family . . . Sam stared into his son's eyes. He'd never heard him use the word in any meaningful sense before. He fleetingly wondered whether he'd learnt the concept at playgroup, or from a Miramax DVD, or Isabel the nanny, or even Rachel. The last sources he considered were himself and Claire.

'That's right,' Sam answered, urging a congratulatory tone into his voice. 'Your family.'

'I'm thirsty now, Daddy,' Archie complained, tugging at the small canvas bag between Sam's tanned, sandalled feet.

Sam rummaged through the spare nappies, baby wipes, biscuits and tiny boxes of raisins which he'd packed before they'd set out that morning. He produced a plastic bottle of fresh orange juice and placed it in Archie's outstretched hands. 'Here you go,' he said.

From up here near the mountain's summit, the island looked more like a map than a real place where real people spent their days. Sam had hoped the view might have provided him with a sense of perspective, of objectivity, even. That was one of the reasons he'd chosen the monastery for this Sunday's outing with Archie: to help Sam see the bigger picture, the way he'd always been able to do in his work. He'd wanted to find a way through the maze his life had become.

Instead, he found himself seduced once more by the thought of Laurie Vale. And the fact that she was out there now, either alone, or with him, James Cadogan, the man who'd called her gorgeous as he'd kissed her by the pool. But then James faded from Sam's mind, and only Laurie remained.

There was no escaping it: Sam had become dazzled by her again, beguiled. Her face had begun to haunt him, not only at night, but in the daytime, too: during meetings, mid-sentence, or as he showered, or opened a bottle of beer and drank. Like the retinal image of something incandescent at which he'd stared for too long, he carried her with him all the time.

How could she have made him feel so much by doing so little? That's what he couldn't figure out. He'd wanted to kiss her there on *Flight*, as they'd lain becalmed in the bay. The urge had reared up inside him like a great wave. All it would have taken for him to surrender to it was the faintest of signals from her. He remembered how he'd stared into her eyes, willing her to close them. He'd wished that the wind would never pick up. The desert island they'd joked about, he'd wanted it for real.

Archie let out a great sigh of satisfaction. 'Finished.' He held up the empty bottle as evidence of his achievement. 'I'm hot, Daddy,' he said.

'So am I.' Sam stood and lifted Archie on to his shoulders. Picking up the bag, he turned his back on the view and climbed the last few steps which led to the monastery's courtyard. 'What would I do without you, Archie?' he asked.

He'd be lost, was the answer which Archie didn't give but Sam already knew. In the same way that, without Laurie, Sam now understood he'd also been lost these last three years and, without her now, he was lost again. Without either Archie or Laurie in his life, it seemed, a part of Sam died. But to have both was impossible.

Or was it? He let Archie down and watched him run ahead through the open cast-iron courtyard gates. He imagined another place, then, far away from here. A colder climate. A walk in the English countryside, with Archie running along a frost-webbed path. With Ararat nothing but a memory and Laurie's hand in his. A different world with different ambitions. Was it really so hard to see?

He walked through the gateway. Plane trees branched out above the courtyard, casting it in shade. Ivy snaked over the cool stone walls and an old man in paint-spattered overalls and scuffed trainers swept dust and crackling leaves across the cobbled ground with a brier brush. Sam wished him a good morning, and the old man grinned back at him, before returning to his work.

'Daddy, Daddy, Daddy,' Archie said, pulling impatiently at Sam's arm.

The blackened chapel door was open and Sam followed Archie beneath the low stone lintel. It was as cold as a subterranean cavern inside. A plain ebony crucifix hung on the whitewashed wall behind a dull oak altar. Light streamed through a stained-glass representation of Christ, dappling the wooden pews with colours.

Archie clambered on to a pew and started to hum. Sam stared at the window, examining the intricate craftsmanship, which showed the thorns around Christ's head and the nails driven through his hands and feet.

Christ, God, the afterlife, Heaven and Hell: they were

concepts which Sam had flirted with as a teenager and at university, but when it had come to the crunch he'd lacked the faith required to believe in any of them. You lived, you died, and that was the end of it. You should seek out happiness and fulfilment while you lived. And you should spread happiness, too, wherever you could. These were the conclusions he'd reached.

But now he was plagued with doubt. How happy should you be? How fulfilled? What if he and Claire were both wasting their lives being semi-happy with each other? He thought again of the young man he'd seen her lunching with in Palma and who he'd later seen leaving their building, the man who he was convinced Claire had had an affair with . . . What if, by settling for one another, Sam and Claire were also denying other people – the other people they could be starting their lives over with – happier existences? What if this chain of mediocre relationships stretched around the whole world and it was up to Sam and Claire to break it?

In the time he'd spent with Laurie in France, she'd taught him so much . . . about art, about history and what it was like to feel young. The world had become a more diverse and interesting place when he'd looked at it through her eyes. Claire, though, partly because of her youth when they'd met, but partly also because she'd always been more interested in her friends' gossip than the contents of newspapers and books, had never taught him a single thing.

'What are they?' Archie enquired.

Sam looked across the chapel to the candlelit table at which Archie was pointing. Then he looked at his son. And what about Archie? he thought. Was staying with Claire for Archie's sake really the right thing to do? Hadn't Sam already failed to recommit to his marriage? Wasn't the resurgence of his emotions for Laurie proof enough of that? Wasn't it inevitable that his marriage would one day collapse into a cycle of bitterness and recriminations? Was that really the future he wanted to bequeath his son?

A tug at his shirt tail. 'Daddy, what are –'

'Candles,' Sam answered.

'Ken dolls?' Archie giggled, confused, wondering whether Sam was making up words or making a joke.

Sam took Archie's tiny hand, which still fitted snugly inside his own, and led him round to the table on which the prayer candles rested in small glass holders.

'Good people light them,' he explained. 'To remember other people they once loved.'

'Good people?'

'Yes.'

Archie pulled free from Sam and ran up to the altar and began tracing out its contours with his fingers.

Good? Evil? Sam wasn't even sure what the words meant any more. Was he evil to have been thinking what he'd been thinking? Would the right choice for him be the wrong choice for everyone else? He didn't know. All he did know was that he was miserable, miserable with Claire, and miserable without Laurie.

The French windows were open in the sitting room when Sam and Archie arrived back at the penthouse. Through the billowing electric blue curtains, Sam caught glimpses of Claire sitting on the spacious balcony outside. She was on the telephone, chattering, laughing.

Archie must have seen her, too, but when Sam put him down he ran not to her, but across the tiled sitting room and into the kitchen doorway, to where Isabel was standing with her arms outstretched. Archie squealed with delight as she scooped him up into the air.

'I saw Ken dolls! I saw Ken dolls!' he began to explain excitedly as Isabel carried him through with her into the kitchen.

As Sam walked out on to the balcony, he remembered the series of sun-drenched landscapes which Laurie had shown him in France. He'd give anything to see what she was working on now. He thought of her there, painting in the boathouse on the beach. Warmth, that's what he craved. Not sterility. Warmth, vitality, creativity, that's what had drawn him to her from the start.

Claire bought, Laurie *did*. That was the defining difference which Sam now saw between them. Claire was a consumer of art, Laurie a creator. Laurie gave to the world and Claire took.

All Claire's talk of setting up an interior design business . . . he saw it now for what it was: a creative screen behind which she concealed an otherwise indolent life, conversational fodder for dinner parties, an excuse to shop . . .

'Oh, there you are, Sam,' Claire said, flashing him a brief, perfunctory smile. She'd finished on the phone. 'I was beginning to think you weren't coming back. Nice trip? Archie happy?'

She might as well have been ticking items off a shopping list. He nodded his head in reply.

She was wearing a black G-string, but apart from that and her Diesel sunglasses she was naked. Suntan oil glistened on her shoulders and her hair was slick with conditioner and combed back from her face. Her smiley face tattoo grinned at him from her ankle. She could have been a model, Sam thought, stretched out on one of the poster hoardings above the road into Palma. Everything about her physique was perfect. And yet she left him cold.

'Here,' she said, 'have a taste.' She held a cigarette, half smoked, in one hand and a tall glass in the other. Carbonated bubbles spiralled up through a mixture of clear liquid, crushed ice and mint leaves.

'No thanks,' he answered. He stared briefly out at the white sails of yachts cutting across the bay, before turning round to face her and leaning back against the balustrade.

'I thought we could serve up cocktails,' she said.

'When?'

'As soon as they arrive.'

'Who?' He noticed her red leather diary on the table next to her, sandwiched between her pack of Marlboros and her phone.

'Sean and Iris. Greta and Sabina. And the gang from the club.' She read something in his face. 'Oh, Sam,' she groaned. 'Don't tell me you've forgotten.'

'How can I forget people I've never even met?' he replied tersely.

'No, not *them*, the party.'

'What party?'

'The party we're having today. I emailed you twice about it,' she remonstrated. 'Twice, because I knew you'd forget.'

'Why didn't you just tell me?'

'Because I've been busy.'

'Doing what?' The question came out more harshly than he'd intended.

'Organising the party, of course. These things don't just happen, you know. There's the food to decide on, and the drinks, and the guest list. I've asked Paula as well, by the way . . . And Antonia and Xevi, who run the new health spa over at Soller,' she went on, stubbing out one cigarette

291

and lighting another. 'It was you who gave me the idea to invite them actually, when you said . . .'

But Sam was no longer listening. When was he last truly happy? That's what he was asking himself as she continued to speak. Completely happy, not partially, not just in his business life, or alone with Archie, but in his life as a whole? When he was with Laurie on *Flight*. And the time before that? When he was with her in France. When he'd decided to leave Claire. Before he'd been told about Archie . . .

'. . . and Alain Tricard, who I thought you might be interested in talking to, because he's no longer working at Zones and I know you've been looking for a chef for . . .'

Everything Sam had built since he'd broken off with Laurie had been built on a lie, the lie he'd started telling himself three years ago: that he no longer cared for her. But all he'd really done was bury his feelings for her. They'd lain there dormant, like foundations, underpinning everything he'd become. But now the cracks were starting to appear. The longer he left it, he knew, the more likely it became that the whole structure of his life would collapse like rubble around him.

'. . . which is forty people in total, and I know it'll be a bit a squeeze, but . . .'

What was he to do? He didn't know. He knew what he wanted to do, but that wasn't the same thing. He wanted to go to Laurie and . . . and see what happened next . . . he wanted to run from here as fast as he could . . .

Claire raised her sunglasses up on to her brow and peered at him curiously. 'Are you OK?'

'No,' he said.

'You're looking stressed again.' She said it like he might have done it on purpose.

'No, I –'

'Only I had lunch with Kayla last week and you know how down she was feeling last year after she broke up with Andy? Well, her doctor recommended a psychiatrist. And I know that might sound a little extreme, but really it's not these days. All kinds of people –'

Sam held up his hand.

'Oh, God,' she said with a look of sudden dismay, 'you don't mind me mentioning it to her, do you? Only I thought –'

'No,' Sam interrupted, 'I don't mind. But no, I'm not feeling stressed, either.' He meant it; his panic attacks had ceased after he'd spoken to Laurie that night in the *Angel's* wheelhouse, as if by acknowledging her and what had once been between them, he'd released the valve on all that pressure which had been building up inside.

Claire took a drag on her cigarette. 'What then?'

'I can't make the party.' His answer had come without thinking about it. The excuse came just as quickly: 'I've got a meeting.'

He marvelled at how easy it was to slip into the pattern of lying, just like it had been when he'd first met Laurie and had spoken to Claire on the phone to tell her he'd need to stay in France for longer than he'd initially thought.

Claire's phone started to trill now and vibrate across the table. 'But it's Sunday,' she protested, ignoring it.

'I know.'

'Well, can't it wait? Can't you just cancel it? Please?' she implored.

'No.'

'Well, what time can you get back by?' she demanded.

'I don't know.'

And he didn't. Truly, he had no idea.

The phone tipped off the table and clattered on to the tiles. The trilling stopped.

Claire growled. Another drag on her cigarette, then another. 'That is so fucking typical of you,' she then exploded, jumping up. 'You're my husband. What's everyone going to think of me, hosting a party on my own?'

Her aggression only succeeded in doubling his determination. 'It can't be helped.'

'Well, fuck you, Sam,' she said, waving her hand at him like she was shooing away a wasp. 'Fuck you. That really is too fucking bad.'

'Hello?'

It wasn't Sam or Claire who'd spoken.

'Hello?' the thin voice sounded again.

Simultaneously, they stared down at the dropped phone from which they both now realised the voice was coming.

'Hello?' it said. 'Claire, is that you?'

Scowling at Sam, Claire picked up the phone and checked the display for the caller's name. 'Leonie, darling,' she cooed, turning her back on Sam, 'I knew you were there all along. Did you like our little joke? Us pretending to fight like that?'

Sam reached Sa Costa in under an hour and parked the Porsche four-by-four by the front door. In spite of the air conditioning, he could feel himself burning up. He jerked his tie from round his neck and threw it on top of his suit jacket which lay draped and crumpled across the passenger seat.

Look at it all, he thought: the Porsche, the black leather attaché case in the footwell, the Jermyn Street tailored suit and Cartier tie, which he'd changed into back at the apartment to make his exit more convincing. Here it was: his

294

fantasy future: the slick, savvy executive lifestyle he'd dreamt up for himself when he'd first left London and moved out here. But what was it really? Laughable, that's what. All of it. Smokescreen. What had it ever done but disguise the extent of his misery? Glamour . . . power . . . success . . . without happiness, none of it meant a thing.

And yet he knew this was insane, being here now. *He* was insane. This wasn't a rational move. He didn't have enough information to base a decision on. The course of action he was embarking on – had *already* embarked upon – he didn't even know where it would lead.

He had to see Laurie, that was all he knew for sure. Seeing her would decide everything. And anyway, what could possibly be worse than what he'd just left behind?

Leaving the keys in the ignition, he got out of the car. Leaving the door wide open, he marched up to the front door. He rattled the handle, but it was locked. He rang the bell. He wondered who'd answer. Laurie? Or *him*. James Cadogan. Her boyfriend. Would he still be here? Maybe down by the swimming pool with her now, performing butterfly dives from the board as she applauded and marked him out of ten? Or upstairs in the bedroom, tangled up among the sheets with her, or grappling for purchase in the shower, lips pressed up against each other's scented skin?

Jealousy coursed through Sam, the same as it had done the moment he'd laid eyes on the other man, the instant he'd realised that they were together. It hadn't even occurred to him that there'd be someone else. But now he couldn't believe his own arrogance. What? Did he really think that just because Laurie was working out here she had no one else waiting for her at home? Just because Sam had failed to move on from her didn't mean she had from him.

But he wouldn't let James's existence put him off. In the same way he didn't know how serious the two of them were, he didn't know how serious they *weren't*. Because Laurie hadn't mentioned James to him, had she? She'd coloured in so much of her life when they'd last talked, yet left that part of the canvas blank. Which could mean one of two things: either James was so important to her that she wanted him kept separate from Sam, or he wasn't even important enough to warrant a mention.

Again, Sam rang the bell: still no answer. He ran to the side of the house and down the pine-needle-matted steps to the lower terrace. The pool was unoccupied, its surface as flat as a drum skin A sprinkler hissed across the lawn, firing rainbows into the air. Dante was standing on a rickety ladder, pollarding the cherry tree which stood on the far side of the pool. Hearing Sam's footsteps, he turned and waved and smiled.

Sam hurried over and shook his hand before quizzing him in rapid Spanish. Laurie was down at the boathouse, he told Sam. And James? The Englishman? He'd flown home yesterday.

Sam set off quickly towards the beach. James had gone. Hope, then . . . Sam still had hope to cling to. But more doubts dug in. Just because James had gone, didn't mean he was forgotten. And even if he was . . . friendship, that might be all Laurie wanted from Sam. At best. At worst, she'd already got what she'd needed: closure on the past.

Lizards scattered before him as he continued his descent along the uneven path. Seabirds cried mournfully in the sky above. The sea flashed blue through the brushwood and then, as he rounded the bend in the path, he saw the sandy beach stretching out along the cove.

There, at the end, nestling against an outcrop of rock,

was the boathouse. Sam ran across the baking sand, his legs growing heavier with each step, like he was being dragged down into a swamp. But he wasn't going to stop. Stop now and he knew he'd turn back.

He flung the door open. She was standing on the other side of the wooden rowing boat, dressed in scruffy denim shorts and an old grey T-shirt. She turned to face him, startled, her paintbrush in her hand. Her red hair was tied up in a knot, stabbed through with a pencil that held it in place. Her legs were spattered with paint: greys and blacks and blues. She was a mess. She looked more beautiful than anyone he'd ever seen.

Behind her was the painting she'd been working on, a great grey canvas of leaden Atlantic waves. A painting from the mind, then, with a sky choked by rain, so different from the view outside. A corked bottleneck glinted on the crest of one of the oil-ridged waves.

'Sam . . . You scared the life out of me.'

Whatever beauty the painting possessed, it had nothing on her. Seeing her was like disturbing a creature in its natural habitat. Her cheeks shifted from white, to pink, to red. It was intimate, personal, a reaction to his presence, as if he'd reached out and touched her skin with his fingertips.

'What are you doing here?' she asked.

Did he love her? he asked himself. Yes. He'd accepted that now. He'd stopped trying to fight it, like he had done at the party on the *Angel*, like he had done during dinner at Sa Costa, like he'd been fighting it every day since he'd made his decision to return to Claire.

Was it real love? That didn't mean a thing. There were a million kinds of love for a million kinds of people. There was the love he felt for Archie, for Rachel, for his parents and, yes, for Claire, as well. All were real, all were different.

297

The love he felt for Laurie was impulsive, like the start of a smile, or the desire to be held. It had nothing to do with duty, responsibility or pride. It was a dancer, shimmering tantalisingly before him, beckoning him to join in. It was an explosion of life and possibility, a promise of hope. It was natural, instinctive and pure.

'What do you want?' she asked.

He strode towards her and stared into her eyes. He could smell the paint on her clothes and feel the heat of the air all around. He was intoxicated.

'You,' he said and, leaning forward, he kissed her.

# Chapter XVI

Bill breathed deeply as he worked, enjoying the blood pumping through his muscles. He twisted the gardening fork's prongs through the sodden peaty earth. It was tough, back-breaking work, and the near-black mud clung to his boots like wet cement. But he shouldn't complain, he supposed. It was good to be outside after so many days stuck indoors watching the rain trail down the barred windowpanes at home.

How many months ago was it since he'd set about clearing the weeds from this land? Four? Five? March, it had been, the same day Emily had walked into the shop looking to buy a gift. It could have been so many years, so much had changed. He'd been up here that morning, readying the soil for planting. Spring had since turned to summer and now here he was reaping that earlier work's rewards, turning over potatoes and carrots and beets, slinging them back behind him into mud-heavy piles. Growth, that's what these last few months had been about for him, growth and progress.

He was lucky, he knew, that the rain hadn't destroyed everything he'd planted. Up until three hours ago, when the sun had finally burnt through the grey clouds and scorched the sky blue, it had been tipping it down for over a week. It had been a worse month than May and no one had thought that possible.

Down in the town below, dripping vacancy signs flapped and rattled under every guest-house doorway. Only the bank had been busy, watching like a vulture over the town's ailing businesses. Vale Supplies had been luckier than most, being less reliant on visitors, but even its takings had dived. People's hopes were now pinned on August to turn the tourist year around. But who knew what August held in store?

'I've never known the like of it,' Bill's mother had complained after church that morning, as he'd wheeled her back through the watery streets.

The vicar's sermon had been about Noah and the Flood. About God's anger over mankind's decadence and ungodliness. About punishment and purification and the need to wash away our sins.

But Bill hadn't cared. He'd thought instead of lying naked in Emily's bed the evening before as a coal fire had smouldered in the grate, and he'd wanted to sin again and again and again.

He let the gardening fork fall to the ground and took the tin bucket and filled it with the freshly dug potatoes. They rumbled like a drum roll as he tipped them out, adding them to the pile on the allotment path. He drank water from the flask he'd left there. Pulling his shirt tails free, he ruffled the coarse cotton material and fanned his skin beneath.

The wind rose suddenly like the laughter of a child and he stared across the ground to where the raspberry canes had once stood, remembering again his father and mother and sister, chasing each other in circles on that distant summer day.

But then he heard her, Emily, calling to him as she trudged across the heavy ground from where she'd been salvaging what was left of the runner beans she'd planted here soon after they'd begun seeing each other. ('Think of all the money you'll save if you grow what you need for the café here,' he'd suggested at the time, even though they'd both known he'd meant it more as an excuse for them to spend time together.)

She was dressed in her brown leather work boots, baggy black trousers and a loose-fitting pale orange shirt with its sleeves rolled up. She combed her fingers through her glistening blonde curls, which she'd cut fashionably and daringly short the week before in the bathroom above the Sea Catch Café, as Bill had watched her from the comfort of a steaming hot bath.

'What were you doing?' she asked, stopping before him now.

He stared at her blankly.

'Gazing off into the distance like that,' she elaborated. She pointed back towards the bean canes. 'I was waving like mad . . . but it was like you were looking right through me. Like I was a ghost.'

Ghost. There, she'd said it.

It was time to let go. He could see that now. It was time to turn his back on the past. All the guilt he'd loaded on to his shoulders over not having been there to save his father, all the resentment he'd racked up about his subsequent return to Stepmouth . . . what had any of it brought him but more misery? Ghosts and memories . . . his mother had lived off them for eight years now, but he wouldn't, not for another minute.

'I don't believe in ghosts,' he answered Emily. 'Not any more.' He didn't. He felt like his own life had only just begun. With time, he hoped to help his mother feel the same. All of them should move on. The whole family. All of them, together.

Tiny wrinkles appeared at the corners of Emily's grey eyes as she smiled. 'I was hoping you'd say that.'

Whenever he kissed Emily, he felt she was breathing life back into him. His life before her arrival was a darkened room. He pulled her towards him and kissed her now.

'There!' she said, as they broke apart. She looked up, distracted. 'They're back.'

Bill turned to see two aircraft, lancing low and fast above the moor, before disappearing into a bank of clouds gathered on the horizon. The roar of their jet engines grumbled down the valley towards them.

'Do you think it's true?' she asked. 'What they say?'

Bill didn't need to ask her what she meant by this. A rumour concerning the appearance of the war planes over the moors had been growing in the town for weeks now, amplified by the recent bad weather. Auxiliary staff from the nearby RAF base drank in the town's pubs at the weekends and, just as during the war, secrets got spilt along with the beer.

'Cloud seeding.' That was the phrase which had slipped from the drunken auxiliaries' lips. They'd found a way to make it rain. By firing chemicals into the clouds. To burst them. To tear the heavens open and let the waters cascade down. They were going to use it on the communists, to flood their dams and smash their cities.

'I think it's a load of old rubbish,' Bill said. He thought back to his time in the army, remembering the tired old uniforms and rifles they'd been issued with. 'Even if they had the technology,' he added, 'which I doubt they do, why would they test it here?' Only two years before, he'd watched pictures in the cinema of the Arizona Desert being rocked by atomic bomb tests. 'Why not somewhere safe and far away from anyone who might be affected?'

302

'Maybe they want us to be affected. Maybe that's what a proper test is. That's what Dad reckons, anyway. That's what he said when I spoke to him on the telephone last night.'

Bill snorted. 'This from the man who believes that one day they'll put men on the moon,' he teased. Alun Jones had told Bill as much when Bill had taken him out for a pint two weeks before, when he and Mavis had driven over from their new home in Wales to see how Emily was getting on.

'And who also approves of me seeing you,' Emily answered back, jabbing Bill in the ribs.

'Good point,' he conceded with a laugh, 'maybe he's not so mad after all.' Hugging Emily, he looked back at the sky. 'I still think the rumours are rubbish, though. Big talk from the air force boys to impress the girls.'

'Want to know how to impress this girl?' Emily asked. Before he could answer, she'd grabbed his hand and had started pulling him up the hillside to where the small wooden potting shed stood at the top of the allotment.

Spiderwebs covered the tiny smudged glass window set into the warped wooden door. Emily kicked off her boots and stepped inside.

'What are you doing?' he asked.

'What does it look like?' she replied with a giggle, as she hurriedly pulled down her trousers and knickers. Balling them up into a makeshift pillow, she lay down and held out her arms to him. 'Quickly,' she told him, shivering, 'I need impressing. Now.'

Stepping inside, he pulled the door shut behind him.

They made love there on the floor, the sunlight streaming in through the knot-shaped holes in the sides of the shed, making their skin shimmer like fish beneath the water as they slowly twisted and turned. Afterwards, she lay draped across him, breathless, with her mouth pressed up against his neck. Whipped up by their exertions, dust motes danced like tiny fireworks above them in the air.

'God, I love fucking you,' she said.

The word didn't bother him. Not the way she said it. It contained too much joy to be crude.

'Me, too,' he answered. When he thought back to what it had been like being in bed with Susan Castle, he marvelled at his ineptitude. *In bed*: that said it all. They'd never done it anywhere else. The same as they'd never done it with the lights on, as if seeing one another naked might have somehow spoilt the romance of it all.

Oh yes, he marvelled at that, but not half as much as at the years which had passed between Susan's departure from his life and Emily's explosion into it. How had he survived? That's what he could no longer understand. How had he managed without Emily's company, without her laughter and frankness, her openness and determination? In short, how had he managed without her at all?

Optimism leapt up inside him. There'd been something he'd been wanting to tell her all day. He'd been saving it up for the right moment. He saw that moment was now.

'I've got something to –' they began simultaneously, before bursting out laughing and rolling apart.

'You first,' he said.

'No, you.'

'I've got something to show you.'

'And I've got something to give you,' she replied.

'What?'

'This,' she said, before kissing him lingeringly. 'Well, I've shown you mine,' she then said. 'What's yours?'

'You're going to have to get dressed first . . .'

Her eyes narrowed in suspicion. 'Why? Where are we going?'

He picked up her knickers and tossed them on to her lap. 'Wait and see.'

'William?'

It's was Bill's mother, calling him from the parlour. Bill and Emily had just driven back from the allotment and Emily was waiting for him in the car outside. Annoyed, Bill stared down at the creaking step which had betrayed his attempt at sneaking up to his bedroom undetected.

He walked through to find his mother with Edith Carver, still dressed in her black church dress, and Giles Weatherly, the ironmonger from across the alley. Edith was sitting at the table pouring tea into cups and Giles stood by the barred open window, smoking a pipe. The sweet scent of cherry tobacco pervaded the room.

'Edith,' Bill said, enjoying the wince in her face which the deliberately overfamiliar greeting had inspired. 'Giles.'

'William,' Giles replied, running his thumb along his thick black moustache.

Bill liked Giles. He was a widower, childless, a few years older than Bill's mother. His wife had died from tuberculosis before the war. He'd been great friends with Bill's father and had been the first to arrive after hearing the shooting on the night Keith Glover had robbed the store. He'd given evidence against Keith Glover during the trial.

Bill noticed his mother was wearing the white silk neck scarf he and Rachel had bought her for Christmas.

'You look pretty, Mum,' he said.

'Doesn't she just,' Giles agreed.

Mrs Vale blushed. As Bill looked between her and Giles,

the absurd notion entered his head that perhaps they might one day end up as more than just good friends. Hot on its heels came the less absurd notion that that's what his father might have wanted, for his mother to move on, the same as Bill was now moving on himself. Why not? he thought. Stranger things had happened. And anything seemed possible, especially the way he felt right now.

'You know what, Giles?' he said. 'You should come over for dinner one night. I might be able to talk Emily into cooking something up for you and Mum. It would be fun.'

Edith Carver cleared her throat, looking sharply between Giles and Mrs Vale. Sniffing out the potential for gossip? Signalling her disapproval? Bill could neither tell nor care.

'I really don't think –' his mother began to protest.

'What a lovely idea,' said Giles. 'I haven't had a decent home-cooked meal in ages.' He turned to Bill's mother for approval. The burnished brass watch fob hanging from his brown woollen waistcoat pocket glimmered. 'Laurel?' he asked.

'Well, yes,' she said, flustered, 'I suppose there wouldn't be any har —'

'Good,' Bill said, 'that's decided then. You've got a real treat in store,' he confided in Giles. 'Emily's an amazing cook.' He turned to his mother. 'Isn't she, Mum?'

Bill walked over and kissed his mother on the brow. He knew she was annoyed with him, for demonstrating in front of Edith Carver that the scandalous Emily Jones was now an accepted face in their home. But Emily wasn't scandalous. Not to Bill. And not to his mother any more, he didn't think, not now that Emily had put in the effort to win her over. The sooner everyone else got wise to the fact, the better.

'You should give the Sea Catch Café a try, you know,

Giles,' he went on. 'Everyone should. It's the best in the town.'

Giles laughed. 'Nothing like a partisan recommendation, eh?'

The comment had been directed at Bill's mother, but it was Edith Carver who responded. 'Hardly the most popular place in town, though, is it?' she remarked frostily.

'Only because certain small-minded people, on account of their peculiar – and if I might say so – *un-Christian* prejudices, won't give it a chance,' Bill answered back.

'Well, really,' Edith Carver objected. She looked to Bill's mother and scowled. 'Even putting Emily Jones's own indiscretions aside,' she continued, 'you can't get around the fact that she still employs that vicious Glover boy and –'

'Who she employs has nothing to do with you,' Bill cut her off. He noticed his mother staring fixedly at him. He'd so far avoided discussing Tony Glover's continued employment at the café with his mother and certainly didn't intend to allow Edith Carver to agitate matters now. 'Or anyone else, for that matter,' he added pointedly, 'including myself.'

His mother looked at the clock and said nothing. He knew he was letting her down, but at the same time he could no longer summon up the same venom he'd once felt for Tony Glover. Hatred, yes, he held a reservoir of that for Keith. But not Tony. Tony's presence was something to be endured, not suffered, Bill had decided. Emily was more important. He knew this was something his mother would never understand.

Giles broke the uneasy silence. 'I'm surprised you're back,' he said. 'Your mother said you were out for the afternoon.'

'I forgot something,' Bill answered. 'Where's Rachel?'

he then asked, noticing her absence and using it as an excuse to change the subject.

His mother's expression was unreadable, as blank as a waxwork doll's. She was dwelling on Tony Glover. Or if not him, then Keith. The thought had switched her off like a light. All because of Edith Carver and her big mouth.

'Over at Anne's house,' she finally replied, still without looking at him.

'Of course,' he answered. 'I'd best get going,' he said. 'Emily's waiting for me in the car.'

He rushed up the stairs, buzzing, taking them one, two, three at a time, and then on into his room.

Bill's bedroom looked more like a draughtsman's office than a place where someone daydreamed and slept. The day he'd asked Emily Jones out on their first date, he'd come back here and pushed his iron-framed bed up tight against the far wall, underneath the window which hung out over the River Step. In its place, at the centre of the room, his drawing board now stood.

He'd dug out his old drawings from university like she'd said. The bridges and art galleries and fantastical houses he'd designed in his leisure time while studying for his engineering degree now covered the walls. Architecture, that's what he'd dreamt of pursuing once he'd finished his course. And architecture, that's what surrounded him now whenever he slept.

Pinned on the wall above the bed were two photographs. One was of Emily, taken on their second date, when he'd driven her to a pub along the coast for lunch. He took it now and slipped it inside his wallet, suddenly wanting it close. The other was a photograph of the Bathers' Pavilion, the derelict building overlooking the beach which Emily had pointed out to him in May, when she'd told him it was a terrible thing to allow ambition to go to waste.

Neatly ordered on his bedside table were his draughtsman's tools. On the drawing board was what he'd come here to collect. He'd been working on it for the past few weeks. It wasn't finished yet, but it was near enough there, and he couldn't wait any longer. The timing felt right. He wanted to show it to Emily now.

Rolling the drawing up under his arm, he ran back down the stairs. Nerves stretched and snapped inside him with each step down he took.

'Hey, guess what?' he said to Emily as he climbed into the Jupiter beside her. 'Rachel's over at Anne's house again.' It was a running joke between them. Rachel had a mystery boyfriend. She'd told Emily and Emily had, in turn, told Bill. Anne was the excuse she used for getting out of the house. Bill wanted to know who it was, but Emily had so far stopped him from prying. Still, Rachel couldn't keep it a secret for ever and, meantime, whoever it was, they'd better be taking good care of her. And Rachel had better be behaving herself, too.

'So has she told you who he is yet?' he asked.

Emily's eyes were fixed on the tube of paper in his hand. 'No, and I haven't asked. And nor should you,' she warned. 'Girls her age like to keep their affairs mysterious. I know I did.'

'Quite,' he teased, starting the car, 'and look where it got you.'

'Enough of your stalling,' she said, snatching the paper from him. 'Where are we going now and what's with this?' She started to unwind the paper cylinder.

'Don't,' he said, gently touching the back of her hand.

'Please. I promise: it'll be worth the wait.' He hoped it would. He prayed.

She rested the paper on her lap and they set off down the high street towards the harbour.

They turned right at the end of the high street and on across Harbour Bridge to the east side of town. Instead of turning right along East Street towards the Sea Catch Café, however, as Emily (judging by her look of surprise) had obviously been expecting, Bill pulled up outside the Bathers' Pavilion.

'What are we doing here?' Emily asked

'I'll show you.'

Taking the roll of paper from her, he got out of the car.

The dilapidated building was rectangular in shape, one hundred and twenty feet long and forty wide. It had been built at the turn of the century as a changing and wash-ing facility for the prudish tourists to undress in, before they stepped out on to the beach in their striped cotton knee-to-neck bathing suits. Its roof had been torn off and its insides shredded in the great storm of 1933. But even before that, its use had gone into decline. People had no longer required such extreme levels of privacy. It had become unfashionable and the funds to rebuild it had never been raised.

Emily sidled around a rust-scarred oil drum which half blocked the front entrance and followed Bill inside.

Rusted pipes hung from the walls like jungle vines, the wind blowing through them, making them groan like the timbers of a ship at sea. Emily slipped her hand into Bill's.

'This place gives me the creeps,' she said.

'You soon get used to it,' he answered.

They hurried on beneath the dripping, mildewed rafters which carved the open grey sky above into squares.

'It's such a shame,' Emily remarked.

They walked on, negotiating their way around smashed roof tiles, broken bottles and papier-mâché mounds of old fish-and-chip newspaper wrappings. When they reached the corridor which ran along the back of the rows of doorless changing cubicles, Bill stopped.

Releasing Emily's hand, he knelt down on the ground and unrolled the sheet of paper, spreading it out and weighing it down with pieces of broken masonry. It was a scale drawing for the structural alterations he'd planned out for the building. Every last detail had been etched into the paper with ink.

He knew Emily was standing behind him, looking down over his shoulder. He took a deep breath to steady his nerves.

'It's just an idea,' he told her without daring to look round. 'And I know it might sound crazy, thinking about taking out another loan, because the café's not yet making money. But that's only because of the weather. And bad weather passes, doesn't it? It always does.'

He was talking faster and faster, afraid now of her silence, afraid of what it might mean.

'And this building's cheap,' he went on. 'Really, it is. Even when you take into account the amount of work which will be necessary. I've compared prices from all over. Other resorts not half as busy as Stepmouth usually is and you'd be paying double for a building this size and this close to the sea, and . . .'

He finally paused, praying that she'd speak. But she said nothing. He still didn't dare turn to face her. Instead, he stabbed a finger down at the plan.

'I thought that what we could do was clear this whole area here,' he said, sweeping his arm expansively to indicate the entire changing area, 'and then divide it up. We could put a wall in there,' he hurriedly continued, pointing first at the drawing and then at the far side of the room, 'with the kitchens behind it –'

'Kitchens?' Finally, she'd spoken.

'Yes, because that way we don't use up any of the space at the front of the building, which means we'll be able to offer more tables with a sea view –'

'Bill,' she said. He felt her hand on his shoulder. Her voice was firm. 'Slow down. Stop.'

'But –'

'You mean you want me to buy this place, don't you? Is that what you're saying?'

'Yes. No.' He turned at last to face her. He stared at her perplexed. Hadn't he already made it obvious? 'Not you. Us. I thought you realised. I thought we . . .'

Like a meteorite, he felt his ardour crashing back down to earth and starting to cool. He'd gone too far. Too quickly. He could see it in her eyes.

She knelt down beside him and stared at the drawing and then at him.

'I'm sorry,' he said. His voice was dull, defeated. He closed his eyes.

'No,' he heard her saying, 'don't be.' She was kissing him then, planting tiny kiss after tiny kiss on his face. 'Don't be, you wonderful, wonderful man.'

# Chapter XVII

**Mallorca, Present Day**

Laurie couldn't open her eyes. The feeling that enveloped her was so unlike anything she'd ever experienced before, that she had to repeat the fact that had caused it in her head several times before she could believe it was real: Sam Delamere had just made love to her.

She was lying on her back in the old boat, cushions squashed uncomfortably around her. Sam was above her, holding her hands above her head. Both of them were sweating, their breath syncopating with the rhythm of the waves breaking on to the shore outside the boathouse.

Slowly, she opened her eyes. Sam was staring down into her face. He was still inside her, but he made no move. She felt glued to him, as if the surface of his naked body – at once so familiar and yet so strange – had fused with hers. She realised that her legs were wrapped around him, her heels pressing hard into the small of his back. She felt her heart pounding, failing to slow down from the climax that had just rocked her and made her cry out.

Tentatively, she started exploring how her body felt. Her face was hot, her lips sweetly stinging from the violence of their kisses, her hair was dishevelled, sprawled across her face, her back aching from where it had scraped along the bottom of the wooden boat.

That first unexplained kiss of Sam's had been like a

match that had sparked an out-of-control firework display. Now she felt as if she were a survivor, staring at him through the smoke.

As if reading her mind, Sam let go of her hands, so that he could gently stroke the hair from her face. His eyes seemed huge. They seemed to fill her vision, blocking out all her thoughts.

Slowly, she moved her legs down his back. When he pulled away from her, it felt as if they were ripping apart. She sat up and shakily shifted back into the corner of the boat on a jumble of cushions. He sat up too, holding on to the sides of the boat, as if for support. Their legs were overlapping, as they faced each other, the scent of sex, the sound of the sea overwhelming in the hot, damp air. She was trembling all over.

Sam reached out and grabbed her hands, as if he were stopping her from sinking. Then he squeezed them, as if she were his own lifeline.

'Did that really just happen?' she asked, finding it difficult to talk. Her throat was dry and she was panting. 'Tell me this isn't real. That we didn't . . . I thought . . .'

She thought what? She didn't know. She didn't know whether this was the start of something new or the end of something old. All she knew was that this was real and it was happening now. She could feel a hundred questions stacking up in her head, but she couldn't think of any of them clearly. She stared at him, willing him to have some answers.

'I didn't come here just for this, I promise,' he said. 'Oh, Laurie.'

He pulled her tight towards him and Laurie felt her body willingly melt against his once again. Her mind was racing, but it felt as if she wasn't getting anywhere. It was as if there was no resistance, like trying to pedal on a bike which was going too fast downhill.

Why did it feel this wonderful to be naked with him? Why did it feel so natural and right? They'd both just been unfaithful to their partners. Not just physically, but emotionally, spiritually, completely. On every level. Why didn't she feel even the least bit guilty? Maybe she was still riding high on an endorphin wave, she thought. Maybe in a minute –

But she didn't want to think about the future. She closed her eyes, pressing her cheek against the damp hair on Sam's chest, breathing in the scent of him, hearing his heartbeat beneath her ear. All that mattered was right now. This feeling of being in Sam's arms again, of feeling as if she were home.

Sam kissed her again and again, feather-light kisses starting in her hair, until he reached for her face, his lips exploring every crevice of her skin, as if greeting her eyelids, her temples, the sides of her nose and claiming them once more for himself.

'I can't believe this is happening,' she said.

They stared wide-eyed at each other, grinning like idiots.

'OK. We have to swim,' he said and she laughed, realising they were both dripping with sweat.

Sam helped her out of the boat and, as her feet touched the floor, her legs were shaking. Sam went to retrieve his shorts.

'Ah, forget it!' he said, throwing them on the floor again. 'Come on.'

He stretched out his hand to her and they ran out of the boathouse, on to the hot sand. It was still baking, the calm sea warm from the sunshine. Laurie didn't stop running, or holding Sam's hand until they were right in the water and were diving simultaneously under the surface together.

Sam grabbed her as they surfaced. They were both laughing as they stood up.

'This feels like a dream,' she sighed.

Laurie hugged him, and kissed the rivulets of water on his tanned shoulder. She realised now how much she'd wanted to touch him when they'd been sailing. How the agony of denial had now gone. She wanted to scream for joy at the freedom she felt. She kissed his skin over and over again, as if he were quenching some inner thirst she couldn't satisfy. Soon her legs were around his waist again and he held her.

He drew back slightly so that he could look at her.

'You're so beautiful,' he said. 'I didn't tell you that enough. Ever. You're the most beautiful woman I've ever seen.'

She smiled, feeling it, as he looked into her eyes. Sam put his finger to her lips to stop her from replying.

'I love you, Laurie. We have been together. I can't live knowing that you're out there and not with me.'

And as the words she'd most longed to hear finally reached her, she realised that they hardly mattered. It was like receiving the confirmation letter for a job she'd already accepted. She didn't need proof in words that he loved her, she'd been able to feel his love from the second she'd turned round and seen him standing in the doorway of the boathouse.

'But . . . but what about?' Doubts, fears filled her head. She searched his face for them too. 'You've got a family, Sam. There's Claire . . .'

'And James,' he pointed out.

Laurie shook her head. She couldn't even begin to describe the world of difference between how she felt for

James compared to what she was feeling now.

'I don't want James,' she whispered. 'I love you. I never stopped loving you. Not for a second.'

Sam leant his forehead against hers. 'We're in this together.'

And then she felt his hardness below her in the water. And as he gently pushed inside her again, the waves gently caressed their naked skin. She felt completely weightless as Sam held her, but more alive than ever, as if she'd just woken up from a very long sleep and that being apart from him had just been a bad dream. As they made love in the sea, she never stopped looking into Sam's eyes, knowing that he'd meant what he'd said. Knowing that this was the most intense moment of her life. Knowing that whatever lay ahead, that this moment was the start of her future.

It was only later, when they were retrieving their dishevelled clothes from the sandy floor of the boathouse, that it occurred to Laurie that anyone could have seen them. That anyone could have been watching them in the sea and that it hadn't even crossed her mind to care.

But as they strolled back up the path towards the villa, Laurie did start to care. She closed her eyes for a second, desperate to hold on to the magic of the afternoon, clinging on to the feeling of being totally absorbed in one another, as they'd kissed and made love.

By the time they reached the top of the path, her heart was beating hard – not only from the exertion of the climb, but from the delayed shock of her recklessness. Stopping by the eucalyptus trees, she broke away from Sam. Dante was standing on a ladder with his back to them, pruning a tree. He'd already seen her at the villa with James this

317

week. Whatever would he think if he turned round and now saw her with Sam?

Why was she suddenly worrying about what the gardener thought of her? Why were her morals suddenly kicking in? Surely it was far too late for that.

Sam stole a quick kiss, as if he were sealing the afternoon, but Laurie sensed a change in him, too. It was then that Laurie knew whatever wild abandon they'd shared on the beach, couldn't exist up here.

Laurie stopped by the terrace steps. 'What's going to happen, Sam?'

'Don't look like that,' he said. 'Don't look like you're scared.'

'I am scared. I'm happier than I've ever been and more frightened.'

'So am I, but everything's going to be . . .' He paused and they stared at each other. 'We're going to make it.'

She nodded, too emotional to say anything. They walked in silence through the terrace doors. Everything was just as perfect as when she'd left it this morning – the kitchen immaculate, the low table on the rug polished and clean. And yet it felt different, as if the familiar living room was at once detached from her and yet charged with emotion.

As she walked towards the two large white sofas, she saw the framed photograph of Tony on the wall. He was smiling, holding up a fish on a sailing holiday. Laurie turned away from the image of the man she'd never met. She felt as if she'd betrayed him in his own home. If she felt like this, how must it be for Sam?

'You know that Rachel's coming tomorrow, don't you?' she said.

'You invited your dad here, after all?' Sam guessed. 'Without telling him whose house this is?'

She nodded, thinking about her father. Her heart seemed to lurch with terror at the thought of him being here. What the hell had she done?

'Oh Christ. This is such a mess.'

'Can't you put your dad off?' Sam asked.

'But what about Rachel? Surely I owe her something, before . . . before . . . ?'

She couldn't bring herself even to begin to imagine before what. Before she exploded Rachel's world. Before she hurt her unwitting father. Before she blew everyone's trust.

'Don't back out on me now, Laurie. Not after this.'

'I'm not! It's just . . . I don't know . . .'

'We can't avoid telling them,' Sam said. 'We can't just run away.'

'I know.'

'Maybe it's best if Rachel *is* here. Do it properly. Wait for her to sort things out with your father and then . . . then . . . it'll be good for Claire. I can't tell her tonight because she's having some stupid party. Yes, it'll be much better if I tell her tomorrow when Rachel's here to, to . . .'

Clean up the mess? Laurie thought, the reality of him mentioning Claire taking her breath away. There seemed to be so many people involved. So many people who were about to get hurt. It felt like too high a price to pay. She hadn't realised that to be selfish would be so much harder and more painful than being selfless.

She felt as if she'd trodden on a stepping stone in the middle of a river which had given way and now she didn't know how to proceed, didn't know whether to advance or go back.

'What's going to happen? I mean now, right now?' she asked.

She was met by her own look of fear in his face. She

couldn't bear for this afternoon to have ended already.

'I've got to go. Just for a little while. There are a few things I need to do before . . . before . . . well . . . I should be prepared.'

They both knew that he might be leaving everything he'd worked so hard for. There was no way Rachel would let him stay when she found out he was leaving Claire.

Sam cleared his throat. 'And there's Archie to think about.'

The sudden uncertainty in his voice frightened her.

'Sam, you have to believe in us,' she said. He walked to her and held her wordlessly, as if the strength of his hug would make her believe that he did. And yet she could hear his heart beating as hard as hers beneath the soft fabric of his shirt.

Sam dropped her off by the cafés on the seafront in Sóller and told her that he'd join her at the villa tomorrow. It was an awkward goodbye, too loaded with the pressure of the immediate future. They'd agreed that he would tell Claire as soon as it was feasibly possible and that he would come to Laurie straight away.

But now, as she walked slowly along the pavement, the cafés filling up with tourists basking in the early-evening sunshine, the waiters clipping fresh paper tablecloths to the square tables, Laurie felt as if she were tied to Sam with elastic. As if the connection between them was being stretched. All she wanted to do was to jump up and spring back to him.

She had felt so safe in the sea this afternoon. She had felt as if everything was right with the world, as if she'd finally made peace with herself. She'd felt light and happy and free. But as she walked into an Internet café, she felt weighed down with the seriousness of what she and Sam were about to do. Their plans suddenly seemed too irresolute and she'd wished they'd spent longer deciding exactly what was going to happen. Sam's promise to tell Claire about them at some point in the next twenty-four hours seemed too open to flaws, too lacking in guarantees.

She bought a bottle of Diet Coke and sat down in the small booth, shivering slightly in the chill of the air conditioning. She wished now that she'd used the computer in the house. Rachel had said she could use it, but perhaps she should trust her first hunch that being somewhere neutral was better.

She had decided to write to James straight away. If she was honest with James and finished their relationship, then it would be the first step to making her and Sam real.

She opened her email account, astonished by the amount of messages. She knew her friends were annoyed with her for being such a recluse, but she couldn't face opening any of them. She felt too disconnected and too guilty. Her life had totally changed. It would be almost impossible to explain to Heather or Roz in writing what had happened since she'd been in Mallorca.

But she must try to with James. She clicked on the button to compose an email and stared at the cursor on the screen for a long time. There was nothing for it. She would have to tell the truth.

Now she forced herself to think about James, it shocked her that they'd only parted just a few days ago. She'd been so confused when she'd seen him standing at the poolside in Rachel's villa, so guilt-ridden when Sam had left, that she'd been tempted to tell James to go. But he hadn't given her the chance.

Instead, he'd listed off all the places he'd wanted to see

321

in his short visit: the bar in Palma where his friends had recommended cocktails, the restaurant in Pollença, the posh spa at the exclusive resort in Deià, a day at the nudist beach for laughs . . .

She'd been happy to go along with him for the ride. After all, she'd hardly seen any of the island since she'd been at Rachel's and it was fun to sightsee with James. It had been an arrangement that had suited her well: he'd wanted to spend every moment squeezing the maximum fun out of every situation and she'd wanted to spend the minimum time being reminded of Sam.

And she couldn't deny that they *had* had fun. It had been made easier by the fact that she'd drunk more in three nights than she had done in all the time she'd been in Mallorca. They'd partied late into the night, finally falling into a taxi and into bed. They'd had sex a few times, but Laurie had been too drunk to care too much about it or analyse her feelings too deeply.

It was only on the last day that things had become tricky. It had been ten in the morning and they'd been shopping in the market at Inca. Laurie had bought a bag of ripe peaches from one of the stalls and they'd sat down on the worn step of the old church in the square to eat them.

'I missed you,' James said, suddenly. 'Back in London, I mean. I didn't tell you before, but I did. I missed you.'

'No you didn't,' Laurie teased him.

'I did. I swear. It was the strangest thing. I've never really missed anyone before, so at first I thought I was hungry. You know, I felt a bit odd inside. Then I realised I was actually missing your company.'

Laurie laughed. 'Good. I'm glad it was only me. I wouldn't want you to get fat or anything.'

'I'll miss you even more now.'

She pulled a face at him, trying to jokily dismiss his first real admission of affection.

'It's not me. You just like being on holiday.'

But then, when James didn't make another joke, Laurie looked into his eyes and realised he was serious. He *was* going to miss her.

She turned away. James wasn't supposed to fall for her. James was the man who never fell for anyone. All his friends had told her as much. She saw now that that was half the reason why she'd gone out with him in the first place – because it wasn't serious. Because she'd had the impression that he never *would* be serious.

James nudged her knees with his, breaking the tension. 'I'll be back,' he said.

'You will, will you?'

'I'm going to call Rachel and ask.'

'You two really are the big pals,' she said, taking another bite out of her peach to avoid his question.

'It's important to me to suck up to your family.'

She could feel herself shrinking away from the conversation and despaired of herself. She wanted to encourage him, to tell him that she did want him to come back, that it was important to her, too, that he made an effort with her family. But something stopped her.

Sam again. They'd made it clear to each other on the boat that there could be nothing between them, hadn't they? They'd put the past to rest. Sam wasn't in her life any more, other than as the husband of her newly found cousin. She had to get him out of her head.

'We've had a good time, haven't we? I'm glad you came,' she managed, keeping things light.

James paused. He took off his sunglasses and his greeny-blue eyes sparkled in the sunlight. 'You know, I was thinking . . . if you're stuck for a place to stay when you get back, you can always come and hang out at mine.'

'You want me to *live* with you?'

'Why not? We've had three days together and it went OK, didn't it?'

'This was a trial run? You came out here to see whether I'd be a good flatmate?'

'No. I came out here because I think you're cute and, as I said, because I missed you. And I don't want you to stay out here, if you're staying just because you're homeless. I'd rather we were together.'

This time, the peach remained in Laurie's hand, halfway to her mouth. This time she couldn't dismiss his comment with a flippant remark. She turned on the step and looked at James, as if seeing him for the first time. She'd always treated him as such a boy, deliberately not taking him seriously, just because he was a few years younger than her. But now that he'd finally come to express his feelings, she felt ashamed of herself for disregarding his emotions so readily.

She'd been so naive. Not being seriously interested in James had inadvertently been exactly the right tactic to get him seriously interested in her. And he was interested in her. He'd come to Mallorca to see her, for God's sake. He'd spent the three days tirelessly entertaining her in an effort to show her how much he didn't care. But now she could see that it hadn't been ironic for him when he'd bought her a rose from the gypsy seller in the restaurant. He hadn't been joking when he'd aped along with the romantic aria on the balcony of the cocktail bar. And now, sitting on the cool step of the church in the square, with peach juice dripping down their chins, she was aware that this was yet another in a long line of romantic moments she'd failed to acknowledge.

Now she was truly speechless. She felt hopelessly caught out. What was wrong with her? James was offering her a serious relationship and a solution to all her problems. Why wasn't she screeching with gratitude and delight? Why wasn't she signing on the dotted line? James was everything she should want. Everyone back home loved him – his friends and hers. So why was she so tied up with her past? Sam had brought her nothing but heartache.

Do it! She told herself, not trusting herself to say the right thing, but the moment couldn't go on any longer. She had to say something, or do something. Panicked, she smiled and opted to kiss him, leaning forward and squashing her peach-covered lips on to his.

Back at the villa, she got herself into even deeper water. She shouldn't have kissed James so readily at the church, she realised, as he'd gently undressed her. And as they'd embarked on sober sex for the first time in James's visit, she realised that he wasn't laughing it off, as he usually would have done.

Afterwards, he'd stayed next to her, not saying anything, as if he was revelling in an intense moment, but Laurie stayed frozen next to him staring at the rafters above her bed, unable to shake the feeling that Sam was somehow in the room watching her. She tried to visualise Sam in bed with Claire, in *this* bed, but thinking about him had only made it worse.

When James had sighed and had tried to kiss her, she'd rolled away and had started babbling about him missing his flight.

Now, in the Internet café, as she stared at the blinking cursor on the white computer screen, she could see so clearly how much she'd been deceiving herself. She'd been in love with Sam all along. From the second she'd seen him and James side by side, after they'd come back from sailing, she'd known it.

*Dear James*, she typed. She sighed and rubbed her face, picturing James's smiling face. He was so handsome. He would be so right for someone else. *This is not going to be an easy thing to write . . .*

Later, back at the villa, Laurie paced by the telephone anxiously waiting for Sam to call, flexing her fingers against each other, as if they'd somehow seized up with guilt after the email she'd typed to James. She'd recounted the whole story of her affair with Sam and how she'd come to see him again. She'd been brutally honest, hoping that the intensity of her feelings for Sam would somehow excuse her.

But as she waited now for some word from Sam, there was no way of squaring it with herself, or pretending that she could come out of this in any way as a nice person. She should have been honest with James from the start. She should have told him the truth about Sam, as soon as he'd arrived. Instead, she'd strung him along, let him think that she was going to move in with him back in London. She'd treated him like a child, made a fool out of him, and she knew that when he read her email, he would be justifiably furious. It made her wince, just to think of it.

And then another thought occurred to her. What if James called Rachel? What if he was so angry that he told Rachel all about Laurie's affair with Sam? She knew that Rachel would have to find out, but to find out from James? It didn't bear thinking about.

By ten o'clock that night, Laurie was going crazy. She should never have let Sam out of her sight. She should have gone with him. How was she supposed to fight for their future alone? She'd been so struck with guilt about Rachel and her father, she hadn't been thinking clearly when Sam said they should wait until tomorrow.

But waiting until tomorrow gave Sam one whole night to be with his family. Hours and hours in which he would realise how much he was about to hurt Archie and Claire. Hours and hours in which he might realise all he was about to give up.

And what if it happened all over again, as it had done three years ago? What if Sam lost his nerve and didn't tell Claire?

Panicking, Laurie dialled Roz's number.

'Just hear me out before you say anything,' she implored, when Roz picked up. She knew Roz would be able to detect the urgency in her voice and that if she blurted out how she was feeling, Roz wouldn't have a chance to be cross with her for being so lax about staying in touch.

'OK,' Roz agreed, 'but what the hell's the matter? You sound dreadful.'

'Oh, Roz,' Laurie began, feeling tears threatening to choke her. 'I don't know what to do.'

'Just tell me everything,' her friend soothed. 'Start from the beginning.'

But five minutes later, when Laurie had filled her in on the details of her current predicament, rather than issuing the much needed words of comfort Laurie needed to hear, Roz was furious.

'You bloody idiot,' she stormed.

'Roz, please understand,' Laurie begged. 'I love him.'

'Do you have any idea how pathetic you sound?'

'But –'

'Once was bad enough, but to get bitten by the same snake *twice*? That's just suicidal.'

'It's not . . . he loves me too.'

'So where is lover boy now? Why are you calling me if he's so bloody marvellous.'

'He's . . . gone. He's with Claire.'

'He's telling her?'

'No, she's . . . she's having a party.'

'A party! Of course!' The sarcasm in Roz's tone cut Laurie to the quick. 'You're tearing your hair out, but he's at a fucking party? I can't believe you've done this again, Laurie. I thought you were over him.'

'I did too.'

'Look, why don't you just come home, honey?' Roz said, more gently. 'You've got all your friends here. Your life is here. Your career. Just walk away.'

'I can't.' Laurie hadn't even begun to tell Roz about her father arriving at the villa tomorrow. Now she buried her head in her hands, but the more she tried to explain her situation, the more confused she became.

Her nerves were shot to pieces by the time she'd rung off. Roz was right, she decided. Why should she be feeling like this? What did a party matter, when she and Sam were supposed to be changing their lives for ever? Why was he stalling with such a lame excuse? Laurie imagined him in his home right at this moment, smiling and greeting all his friends with Claire as if nothing had happened.

*You have to believe in us*, she'd said earlier. And she had. She'd finished with James. James, who had proved himself to be so much more emotionally together than she'd ever suspected. James, who had been ready to make a commitment to her, to their future together. And she'd thrown him away. Finished with him – callously – by email. And as Roz had so plainly put it, nobody deserved that, surely? Especially not James. And what had Sam done in return?

328

Laurie dialled his mobile phone.

'Hello?' Claire slurred in the kind of sing-song voice that immediately told Laurie that Sam hadn't breathed a word of what had happened. She was drunk and clearly in the middle of her party, judging from the noise in the background.

'Is Sam there?' Laurie asked, pretending that she didn't recognise Claire's voice.

'Laurie, is that you?'

'Er . . . yes. Oh, hi, Claire.' Laurie's face contorted into a grimace. She was a hopeless actress.

'Hang on, I'm walking through. Sam's hiding in the wet room having a shower,' Claire shouted, above the noise of the party. 'Would you believe it – he hasn't had the courtesy to turn up to his own party all day and now he's complaining that everyone is too pissed to talk to!'

Laurie could hear the noise of the party abruptly being muffled and then suddenly the sound of running water in the background. Sam was naked, just a few metres away from where Claire was talking to her on the phone. Here she was, all alone, agonising about their future, and Sam was *in the shower*?

'That's better,' Claire said, obviously referring to the noise level. 'I'm so glad I got a chance to speak to you. Tell me, tell me, is that divine boyfriend of yours still at the villa?'

'No . . . no. He's gone,' Laurie mumbled, her pulse racing. She could feel her hair prickling and she was finding it difficult to breathe.

'Pity. I was so hoping the four of us could get together for dinner. Rachel said he was to die for. She planned his surprise visit, didn't she? She was so excited, but so nervous too. Was it wonderful? No wonder you've been so

329

quiet! I've been dying to come over there, but I stopped myself.'

'We were . . . busy.' It came out as no more than a whisper, but Claire didn't seem to notice.

'I bet you were!' Laurie heard her lighting a cigarette. 'You're not offended about the party, are you, Laurie? I would have invited you –'

'No, no, don't worry.'

'Ugh! Sam's taking ages in the shower. Did you want him for anything?'

*Only the rest of my life*, Laurie felt like saying, but as soon as she thought it, yet more guilt kicked in. Out of nowhere, she noticed that hot, silent tears were suddenly popping out of her eyes. 'Oh, really, no, I don't want to disturb him, Claire. It's late and I'm sure he's very busy . . . especially in the middle of a party –'

'No, go on . . . what's the problem?'

What was the problem? How could Claire even begin to comprehend the magnitude of the problem!

'It's the electronic gate,' she managed. It was the only excuse she could think of. It took all her effort to keep the emotion from her voice. 'I can't seem to get it open. I was wondering whether . . . Sam had Fabio's number?'

'Oh, boring! Don't disturb Fabio at this time of night. I'll get Sam.'

'No, don't. I'm sure you have things to . . . it can wait . . .'

But it was too late.

'Darling?' she heard Claire say, knocking on the door of the wet room.

*Darling.* Laurie heard the shower in the background. She imagined Sam washing the scent of her from his skin. She felt sick.

330

'He's not answering. He probably thinks it's someone trying to get in there for a shag. I'll tell him you called. Don't worry about the gate. I'm sure someone will fix it by the morning. Now I must dash, I've got guests waiting.'

And then Claire had gone. Laurie pressed the call-end button and, with a howl of rage, threw her phone at the wall.

# Chapter XVIII

Even on a day like today, with the rain slashing against the glass shopfront, leaving angry diagonal stripes on the glass, Emily Jones was as breezy and cheerful as the summer day it should have been. Rachel stood behind the counter in the dark corner of the shop, folding a pile of new yellow dusters, but her attention was entirely focused on Emily, who seemed like a luminous butterfly fluttering in the middle of the dreary shop.

Rachel had always felt a curious mixture of envy, pride and longing whenever she saw Emily and today wasn't any different. There was something so unique about her. In all the months since she'd reappeared in Stepmouth, her style had been unfailingly modern. Rachel didn't know one single girl in the town who didn't want to be exactly like her.

Today she was wearing a felt hat, pulled down at a rakish angle over her blonde curls and a polka-dot raincoat, which matched her umbrella. A silk scarf printed with a motif of sweet williams was tied around her neck. Her cheeks glowed with pretty pink rouge and the scent of her perfume filled the musty air, even overpowering the box of boot polish next to Rachel. It was as if Emily was stamping her personality on everything, forcing everyone to be cheerful. No wonder Bill was behaving like a lovesick puppy.

Rachel watched as Emily smiled, pushing the large Coronation sweet tin housing her latest offering across the counter towards Mrs Vale.

'You really don't have to bring cakes all the time,' Rachel's mother was saying, her tone at once disapproving as well as begrudgingly grateful. 'I've told you before, I'm perfectly capable of baking myself, should we want to indulge ourselves –'

'But I was only thinking this morning about who I could rely on to help out,' Emily cut in, 'and I suddenly thought that a smart woman like you, who hates for food to go to waste, must be able to. You see, in this weather, I'm so down on numbers for afternoon tea. My cake's only going to go in the bin. And it's fresh cream and –'

'It's chocolate,' said Rachel's mother, easing up the lid of the tin and peering inside. She said it as if it were coated in rat poison.

'Mrs Vale, is it really worth living, if we don't have a few treats once in a while?'

'Let me pay you for it.'

'No, no, it's a gift. And if you can't eat it, then at least you could try and sell it. We might as well spread the wealth. Us businesswomen must stick together.'

Emily winked at Rachel and she had to hide her smile. Emily's tactics to soften her mother with relentless enthusiasm were finally working. She'd been on a consistent campaign recently to gain her approval. She'd visited the shop regularly with little gifts, never missing an opportunity to allude to the similarities between Mrs Vale and herself, rather than their differences.

Personally, Rachel couldn't think of two people more opposite. But Emily was playing a smart game, peppering her conversation with polite, respectful compliments which

Rachel's mother had accepted before realising she'd been buttered up. The result was that Laurel Vale had recently changed her tune about her beloved son's girlfriend, at least to the point of acknowledging her existence.

'I'll take it this once, just to help you out, but no more gifts,' her mother warned, but there was a smile playing in her eyes.

'I'm so grateful,' Emily said, as Mrs Vale put the tin on her lap and wheeled out of the shop and into the hallway, to put the tin in the kitchen.

'You're getting there,' Rachel said, moving back along the counter, so that she faced Emily.

Emily looked after Rachel's mother. 'I'll get the old bat to like me yet!' She said it almost to herself. 'Oh Lord! Listen to me. I didn't mean . . . she's your mother . . .'

Rachel giggled. It was so refreshing that Emily was so normal, that she always said what she was thinking.

'Don't you dare tell your brother I said that,' Emily warned, but she was smiling.

'I won't. He's not here by the way.'

'I know. I came to see you.'

'Me?' Rachel asked, feeling flattered, but at that moment, two kids came in, the bell clattering loudly, and Emily moved away as Rachel served them. They both wanted liquorice and were squabbling over their money as they stretched up towards the counter. Usually, Rachel would have indulged them, maybe given them a sweet as a treat, behind her mother's back, but today she was in no mood. She wanted them gone, so that she could talk to Emily alone.

When the bell had clanged as the door shut behind them, Emily came back to the counter.

'So?' Rachel asked.

Emily stepped in closer and seemed to take a deep breath before she spoke. 'Oh, Rachel, this is so difficult.' Her voice barely more than an urgent whisper.

'What is?' asked Rachel, alarmed. She couldn't imagine Emily ever finding anything difficult.

'The thing is . . . you're going to have to tell Bill about you and Tony.'

Rachel felt her cheeks burn with embarrassment and shock. This was the last thing she'd been expecting to hear. She glanced nervously towards the door, but Emily seemed to sense her fear. She reached out and touched Rachel's hand. Her nails were painted bright red.

'You can't keep it a secret from Bill any longer. And I don't want to tell him. But I'll have to –'

Rachel's head snapped up and she stared into Emily's gentle eyes. 'Please don't! Oh, Emily –'

'It's getting difficult. With Bill, I mean. I'm not lying to him, but I'm not exactly telling the truth, either. He deserves to know. I hate being with him and knowing he's being deceived. You're the only one who can tell him.'

'You know I can't. He'd go mad if I do.'

'Bill's changed. Trust me. He might go a little mad, but not as mad as you might think. He's your brother. It's not as if he's never going to speak to you again.'

Emily smiled but Rachel didn't return it. She felt abandoned. She'd thought that Emily understood about her and Tony, but now she saw that Emily's allegiances had changed without her noticing. Bill had claimed her for himself and Emily wasn't on Rachel and Tony's side any more.

Rachel shrank away. Emily didn't know Bill as she did. Emily saw the kind, romantic Bill, the Bill who was trying to impress her all the time. The Bill who mooned around her as if she were a goddess. Emily didn't know what her brother was really like. She didn't realise that if he found out about Rachel and Tony and their plans for their future, he'd do everything in his power to make sure they would never happen.

Emily sighed. 'I know it seems difficult, but think about what I've said, for me, that's all I'm asking. Now I've got to go.'

As Emily disappeared into the rain, Rachel felt a sense of foreboding that she couldn't shake. But what if, just by chance, Emily was right? she wondered, as she started folding the tea towels. What if Bill had changed? What if he did understand that Tony had nothing to do with Keith? What if, through Emily, he had learnt the power to forgive at long last?

Rachel felt a glimmer of hope, but at that moment the door to the hallway slid open and her mother was back. And that was when Rachel's hope died. She couldn't trust Bill. If he found out about Tony, then he'd tell their mother and she knew for certain that there would never be any understanding in this household.

Pearl's mother had come from a wealthy family, before marrying Dr Glaister and settling in Stepmouth. They lived in one of the Victorian town houses by the harbour and their front garden ended at the sea wall. The surgery was downstairs and was bleak and austere, with ripped posters of skeletons and medical adverts on the peeling mustard-coloured walls. Rachel was as familiar as the rest of the town with the wooden benches in the waiting room and the smell of disinfectant by the sliding surgery door with its intriguingly shadowy frosted glass.

But upstairs, unlike the rest of the town folk, Rachel was

privy to Pearl's mother's extravagant taste which nobody would ever guess from the dank surgery below. An old-fashioned chandelier, a family heirloom, hung from the high ceiling on the landing and everywhere there were frills and fancy decorations, with floral curtains and pelmets framing all the windows.

Pearl's large bedroom overlooked the harbour wall and the small estuary with its constant chugging fishing boats, but despite its proximity to the water, it always felt warm and cosy. Rachel had played in the room since she'd been a little girl and knew every one of the dolls and teddy bears that lined the wooden bookshelves.

Later that night, as she stood behind Pearl, who was sitting at her flouncy dressing table, Rachel felt a sense of security from the familiar surroundings, which she'd failed to find in her own home recently. They were both looking at their reflections in the long mirror. Pearl was wearing a padded pale dressing gown, her hair in the new pink curlers she'd bought in her latest attempt to bring some life into her fine blonde straight hair. Rachel had pulled the curlers so tightly that Pearl's perfect pale skin was pulled taut at her cheeks and forehead.

'Emily mentioned she's got some magazines coming from America,' Rachel said, knowing this would impress Pearl. She'd already recounted every detail of Emily's outfit today. 'We might be able to order some new patterns. Well, I could ask her anyway.'

'Would you? I mean, ask her for me as well?'

Rachel nodded and turned her attention back to Pearl's hairdo, pleased she'd found a way to ingratiate herself with her friend. She'd been feeling so guilty that she'd kept Tony a secret from Pearl all this time. And now she longed for the closeness they'd once shared. As they fell into a contented silence, Rachel plucked up her courage to consult her friend on a matter which had been plaguing her for days.

'You know there's this girl,' Rachel began, not looking at Pearl, as she retwisted her hair at the back around the pink curler. Pearl was humming, playing with a large talcum-powder puff and Rachel didn't look at her as she continued. 'She comes into the shop sometimes. She's not from here, but she must be about our age. Younger even. Anyway, she came in the other day and she looked dreadful. Someone told me she might be, you know . . . knocked up.'

Rachel managed to inject enough horror into her voice in order to gain Pearl's attention. Pearl looked up at Rachel in the mirror. There was a blob of white powder on Pearl's cheek, as if a snowball had landed on her.

'Pregnant?' Pearl exclaimed. 'And she's our age? How terrible. She's obviously not from around here.'

'No, no. I mean, she's not like you think. She's from a nice family and everything. Just like us. But she's definitely not married, or engaged. I mean, it would be awful, wouldn't it? I wouldn't know, would you? Assuming we'd done it, that is, which we haven't,' Rachel continued, quickly. 'But assuming you had, how could you tell you were . . . pregnant . . . for sure?'

'You miss your time of the month and you get sick in the mornings and stuff, Dad says.'

'What would you do if it was you? Just in theory?'

'Me? I'd kill myself,' Pearl said. 'Can you imagine what my parents would say? I'd rather die than face them.'

Rachel smiled uneasily. She'd known Pearl's parents all her life. She could imagine that they'd have a lot to say on the subject and none of it would be pleasant, or understanding.

'I wouldn't be able to live here if something like that happened,' Pearl continued, warming to the subject. 'I mean, everyone would know, wouldn't they? You wouldn't be able to hide it. And my parents would be so ashamed. People would whisper about them behind their backs everywhere they went.'

'Not if you got married.'

'But who's going to marry you if you've already got a child?'

'What about the man who got you pregnant?' Rachel asked.

'Think about it. You wouldn't be able to go to him, would you? Not once you'd got yourself in the family way. There'd be no point. No man, especially a nice one, is going to stick by a girl who's slept with him before getting married.'

Rachel didn't say anything. She longed to tell Pearl about Tony and had nearly let slip on so many occasions, but she knew now why she hadn't. Pearl wouldn't understand. She was just the same as Anne.

'There was a girl up on the base who got knocked up a few years ago,' Pearl said, leaning her elbow on the dressing table. 'I remember Dad took her in late one night. Don't tell anyone, I'm not supposed to say.'

'What happened?'

'She'd tried to get rid of the baby herself.'

'You can do that?'

'She tried to get it out with a wire coat hanger!'

Rachel felt sick.

'She was in a terrible mess. There was blood everywhere. She bled all over our kitchen floor. I heard Dad telling Mum that this girl had said that she wanted to go to a doctor in Exeter who would get rid of it, but Dad said that those people are not real doctors, they're quacks and they'll kill you as soon as fix you.'

'Oh,' Rachel said. She hadn't expected Pearl to be so forthcoming, or so full of gory details.

'Imagine, though,' Pearl continued. 'I mean, you'd have to kill yourself, or go away for ever, wouldn't you? Especially if you were on your own.'

Rachel nodded mutely. She couldn't think of anything to say. 'But if you didn't have any money . . .' she said finally, '. . . if you didn't know anyone apart from where you lived . . . and you had no family anywhere else?'

Pearl picked up the magazine off the dressing table and started to flick through it. 'Then you'd probably die of starvation, or wind up in some big city being a prostitute. Do you think I should dye my hair, Rach? What about if I was a redhead like you? Or do you think Emily's style really will suit me?'

That night, in Rachel's room, the rain drummed on the skylight. It was such a rhythmic, soporific sound that Rachel would normally have been asleep in minutes, but as the night moved into dawn, she was still awake, staring at the shadow of the branch of the old oak tree moving across the ceiling of her room.

She ached for Tony. She'd started a dozen letters to him and had torn them all up. She imagined him in his shed and worried about him being safe and dry. She imagined him on his box bed, right now, light flickering from his stove. It was all so wrong. Tony deserved so much more.

If only there was a way of them being together. But the more she thought about her conversation with Emily earlier, the more she was convinced that the possibility of them ever being together was slipping out of her reach.

It was like a torture, this living in secrecy. Rachel felt bound up by so many lies, she hardly dared speak to anyone with the fear of tripping herself up. Only Tony would understand, she thought. But that was what scared her the most. If she saw Tony, if she went to him, or spoke to him, then he'd be able to tell that something was wrong.

And something was wrong. Very, very wrong. Every time she thought about the possibility of it, it was like dipping her toe in scalding water. She'd thought that talking to Pearl would help, but now she knew for sure that her symptoms could only mean one thing. And couldn't lie to herself any longer.

As Rachel stared at the ceiling, clutching the cold sheet and blanket around her chin, she finally admitted the truth. She was pregnant with Tony's child. She could feel it in her bones, as if a parasite was sapping all her strength.

Rachel cried to herself silently. What if Pearl was right? What if she had been duped by Tony? What if he had said he'd marry her so that she carried on giving herself to him? What if he'd promised himself to a dozen girls before her?

But Tony loved her. She knew it. He'd told her. He wanted to be with her for ever, didn't he?

But no matter how much she held on to the image of Tony holding her in his arms, she knew that everything had changed. What if she told him about the baby and he hated her for it? After all, he wouldn't want a baby now, would he? At his age . . . he had his future waiting for him. He was young, with prospects. And if he found out about the baby, he'd realise his future had been robbed from him, too.

*You'd have to kill yourself, wouldn't you?* That's what Pearl had said. Rachel felt the cold terror of her dilemma, as she sat up in bed and reached for the chamber pot by the side of her bed. It must be dawn, she thought, knowing only too well that once the nausea started, it wouldn't stop.

It was then that she heard the tell-tale creak of the door downstairs and knew that Bill had finally come home. Rachel whimpered to herself. She knew that just below her Bill was trying to creep into bed without waking up their mother, after having spent the night with Emily. She could imagine the dreamy look on his face and hated him for it.

It wasn't fair, she thought, as she was silently sick into the chamber pot. Why was it fine for Bill to skulk about at all hours of the night, when she knew perfectly well what he'd been up to with Emily, and yet Rachel was trapped here all alone?

An hour later, Rachel had found no peace. She crept down the stairs to empty the chamber pot in the outside lavatory before either Bill or her mother got the faintest whiff of her vomit. She dipped her finger in the pot of white toothpaste powder and put it in her mouth, so that it coated her tongue. She almost gagged again, but she had to hide the rancid stench of her breath before she faced her family at breakfast.

Bill was up first, whistling as he shaved in the kitchen, his braces hanging down beside his trousers as he stood by the sink. He didn't seem the least bit tired, given the fact that she knew he'd only had a few hours' sleep.

Rachel, on the other hand, felt more weary than ever, as she cooked bacon and eggs on the stove and tried not to gag. As they sat down to eat breakfast together, she could feel her mother and Bill exchanging worried glances.

'Are you OK, Rachel?' Bill asked. 'You're looking very pale.'

'I'm fine,' she told him. She didn't dare look up. Instead, she forced in another mouthful of fried bread. 'Are you going to tune that thing to the weather forecast?' she asked, nodding to the radio. 'The rain is definitely getting worse.'

Her diversion tactic seemed to work. Still, she could barely bring herself to acknowledge Bill, as he left, agreeing listlessly to another shift in the shop. Now that she'd passed her exams, he expected her to work more rather than less. It wasn't fair, but she had no energy to argue.

When her mother followed him into the hallway, Rachel seized her moment, leaping from her seat and racing silently to the sink in the kitchen, where she threw up her breakfast.

Quickly, she ran the tap, watching the evidence drain away as the tap clunked and coughed and the water spurted out in an angry gush. As Rachel pushed the food chunks down the plughole, a small groan escaped her.

'Rachel?'

Leaning on the sink, Rachel turned to see her mother silhouetted in the doorway between the kitchen and the parlour. She watched her close the door quietly and then, to Rachel's dismay, she lifted the large key chain from around her waist and turned the lock.

'What are you doing, Mum?'

'You've been sick, haven't you?' Her mother wheeled herself down the ramp into the kitchen. Rachel shrank back against the sink away from her.

'No.'

'Don't lie to me.'

Rachel looked at her feet, fighting the nausea, fighting the fear she felt at her mother's tone.

'I've been watching you,' her mother said.

Rachel turned her back on her mother and pretended to do the washing-up. But then, as her mother spoke again, she froze.

'I know, Rachel.'

'Know what?' Rachel could barely speak, as she leant on the edge of the sink.

'I know what's wrong with you.'

Rachel could feel her eyes filling up with tears. No, she told herself. She couldn't cry. Not in front of her mother. If she cried, then she'd know for sure. And yet the childish part of her was too strong. She needed her mother to understand. She needed a hug. She needed to be told that everything was going to be all right.

'Look at me!' her mother snapped. Rachel could feel herself starting to shake. 'Look at me!'

Rachel thought that she managed to conceal most things from her mother, but she knew instinctively that this time she'd failed. Her secret was out. As she turned round, her mother gasped. Even if she'd had the energy to, she knew that there was no point in pretending any longer.

'It's not how you think,' Rachel whimpered.

'You're pregnant,' her mother hissed. 'Any damned fool can see it. Do you think I couldn't hear you this morning? And yesterday. And the day before. Do you think I'm stupid? That I can't tell what's wrong with my own daughter?'

Rachel could feel her tears spilling out on to her cheeks. All she wanted was her mother's understanding, and realising now that her mother had witnessed her suffering and felt nothing but contempt, rather than any form of compassion, made her feel more desperate than ever.

Her mother wheeled in closer. 'Who did this to you? Tell me? Tell me now.'

'I can't.'

Her mother reached up and yanked Rachel's arm, pulling her down so that she fell to her knees by the wheelchair, their faces level. Rachel yelped in pain. She thought her mother was going to slap her, but she seemed to stop herself on the brink of violence and, instead, let out a long sigh. Rachel could tell she was making a supreme effort to compose herself. She heard her mutter a brief prayer.

There was a long pause. Rachel wiped away her tears, bracing herself for the onslaught of her mother's wrath. But then her mother smoothed the hair away from her face.

'Oh, my poor baby. I mustn't be cross. I'm sorry. I'm sorry,' she sighed and stroked Rachel's cheek. Rachel felt something inside her let go. Her mother did love her. She did understand.

'Oh, Mum, I'm so scared.'

'Did he force you into it?' her mother asked.

'Who?'

'Whoever did this to you.'

Rachel stiffened and sniffed. 'It's not how you think. I love him –'

'Love!' Her mother's compassionate tone had vanished. 'What do you know about love?'

'Plenty,' Rachel countered, feeling her strength returning. 'Tony and I . . .'

She stopped, realising that she'd said his name. She saw her mother's eyes cloud with a fury she'd never seen before. Rachel willed herself to go on, to tell her mother the truth, but she was too scared.

'Tony? You don't mean the Glover boy? You mean . . . you mean to tell me he did this to you?'

Rachel had been kneeling all this time, but now she shifted back to stand up. 'Not on purpose. It's not his fault. It was both of us. We love each other.'

Her mother suddenly struck her in the face with such

force as she stood up that Rachel lost her balance and fell back against the range and hit her shoulder hard. She cowered by the cold metal door, too shocked to move. Her mother had never hit her. Rachel's lip pulsed. Blood splashed on the floor.

'You will get rid of it!' Her mother didn't shout, but her voice was deadly.

'No,' Rachel cried.

'You will never have his child. Do you hear me?'

'No, Mum, no! We're going to get married –'

'Over my dead body!' her mother hissed. Then she leant forward lunging so that she could grab Rachel's shoulder. Her fingers bit into her flesh. 'How could you do this, Rachel? How could you do this to your father and me? To your family?'

'I'm sorry.' Rachel was sobbing so hard, protecting her face from yet more blows, that she hardly registered her mother's own low wail of pain.

She couldn't say how long the silence between them lasted, but when she glanced up, she could see tears on her mother's cheeks. As their eyes met, she suddenly pulled Rachel into a stranglehold.

'You must never tell anyone about this. Never tell Bill, or that wretched boy. It will be our secret, Rachel, do you understand?' Rachel could feel something inside her squirming as she caught the gist of what her mother was saying, before she said it. 'Nobody need ever know. We'll get rid of it. I'll arrange it and then it'll be all over.'

'Mum, no, please, no.'

Rachel tried to break away, her sobs turning into cold terror. But her mother didn't hear her. Instead, she held her in a vice-like grip forcing Rachel's head on to her knee.

'My little girl. There, there. You're still my little girl. It's not your fault. It's all going to be all right now. You'll see.'

Rachel bolted for the back door, as soon as her mother had left her to open up the shop. Her only thought had been to get to Tony as fast as possible. She didn't stop to put on a coat, but ran blindly into the rain.

Tony was sweeping the water away from the concrete slab outside his hut, when Rachel reached him. She collapsed into his arms, her clothes sticking to her body, her teeth chattering.

'What's happened?' he asked, his voice panicked as he grabbed the top of her arms. He looked into her face, tentatively touching her split lip. 'Who did this to you?'

'She found out,' Rachel sobbed. 'She found out.'

'Who? Who found out.'

'Mum.' Rachel burst into fresh tears, thinking again about her mother striking her. 'I hate her. I hate her so much! I wish she was dead.'

'She found out about us? How? Who told her?'

Rachel swiped at her tears. She had to be brave. Only Tony would understand. He had to. He was her last chance. Oh God. What if he left her? What if he didn't want her? What if he didn't want the . . . what then?

She could feel him gripping her shoulders and she forced herself to look up into his face. She had nowhere else to run. He was her last chance.

'Oh, Tony, it's worse. So much worse than you think.'

'What do you mean?'

'She found out about the baby.'

Tony seemed to stop breathing. He didn't let go of her shoulders.

'Our baby? You mean you're . . . ?'

347

Rachel nodded. She was shaking. 'She wants me to get rid of it. She told me never to tell you. She hit me. She, she . . .' Rachel burst into fresh sobs again.

Tony folded her into his arms, so that her face was buried against his chest. 'She said that?' he asked.

'Oh, Tony. I didn't want to tell you like this.'

'Shhh. Don't cry. Please don't cry. You leave it to me,' he said. 'You leave everything to me.'

# *Chapter XIX*

## Palma, Present Day

Laurie drove the red hire car into the concrete maze of roads around Palma airport. She'd arrived in a taxi from the villa and had intended to get one back once she'd picked up her father, but she'd changed her mind. It would be foolish not to have transport on today of all days. So this, an outrageously expensive Fiesta, was going to be her getaway vehicle – if it came to that.

It was only ten in the morning, but it was going to be one of the hottest days of the summer – even by Mallorcan standards – according to the staff in the car-hire office. The sun was already relentless, making her feel dry-throated and nervous as if she were being picked out by a spot-light. She glanced at the temperature gauge on the car and saw that it had already crept passed forty degrees.

Outside, the palm trees were the only things that seemed to be motionless beneath the ultra bright sky. Everything else, from the pavement to the idling coaches in the car park, vibrated in a mirage of heat. By the airport terminal, Laurie could see gangs of holidaymakers stepping out of the air-conditioned arrivals hall. Like disorientated insects, they seemed to dither and wilt, losing any sense of direction.

Laurie knew just how they felt, but today she had to remain focused. Dipping past a No Entry sign, she took a short cut and veered across the car park to a stop. She turned off the engine and swore at the heat, fighting against it. She was sweating all over now and her legs felt as if they were melting on to the black seat. Pulling up her straw handbag from the footwell of the passenger seat, she took out her bandanna and wiped her face and neck. The sooner she got inside the better.

But the cool air inside the terminal didn't diminish her jittery nerves, as she looked up the flight arrivals information on the TV screen and saw that her father's flight was due to land in forty minutes. Forty minutes! Forty minutes was nothing. So little time until . . .

Suddenly, the reality of the situation hit her and for a moment Laurie thought she might faint. She grabbed the water bottle out of her bag and took a sip of the lukewarm liquid, but it didn't quell the anxiety she felt pumping through her. Every instinct told her that she was making a monstrous mistake.

Behind the glass screen, she could see the busy baggage carousels surrounded by crowds of stressed passengers jostling for their suitcases. The only people who seemed totally unfazed were the official airport staff, who moved around in their uniforms at a nonchalant pace, unperturbed by the hustle and bustle around them and the seemingly urgent overhead announcements in Spanish.

Laurie felt utterly trapped. There was nowhere to run to. How the hell had she got herself into this mess? What the hell had she been thinking? Her father was coming for a whole week, under the impression that they were going to spend a quiet holiday together. She hadn't given one hint of the surprise she had in store for him, when she'd spoken to him a few days ago. Instead, she'd listened to him talk about his expensive flight and the fact that this would be his first solo trip abroad since her mother had died, two facts that had made Laurie cringe to her core.

But now? Now it was a million times worse. Now, not only had Rachel arrived early this morning, full of excitement about being reunited with her brother, but everything had happened with Sam. Laurie had barely spoken to her aunt before she'd left the house. She hadn't even been able to look her in the eye. Because there was every chance that in a few hours Rachel may just hate her guts.

And her father would too.

Laurie wanted to cry. How had she managed to let Rachel persuade her into doing this? Could the timing possibly be worse? Did Rachel really think that Bill would take one look at her and forgive whatever differences there were between them? And even if, by the remotest chance, they did kiss and make up, what would they both say when they found out about Laurie and Sam? Wouldn't that rip them apart all over again?

This was all her own fault, Laurie panicked. She should have put Rachel off the idea of a reconciliation right at the start. She shouldn't have let her get her hopes up. Now she remembered with searing clarity her father's reaction when Laurie had mentioned his sister. He would never forgive Rachel, because the truth was that he hated her.

And she knew, standing in the arrivals hall, that once Bill realised the level of Laurie's deception, he might go through with his implied threat. He might cut her off, too. OK, so her father loved her, she knew that, but she'd also discovered that she knew very little else about him. After all, he was stubborn enough to keep his family a secret for fifty years. And if he was stubborn enough for that, he was stubborn enough to never speak to his only daughter ever again.

She thought back to their first argument after Rachel

had called when she'd been at her father's house for Sunday lunch. It seemed so long ago. But after all this time, she could finally see why her father had been so angry. He'd made a decision to cut off his family all those years ago and had stuck by it and created a new family of his own. Just as she now wanted to with Sam.

Sam. Laurie's stomach lurched at the very thought of him. How would her father, or Rachel, ever understand the kind of all-consuming desperate love she felt for him? Her father wasn't a passionate kind of person. He'd never lost love the way that she had, once. So how would he begin to understand that she was prepared to risk everything – even her only true family – not to lose it again? And Rachel? Well, Laurie couldn't even begin to imagine what Rachel was going to say.

'Sam, oh, Sam, where are you?' she muttered to herself. She hadn't spoken to him since he'd left her yesterday and she was desperate to hear his voice, desperate for reassurance. But there'd been nothing. No word, even after Laurie's conversation with Claire. And that was her fault, too, no doubt, because in her anguish, her phone had broken after she'd thrown it against the wall. Now she marvelled at the roller coaster of emotions she'd experienced since that moment.

If Sam had come to the villa right after her phone call with Claire, Laurie was sure she would have beaten him up. She felt utterly betrayed, racked with jealousy and guilt. She couldn't shake the image of him naked near Claire. And after everything Roz had said, Laurie was convinced that Sam was going to break her heart all over again.

But as the night had worn on, her anger had turned into distress. As she thought of Sam back at home with Claire, she'd started to feel sorry for him. She'd tried to put herself in his position and could only imagine that he was having a terrible time. What if he was having to make small talk with people he hated, when he knew Laurie was waiting for him? What if he felt trapped? What if everything Claire was saying was making it worse?

There were so many what ifs that Laurie's head felt as if it had been scrambling, like a computer trying to defend itself against a virus. She'd forced herself to stop panicking and get practical. She had to think of her immediate course of action. And that was to prepare to leave – in a hurry, if necessary.

Which was why she had packed up all her clothes, gathered up her possessions from around the villa and had gone down to the boathouse as soon as dawn had started to break, in order to dismantle the makeshift studio. She had to get away. Whether together with Sam or alone, she would have to leave and start again somewhere else.

Yet, as Laurie had stacked up the paintings in the dim light of the boathouse, she'd realised that she couldn't handle the possibility of her move being alone. She loved Sam. She needed him and wanted him. She stroked her hand along the side of the boat, remembering how they'd made love there just the day before, remembering his touch, his smell, the sound of his breathing. And she made a vow there and then to banish her doubts. She knew that having them was just damaging all their chances of being together.

But still a part of her head nagged her. There was Archie to consider. That's what Sam had said and it had been at that exact moment that he'd suddenly seemed uncertain. Would Sam really leave him? Would he make that level of sacrifice for her? And more to the point, was it fair to ask him to?

If she was being hard-hearted, she could convince herself of the facts. Children were resilient. They could bounce back from broken families, couldn't they? Archie would be fine, after a while. But then, she thought about Archie being alone in Mallorca with his mother and how rejected he'd feel. And then she thought about Sam trying to say goodbye to his son and it made her eyes fill with tears. Archie needed Sam – anyone could see it. In the dawn light, Laurie stood and looked out one last time at the sea. The sky was starting to lighten, the stars above the horizon slowly fading. She watched as the flat sea and sky turned through shades of milky blue to pale oranges. She could smell the promise of a hot day in the air.

She'd been so happy in the villa, being a recluse and working away at her paintings. But she was ready to go now. The sunrises and sunsets she'd painted seemed now to her to be markers in time rather than a true expression of anything creative. She felt as if she'd been on hold, waiting.

But now she knew what she'd been waiting for, now that she'd found Sam again, Rachel's villa had started to feel like a trap and she needed to be free. She needed to be the person she was going to be with Sam and she knew that it was impossible in the context of her family.

She could feel her need to escape right down in her bones as if there were some internal force egging her on. She was amazed that she'd come such a full turn. All her life she thought she'd wanted a large family and discovering Rachel had seemed to fulfil such a deep-down need in her. But she could see now that all she'd really needed was someone of her own. And a big family was no substitute. In fact, being part of Rachel's life brought more complications and obligations than she could ever have envisaged and now all she wanted was to get back to her life. With Sam. And with Archie, if that was what it took.

She'd been such an idiot! There was so much that seemed to have been left unsaid in the hazy passion of the afternoon. So much that was so important. She hadn't told Sam that she'd be prepared to include Archie in their plans. That she would do her best to love him like her own child, if it meant that she and Sam could be together.

She allowed herself to fantasise, imagining herself kitting Archie out in his little school uniform, walking with him to the local school. She imagined decorating his room for him, making him happy and secure. And she imagined having her own children with Sam. Of making brothers and sisters for Archie.

Who was she kidding, she thought, snapping back to reality. She'd never even changed a nappy! Her married friends teased her about being hopeless and tongue-tied with their kids. She'd never been asked to be a godparent, or been considered patient enough to babysit once for any of the kids she knew. So how could she possibly expect to step into a mother's shoes? Claire might have her faults, but compared to Laurie she was a saint. And what's more, Claire was Archie's mother. Archie was hers. She wouldn't want to let him go any more than Sam. Whichever way she looked at it, it was bad.

As Laurie had come back up to the house, she'd still had no answers, but at least there was resolve in her heart. She loved Sam. That was all that mattered. And if she held on to her faith in him, she was sure she would be able to deal with anything that life threw at them.

But now, a few hours later, Laurie felt her confidence wavering. Her heart seemed to skip a beat as she looked through the glass in the arrivals hall towards passport control and spotted her father queuing. He was wearing a new straw panama hat and a white shirt, the short sleeves ironed into neat turn-ups. His passport was sticking out of his top pocket and the sunshade part of his glasses was hinged up as he consulted his miniature guide to Mallorca. She knew him well enough to know that he was planning on saying the appropriate phrase to the passport officer.

To everyone else, he looked like just another holiday-maker, a retired man, but to her, he looked like the most precious person, and she realised now how much she'd missed him. She felt tears stinging her eyes. She was about to hurt him so much. She was about to destroy all his trust in her. Could she really do it?

'Dad,' she said, reaching up to hug him, a few minutes later. She wondered whether he could sense how tense she was. She felt as if she were approaching the top of another death bend in the roller coaster. 'You're here.'

'Laurie,' he said, kissing her on the cheek. 'You look tanned.'

She took one of his bags, dragging it on its wheels across the polished floor. She'd been dreading this moment, but as he started to talk about the Residents' Association and the neighbours she barely knew and how the strawberries had flourished in the record-breaking English summer, she was taken aback by the normality of him. It made his visit so painfully real.

'How's the work been going?' he asked, when he'd exhausted his round-up.

'Oh, you know. Good. I've done about fifteen paintings in the last few months.'

'Quite a collection. I can't wait to see them.'

Laurie hesitated by the revolving door. She begged him

to see into her eyes, to read all the anxiety in her mind and to fix it all. Instead, he seemed to take her silence as his cue for an apology. He took off his glasses. She noticed how many wrinkles there were around his eyes.

'I suppose we should clear the air, before we go any further,' he said, with a sigh, as if she'd challenged him. 'Now I know I overreacted a bit when we last saw each other, but you see, I was just so worried that you'd get involved with Rachel. But you've been such a sensible girl as always and got yourself out here and put some distance on the whole situation.'

'Dad, I –'

'I know you're sorry, Laurie, you don't have to say it. Inviting me here was enough. We should never have argued. It made me feel terrible. But there you go. And now I'm here and we can have a lovely break together.'

Laurie opened her mouth to speak, but couldn't find the words.

'Come on,' he continued, squeezing the top of her arm. 'Let's not say any more about it. I want you to show me this place you've been raving about.'

And with that, he pushed her through the doorway into the blazing day.

# Chapter XX

**Stepmouth, 6.30 p.m., 15 August 1953**

Tony stared through the onslaught of rain, but there was still no sign of Rachel. He was standing pressed up against the blistered wooden doors of the garage on Lydgate Lane, sheltering beneath the lip of its corrugated-iron roof.

Water spattered down over its edge and on to the toes of his best black leather boots. The moaning rise and fall of the wind came at him in blasts, howling wolfishly down the funnel of the street, forcing him to pull his cap down tight on his head.

It had been a crazy day already and now Tony was worried that it was getting worse. He wasn't superstitious, but even he had to admit that something wasn't right. The air felt wrong: dense, heavy. His temples had been throbbing for hours and now his ears had started to ache.

'Plain weird' was how Emily had put it before he'd said goodbye to her two hours ago. 'The sooner this day's done with, the better.'

He'd kissed her on the cheek when he'd said goodbye, something he'd never done before. She'd looked at him strangely, but whatever she might have guessed, she'd kept it to herself. She'd been a good friend. He'd nearly told her everything.

Plain weird . . . Well, she'd been right enough about that. By ten this morning the sky had switched from blue to white to grey. It had grown so gloomy by noon that

358

they'd needed to switch on the lights inside just to see. Then he and Emily had huddled by the kitchen window's whitewashed sill, and watched in wonder as a vast cumulus nimbus cloud with a mauve-and-purple base had settled over the town, stretching up into the sky. It had been the shape of a hammer, balanced and ready to fall.

He looked up now. But if the hammer cloud was still there, it was now hidden behind a greater mass of churning grey. Tony shivered. The quicker Rachel got here, the better for them both.

The spring of apprehension inside him was tightening into alarm. What if something had happened? What if she was there at Vale Supplies right now with her mother and Bill? What if they were keeping her there? Or what if she'd changed her mind? Tony rubbed his freezing hands together. How much longer should he give her? Another five minutes? Less? And then what? Go there? To Vale Supplies? Go there and get her and bring her back?

It was almost as if she'd heard his barrage of questions, because there she suddenly was, in a shining green raincoat and a waxed yellow sailor's hat which he recognised from her room, lurching awkwardly towards him under the weight of the red carpetbag she was carrying.

Waving, he charged towards her through the overflowing potholes and swelling puddles. Taking the bag from her, he led her back by the hand until they stood beneath the shelter of the garage roof. He wrapped his arms around her and kissed her wet face, pressing his shivering body against hers.

'No one saw?' he asked.

'I'm scared.'

*I'm scared, too*, he wanted to answer. He was: more scared than he'd been in his life, frightened of the looming gap which their future had just become. But what would be the point of telling her that? It would only make her feel worse. Show doubt and, chances were, they'd both end up in a panic. He had to pretend to be strong. For them both. For all three of them, he thought, aware of her midriff pressed up against his, absurdly conscious of what it contained. They were a family now and they were under threat.

'Did you get them?' he asked.

She nodded. 'I still don't know if this is a good idea . . .'

'We've got no choice.'

It was true. He hadn't slept a wink last night, racking his brains for an alternative plan to the one they'd concocted after she'd told him she was going to have their child. But there was no other plan that would work. Rachel's mother would never change her mind. About Tony or the baby. No choice: that's what they'd been given. No choice for Rachel to stay behind. No choice for Tony to keep on working with Emily. No choice to do anything but run. Rachel knelt down and unzipped her carpetbag. She rummaged through it and produced a set of keys.

'This is it, then,' she said.

Even in the gloom, he could see the sparkle in her eyes. What they were doing was frightening, all right. But it was exciting, too. He checked up and down the lane, but the only person he saw was the blurry figure of a man a good hundred feet away, darting between buildings for shelter. Tony turned and matched a key to the padlock on the heavy wooden garage doors. Within seconds, they were inside.

It stood there in the centre of the room, as pristine as a newly minted coin, the Jowett Jupiter: Bill Vale's pride and joy. Not for much longer, though, Tony thought, breathing in the warm oily air and hurrying over to the car.

He unlocked it and slung in his bag, Rachel's too, then climbed inside behind the steering wheel and looked over the controls. The set-up wasn't so different from his step-father's Vauxhall in which he'd learnt to drive. He tried the key and the engine started first go.

'He's going to kill us when he finds out, you know,' said Rachel, getting in next to him.

'He's going to have to find us first.' Tony switched on the headlights.

'We could still catch a bus . . .' Rachel's voice was now fluttering with panic. 'There'll be one leaving –'

'No. The moment they realise we've run, they'll think we're on the bus and they'll call ahead and have the police pick us up.'

'But –'

He reached for her hand and squeezed it hard. 'We'll take the quiet roads across the moor. Let them search the bus routes all they like. Bill won't notice the car's gone till morning and we'll be long gone by then.'

She took a deep breath. 'Tell me, Tony: everything is going to be OK, isn't it?'

He nodded and put the car into what he guessed was reverse. He looked over his shoulder and eased out the clutch. The car leapt forward and stalled.

They looked down at the gearstick and then at each other. For the first time since Rachel had fought her mother the day before, they both burst out laughing.

'Nothing like a smooth start,' he joked, finding reverse for real this time and slowly backing out of the garage and into the lane.

If anything, the rain seemed to have intensified since they'd been inside, rattling down now on the car roof, so that they had to shout at one another to be heard.

'How long do you think it's going to take us to get there?' Rachel asked.

To Scotland, she meant, of course. To Gretna Green. Because that was where he was taking her. To the one place in Great Britain where he could marry a seventeen-year-old woman like Rachel Vale without her parents' permission. They were to elope, then. And make them and the baby safe. This was the plan they'd come up with. And after that? They could sell the car, perhaps. And he had the money he'd saved while working for Emily, which would last them for a while. Then they'd improvise. He'd make it work. He'd take care of his new wife and child like no man had ever done before.

'I don't know,' he answered, staring ahead as the headlights cut a path through the swirling opaque rush of rain. Neither Tony nor Rachel had ever been out of the county before, let alone anywhere as distant as Scotland. He'd only thought as far as taking the car, and driving west across the moor to fool anyone following, before looping back round towards Bristol and the east. 'A few days,' he guessed. 'We'll need to pick up a map somewhere along the way.'

They drove slowly, because they had no other option. Rain drenched the windscreen as quickly as the wipers cleared it off. At the end of Lydgate Lane, they turned right. The streets were empty, the same as they'd been a year ago when the TV mast across the Bristol Channel had started transmitting and brought television to the town for the very first time. He remembered huddling in the town hall that night, along with a couple of hundred other people, marvelling as the miracle arrived. He'd thought the world had changed that day. But it had nothing on now.

He would have rather raced, of course, and got as much

distance between him and the town as possible. But maybe it was better this way, crawling along past the white clapboard cottages of Granville Road which ran parallel with the high street. There was certainly less chance of drawing attention, which meant less chance of someone spotting them and calling the police. Already, he was breaking the law, running away like this. If they caught him, he'd be charged. Through the rain, the whole town looked smudged, like a charcoal drawing. Like it was disappearing into a fog.

He fastened the top button of his old waxed poacher's jacket which he'd gone back to his mother's house to collect less than an hour before.

She'd been leaning over the stove as he'd stepped in through the kitchen door, stirring a saucepan which he knew from the smell had contained the thick Scotch broth with which he'd grown up.

'You look like you could do with a bowl' was all she'd said when he'd cleared his throat and she'd turned round to see him standing there. 'Don said you were doing a good job of looking after yourself, but you look thin to me.'

'I've come to say goodbye,' he'd replied.

'Isn't that a bit late? You've been gone for five months.'

'I mean for good.'

'More trouble?' she'd asked reproachfully.

'Not the kind you think. No.' He'd just got on and said it: 'I'm going to be a father.'

The colour had drained from her face. She'd stared at him open-mouthed. 'Who is she?' she'd then asked.

'I can't tell you yet.' He'd decided against it already. It would have led to too much talk, and he hadn't got the time. 'But I will,' he promised her. 'I'll write to you as soon as I can.'

Tears had filled her eyes. 'But you're only a boy.'

'No, Mum, I'm going to be a dad and I'm going to be a good one. I'm sorry . . .' he said. 'I'm sorry things didn't work out for me the way you wanted . . .'

As soon as he'd spoken the word 'sorry' her mouth had seemed to stretch downwards, like rubber. She'd covered her face with her hand and he'd walked over to her and held her like a parent would a child, as she'd sobbed into his arm.

Now he followed the curve of the road round to where it terminated at a crossroads at the end of the high street. So far so good: they'd yet to see another vehicle, let alone a person. The high street ran to the left, its neat row of shops and houses backing on to the River Step, all the way to Harbour Bridge.

Two doors down the high street was Vale Supplies. Silently, they both stared at its dimly lit, weeping windows.

Tony rested his hand on Rachel's leg. She was shaking.

'Keep going,' she said.

Straight ahead over the crossroads was the great stone humpback of South Bridge, leading to the east side of town. But Tony turned right and they set off up the steep Barnstaple Road.

Neither of them spoke until they reached the top of Summerglade Hill. A thin film of water covered the road, glistening like oil. Tony glanced in the rear-view mirror. A mile away, eight hundred feet below, was the town, its houses huddled together in the encroaching darkness and strangling rain. He wondered if he'd ever see it again.

He thought of the twins, further along the road at Brookford. His mother would have tucked them up safe in bed by now, maybe even told them that he'd left town. They'd been out with Don when he'd called round. He'd write to them just as soon as he could. He'd write to them all to let them know that he was happy and safe.

He thought about Keith, about writing to him as well. He'd have to tell him about Rachel. And he'd have to tell him to stay away. They were going to have a child and Tony could never tell that child what his brother had done.

He turned off on to the coast road which ran along the moor.

'Still scared?' he asked Rachel.

'Yes.'

They were driving at forty miles an hour now, straddling the middle of the bumpy road. There wasn't a chance, Tony reckoned, of encountering another car up here. The wind – suddenly heavy up here on the open ground – began violently buffeting the car.

'Don't be,' he said, as a sudden sense of freedom burst inside him. He glanced across at her shadowed form. 'This isn't the end of anything,' he told her. 'It's just the st—'

The noise she made was soft, not a scream at all, in fact. More an expression of mild surprise. Automatically, he reached for the brake.

As they hit it – whatever it was Rachel had seen on the road ahead of them – all Tony was aware of was his body twisting violently, before his world turned utterly black.

# Chapter XXI

**Mallorca, Present Day**

At Sa Costa, Rachel stood beneath the whirring wooden ceiling fan in her bedroom, feeling like a teenager again. She hadn't felt this sick with nerves since . . . well, since the night of the flood. She could hardly breathe with the expectation of what was about to happen. Laurie was picking Bill up from the airport and bringing him back to her. Right now. She hardly knew what to do with herself.

She was wearing her coolest summer outfit – the thin white muslin trousers and tunic top that she'd had handmade in Morocco and leather thong sandals – but even so, she was uncomfortably hot. And she loved the heat. She shook out her top, away from her body, the silver bauble on her necklace tinkling, along with the charm bracelet she was wearing for luck. Then she reclipped the stray hair that was flying in the draught from the fan into the large tortoiseshell clip at the nape of her neck.

Once again, she couldn't resist angling down the wooden slatted shutters on her window and looking out on to the driveway below, but it remained empty. Everything was still, not even a murmur of sea breeze in the trees. Even the birds seemed to be having an unusually quiet siesta. It felt as if the whole house and its surroundings were holding their breath. The only sound was from the sprinklers which were working overtime in the gardens. She watched as some of the overspill hit the sparkling tarmac, the water evaporating immediately, like footprints in wet sand.

Rachel turned away from the window. The shutters cut the bedroom into diagonal stripes of light and shade. She walked from the window to the French-made teak bed. The thin red silk quilt was folded back on itself to reveal a monogrammed linen sheet covered in some of the framed photographs she'd brought up from downstairs.

She'd done so on Laurie's suggestion, so that when Bill first came into the house he wouldn't realise it was Rachel's, until Laurie had had the chance to explain properly. Rachel picked up one of the framed photographs she'd taken from the kitchen wall and dusted its surface with her hand. She couldn't remember who'd taken it, but it must have been either Christopher or Nick. It was of her and Tony a couple of years ago here at the villa. He had his arm around Rachel, pulling her in close and they were both laughing, their faces tanned. They looked like young lovers, not the grandparents they were. It had never crossed her mind back then to think that one day so soon she'd be left on her own.

Rachel touched Tony's smile. Was she really doing the right thing? she wondered, her nerve wavering. Tony had always been so adamant in his burial of the past. He'd been so confident with the decision he'd made to shut the door on that part of their lives and to move on. A decision he'd never once, to her knowledge, questioned. She was the one who'd always been peeping back through the keyhole, in secret.

She knew that Tony would be furious with her for having such a point to prove, after all this time, but Rachel knew it was too important to obey Tony's wishes any longer. Because even if Tony hadn't cared about it while he was alive, it was important to her to show Bill that Tony had made a success out of his life. She wanted to prove to Bill that Tony hadn't turned out like his brother.

And for herself, she wanted Bill to see the success she'd achieved with Ararat. The amazing legacy she'd now handed over to Sam. For what? she wondered. Why did her brother's opinion of her matter after all this time? Why did she seek his approval, when her success was affirmed to her every day?

Because she was proud, she admitted to herself, practising the speech she was going to deliver. She was proud of her children. She wanted Bill to meet them all. She wanted him to see how stable and secure they all were. She wanted to prove to him that she wasn't controlling and judgemental as their mother had been, but that she had a special bond with each and every member of her family and that they embraced her being part of their lives.

And most of all, she wanted Bill to know that he could . . . *would* be part of her happy, loving, open family, if he'd only say the word. Just as Rachel had grown to love Laurie, then perhaps Bill would learn to love and respect her family, too. She and her brother were both getting older, after all. Surely, in their twilight years, it would be nice to think of them sharing the bond of family, of having found each other again.

It seemed to Rachel that the void Tony had left in her life had never felt bigger than it had in recent weeks. She'd been through so much anguish, so much pain, so much grieving. Would spending time with Bill make her feel better? she wondered. Even a tiny bit? Because even a tiny bit would help.

Rachel placed the photograph on the bedside table and listened, as she heard a car in the distance. But it passed the gateway and, as it did, she realised she'd been holding her breath. This was no good, she decided. This waiting around was disastrous for her blood pressure. It was pointless hovering by the window, waiting for him to come. It felt too weird. As if she were waiting for a long-lost love.

Rachel knew from her previous visit that Laurie had taken over the top attic room, so when she pushed open the door, on a last-minute inspection of the house, she was expecting to see Laurie's clothes and belongings everywhere. Instead, she stopped in the doorway, as she saw Laurie's suitcase and bags stacked by the door, her canvases leaning neatly against the wardrobe.

What was going on? She'd only seen her niece briefly this morning, but even so, Laurie hadn't mentioned that she'd packed up. Was there something wrong?

No, there must be a perfectly logical explanation, she thought, as she went back to her own room. Maybe Laurie was just being her usual considerate self. Maybe she felt it was better for Rachel and Bill to have some time alone. And anyway, Laurie had her own life to lead. She was probably anxious to get home to James. That was it, Rachel thought, feeling relieved. She wanted to be with James. But, even so, it would be ridiculous for Laurie to leave now, especially when Rachel had a surprise for her. She'd asked Anton, her and Tony's art dealer, to come out later on in the week to see Laurie's paintings. It was the least Rachel had been able to do for Laurie, considering all her niece had done for her.

Just at that moment, she heard a car turning into the driveway. She raced to the window. She watched as Laurie stepped out on to the drive from what she assumed must be Bill's hire car.

Then the passenger door opened and Rachel saw an

elderly man supporting himself on the edge of the car door, as he got out. When he removed his hat and looked up at the house, she gasped, putting her hand to her mouth to stop herself from calling out Bill's name.

It was such a shock seeing him after all these years. In her mind's eye, when she'd been addressing him, rehearsing what she was going to say, she'd imagined his twenty-six-year-old face. But he was old, she realised, watching as he fanned his face with his straw hat. She looked down on him, recognising his features, yet feeling the weight of time so acutely she couldn't stop the tears in her eyes from spilling out on to her cheeks.

She flattened herself against the cool brick of the bedroom wall, out of sight of the window, not knowing what to do. Why was she being so childish? It was as if Bill were in charge of her home again.

But this was the way Laurie wanted it to be. Laurie had insisted that she wanted to talk to her father and settle him in first, before she announced that Rachel was in the house.

But discovering Laurie's bags all packed up had shaken Rachel's confidence. Now that he was here, what if it was harder than she thought to convince Bill that they should heal their past? What if he was happy to remain stubborn and not speak to her for the rest of her life, as he'd once declared was his intention?

She glanced across to the dressing table by the door. On it were all the returned letters she'd written to Bill over the years, which she'd brought from Dreycott Manor. She tiptoed over to it and picked up the letters and newspaper cuttings.

She looked at herself in the full-length mirror, smoothing her hair for the fiftieth time and touching up her make-up. She wondered, now that she'd seen Bill, how he would see her. She'd spent so many years trying to retain her youth, but she knew she hadn't really escaped time. She could see it on her face. She thought of all the tragedies she'd assimilated into her life: her father, the flood, her mother, Anna and now Tony. Heartbreak after heartbreak. It was amazing she'd survived at all. And now she hoped to cover it all up with make-up. It seemed laughable.

And pointless. A lifetime's worth of highs and lows had become part of who she was. And she'd lived through them all, because she'd always had hope. She'd always managed to tell herself that however bad things got, the future would somehow be brighter.

Now, as she took a deep breath, she forced herself to reach her last reserve of hope. Bill was here. And that meant that she would find peace at last and lay the ghosts of the past to rest.

She glanced at the newspaper articles in her hand. She thought of the first time she'd seen the facts of the flood in print, the first time she'd seen the list of the dead in these very cuttings. It had been so raw, but now, over time, she could barely remember half of the people the newspaper mentioned.

In the meantime, generations had come and gone. These newspapers she'd kept and cherished would have been through someone else's compost heap several times over, would have served to mop up the floor of a hundred rabbit cages, no doubt.

But it hadn't stopped mattering to her. It hadn't stopped being real. Of course she hadn't thought about it every day, but it had always been there: the tragedy she'd walked away from.

That was it, she thought, straightening up. That was

how she would set the tone of her reconciliation with Bill. She would start by thanking him. She would be gracious and magnanimous. She would start by acknowledging that he'd helped save her life once. Was it too late to thank him? Was fifty years too long? she wondered.

Fifty years. Could it really be that long ago? She closed her eyes for a second, listening to the whirring of the ceiling fan, the noise blurring with a vivid memory of being in Bill's car, up on the moor, on that terrible night.

# Chapter XXII

**Stepmouth, 7.30 p.m., 15 August 1953**

It was ink black, black as Guinness, black as the night-time sea.

The rain beat down like a thousand tiny drumsticks against the walls and windows and roof, muffling the slow tick-tock of the clock. Crouching over the stove, Bill felt for the match head with his fingertip, then scraped it across the big box of cook's matches. A phosphorescent flame flared up. Yellow light flickered nervously across the kitchen. Shadows danced.

'Have you found them?' Mrs Vale called from upstairs.

Bill could smell the lamb stew left over in the pan from supper. 'Yes,' he shouted back.

He dug out a fistful of candles from the table drawer, along with an army surplus battery-powered torch, which he briefly tested, before pocketing. He set about lighting candles, melting their bases and sticking them to saucers. The shadows shrank back into the corners. The whiff of wick and wax filled the air.

Out in the corridor, Bill examined the fuse box beneath the stairs, but could see nothing wrong. The town received its electricity from the power station further up the valley at Watersbind. All this water and debris, Bill thought, careering through the turbines, maybe that was what was to blame.

Mrs Vale was waiting for him upstairs in her bedroom,

sitting in front of her dressing table, with her nightgown on and a black crocheted shawl around her shoulders. She'd been just about to have a bath when the electricity had cut out.

'Put it on the window sill, will you?' she asked, twisting her wheelchair round to face that way. She smiled at Bill, comforted by the warm glow of the candle he'd brought with him. 'I hate the dark.'

Bill did as he was told and Mrs Vale wheeled herself over and peered outside. The high street was wrapped in shadow as thick as wool. You could see candles and oil lamps glowing like fire embers in the windows of the buildings opposite. The power was down across the whole town, then.

'What a filthy night,' his mother complained.

'Worst August on record,' he told her. He'd heard it on the radio that afternoon. There'd been six and a half inches of rain in the last two weeks alone. Half the crops in the county had been decimated, the news presenter had reported. A river bank had burst over in Moxborough Valley, drowning six rare piebald ponies which had been put out to pasture on the flats.

'I think it might be a good idea to go and bring Rachel back from Pearl's,' his mother said. 'I don't like the look of it out there. It's going to turn worse before it gets better.'

'I'll go now,' he answered, taking out the torch and switching it on.

He was already dressed to go out: boots on, raincoat tied. He'd been planning to call in on Emily to see that she was all right. He'd tried telephoning her already, but the line was dead, the telephone exchange down.

Throughout the day, he'd been monitoring the condition of the River Step where it ran between their two streets. It had grown turbulent and swollen. All afternoon, it had risen steadily. There was nothing to worry about yet, he didn't think, though the waters were blackening, heavy with peat. But if the rain carried on this way for many more hours, then there'd be a real danger of the river breaking its banks and seeping out across both his and Emily's backyards.

Bill had a stack of sandbags left over from the air-raid shelter he and his father had built in the war. He'd already dragged two across the yard door just in case. He'd wheelbarrow more round to Emily if she hadn't already taken precautions of her own.

As he hung an oil lamp from the ladder leading to Rachel's room, Bill shivered, remembering the water damage he'd seen over at the nearby village of Castleton as a child, after the 1933 storm. He'd driven out there on the old cart with his dad to deliver blankets after the swollen River Lox had forced people from their homes and left their possessions rotting and sodden. He hated the thought of all the work Emily had put into the Sea Catch Café going to waste for want of a little preparation.

Downstairs, he pulled out his set of keys to unlock the alley door, but the door started to shake, being pounded by something from outside. Bill froze. Then the noise stopped, then started again.

Quickly, Bill unlocked and opened the door. He shone the torch outside. What he saw made his heart lurch. A man – he didn't recognise who it was at first – was slumped against the door frame, clinging on to it like he was about to collapse. The man's head hung low. His fingernails were filthy and his black hair soaked. As the man looked up, Bill saw that his lip was split wide open and a great scab of freshly congealed blood clung like an obscene parasite to his jaw. He was out of breath. He looked like he'd been in a fight.

'If it's help you're after, you can forget it,' Bill told him the moment he recognised him.

The man showed no surprise at Bill's welcome. But he didn't move either. He opened his mouth to speak but he was panting too heavily and whatever it was he said came out in a wheeze.

'Scat,' Bill told him, starting to shut the door.

'No,' the man gasped, lurching forward and unsteadily planting his foot in the doorway, 'you've got to come with me.'

'Like hell I –' But then Bill saw that it wasn't only rain running down the man's face, but tears as well.

'It's Rachel,' the man said. 'There's been an accident.'

Bill Vale stared with disbelief into Tony Glover's eyes.

'Who's there?' Mrs Vale called from upstairs. 'What is it, Bill? What's going on?'

Bill grabbed Glover, spinning him round and slamming him up against the soaking outside wall. His voice turned sharp and cold. 'Tell me what you've done.'

Glover's eyelids drooped like he was about to pass out. He stank of fuel. All around them, drainpipes cascaded like waterfalls. 'We were eloping,' Glover croaked, 'we were in the car . . .'

*Eloping.* Bill's expression crumpled. Glover . . . eloping with Rachel? But how was that –

'A baby . . . we're having a baby . . .'

Bill jammed the torch up under Glover's throat. 'Where is she?'

The savageness of the question seemed to straighten Glover out. 'Up on the moor,' he said. 'I left her there and came to get help. You were the nearest . . .' As Glover

376

looked Bill in the eyes, strength seemed to gather in him. He struggled from Bill's grip. 'Don't you get it?' he snarled, throwing his arms up as he stumbled back. 'We crashed. *I* crashed the car. She's unconscious. She needs a doctor. Now.'

This last word came out as a roar.

Now.

Glover was right. They needed to act immediately. Think of Rachel, Bill told himself. Only her. Forget everything else you've just heard.

Rachel . . . unconscious . . . up on the moor . . . he started running through the options. They could pick up Pearl's dad, Dr Glaister, on the way. But the doctor was away at a conference . . . Pearl had said so that afternoon when she'd popped in to see Rachel . . . That left Dr Barnard, who lived in a hamlet two miles out on the east side of town. But with the telephone lines down, there was no way of knowing if he was at home . . . he might be out on a call . . . And they were wasting precious time already. And what if Rachel needed more than a small-town doctor? Then he'd need to get her to Barnstaple General Hospital as quickly as possible . . .

Go to Rachel now, that was the decision Bill made. Get to her as fast as he could. Then he could make his choice, once he saw what sort of state she was in: either to bring her back here into town and search for the doctor, or to rush her to Barnstaple and the surgeons there . . .

'You'd better pray she's all right,' he told Glover.

Glover nodded dumbly back.

'My car's over on Lydgate Lane,' Bill said, turning to run upstairs and get the keys.

Glover shook his head. 'No. We took it. It was your car we crashed.'

Bill said nothing. He didn't care about the car. The thought of Rachel wiped it from his mind.

'Answer me, Bill!' Mrs Vale called again. 'What is it?'

She sounded closer, like she'd moved to the top of the stairs. Bill didn't turn round to look. She'd worry herself sick if he repeated what Glover had just said. Better to lie to her until he knew how bad Rachel was. He stared down the alley and that was when he saw a way to make everything work.

'It's Giles,' he called up through the doorway to his mother, 'he's going over to Lewis Cook's house to see their new television. He's going to give me a lift over to Pearl's house, so I can pick up Rachel.'

Without waiting for a reply, Bill ran through to the shop and grabbed the first-aid kit from underneath the counter.

'Move it,' he told Glover, back outside, pulling the door shut behind him.

'But without a car . . . how –'

The Norton motorbike was too unstable to use to get Rachel, but parked in front of it was a white Citroën delivery van, belonging to Giles Weatherly. The ironmonger, who Bill really had watched set out on foot for Lewis Cook's house over an hour ago, let Bill use the van from time to time for big deliveries, and now Bill reached beneath its front right wheel arch and unhooked the spare keys which he knew Giles kept there.

Bill thought of Emily. The Sea Catch Café was sited next door to Lewis Cook's. All of a sudden, he wanted her close.

'Get in,' Bill ordered Glover, unlocking the door and climbing in.

The electricity flickered back on in the town as Bill pulled out of the alley and on to the high street. The street lamps blazed, restoring a sudden reality to the insanity of the last few minutes. Bill hoped his mother wasn't look-ing down, or if she was, he hoped the old oak tree obscured the fact that it was Tony Glover sitting next to him. It was only then that he realised that, for the first time since his father's murder, he'd left home without locking the alley door behind him. He gripped the steering wheel tighter. Glover's blood from when he'd grabbed him was on his hands.

'Patch your face,' Bill told Glover, taking the first-aid kit from his lap and holding it out to him. But Glover didn't move. Bill shoved the first-aid kit at him.

'I don't matter,' Glover responded. 'Just get to Rachel.'

As he accelerated over the crossroads, Bill glanced left towards South Bridge. For an instant, he imagined it looked awash, as shiny as treacle beneath the street lamps, like the river had already crept up over it and any second now would start spilling out on to the streets. But that couldn't be true, could it? It must have been a trick of the light. The river couldn't possibly have risen up so high so soon.

Forcing the van up Summerglade Hill and into the wall of wind and rain, Bill thought of his mother, alone at home, then of Emily, alone at the Sea Catch Café. He wished he'd called round earlier to see that she was OK. But the sand-bags could wait. Rachel was the priority now.

As the engine screamed in protest and the town dropped away below them, Bill's mind reeled. A baby. A baby. A baby. *His* baby. *Glover's* baby. The thought kept slipping from his mind. He couldn't face it. Glover and his sister. A baby. *Their* baby. Rachel had been eloping with Glover? Glover was the boy she'd been seeing all this time? Had Emily known? Was that why she'd refused to tell him who it was? Had she known they were planning to elope, too?

They reached the hill's summit and turned right on to

the moor road, the same road Bill had driven along with Emily on that hot summery night. He glanced at Glover, at the blood on his face, then down at the blood on his own hands. He pictured him running back towards the town, fighting to get there, fighting to bring help. He thought of Rachel, little Rachel. He didn't want to see her blood. He'd give anything so long as she didn't . . . just so long as she was safe . . .

Suddenly, he didn't care that it was Glover sitting beside him. He couldn't give a damn if Rachel wanted to marry him, have his baby, anything. She could do whatever she wanted. So long as she was OK. So long as nothing had . . . So long as she wasn't already . . .

'There,' Glover shouted, pointing straight ahead.

'Jesus wept,' Bill gasped. A great horse-chestnut tree lay across the road. Buckled, broken and crushed up against it was the torn form of the Jowett Jupiter which Bill and Richard Horner had spent so many months working on.

Desolation . . . even in the storm, Bill knew that this was where Emily had brought him that night in the car.

Before the van had even stopped, Glover was swinging out of the door with the first-aid kit in his hand. Bill slammed on the brakes and climbed out into the gale, running after Glover through the hissing rain. He joined him ten feet from the car's carcass, where Rachel was lying slumped up against the tree's thickened foliage. A red bag was open at her side, its contents – sweater and trousers and shirts – had been thrown haphazardly over Rachel in a frantic attempt to protect her body from the rain.

Glover was down on his knees in the mud, crouching over her, kissing her face, whispering her name. Bill stood behind him, looking down. His little sister wasn't moving.

He realised that Glover was sobbing, desperately, pitifully, now. Bill took the torch from his pocket. He swept its beam across Glover's drenched back and on to the parts of Rachel's face he could see. Her ear was cut and the right side of her face livid and bruised. Still no movement: nothing. Bill reached out to push Glover out of the way.

But then he froze. Because then Rachel stirred. Her lips parted.

'Tony' was the first word she said.

Bill stared at them. These two people together. This unit. Thank God she was all right.

'Can you move?' Glover was asking Rachel. 'Can you move your legs?'

'Yes. It's just my head aches . . . my ribs . . .' Her voice rose up a notch in panic. 'I woke up and you were gone . . . I went to the car and looked for you . . .'

'I went to get help . . . to get your brother . . .'

'Bill?'

Bill wiped the tears from his eyes and leant in so that she could see him. He pressed his hand against her frozen cheek.

'Oh, Bill,' she said, taking his hand in hers and kissing it.

'We're going to drive you to Barnstaple,' he told her.

'No.' Already, she was struggling to get to her feet. Together, Bill and Tony helped her up. 'I want to go home.' She looked back to the road, into the storm. Fear filled her eyes as she turned back. 'It's too dangerous up here.'

Bill stared at the bruising on her head. It wasn't too severe. She might be concussed, but Dr Barnard would be able to deal with that. Rachel was right about the roads. If there was a tree down here, who was to guarantee they'd make it across the moors to Barnstaple at all?

'Home then,' he agreed. Once he got her back to their mother, he could go out looking for Dr Barnard. 'Back where you belong.' He stared at Glover. 'We'll all go home together.'

# *Chapter XXIII*

**Mallorca, Present Day**

'Home,' Archie announced from his seat in the back of the Porsche four-by-four, as Sam switched off the engine.

'Did you enjoy today?' asked Sam, peering round the seat at him. 'Did you have fun?'

'Yes, Daddy. I seed fish.'

'Saw,' Sam corrected him.

'I sawed fish . . .'

'No,' Sam started to correct him again, before his face clouded over with weariness. 'Yes,' he said instead, 'that's right, Archie: you sawed fish.'

They were in the apartment block's underground car park and had just got back from a trip to the Reserva Africana over near Porto Cristo. Sam switched off the crackling radio and stared through the bug-dashed windscreen at the breeze-block wall in front. His heart was beating erratically, thumping like a trapped bird against his chest.

Deliberately – to remind him of her – he was wearing the same clothes he'd worn the day before to see Laurie. He could smell traces of her perfume on his shirt. If he closed his eyes – as he did now – it was possible to pretend that she was here with him. It filled him with longing. Even something so simple as her and him sitting in a car seemed miraculous right now, because so much still had to be done, before that could be achieved.

He knew she'd be going crazy, wondering what was

happening. He wanted to call her, but he couldn't. Not until he'd spoken to Claire. Not until he had something concrete to say.

And Claire had been in no fit state to speak to about anything when he'd seen her this morning. And so he'd had to wait and bide his time until now. His nerves were making him feel physically sick.

'Daddy . . .'

'OK,' he said, opening his eyes and reaching for the door. 'Let's do this now.'

He got Archie out of the car and walked with him across the neon-lit car park to the lift. He counted the yellow apartment numbers painted on the parking spaces as he passed them, then listened to the hum of the lift as it descended towards him. Archie scuffed his trainers across the concrete as they waited. The tiny red bulbs set into their heels flashed quickly on and off.

These sights and sounds . . . already they felt like memories. Was that what this place was about to become?

As the lift carried them up towards the penthouse, Sam sifted back through the day he'd spent with his son. He'd slept on the sofa in Archie's room the night before to escape from the party. When he and Archie had woken and dressed, Claire had been on her way to bed.

'I need to speak to you later,' he'd said.

'Whatever,' she'd answered as she'd disappeared into her room.

The living room had been choked with smoke and he'd started to help Isabel clear the bottles and ashtrays away.

'Go,' she'd told him. 'Take Archie out.'

So that's what he'd done. To the first place he'd been able to think of which Archie had never seen: the Reserva Africana. Sam had driven slowly through the auto-safari's feeding grounds, with Archie standing on his lap, shouting with delight at the monkeys who'd dropped down on to the car from the trees. Then they'd driven to the beach for lunch and had eaten ice creams and drawn zebras and antelopes and wildebeest on the sand with sticks which they'd found washed up on the rocks.

All memories. All wonderful. Even though not a second of the day had gone past without Sam thinking about Laurie, and what they'd done, and how everything had changed.

Archie and Laurie . . . Laurie and Archie . . . he didn't want either of them to be memories. He wanted them both. Always. He didn't want to have to give either of them up.

He was back where he'd started, then: torn between his family and the woman he loved.

Claire . . . he felt guilty about wanting to leave her. But would it really be so bad for her if he went? He couldn't bring himself to believe that. He thought of her at the party, and on her way to bed this morning as he'd been getting up. Hadn't their lives been unravelling for a long time now?

He remembered the resolve which had filled him as he'd flown back from France to Mallorca three years ago. He'd been prepared to throw everything away then, to be with Laurie. He'd have set Claire and himself free from one another. He'd have willingly betrayed Tony and Rachel, and given up on the future which they'd so clearly marked out for him. He'd have thrown it all back at them and struck out with Laurie on his own.

And yet his resolve had failed the moment he'd found out about Archie. And his resolve was failing again, because Archie was now so much more than a nameless bundle of cells in Claire's belly. Now he was walking and talking and holding Sam's hand. And Sam didn't want to let go.

The floor numbers continued to flick past on the digital display. He squeezed Archie's hand.

But who was to say he *would* lose Archie if he left Claire? Wasn't it possible that he could take him with him? He hadn't discussed it with Laurie yet – let alone Claire – but who was to say that Laurie wouldn't want to be a parent to Archie? If she loved Sam, then surely she might learn to love his son.

But, equally, he knew it was impossible. If he tried to take Archie from Claire, she'd fight him harder than she'd fought for anything in her life. Not only because of Archie – although Sam knew she loved him in her own way – but because of Sam. Because he'd have left her. Because he'd have rejected her. And because that would mean that, for the first time in Claire's life, she wouldn't have got her way.

And Rachel . . . wonderful, wise and understanding Rachel, who Sam loved and who'd loved him and welcomed him into her family and business. Rachel would turn on him the moment she saw her family was under attack. A cuckoo, that was how she'd see him. A cuckoo she'd let into her nest. A cuckoo who was now trying to steal her beloved great-grandson away. Not to mention a cuckoo who owned a 5 per cent stake in her family company.

Sam sighed. What was he thinking? Laurie as a parent to Archie? Claire fighting him to the bitter end? And Rachel joining in on the attack? Slow down, he told himself. He was so many jumps ahead of himself already. He hadn't even found the courage yet to tell Claire that he was going to leave. He didn't even know if he had that courage left in him.

The lift doors hissed open and Sam and Archie stepped

out into the hallway. Sam and Claire's was the only apartment on this floor. Sam stared at the white door to his home.

'Archie,' he said, kneeling down in front of his son and gripping him by the shoulders.

Archie laughed, and began to wriggle, thinking that this was some kind of a game.

'No,' Sam said, 'I need you to listen to me.'

Archie frowned, reading something in Sam's eyes, becoming still.

'If Daddy had to go away for a little while . . .' Sam began.

'Away?'

'That's right. Go away, like when we go on holiday, or –'

'Holiday?' Archie smiled brightly.

'No, not you,' Sam said. OK, he'd try explaining another way. 'Sometimes,' he said, 'when grown-ups love each other . . . sometimes mummies and daddies . . .'

'I want *Shrek*,' Archie said.

Sam released his son and watched him walk to the penthouse door. It was hopeless. Archie was too young to understand. And if he was too young to understand Sam's explanation for leaving, then how much less would he understand it if Sam actually left? Or should he be seeing it the other way round and taking solace from Archie's lack of comprehension? If he was too young to understand, might that mean that he was also too young to remember? And therefore too young to apportion blame?

'Mummy!' Archie yelled excitedly as he pounded on the door.

Sam stood up. Too young to remember? With Rachel and Claire to remind him? What chance was there of that?

It was Isabel who answered the door.

'*Shrek*!' Archie yelled up at her.

'No,' Sam said.

'No?' Isabel asked.

'No, I want you to take him out for a walk, to a cake shop, anywhere. Take a phone and I'll call you when I want you to come back. Now, please. As quick as you can.'

Isabel collected her bag from the stand just inside the doorway. Embarrassed, probably thinking all this had something to do with the mess Claire's friends had made of the apartment, she wouldn't look Sam in the eye as she walked past him and pressed the lift call button.

'I love you,' Sam said, picking Archie up and hugging him. Sam couldn't look him in the eyes.

'I love you too, Daddy,' Archie answered, before running off to join Isabel. 'Cake!' he exclaimed as the lift doors opened.

In the sitting room, Sam stared around him at his home. In the centre of the room was a Robin Day black leather sofa which Claire had had shipped over from London, a David Design's 'Bob' beanbag and a Merrow Associates glass coffee table. Hanging from the ceiling was the Tom Dixon 'Ball' chandelier she'd brought back with her from last year's Milan Furniture Fair, and against the wall to the right was the custom-built drinks bar, along with its four Azumi brushed stainless-steel and walnut bar stools.

He knew the names of the various designers, not because he was into this latest wave of retro chic like Claire, but because he'd heard her brag so many times to her friends about the individual pieces of furniture.

He searched the room for a single item which he'd bought himself, just one contribution to this, the public face of their family home. He found none.

His stuff, Archie's stuff . . . there was none of it here.

Not even a photograph of either of them, or of Sam's brother or parents. His mother had remarked on it the last time she'd visited (nearly a year ago now). 'I don't want the room cluttered,' Claire had replied, knowing full well that Sam's mother's sitting room was a gallery of family photographs. Claire used a similar excuse for keeping the sitting room a toy-free zone: 'This is an adult space. I don't want it ruined.'

Sam's stuff, Archie's stuff . . . it was all kept separate: Sam's in his study; Archie's in his bedroom. Separate. Compartmentalised. Was that what they'd become?

Sam's eyes settled on the oil painting of Sant Bartholomew, the monastery he'd visited the day before. It was a late nineteenth-century piece, not in keeping with the rest of the room at all. It had been a gift from Tony to Claire. It was the same painting which Sam had found himself staring at nine years ago in Claire's old apartment, after he'd slept with her for the very first time.

Who knew, Sam had wondered then, how different and amazing his own life might become in a few years' time? Well, now he had his answer. He'd fallen head over heels in love with Claire's life, all right, and he'd become a part of it, a part of the great Glover family bandwagon. Subsumed. Sam Delamere, the individual, the dreamer who'd once been, was as anachronistic in this room as the painting itself. Sam Delamere, the company man, who'd imprisoned himself with each decision he'd made: that's who lived here now.

'God, I feel like shit,' Claire announced. She was standing in the doorway which led to the master bedroom, dressed in a green dragon-patterned silk kimono. Her hair was still wet from the shower.

'Does that surprise you?'

'Oh, don't start, Sam,' she said. 'I'm not in the mood. Oh,' she suddenly said.

'What?'

'I forgot to tell you: Laurie called last night, while you were in the shower . . .'

A momentary panic ran through him. What if Laurie had changed her mind? But he fought it down. He loved her. He'd always loved her. And she'd never stopped loving him. All he had to do now was prove himself worthy. 'What about?'

'Something about the gate not working. I can't really remember.' She gazed around the room. 'Isabel!' she called. 'There's no bloody hair conditioner again,' she complained to Sam. 'Isabel!' she shouted again, louder this time.

'She isn't here,' Sam said. He could feel the sweat forming on his brow. His heartbeat was stuttering now. He tried not to think of the attacks . . . the one which he'd had at Tony's funeral . . . and later, in bed with Claire . . .

'Why not?'

Sam slowed his breathing, counting one hippopotamus, two hippopotamus, three . . . The other attacks, they'd been a result of his deceiving himself about Laurie. They'd stopped when he'd spoken to her that night in the *Angel*'s wheelhouse.

'Why not?' Claire asked again.

But he wasn't deceiving himself about Laurie any more, was he? He wasn't pretending he didn't want to be with her, was he? *Was* he? Was that what this was? Was he about to let her down again? 'Because I told her to take Archie out,' he answered.

'Why?'

His heart jolted hard. Archie . . . his little boy . . . 'Because we need to talk.'

'Look,' she said, 'if it's about Toby breaking the glass table top, then don't worry, I'll be able to get it fixed.'

'It's not that.'

She didn't look like she believed him. 'Fine,' she said. 'But let me get dressed first.'

'Fine.'

Outside on the terrace, Sam took a cigarette from a packet of Marlboros which someone had left on the table. He hadn't smoked since the day Claire had told him she was pregnant. He lit the cigarette now and took a long drag. When he looked down, he saw that his fingers were shaking and realised his breath had grown shallow again.

# Chapter XXIV

Tony could feel Rachel's breath against his throat. His arms were cramped from holding her tight, but he wouldn't let go. She was alive. She hadn't died. He hadn't killed her when he'd crashed the car, as he'd been so terrified he had.

They were sitting in the front of Giles Weatherly's Citroën van, halfway down Summerglade Hill. Between the sweep of the wipers, rain slapped the windscreen in sheets. Bill was at the wheel, silent, focusing intensely on the road ahead. Whatever he was thinking he was keeping to himself. Up on the moor, he'd dug a blanket out of the back of the van and they'd wrapped it round Rachel as tight as swaddling clothes.

Tony's muscles burned, like they'd been squeezed in a vice, from when he'd run to get Bill. His face felt raw, sand-papered by the wind and rain. The cut on his jaw throbbed steadily in time with his pulse. But then came the image of Rachel's mother. She'd be waiting for her son and daughter. And when they returned – they'd call the police, of course – and, then . . .

Tony placed his hand gently on Rachel's stomach. Let them do their worst, he thought. He was going to be a father. A father. That's what had given him the strength to get as far as he had, before the storm had shredded his plans. And that's what would keep him going now. He'd take on this night and whatever it threw at him. And he'd win.

The van slid to a halt.

'What is it?' Tony asked.

Ignoring him, Bill yanked on the handbrake and climbed out into the night.

'Bill?' Rachel called out, but got no reply.

Rachel groaned from the pain of her bruised ribs as she leant forward to see what Bill was doing. Ahead of them, the lights of Stepmouth shimmered in the torrential rain, like a fleet of fishing boats on a storm-racked sea.

'I'll go and look,' Tony said.

Other than the vicious sting of the wind, the first thing he noticed as he stepped from the passenger door and on to the road was the back of his feet turning freezing cold. Then he looked down and saw why: he was standing in a stream of running water, ankle-deep already, and gathering pace in front of him, onwards to the town below.

Bill stood on the other side of the van, rigid as a gundog with a view to a kill. Following his line of sight, Tony joined him in gaping speechless ahead.

From where the van was parked, the road ran another twenty yards down a steep incline until it reached the crossroads which signalled the start of the town. Tony had been up and down this road so many times before that he knew it better than his own reflection.

But the crossroads had vanished. Or it was no longer visible, at least. In its place was a river, a rising flowing river.

At first, Tony assumed it was a continuation of the streaming water in which he stood, but then his eyes moved to the right of where the crossroads had once been. South Bridge was still there, only now it seemed to be half submerged itself and acting not only as a bridge, but also as a dam.

Something must have blocked the channel which ran beneath it. And the river had done what water will always do: it had found another way through, pouring from the river bank like blood from a ruptured artery, searching out the path of least resistance. So that now the great black snake of the River Step slithered down the high street, lapping hungrily at the walls and doors of the terraced houses, trapping the people who lived there inside.

'Wait here,' Bill shouted.

Tony watched him run back to the van and get in. The gears ground noisily. Then the van was reversing up the hill, away from where Tony stood. Shielding his eyes from the glare of its headlights, Tony watched it retreat: ten yards, twenty, more . . . He waited: nothing. Thirty seconds past, forty-five . . . then the headlights dimmed and died . . . he caught the sound of a van door slamming . . . and a figure lurched towards him, splashing through the gloom.

'My mother and Emily,' Bill said. 'We need to get them out of there.'

Tony was tired enough to lie down and sleep where he was. He wasn't going anywhere. He wanted to stay close to Rachel, no matter what. 'But why?' he asked. 'Why not wait till morning? We can get them then. They'll be safe enough inside. Not like us, freezing out here in this –'

'Because I think that what's happening down there is going to get worse. A lot worse.'

The two men stared at one another. Tony glanced over at the high street. What did Bill mean, it was going to get much worse? How much worse *could* it get? Chances were that the ground floors of all the high street properties had already been flooded and ruined. And what were those people to Tony? What did it matter to him if their tables and sofas got soaked?

'Forget it,' he started to say.

But Bill wasn't listening. Shielding his eyes from the rain with one hand, Bill pointed with the other at South Bridge. 'All this rain,' he shouted, 'it must have washed stuff down-river . . . branches, leaves, fallen trees, even boulders . . . and that's what's blocked the bridge . . . The water that's draining off down the high street,' he continued, swivel-ling round now and pointing straight ahead, 'it's two feet high already and I'm worried it'll soon be enough to rip the foundations clear out from underneath some of those houses . . . They're structurally weak . . . I've lived in one of them all my life and studied enough engineering to know . . .' He pointed back at the bridge. 'And there,' he said, 'the river's burst its banks on the other side, too, which means it's flowing down East Street and Emily's place will be in exactly the same danger . . .'

He was right: from this elevated position, again illumi-nated by the street lamps, Tony could clearly see another rippling black river, pouring itself out into the town beyond the bridge. 'But Emily might have already got out,' he said.

'Why would she have? She can't see what we can from there. No, I need to be sure.'

'What about Rachel?' Tony asked. 'We can't leave her here.'

'It's the river that's the real danger, not the water running down here.'

Tony hesitated. So it was safe here. So why not just stay put? Why should he help Mrs Vale? And Emily: Tony liked her all right, but his place was by Rachel's side, not hers. He opened his mouth to protest.

'It's what Rachel wants,' Bill cut him off.

Tony knew Rachel well enough to know that Bill was telling the truth. He also knew she'd be out here herself to help if she had the strength.

He stared at Bill, resigned. 'What do you need me to do?'

'We split up,' Bill answered. 'It'll be quicker that way and I don't know how much time we've got.'

'All right,' Tony agreed. Of the two journeys Bill was suggesting, the one to reach Emily, being the further, looked the more difficult. 'I'll get Emily,' he volunteered, not because he wanted to prove anything to Bill, but because the last person in the world he wanted to see right now was Mrs Vale, and he'd take the harder journey over that any time.

Bill said nothing. Tony watched as he closed his eyes, as if struggling to reach a decision. Then Bill nodded, as if drawing whatever internal debate he'd been having to a close.

'No. You haven't the strength to get across South Bridge,' he said, 'not after doing what you've done already . . . And I won't forget that, Tony, not ever . . .'

What did he mean? Tony wondered. Was he forgiving him? Or warning him that he hadn't forgotten everything else? Had they become allies now? Or were they still enemies? There was no time to ask.

'It's got to be me who crosses the bridge,' Bill finished.

'But what about your mother? She can't walk. How am I meant to –'

'You get help. Get the neighbours out of their homes. Warn them all of the danger. Get them to help you move Mum. Tell them what's happened to the bridge. Tell them to get the hell out of there, out of their houses and up to higher ground.'

Tony turned and waved at the van behind them. Although he couldn't see Rachel, he knew she'd be watching. He couldn't believe he was leaving her. Not after what they'd already been through. And yet he realised that saving Mrs Vale might be the only hope of acceptance that he and Rachel had left. He'd do it, then, not for the old woman who hated him, but despite her. He'd do it for himself, for Rachel, for the family they'd soon be. He'd take this chance to prove to Bill and Mrs Vale, and everyone else in the town who thought he was no good, how wrong they'd always been.

He set off with Bill down the last twenty yards of Summerglade Hill. The closer they got to the town, the more signs of life they saw: the silhouettes of people watching from their windows; a dog paddling desperately against the current, before being spun around and disappearing, yelping from sight. There were noises, too: thunder rolled and lightning cracked; the water roared where it was bursting free from the bridge. In the distance, at the harbour end of the street, Tony glimpsed what looked like a dirigible, but then it was gone.

As they reached the crossroads, neither Bill nor Tony broke their stride. They waded into the freezing water.

'What time is it?' Tony called out to Bill.

'Twenty-five past eight,' Bill yelled back.

By a quarter to nine, Tony swore to himself he'd be out of this water and somewhere safe, with Rachel's mother by his side. Everything would be over, he swore, by then.

'I'll have her safe by a quarter to,' he called to Bill, as if committing to it out loud might somehow make it more possible. 'I swear it. I'll see you back on the hill. Good luck.'

'And to you.'

Then they separated, Bill pushing off into the oncoming

waters which came from the right and Tony downstream, over the crossroads towards the high street.

The hidden road beneath his feet was as slippery as a salmon's scales. Tony stretched out his arms like a tightrope walker. He felt like he was trying out roller skates for the very first time as he slid and stumbled on. A piece of debris jarred against his hip.

On the other side of the crossroads, Tony steadied himself against the brickwork of the corner house where Granville Road and the high street met. Further down the high street, the gaudy wooden signs above the doorways to the Channel Arms and the Smuggler's Rest banged in the wind, still glowing invitingly beneath their spotlights. Up above Tony, someone called his name. He looked up and saw Mr Tyler, the teacher who'd first taught him how to read, hanging out of an upstairs window.

'The bridge,' Tony shouted up, 'it's logjammed. Get your family out and up the hill to safety. Bill Vale . . . he says it's too dangerous to stay.'

Tony didn't hear what Mr Tyler called back. A great gust of wind tore into him, screeching into his ears. Clinging to the brickwork, Tony worked his way along the corner house on to the high street, and then on to the next house along. He wedged himself up against its front door and pounded his fist against it, over and over again.

'Who's there?' someone finally shouted through the letter box.

Tony crouched down, his legs and waist now submerged in water. A pair of terrified eyes stared back at him through the letter box.

'Tony Glover,' the voice shouted over the wail of the wind, 'is that you?'

Thank God. It was Wilfred Lee. Tony's mother had known

him since school. Hurriedly, Tony passed on Bill's warning about the bridge, then explained why he was here: to fetch Mrs Vale. Without being asked, Wilfred offered to help Tony carry her to safety.

'I'll get dressed,' he said. 'Go get her ready to leave and I'll join you there.'

Tony stood and faced across the street. Already the water seemed to have risen. Now it was nearing the tops of his thighs.

Opposite him was Vale Supplies and to its right was Giles Weatherly's ironmongery. At the head of the alley which separated the two shops was the great old oak tree which Tony had clambered up in June to see Rachel. Its solidity brought him comfort now, even though he saw its trunk was surrounded by water and that the alleyway was flooded, too.

None of the lights in the ironmonger's were on. But in the lit upstairs front window of Vale Supplies, Tony suddenly saw the silhouette of a head appear. It had to be Mrs Vale. Had she seen him, too? He raised his arm to wave, but just as he did, the street lamp above his head fizzled and died. Sparks cascaded down.

Tony opened his eyes to discover the town thick with darkness. The sense of isolation that accompanied it was terrible, like the conversation he'd just had with Wilfred Lee had been nothing but a trick of the mind. Like he was truly alone.

At first, it was like trying to look through oil. But then shapes began to distinguish themselves from one another – houses, windows, doorways – as his eyes took advantage of the scant light thrown down from the flickering night-time sky which swirled above him. Soon, only the water in which he stood remained as black as pitch.

The power was down. He thought of Don. Was he up at the power station on night shift? Tony hoped not. He hoped he was somewhere safe. He thought of his mother . . . and the twins . . . and Rachel . . . everyone he loved . . .

Then he saw candlelight spread across the upstairs window of Vale Supplies and remembered why he was here. Everything slotted back into place. How many minutes had it been since he'd split off from Bill? Five? Ten at most? He wanted this done with, and now.

He'd use the candlelight as his beacon. He'd let it guide him home. He braced himself and stepped out into the street. Immediately, he noticed the change: the water level was now up to his waist, now faster, now dragging him downstream.

Shoulders forward, head down, he pushed out in what he thought was a straight line. But with each stride he took, the weight of oncoming water forced him further down the street, leaving him crossing it in frantic, faltering, sliding steps in a diagonal line. Three feet . . . four . . . six . . . Already, by the time he got halfway across, he was two houses down from Vale Supplies.

The water ran fastest here and nearly threw him. For an instant he felt both his feet leaving the ground. But somehow he kept himself from toppling over, and got a foot down. Then another. He steadied himself against the onslaught. Then onwards. One step . . . two . . . just one more and he'd be –

Something loomed at him out of the darkness and he threw himself at it, got a hand to metal, something solid, and gripped it tight. He hauled himself upright and caught his breath.

Now that he was on the same side of the street, he could no longer see the candle in Vale Supplies. His beacon of hope had vanished and he felt his spirits drop.

He searched through the darkness till he saw where he was: at the bus stop outside the church hall, where back in March he'd fought Bernie Cunningham and lost. Film posters lolled from the side of the bus stop, licking at the passing water like thirsty tongues.

Tony stared across the street at the shadowy awning of the fishmonger's which flapped like a wing in the dark. He counted two doors up from there, to where he'd only a minute before been talking to Wilfred Lee. A burst of panic. What help could Wilfred be now? Even if he made it across, what chance would they have of getting Mrs Vale back upstream to safety?

He should never have come.

But he *had come*. So now he should get on and see what he could do. Upstream. Upstream then, on to Vale Supplies. He stretched out and grabbed the church hall door handle and began the slow process of clawing himself back up past the remaining two houses which separated him from Rachel's home. He pounded against each door and window he passed, but got no answer.

Finally, he reached the front door of Vale Supplies. He hit it, shook it, screamed up at the window above. Nothing. As the water continued to pull at him, his strength began to wane. But he wouldn't let go. He thought of the dog he'd seen swept away. It would have drowned by now, sluiced across the quayside at the end of the street and into the harbour like a piece of rubbish. There was no way Tony was going out like that.

Then, as he gave the door a final shake, he remembered something else: the great bunch of keys Rachel had shown him on the bus. Keys for the windows, keys for the front door and yard door and the door to the alley.

Of course: the alley door. Had Bill locked it when he'd

401

left? Tony couldn't be sure, but it was worth a try.

Another two minutes and he was there.

It was wide open. The same water which had flooded the alley to waist height now swamped the downstairs of the house. He pushed his way in.

Eerily silent, it was like a shipwreck inside, like the tomb of the vessel which Tony had once watched Robinson Crusoe search through for salvage in a film. Water dripped. A candle flickered on a saucer on the hexagonal wooden post at the bottom of the stairs. Six inches below it, floating on the surface of the water, were straw table mats and a magazine cover featuring the watery visage of Marilyn Monroe.

Yellow light glowed at the top of the stairs. Tony dragged himself free of the water and sloshed up the remaining dry wooden steps which hadn't yet been submerged.

'Mrs Vale?' he called, as he reached the landing and saw that the source of the yellow light was an old oil lamp which had been hung from the wooden ladder which he guessed led up to Rachel's bedroom.

No answer.

'Mrs Vale?' he called again.

He was about to turn into the room on the left: the room at the front of the house, where he thought he'd seen Mrs Vale peering out at him. But something else snagged his attention: a faint flicker of light, in the room to the right. Someone was there, huddled in the gloom at the back, shielding the candle which they held with their hand.

'Mrs Vale?' he asked, gently now, not wanting to scare her. He stepped into the room. The window behind her which must have overlooked the river channel was a stamp of black. 'It's me: Tony Glover,' he started to explain.

'Keep away.'

Even after what he'd just been through – perhaps *because* of what he'd just been through – the hatred in her voice stunned him. It was the first time she'd ever addressed him. But what had he expected? He told himself to keep calm.

'The houses aren't safe. We need to get you out of here. Bill sent me here to help.'

'Liar.'

He could see now that she was next to a drawing table. The candle she was holding flared, briefly illuminating a drawing of what looked like the old Bathers' Pavilion on the wall.

'But I swear to you, Mrs Vale,' he insisted. 'Wilfred Lee across the road. He's going to try to –'

Something fell from her hand, rattling as it landed on the floor. He looked down to see a small silver crucifix on a silver chain. Then the candle guttered and the only light left was that which came from the landing behind him. His shadow stretched towards her.

'Get out.' She screamed the words. 'You think I don't know why you've come here?' Panic was rising in her voice. 'It's because of Rachel. It's because –'

'Yes,' he said, 'because of Rachel. Because she's going to have my child. Because I love her and she loves you.'

'To shut me up. Because you know I won't allow it. That child. Never.'

He tried to close his ears to what she was saying. He'd come too far to let Rachel down now. 'You're coming with me,' he told Mrs Vale, 'whether you like it or not.'

Get her out of this bedroom, that's what he was thinking. Carry her, if that was what it took. Over to the window at the front of the house. Then look out for help. Someone might come. What about the dirigible he thought he'd

403

seen? Maybe that was working the high street this minute even, pulling people from their upstairs windows and carrying them off to safety . . .

'You've come here to kill me, the same as your brother,' she told him as he walked towards her.

'No,' Tony said, 'that's not . . .' But the virulence of her hatred had infected him and suddenly he was cursing himself for having been so weak. He should never have listened to Bill. He should have stayed with Rachel, no matter what she'd said she'd wanted. He should have taken care of her and left the rest of the Vale family to rot.

'Well, he didn't manage it,' she spat, 'and neither will you.'

The first thing he knew of the poker in her hand was when it swung past his head, missing his face by mere inches. He stumbled backwards into the corridor. She pushed herself after him, catching up to where he'd fallen and lashing out at him again. They were both at the top of the stairs now. As Tony struggled to his feet, she struck down at him. But this time he was quicker than her and snapped his hand around her forearm. He closed his other hand over hers, so that both of them now gripped the poker together.

He wouldn't have thought it possible, the strength she had. It took everything he had to prevent her from tearing the poker from him. Her teeth were bared and she was twisting and snarling like a cat. He grappled his hands along the haft of the poker and gave it an almighty yank.

In the same instant it came free, Mrs Vale went tumbling down the stairs. Her wheelchair went with her. Together they flipped over once, then smashed against the wooden banister. Her bare foot had got caught between two spindles, locking her there. But there was something wrong about the angle of her head. She stared up at him, unmoving, through wet-pebble eyes.

That's when Tony first heard the noise: rumbling, rising, coming closer, quickly now. Like a train, he thought. Like a freight train hurtling towards him through the night. He felt the floor begin to vibrate and watched in horror as, with a crack, Mrs Vale's foot slipped free, and then she and her chair toppled over into the black waters which had gathered at the bottom of the stairs.

# Chapter XXV

**Mallorca, Present Day**

Laurie opened the large fridge in Rachel's kitchen and pulled out the jug of filtered water. Her hand was shaking as she took two glasses from the cupboard, filled them with ice and water, and put them on the worktop. She could sense Rachel upstairs. She could feel her presence, as if she were seeping through the floor.

Her father put his hat down in Rachel's kitchen and looked around the large open space of the villa's living area. How could she love her father so much and yet he could cause her so much stress? The nostalgic affection she'd felt towards him when he'd been on the other side of a no doubt bulletproof, soundproof piece of glass in the airport earlier had vanished. In its place was a seething frustration. It was as if by the sheer fact of being together, she couldn't be herself, only a version of herself that she'd long since outgrown.

Now, everything from his happy-go-lucky comments about the perils of mixing with the locals, to his gung-ho war mentality towards the 'infernal heat' was making her head ache. Not to mention his relentless criticism of her driving! She longed to put her hands over her ears and scream like a little child.

She took a long sip of water, feeling the coolness soothe her scorched throat. She must be patient and stay calm, she cautioned herself. She had to stay in control. It was her guilty conscience that was making her feel this way, and not her father's fault at all.

Laurie washed her hands in the sink, running the tepid clear water over her wrists in an attempt to cool herself down. It didn't work. As she dried her hands on a towel, she noticed that Rachel had moved the pictures of Tony as she'd asked her to, but it still didn't make it any easier. She had thought that she'd be able to handle the situation with her father and that she'd easily be able to engineer a suitable time to tell him about Rachel. But it was more difficult than she could possibly have imagined.

The fact that they were together in Rachel's villa was almost unbearable. She felt like an absolute traitor. Everything her father had said from the second she'd picked him up at the airport, every little remark, was made poignant by her deceit.

'My goodness, you've landed on your feet.' Her father whistled appreciatively as he accepted the glass of iced water that Laurie handed to him. She could hear the ice cubes clink in the glass. 'I can see why you've been a recluse. This place is something special, isn't it?'

'Listen, Dad, there's something I've got to tell you.' Laurie placed both hands on the worktop and faced her father. But to her dismay, her father totally failed to pick up on the seriousness of her tone and, instead, he laughed. It was one of his I-knew-it chortles which always grated against her.

'Oh,' he said. 'Oh . . . I thought so. I thought you looked different. There's someone special, someone new, isn't there? Is that why I'm here, to put my seal of approval on the new boyfriend? You know, I may be a little rusty, but I can still read the signs.'

Laurie hardly knew what to say.

407

'Is it that obvious?' she asked, faking a smile.

Her father slapped the worktop, pleased with himself. 'I've been wondering why you've been so quiet and now I have my answer. I've never seen you look so nervous and lovesick.'

Laurie gestured to the terrace doors. She couldn't discuss Sam inside, not when Rachel might come down at any moment and eavesdrop.

Outside, she managed to stall her father for as long as it took to show him briefly around the garden, but once they'd sat at the table in the shade, she knew the conversation couldn't be put off any longer.

'So where is the lucky fellow?' her father asked, sipping his water. There was something in his enthusiasm that made her shrink away. He'd obviously been waiting to have this conversation with her for a long time. She wondered now whether he'd discussed her continued single status with his friends, whether his neighbours enquired about her love life. She couldn't help feeling defensive. She hadn't even told him about James, let alone Sam. Had her father assumed she was some kind of hopeless spinster all this time?

This was why she'd never discussed anything personal with her parents, she remembered. Because she couldn't handle their enthusiasm, or their disappointment, or the way they seemed to judge her by being so eager not to. Besides, talking about her private life seemed so embarrassing, especially with her father. She wished that her mum was here.

She realised that for all her adult life she'd been telling her father an edited and highlighted version of the truth. Now, coming clean about Sam seemed as if she was breaking all the rules of their relationship. She was about to shatter her father's illusions and reveal herself as an adult. It was new territory that seemed fraught with danger. Just starting out on the journey of explanation felt as if she were stepping on to quicksand. The only chance she had of survival was to get it over with as quickly as possible.

'Where is he right now?' she repeated, feeling an echo of her conversation with Roz, yesterday. But she knew she had to be brave. This was too important to start lying now. 'Well, right now . . . he . . . Sam . . . he wants to be here and he's longing to meet you, but the truth is that he's with . . . he's with his wife.'

'Oh . . .' her father's face crumpled. He stared at his glass.

'It's not as bad as it sounds.'

'But . . . but you could have anyone . . .'

She knew it was going to be hard to make her father understand, but this was impossible.

'But he's leaving his wife. That's what I'm trying to tell you.'

'Well, I certainly don't approve of you breaking up some-one's marriage,' her father countered. 'You're so much better than that.'

She could see the disappointment in his face. This was all going wrong. She wanted nothing more than for him to like Sam, to accept him, and now she'd already blown it.

She shook her head, growling with frustration at herself as she sat up in her chair and leant towards him. 'You don't understand. I'm saying it all wrong. You see, we met before. I mean, we had an affair before. Three years ago, before Mum died. You remember I wrote you a postcard, saying that I was in love? Well, that was Sam. The same person.'

'And was he married then?'

'No, no, he wasn't. Not then. We were supposed to be together, but then, then he found out that his girlfriend was pregnant –'

'Oh, this just gets better and better,' her father exclaimed. 'Laurie, what are you playing at? Is that what you've been doing all summer? Dallying around with someone else's husband? I know it's none of my business, but it sounds to me as if you've got yourself into a bit of a mess.'

He was right. She was in a mess. He made her affair with Sam seem so sordid. And telling him the details like this made her feel more anxious than ever.

'But . . . well . . . the thing is . . . I thought I was over him,' Laurie said, determined to get the truth out, before her doubts subsumed her. 'Really, I did. I had a new boyfriend and then, then, I met Sam again a few months ago and I realised – *we* realised – that it wasn't over at all. And the whole point is that he, Sam, made a mistake with her . . . with Claire. He shouldn't have married her, but he didn't feel he could back out . . . because of the baby –'

'But now he does?'

'Oh, Dad, I don't expect you to understand, but Sam and I love each other. We have to be together. It's special. More than special. He's the man I want to be with for ever.'

Bill Vale retrieved his handkerchief from his pocket and flicked it out, before using it to dab his face. 'Are you sure you know what you're doing? Are you sure he feels the same way? I mean, you can't know how their marriage really is, can you? Marriage is sacred, Laurie. They made vows to each other. And anyway, is this Sam person honestly going to leave his wife if there's a child involved?'

'I think . . . I hope so.'

'You *hope* so?'

'He is. I'm sure he is. He should be . . . right now.'

Her father's obvious horror at her predicament made her feel as if everything she knew to be true was slipping away.

'I love him, Dad. And he loves me.'

She could feel tears welling up inside her, making her unable to speak. She was determined not to cry. She knew her father couldn't handle seeing her emotions like this. She waved her hand in front of her face.

'Oh dear, oh dear,' he said. He looked away, waiting until she'd composed herself.

She took a sip of water.

'So this place?' he asked. 'Does this belong to Sam?'

She could see him trying to piece together a picture from the information she'd given him. She wanted to rub it out, to try and explain it a different way. There was so much more to tell him. His earlier bonhomie had gone, replaced by a look of suspicion. He glanced around the garden, as if seeing it through different eyes.

'No,' she said. She might as well get it over with. She took a deep breath. 'You've got to promise not to be angry . . .'

Her father frowned. 'You mean there's more?'

'You see,' she started. God, this was hard. 'It's Rachel's . . . and Tony's . . . this place. I've been staying here with Rachel. And Sam is –'

'This house belongs to Rachel?' her father burst out. 'My sister? Is that what you're telling me? But you said it belonged to a friend. You said . . . you . . . you made me come all this way to –'

'Dad, you've got to understand,' Laurie begged.

But her father wasn't listening. He slammed the glass down on the table top, stood abruptly and marched down

411

the terrace. Laurie ran after him, and caught up with him at the far end of the pool. He looked out over the horizon, livid.

'I thought . . . I didn't mean for you to be upset.' She felt utterly pathetic. He'd so rarely been truly angry with her in her life that she had no means of dealing with it.

'Upset? Upset?' Her father's voice was choked with rage. 'How could you do this? Trick me like this? And I thought you were –'

'I did it for Rachel,' Laurie interjected quickly. 'She thought –'

'Whatever she thought, she thought wrong,' her father barked.

'But, Dad, whatever needs sorting out between you, surely –'

'You don't know what you're saying, Laurie, what you're meddling in. Do you have any idea who he was?'

'Who?'

'Tony Glover. He ruined everything. His family . . .'

'What?' She watched her father rub his face. She'd expected him to react, of course, but not like this. He looked as if he was going to cry. 'I mean, whatever it is, surely you've got over it by now,' she continued, trying to be brave. 'It's been fifty years. Isn't it time to let bygones be bygones? Tony's dead.'

'That doesn't matter,' he said, his voice choking.

Why was he reacting so badly? Rachel had glossed over their problems, as if her rift with Bill was just a foolish misunderstanding that had stretched over time until it was now somehow meaningless, but whatever emotions her father felt were obviously as raw as ever.

But even so, surely it was time he started behaving like an adult. OK, so she'd told a few lies to get him to come

412

out here, but that was nothing compared to the lifetime of lies he'd told her. About Rachel's existence. And now, obviously, about what they'd rowed about.

'Like what?' she asked. 'What don't you get over, Dad?'

'I never thought I'd have to tell you this,' he said.

'Tell me what?'

'It was Keith Glover who shot my father – your grandfather,' he said.

Laurie shook her head. 'Keith?'

'Tony's brother. He broke into the shop to rob it and he shot Dad. And then he shot Mum. That's why she was paralysed. That's why she couldn't get out when the flood hit. Because she was in a wheelchair. Because of Keith Glover. He destroyed us.'

'But you told me that Grandpa died in the war. You lied to me.'

'I was trying to protect you from it.' Her father's voice cracked with emotion. Laurie stared at him as he continued to recount, in angry bursts, how his mother's life had been ruined. How she lived a lonely painful half-life without her husband, all because of Keith.

Laurie forced herself to think rationally. There must be a way through all this. But how? What her family had experienced back then was so horrific. All she could see was her father's pain and all she wanted to do was to make it better.

But one thing didn't make sense. 'But surely you can't blame Tony for something his brother did?'

'Oh, Laurie,' he said, turning to her, his eyes full of tears. 'You'll never understand. It wasn't only . . .' he paused, trying to control his emotions. 'There was Mum, too . . . Tony . . .'

Laurie shook her head confused, as he failed to

continue. There was obviously so much more that he wasn't saying. 'What do you mean? Grandma? What's she got to do with Tony?'

But her father's look suddenly turned steely and he seemed to close up. 'It doesn't matter,' he snapped, rubbing his eyes angrily. When he looked at her again, his tears were gone. In their place was a hard frown. 'All you need to know is that Rachel chose Tony. She chose him over her own family.'

These festering emotions he'd been harbouring for all these years . . . she'd always thought her father was so straightforward and normal, but she could see now that she couldn't have been more wrong. She could never have suspected that he had so much bitterness inside him.

'But you can't choose who you fall in love with, Dad. From what I've seen, Rachel and Tony were happy together. He was a good man.'

But her father wasn't listening to the logic of her argument.

'Rachel and Glover, they took something away from me. Something I never got back. It took me until I met your mother to even feel like I was living again.'

Laurie put her hands on her waist, feeling dizzy. She was still reeling from what she'd heard. Besides, it was so hot. Too hot to be trying to decipher her father's emotional riddles in the full glare of the sun.

'And you won't ever give Rachel a chance?'

Her father was silent for ages. He was squinting towards the horizon.

'What did I do wrong?' he asked, suddenly.

Again, he'd thrown her. 'What do you mean?'

'Weren't your mother and I enough for you?'

'Of course you were.'

414

'Then why did you need to see Rachel? Why did you?'

'I don't know,' Laurie mumbled, failing to find a proper reason.

'We gave you everything we possibly could.'

Laurie looked down into the azure water of the swimming pool next to them. She could see her and her father's shadows on the bottom, as if they were drowning. Blurry. That's what her whole life suddenly was. Everything she'd always believed about everyone, apart from Sam, had been ripped from her.

'Look, I didn't tell you before, Dad, but Rachel is inside,' she said, suddenly. There was no point in hiding the truth from her father any longer. She thought she could control the situation between him and Rachel, but now she felt totally powerless. There was so much she didn't know. So much she hadn't been told. 'She's upstairs in the house. She wants to talk to you. Why don't you sort all this out with her?'

This information seemed to stun her father. He turned and gawped at her.

'Oh no, oh no,' he said. 'It doesn't work like this, Laurie. Life isn't about pushing people together to make happy families like a jigsaw puzzle. Only it's not that simple and you should be old enough to realise that by now. Your actions have consequences. Everyone's actions do. And sometimes words can't heal them.'

Laurie knew he was lashing out at her and even though what he was saying stung, she had to be strong. 'Just give Rachel one moment. She needs to see you,' Laurie appealed. 'She's lost Tony and you're all she has left.'

'She's got all of this, hasn't she?' he countered, swinging his arms out wide. 'She's got you.'

'She hasn't got me, Dad. I'm not on anyone's side.'

415

'Yes, you are.'

'Oh, Dad, please,' she said, finally exasperated.

'I don't want to see that woman, let alone forgive her.'

'Fine,' Laurie sighed, giving in. She'd done all she could. 'I'm all packed to leave, we'll just get in the car and leave Rachel behind. If that's what you want, Dad. I'm with you. We'll just go. Together. I promise.'

Laurie touched his arm, but he wasn't responding. Inside, she could hear the phone ringing and her stomach lurched. What if it was Sam? She looked back at her father, before starting up the terrace steps.

'Laurie! Wait.'

She stopped and turned. Her father's look was one of steely determination as he strode towards her. He didn't say anything, or even look at her, as he passed her.

Inside the house, the phone stopped ringing.

# Chapter XXVI

**Stepmouth, 8.25 p.m., 15 August 1953**

Bill waded into the freezing water which now submerged the crossroads. Through the torrential downpour, he could hear muffled shouts, but couldn't figure out which direction they were coming from. Other than the water gliding past the houses, the high street looked deserted. No one was panicking, and no one was splashing out into the street. Apart from Tony Glover, Bill could see no one at all.

So was he wrong to be panicking like this? Sending Glover out into a flood? Willingly embarking on risking his own life, too? Was he overreacting, assuming too much from the limited information and civil-engineering knowledge he had? Would he actually end up putting his mother and Emily in more danger than they already were?

It was possible, but he had to remain resolute and remember the fear, the cold primal fear, that had crept over him when he'd got out of the van and felt the cold water running over his shoes.

What he'd told Tony – his concern over the buildings' weak foundations – was only part of his fear. He'd realised immediately that for the volume of water to have been released down Summerglade Hill, the peat bogs up on the moors must have reached saturation level. But why, he'd immediately wondered, weren't the East and West Step valleys draining the excess waters away as they normally did?

417

Because they were already full to capacity, was the terrifying conclusion he'd reached.

Full and yet the deluge continued. The rainstorm was getting worse. Thunder exploded like cannon fire across the sky. Rain pelted down, more rain with nowhere to go.

It was seeing South Bridge which had made up Bill's mind about getting his mother and Emily out. That the bridge was blocked – or partially blocked, at least – was obvious, and yet Bill couldn't conceive of an object large enough to obstruct that sizeable a bridge. Only several objects, tens of objects . . . only if the engorged twin rivers had started uprooting every tree they'd encountered as they'd raced down from the moor.

And if that was true of South Bridge, then what of Watersbind Bridge further up the valley, and the natural reservoir behind it where the two rivers met? (Not to mention the other sixteen road and foot bridges crossing the East and West Steps between here and the top of the moor.) Was Watersbind Bridge blocked, too? Was the water behind it already backing up and searching for a way to escape?

Bill hoped to God the answers were no. Because if he was right, and the water pressure continued to build behind Watersbind Bridge as more rain fell, then it might become enough not only to flow over and around the bridge, but also to smash right through.

And if that happened . . . well, only one thing stood between the monstrous wall of water that would then rush down the valley to the sea: and that was the town of Stepmouth itself.

'What time is it?' Tony Glover called out.

Bill checked his wristwatch, the silver-plated one which had once belonged to his father. The light thrown down by the street lamps was too weak to read it by. Bill pulled his torch from his coat pocket – glad to have remembered it now, before it had got soaked – and shone it down on to the watch's cracked surface. Cracked by Keith Glover, he automatically thought. Cracked the day he'd killed Bill's dad.

'Twenty-five past eight,' Bill yelled back.

'I'll have her safe by a quarter to, I swear it,' Tony Glover shouted as he pushed on towards the high street. 'I'll see you back on the hill. Good luck.'

Bill would say one thing for Glover: he certainly didn't lack guts. Not after the way he'd run back to get help for Rachel. And not after what he was doing now.

'And to you,' Bill shouted, as enthusiastically as he could.

But already, he'd started questioning his own judgement again. He dreaded to think how his mother would react when Glover turned up. But what other choice did he have? Glover was dog-tired and crossing over South Bridge was going to take a miracle and every ounce of strength Bill had. Downstream, however, the way Glover was heading now, that would be easier. Glover would find help quickly, too, on the high street. Not that he'd necessarily need it, Bill hoped, because Giles Weatherly had probably returned home by now. And if he had, then he might have already spotted the danger and got Bill's mother out of there and somewhere safe.

Which is more than could be said for Emily, Bill thought, as he turned and began slogging upstream towards South Bridge. Emily cared too much about the Sea Catch Café to up sticks and leave it just because the river had broken loose. She was too determined, and had too much faith in her own ability to make things right. She'd be there now, he was convinced, shoring up the doorway, frantically bailing out water with a saucepan, fighting the river with both fists.

Switching off the torch till he needed it again, Bill held it high above his head. As he drew nearer to South Bridge, the water began pushing steadily against his thighs. He threw off his coat, which had started to drag, and hunkered down low like a dog pulling a sledge, dropping his centre of gravity, imagining himself as solid as rock.

But the closer he got to the bridge, the more the velocity of the water rushing outwards from behind it increased. Until finally – while he was still some fifteen feet away – he and the river reached an equilibrium. Matching him strength for strength, it roared defiantly, as he pushed against it with all his might and yet remained quite still.

Sideways, then. If he couldn't go through it, he'd have to go around. He forged his way right – towards the rocky bottom of Summerglade Hill. The water level dropped with each step, uncovering first his waist, then his thighs, until he was only submerged from the knees down.

He staggered out of the water and into the bushes beyond. He stood there panting, as the wind sliced through his soaking clothes and left him numb.

He worked out then what he had to do. Forget about crossing over the bridge. The current was too powerful there. He'd been crazy even to try. He'd head up the valley, away from the town, and attempt to cross the river higher up.

Using the torch to cut out a path through the black night, he hurried around the base of the hill, stumbling on over rocks and mud and grass, before finally lurching back downhill to where the land levelled out. Finally, he burst through the undergrowth twenty-five yards upstream from South Bridge.

Normally, the River Step would have flowed past several feet below where Bill had emerged, but it was now almost level with his feet. In the darkness, it looked as stationary as a fenland canal. It was only when Bill shone the torch across it that he saw its speed. Flotsam rushed by . . . sticks reaching up like the hands of drowning men. And branches too, covered in green foliage . . . the remains of healthy trees ripped from the river banks . . .

Upstream, South Bridge glowed ethereally, its Victorian street lamps casting off rainbows in the rain. Bill could see from this angle that it was only partially blocked by trees, and water still ran beneath it. What was causing it to burst out and branch out into two new rivers on the left and right was the volume of water rushing down from Watersbind above.

The reservoir, then, at Watersbind was so full that it had started to overflow. Which meant that – if the bridge there gave out – Watersbind could also burst.

Bill gave himself no more time to think. He threw down the torch and stripped off his sweater and shirt, then hurled himself into the ice-cold flow.

As he broke the river's surface, he gasped. The water was so cold that it burnt. He struck out with long, powerful strokes towards the opposite bank, as the river rushed relentlessly on towards South Bridge, carrying him with it.

Fail to reach the other side in time and he knew he'd be pinned like a fly against the web of flotsam beneath the bridge: crushed, eviscerated, drowned. Or forced through by the current, bludgeoned by the boulders in the channel beyond.

Another second passed. The water rolled like thunder at the bridge. But Bill had already reached the far bank.

Arms outstretched, he clawed for something – anything – to grab on to. But still he was dragged downstream. His hands tore over rock and mud. Pain shot up his arm as his right thumb twisted and broke. Then his hand latched on to something, and locked around it like a vice.

Water rushed into his face, into his mouth, eyes and ears, as the river swung his body round and tried to tear him loose. His right arm stretched like it was going to snap. But still he clung on, got his left hand to whatever his right hand already had a hold of.

Tree roots. That's what they were. That's what had stopped him from being sucked beneath the bridge. He grabbed another, then another, and finally started to haul himself free from the river.

He slumped forward as soon as his knees found solid ground. He lay face down on the river bank and vomited, spewing up the bellyful of water he'd just been force-fed.

But there was no time to rest. Instead, he willed himself to stand. The rush of water was deafening. He looked around in an attempt to orientate himself. He was ten foot upstream from the bridge. The tree he'd grabbed on to had been the last chance he'd had. If he'd missed its roots, he would have been dead by now.

The land he was standing on was at the very top of the river bank. But still the rain hissed down. Soon the river would breach the banks here, too, and widen the flood to the rest of the town.

The clock of St Hilda's glowed feebly at him through the hammering rain, like a full moon behind a cloud. Bill stumbled on, away from the river, into the shallows of where it had already flooded out beyond the bridge. What he saw before him was a mirror image of what he'd seen on the other side of the bridge. Where the water was flooding down the high street there, so it was charging down East Street here.

It looked the same depth, too: two feet, maybe even higher, maybe three . . .

Bill pictured Tony as he'd last seen him, wading into the water, choosing the fastest route to get him to where he needed to be. Bill decided to do the same. The flow shouldn't be any faster this side, he thought. And the hardest part of his journey – crossing the river – was behind him now. He'd be going with the current, not against it, from now on.

Bill heard shouts. Through the screen of rain, he saw people, loaded with possessions, battling upstream from the roads which ran parallel with Emily's, making for higher, drier ground.

'Richard,' he shouted, seeing his friend steering Rosie and the girls away from the oncoming waters, to the east. 'Have you seen Emily?'

'No,' Richard called back. 'What's happening, Bill?'

'Don't stop,' Bill shouted. 'Get as far away from the river as fast as you can.'

Whether Richard heard him or not, Bill would never know. Already, he was moving in the opposite direction to Richard, skirting around where the new river now ran, before wading into its waters where they began to channel down East Street.

The pull didn't seem so bad at first. He looked down East Street. Emily's place was – what? – fifty yards away. He'd be there in no time. And then what? Then he'd get her out of there and on downstream, before cutting off right along the streets, away from the flood path, to the east.

Then the current shifted, suddenly stronger, ripping at

423

his legs. Bill's heart pounded his ribs. Beneath his feet, he felt the pavement slabs rise and fall, shifting beneath the force of water. Then something struck his hip and he was over, under.

Darkness. Cold. Water all around. An ocean filled his ears, a million rushing bubbles.

He was tumbling now, over and over, trying to right himself. Inside his head, he screamed. He couldn't tell up from down. Something soft brushed against his face. But then it was gone. His knuckles scraped the road. Then came air. A lungful. Enough to raise him up.

He could breathe. But he couldn't see. He thought for a second that he was dead. That he was still underwater. That the reason he thought he could breathe was because he'd already left his body and no longer needed oxygen at all.

Another lungful of air. And another. He clawed at the water with his arms and legs, like a drunk attempting to rise. Then his brain caught up with what his body had already worked out for itself. He wasn't still underwater. He wasn't dead. The electricity, he realised. The electricity had failed again.

He heard a shout. A scream. His name. Light flashed into his eyes. Something tore across his leg, then snagged his belt.

'Pull!' a voice called out.

Then the weight of water tore into Bill's face once more, as he found himself being hauled upstream.

'Take his arms,' the same voice yelled.

Bill felt hands on his wrists and under his elbows. Fingers dug into him. They burnt against his freezing skin. Dragged from the water, he cried out in pain. Brickwork scraped across his ribs. A window of light appeared from nowhere.

He was dragged quickly through. He toppled over on to the dry carpeted floor.

Then another voice, warm in his ear, a voice he thought he'd never hear again: 'Bill, Bill, oh my darling, Bill.'

He lay breathless in the candlelight, staring into Emily's eyes. She was drenched, wrapped in towels. Warmth flowed through him, like none of what had just happened was real, like he and Emily were actually in her bathroom and he'd nodded off in the bath and had woken to find her gazing down at him. He managed to sit up and pulled her close.

But then the real horror of what was happening returned. 'We've got to go,' he said.

He looked up and saw that they weren't alone. Giles Weatherly, drenched and pale, was gazing down at him. Next to him was Lewis Cook, Giles's friend who lived next door to Emily. Lewis was shaking. His left temple was swollen and split. His blue V-neck sweater was ripped, its sleeve hanging off. In his hand he gripped the boat hook he'd just used to pull Bill to safety.

If Giles was here, then that meant that he wasn't there to help Glover carry his mother away from the high street. Had Glover found someone else to help? Was Bill's mother safe? Bill struggled to his feet.

'Where are we?' he asked, looking round the unfamiliar room. Emily's hand was in his, their fingers tightly intertwined. He saw a chest of drawers and a white washbasin, luminescent in the candlelight. Absurdly, a brand new television set – the one Giles must have come here to watch – stood in the centre of the bed.

'My house,' said Lewis Cook. A thickset man with a shock of white-blond hair, he ran the post office and was one of the town's volunteer lifeboat men.

'The café's flooded,' Emily added. 'Giles and Lewis fetched me round here.'

'We thought, because our doorstop's higher, we'd be safe,' said Lewis. 'But the water level kept rising.'

'Here,' Lewis's wife, Josephine, said, hurrying into the room and draping a blanket over Bill's shoulders.

Lewis returned to the window. Wordlessly, Bill, Emily and the others joined him there to take stock. The rain crackled like static. Lightning splintered the sky. The stink of peat and woods and mud rose up.

It was only now that Bill realised they were on the first floor and the others must have already been driven upstairs by the water. He peered into the darkness. East Street must be five foot deep by now. And hurtling by. He'd been lucky not to have been swept out to sea.

The lights were all out in the buildings opposite. Perhaps they would come back on like they had done before. Or maybe, if Bill's theory about Watersbind was right, they wouldn't. Maybe the concrete channel which diverted water from the reservoir to the hydroelectric power station had flooded. Maybe the station itself had now flooded, too.

A torch flicked on and off in the dark mouth of a window across the street. Morse code. Bill read it automatically, like he'd been taught to in the army: SOS – save our souls, the international distress signal.

'It's John Mitchell,' Lewis shouted over the surging waters, 'but we'd never make it across now. They're on their own now, the same as us.' A memory flashed through Bill's mind of John leaning out of that very window back in the spring to water his hanging baskets of daffodils. Was this really the same planet?

'We need to find a way to get out of here,' Bill said.

Even as he said it, though, panic rose inside him. Because how *could* they get out? How *could* he get Emily away from here, when the water was now running so fast it would sweep them away?

'No,' Giles said. 'We need to stay here. Where it's safe.'

'Even if the water gets higher – and I can't believe it will – there's always the attic,' Lewis agreed.

'You don't understand,' Bill answered. 'The bridge is dammed. I'm frightened the same's true of Watersbind. I'm scared that if –'

But before Bill could explain any further, his voice began to quaver. He coughed and cleared his throat, but the same thing happened when he tried to speak again. Then he realised the trembling wasn't emanating from him at all.

Bill dashed to the room at the back of the house and looked out, but the waters were hurtling past there as well.

As he ran back through to join the others, a low rumbling noise began to rise up above the cacophony of wind and rain. It wasn't thunder, though, because it didn't die. Instead, it grew louder, closer, like a goods train accelerating towards them down a track. A carriage clock dropped off the mantelpiece above the fireplace and smashed to the floor.

'Everybody down!' Bill shouted, wrapping his arms around Emily and pulling her to the ground.

It was like the house was coming to life. The floorboards flexed like muscles beneath them. The walls groaned. The ceiling shuddered. Dust showered down. Candles guttered and died. Darkness, thick as velvet, swamped the room.

Bill closed his eyes and pressed his lips to Emily's face, as the thunder rolled on. Whatever it was coming towards

them, it wasn't going to stop. The bridge at Watersbind
. . . Bill knew then that he'd been right. The reservoir had
burst through and loosed its tidal wave towards the town.

Bill understood then that he was going to die. He was
going to die at Emily's side. He'd failed to save her, but
he'd reached her in time. He was glad he'd come for her
and not sent Tony. Being with her and not his mother had
been the right choice. He'd rather die with Emily than let
her die alone. He pulled her face into his chest, and used
every inch of his body to cover and protect her.

He opened his mouth to whisper goodbye.

But then the waters hit.

The noise. It was like being hit by an avalanche. Like
being buried alive.

The house rocked as if from a mighty hammer blow.
The air was sucked from the room as the waters rushed
past. Then wave upon wave burst in, through the windows
and doors. They could have been on the bridge of a sinking ship. Bill clung tight to Emily as they were thrown
across the floor and up against the wall, then dragged back
into a bundle of screaming limbs. They were choking,
drowning in each other's arms, as the water thrashed them
back and forth.

Then nothing.

Wrapped in darkness, Bill couldn't see a thing. The hand
holding his moved.

'Emily?' he asked.

He was prone, wedged into what felt like the corner of
the room.

He squeezed the hand harder.

'Emily?' he asked again.

'Bill,' she answered.

He felt for her face, her lips . . .'You're alive,' he said.

428

He kissed her. Elation ripped through him like sunlight through a cloud. 'Is everyone all right?' he called into the darkness of the room.

A man's voice – Giles's? – called back, 'Yes.'

Josephine, hysterical: 'Lewis! Lewis, are you there?'

A low groan came from the other side of the room. 'My arm . . . I can't feel my . . .'

But Bill wasn't listening. He held Emily's face in his hands. 'It's over now. It's over. That was the reservoir, but now it's gone . . .'

He felt her hands on his. 'I should have told you before how much I love you,' she whispered. 'I should have told you every day.'

'Oh, my God.' It was Giles. 'Oh, my God. Look.'

Bill hauled himself through the fizzing, frothing, slopping water towards where Giles's voice had come from. He made out the shape of the window, grey against the greater dark of the room. He tried to stand, but his legs were still too weak. His skin prickled. He could sense something near the window, moving, sliding by. Like a shadow. He reached the window and dragged himself up by its sill.

Sheet lightning crackled across the sky, flickering like a strobe. What it lit up would stay with Bill for the rest of his life. The river was less than two feet below the upstairs window ledge, rolling past. Monstrous wave chased monstrous wave, tumbling, foaming, leaping upwards in giant crests, seething forwards in a great black mass.

But it wasn't that which drew Bill's eye, but the row of houses opposite, which was cracked and broken like a boxer's teeth. Tiles had been stripped from roofs, bay windows torn off. The window from which John Mitchell had been signalling – indeed the whole top floor of the house – had vanished. Along with the top halves of the houses either side.

Half of East Street had quite literally been washed out to sea.

'God bless them,' Giles was repeating to himself over and over again.

Suddenly, beneath the waters, upstream, they saw two beams of light, stretching impossibly out towards them.

'But that can't be a –' It was Emily, now standing at Bill's side.

'Car,' Bill confirmed.

And it was. They watched in astonishment as it floated towards them down the road, half submerged on the top of the hellish black river, somehow short-circuited, with its headlights on full beam, illuminating the water before it. Just as it drew level with them, the phantom vehicle nosedived, sending up a rush of bubbles as it vanished from sight.

The lightning died in the sky. Darkness returned.

Lewis cried out in pain behind them.

Bill couldn't see his hand in front of his face.

'I'm coming,' Emily shouted.

But then they all froze, as simultaneously, they heard the rumbling noise begin to rise again. Bill's face crumpled in confusion. It wasn't possible, was it? When the reservoir at Watersbind had already burst?

Sixteen bridges, the answer came. Sixteen bridges up the East and West Step valleys. And any one of them could have been blocked the same as South Bridge. Any one of them could have just given way . . .

The walls screamed out. The rumbling switched to thunder. The demonic cacophony rose. Bill shouted Emily's name, but his tongue might as well have been hacked out.

He staggered through the pitch-black prison of the room, as the floor shifted and broke like an ice sheet beneath his feet. He grabbed at thin air, praying for Emily.

Then a flash of lightning: he saw her, a silhouette against the window, arms outstretched the same as him. He ran at her.

But his hands touched nothing but the solid wall of water which blasted past and through the room.

# Chapter XXVII

**Mallorca, Present Day**

'You fucking bitch!'

Rachel held the receiver away from her ear, as the torrent of abuse continued. What the hell . . . ? She didn't have time for this, she thought, flustered. She didn't have time for a crank call, not when she was about to go downstairs and reintroduce herself to her brother after fifty years.

A moment ago, she'd been watching Laurie and Bill on the other side of the swimming pool from the top window. Laurie's explanation obviously wasn't going well. She couldn't hear what they were discussing, but Rachel could tell from their body language that maybe it was time for her to intervene. She'd decided that she couldn't hide in her own home any longer. It was time to take the bull by the horns, so to speak.

She'd been on her way downstairs when the phone had rung. Why hadn't she just ignored it?

'Hello?' she ventured, cutting in once more. 'Can you please –'

Then, through the swearing, she recognised Claire's voice.

'Darling? Darling? Is that you?' But Claire didn't answer. She was hysterical. 'Claire, Claire, calm down,' Rachel raised her voice, above Claire's sobs. 'What's happened? Tell me what's happened? Has something happened to Archie?'

Now all thoughts of Bill and Laurie vanished, as Rachel gripped the phone with both hands. She could feel real fear building up inside her. Claire had her moments of histrionics, but Rachel had never heard her this out of control.

'He's been having an affair,' Claire choked. 'He's been having an affair.'

'What on earth are you talking about?' Rachel felt as if she were falling. As if the floor beneath her had suddenly collapsed.

'Sam. *With her*,' Claire wailed.

'Who?'

'Your precious Laurie. That's who. That bitch, that . . . that . . . I called to tell her . . .'

Rachel sat down heavily on her bed. As she did so, one of the family photographs bounced off the covers and smashed on the floor.

'Are you sure?'

'Of course I'm fucking sure. Sam's just told me all about it.'

She heard Claire emit a guttural wail at the other end of the phone.

Rachel put her hand over her mouth, wanting to cry out herself. She felt something – fear? – adrenalin? – anger? – course right through her from the top of her head to her toes. She gripped the edge of the bed as Claire recounted what Sam had told her.

Not Sam. Oh God, no. Not Sam. He and Claire – they were happily married, weren't they? Sam couldn't cheat on Claire, he just couldn't.

*And with Laurie?*

No, it couldn't be right. Sam didn't even *like* Laurie. Then, suddenly, she thought about him the night they'd had supper here at the house and Laurie had been so subdued. Had Sam been so strange that night because Laurie was there? Because she was his lover?

What about James? Wasn't Laurie supposed to be in love with James? It didn't make sense. She'd spoken to James herself. But maybe James had just been a cover. Maybe Rachel had been wrong about him, too. Snapshots of all the times she'd seen Sam and Laurie together rushed through her head as she searched for meaning.

'It can't be true –' she half mumbled to Claire, but as she did, she thought about Laurie's bags, all neatly packed up in her room and the truth of what Claire was saying finally sunk in. Laurie knew it was going to come out! She knew. She knew she'd have to leave.

'What am I going to do?' Claire wailed.

Something desperate in her voice, in her cry for help made Rachel snap out of her own shock and focus. She had to think straight. This was not going to happen. She would simply not allow it. Whatever had happened between Sam and Laurie, Rachel was sure as hell it was going to finish, right now. Sam was the father of Claire's child. What did he think? That he could just walk away?

Well he could think again! He had responsibilities. And it was because of who Claire was that he had everything he took for granted. No, Sam was going to damn well apologise to Claire and get on with fixing all the damage he'd done. Every marriage had its ups and downs – Christ, she should know. Sam and Claire would be able to put this behind them and move on.

And as for Laurie? Well, damn it! Laurie Vale could take her packed bags and get the hell away from Rachel's family before she did any more harm.

'Claire, calm down,' Rachel tried to get through to her.

It took all her effort to control her voice. 'Darling, please. Stop crying. Try and pull yourself together. I'll sort this out, I promise. Sam is not going to get away with this. Just leave it to me. Is he there with you now?'

'Yes, he –'

Rachel stood up. 'Whatever you do, just keep him there. Everything is going to be fine.'

Rachel slammed down the phone. Every maternal instinct told her to run to Claire, to put her arms around her, to make everything better. And yet a bigger part of her felt as if she was going to burst with anger. She felt as if she'd failed horribly. She'd failed to protect her family. This was all her fault. And she had to fix it, right now.

She staggered down the stairs to the hallway, hardly knowing what she was going to say, but whatever it was, she was going to give it to Laurie straight. With both barrels. Right between the eyes. And right now.

Then she saw Bill, standing before her. He had his arms folded, like a bouncer.

'Rachel,' he said.

She stopped still on the stairs. It was the familiarity of his voice that did it. Fifty years melted away in an instant and it felt as if she'd been caught out, as if she were still the sneaky schoolgirl she'd once been. It was the solidity of him, the reality of him, his stature, even though he was in his seventies, that utterly threw her. She felt all her power draining away.

Now, everything she'd been preparing to say to him vanished from her head. She felt as if the unity of her family, the trump card she'd been planning on showing him, had just disappeared into thin air. Instead, she felt stripped bare, as if he were seeing her at her most vulnerable.

'Bill,' she said. Her eyes locked with his and she remembered now with such clarity the last time she'd seen his face. Then his eyes became harder than ever.

'You listen to me and you listen well,' Bill said. He stabbed his finger at her. 'I don't know what kind of game you're playing, and I don't know what crazy plan you had when you got Laurie to ask me here, but I don't forgive you. I won't ever forgive you. You made your choice. And just because you're widowed now you can't expect to turn back time.'

The coldness of his voice, his lack of sympathy, his lack of compassion overwhelmed her. Her heart raced.

'You married a liar, Rachel. If you're after some kind of salvation for your conscience from me, then you can think again. We're not family, you and I. We stopped being family a long time ago when you walked away.'

In fifty years, nobody had spoken to her like this. Nobody had dared to attack her, or Tony, or her integrity. Nobody had dared impose their will on her, certainly not in her own home.

She was shaking now. All the hope she'd felt earlier had gone, all the expectations she'd had now evaporated. This was hopeless. Nothing had changed. She'd been a fool expecting Bill to have mellowed over time. How could she ever have thought that he would forgive her? She'd assumed that once they saw each other, the past would have been magically swept away. But now they were finally face to face, she could see how rash and unrealistic that notion had been. She felt all the fantasies she'd entertained about being reconciled with Bill crashing down around her. He'd just become more stuck in his ways. He didn't want or need the same things that she did. He didn't need forgiveness, or understanding. He would live with his hatred and bitterness until the day he died, like their mother had, firmly believing he was still in the right.

'You were the one who walked away, Bill,' she corrected him.

Bill shook his head, as if trying to stop her words entering his ears. 'I don't want to discuss this. It's too late.'

'So why are you here? Why are you standing here?' *Why are you tormenting me*, she wanted to ask him.

'For Laurie. Because she shouldn't have to say this for me.'

'Ha!' Rachel spat, the irony of the situation, the irony of this meeting suddenly hitting her. All the time she'd thought Laurie was helping her. But the truth was that she was bringing Bill to her to hurt her even more. Father and daughter. They were just as bad as each other. Just as selfish. Just as blinkered and stubborn. How appropriate that Laurie was named after her mother.

'I think it's utterly despicable that you have drawn Laurie into this,' Bill continued. 'Why do you think I kept you a secret for all those years? To protect her from you. To stop her having to know what happened to her grandparents. But I should have known you would be this devious. I should have known you would take the first chance of taking advantage of her good nature. That you hadn't stopped being selfish, or thinking of yourself. How pathetic that you had to wait until your husband died.'

Rachel wanted to yell out for Tony. She'd never felt so acutely that she'd betrayed him. She'd courted Bill from the moment he'd died. She'd gone behind her husband's back and sought this. This punishment.

She should have trusted Tony. She had when he'd been alive. Why had she stopped the moment he'd died? Because he'd been right about Bill all along. She tried to picture

Tony's face. She thought of all the photos she'd taken upstairs to protect Laurie and Bill, when they arrived at the villa. How could she? She wasn't ashamed of Tony. Not for a moment. She should have kept the pictures where they were.

'Laurie's good nature? Laurie's good nature?' Rachel's rage burst through. 'How dare you walk into my house and say all this to me. How dare you act like you're still in charge. I don't have to put up with this from anyone, especially not from you. Especially when you've got your facts wrong now, the same as you always did.'

It was time to put Bill straight about his own family, before he started judging hers. She stormed towards him down the stairs, forcing him back into the hall.

'And after what Laurie's done!' she shouted. 'You dare to lecture me about Tony, when you didn't even know him? You didn't even see the man he turned out to be. He was good and kind and honest and true. Unlike that vile daughter of yours.'

'What on earth do you mean?'

Rachel wanted to scream. 'If you'd just shut up and listen for one second . . . I'll spell it out for you, Bill.'

# Chapter XXVIII

**Stepmouth, Midnight, 15 August 1953**

Rachel sat shivering on an upturned crate, clutching a blue tin mug of tea that had gone cold in her hand, a grey army blanket around her shoulders. Her teeth chattered as she stared out at the road leading down Summerglade Hill, but it was shrouded in a darkness so complete, it was almost like a void. She tried and tried to focus on it, praying for Tony to step out of the darkness, but all she could see was a veil of drips coursing from the edge of the green tarpaulin above her, splattering on to the waterlogged ground below. She had no idea what time it was. All she knew was that this nightmare had been stretching on and on for hours.

It seemed a lifetime ago that Tony and Bill had left her alone in the van. She'd been so terrified, listening to the howl of the wind, as the rain had drummed on the metal roof in time with the throbbing pain in her chest. She'd hoped when she'd seen some people outside the van illuminated by a shaft of lightning, that her ordeal would have been over, but it had only been the beginning.

Even though Rachel had only had the vaguest glimpses of the mud-covered bedraggled crowd as she'd peered through the windscreen of the van, she'd seen enough to know that quite a few of them had been injured. She'd banged her fist on the window, yelling at them to stop and wait for her, but nobody had heard her. The roar of the

439

wind had been deafening. In desperation, she'd clambered out of the driver's door.

There had only been once source of light, from one man holding a torch, but as Rachel had joined the group, struggling against the rain, the weak beam had flickered and died. She'd groped her way in the darkness, holding on to somebody's wet coat, as the group hobbled together up Summerglade Hill, to higher ground.

Suddenly, a fork of lightning had opened the sky and Rachel had had a glimpse of the terrible drama below as if through a crack in the black curtain of sky. It was a scene she had barely been able to comprehend. She'd seen an unthinkable torrent of water, rushing through the town.

The survivors had only made it as far as the clearing halfway up the hill near the viewing gate, before the group had started to disperse. Someone had shouted above the howl of the wind and the roar of the water, and had managed to corral the survivors through the gate to the disused gypsy caravan where Rachel had once made love with Tony.

They'd all waited in the darkness, huddled together as the rain poured through the roof of the dilapidated caravan, the sour smell of mud mixing with mould. No one knew what had happened. Only that they'd managed to escape the waters that had come. Rachel had found a candle in a box under one of the seats and someone had lit it. In the gloom, she'd been able to identify the wet faces of her companions: Mrs Tamar from the butcher's; Janet from the ice-cream parlour and her two sisters; Mr Barry and old Mr Stebbing. Another woman, probably from the hotel, had nursed a baby, silently weeping while a small girl had whimpered by her side. Meanwhile, Mr John had shaken the torch so that it flickered intermittently and had volunteered to take the first watch outside, plaintively calling for survivors to come and join them.

Nobody had asked Rachel how she'd come to be alone inside the van on Summerglade Hill. The collective numbness of pain and shock had subdued her companions into silence, as they'd all strained to listen against the buffeting of the wind for other survivors, or for signs of any sort of help. Rachel had hardly been able to sit upright, such was the pain in her chest. Unnoticed tears had coursed down her cheeks, as she'd pleaded with the vengeful God outside to let her wake up from this terrible nightmare.

It must have been an hour later that the first ambulance had arrived from Barnstaple. Rachel had no idea who'd managed to raise the alarm, as according to Mr John all the telephones were down as well as the electricity. And then more ambulances had arrived from the army base. They'd declared that the roads were too bad to evacuate the group and had set up next to the gypsy caravan, constructing tarpaulin over the clearing to form a makeshift camp. A kind woman in a grey uniform had handed out hot tea and blankets.

Now, from where Rachel sat, she could hear the occasional moans of the other survivors when there was a lull in the wind and the tarpaulin stopped flapping so loudly. Yet despite the flickering gas lamps the army had rigged up, it was still almost impossible to see much beyond her feet. The lightning had stopped now but the occasional sweep of a vehicle's headlamps illuminated a hedge or a tree, reminding her that she was on Summerglade Hill, sitting by a road she knew like her own skin.

Behind her, the army medic who had treated her, wrapping a bandage around her ribs and cleaning up her face, jumped down from the back of one of the ambulances and

441

startled her. He'd just checked on Mr Barry, having sedated him and laid him on the bed in the back of the ambulance. Rachel knew that the others were concerned over Mr Barry being manhandled like that, but he'd been ranting so hard at the army staff that Rachel had seen they'd had no choice but to silence him.

The rumours of the RAF's cloud-seeding to make rain deliberately that she'd heard in the shop were obviously more widespread than she'd thought. And Mr Barry, who was missing a son and obviously thought the armed forces were to blame, had wasted no time in venting his fury.

Rachel pitied the harassed medic. She wanted to do something – anything – to help, but she already knew what the answer would be. She'd been told that she had two broken ribs and must stay still. She also felt slightly woozy from where she'd hit her head when the car had crashed. She wondered whether she'd lose the baby now. Her stomach felt bruised and battered.

But it didn't seem to matter any more. All that mattered was that Tony made it through and came back to her . . . and, for that matter, Bill and her mother. Rumours had been reaching them of great waves of water . . . of collapsing buildings. But Rachel wouldn't believe them. How could they be true when it was still too dark to see?

But fear still gripped her. What if a wave of water hit their home? What if her mother hadn't been able to get out? Rachel felt desperate, just thinking of her mother left frightened and all alone in her room, with only a candle, unable to get out. Rachel thought back to their argument the day before, how she'd hated her mother with all her heart. It seemed so long ago. But what if that was the last thing her mother remembered? What if Rachel never got the chance to tell her mother how much she loved her?

What if she never got to understand that she loved both her and Tony?

And Tony? What if the flood had taken him? What if he was down there injured, waiting for someone to rescue him? What if he was in pain? It would all be her fault.

It was all supposed to have been so different. She should have been far away with him by now. And tomorrow, or the next day, or the day after that, they'd have arrived in Gretna Green to get married. Just the two of them, pledging themselves to one another for ever. And then nobody would ever have been able to split them up, or take her baby. Not even her mother.

But now, as she thought about everyone she loved, she couldn't imagine the danger they were all in. South Bridge couldn't really have gone, could it? The water in the valley simply couldn't have got that high, could it? It was impossible.

This was Stepmouth. Disasters didn't happen in Stepmouth. It wasn't a place that anyone cared about. It wasn't a place that could be devastated like this. This kind of thing happened abroad, to other people. Floods happened on the Pathé newsreels, not here in her backyard.

But the glimpse she'd seen of the torrential water haunted her. What if people had died? What if the reason there weren't more people here was because they'd all gone? Rachel felt dizzy with panic. What if this was all there was left of the world that up until yesterday had seemed so ordinary and boring?

'Is there any news?' she shouted, grabbing the arm of one of the rescue workers, who'd recently arrived. He stared out at her from under the hood of his dripping souwester.

443

'Nothing, yet,' he replied, above the din. 'We've tried to get through, but we can't get beyond the bottom of the hill. There's too much water. We're doing all we can. We'll let you know as soon as there's any news. Don't worry, love, the rain's easing up at long last.'

Rachel wasn't comforted. She slumped once more into black fear, staring at the road, willing Tony and Bill to come into sight. She had no idea how long she sat for, but she jumped when she felt a hand on her shoulder. She turned, expecting to see a policeman, or a soldier, but it was Bill. Her mug of cold tea clattered to the floor, the liquid spilling on to her sodden skirt, as she sprang to her feet, wincing at the pain.

He was drenched. Standing only in a vest and trousers. He looked as if he'd been swimming. Even his shoes were gone. Rachel could see that he was covered in scratches and bruises. He was holding his left arm up in front of him and Rachel could see that he was in a lot of pain.

She had been expecting him to be angry. She'd been expecting a showdown about how she and Tony had stolen his beloved car, or worse, a furious lecture about her being pregnant, but in an instant she forgot all of it, such was her horror at his appearance.

She gasped and he held out his arms to her.

'Thank God,' Bill said, holding her tightly to him. He was shivering violently. 'Thank God, you're alive.'

She took the blanket from her shoulders. Then she forced him to sit on a packing crate and put the blanket around him. He was soaked through, his face smeared in mud and blood.

'I was so worried,' she said. 'Oh, Bill, it's so horrible. Where have you been?'

'Oh God!' He broke down crying, clinging to her.

'What is it?'

'Emily,' she thought she heard him say. 'She's gone.'

Bill's eyes were bloodshot as he looked up at her. 'I tried to hold on to her, but I couldn't. I couldn't,' he said, his voice catching in his throat. 'I watched the water take her, Rachel. I didn't reach her in time.'

He pressed his head against Rachel's chest. She gasped at the pain.

'They'll find her. Someone will have found her. Don't worry.' She tried to find strength to put in her voice, rather than the cold terror she felt.

'I'm going,' Bill said, suddenly releasing her and springing up from the crate. 'I'm going to look for her.'

Rachel clung on to him. 'But you can't. It's too –'

'Let me go.' He shook her off, shouting now.

'What's going on back there?' someone shouted.

Then Rachel saw two soldiers rushing over. They took hold of him.

'No one goes out,' one of them said. 'Not until we've got the all-clear.'

'Medic!' the other soldier called. 'We've got another one in need of attention.'

It must have been several hours later, just as dawn was breaking that the all-clear was finally given. Shortly afterwards, a crowd of people started walking up the hill, chaperoned by several policemen and soldiers.

And then, as the darkness faded into a dark grey, suddenly there were people and noise everywhere, lights and sirens as the ambulances and fire engines fought to get through the throng to the injured.

Desperately, Rachel left her position under the tarpaulin, her legs stiff. She started hobbling as fast as she could through the crowd, scanning each ravaged, harrowed face for Tony. She felt sobs escape her, as each person passed her.

And then she saw him. He was being supported by a policeman. But he was alive. Her Tony was alive.

His face looked ashen, his hair plastered to his face. She could see that his shirt was a rag and his trousers were soaked and torn and he was limping, but Rachel thought he was more beautiful than ever.

She pushed through the crowd and ran to him, flinging her arms around his neck, kissing his face.

'You're here, you're here,' she gasped, through her tears. It didn't occur to her to worry about who saw them together. Everything that had seemed so important yesterday now seemed so trivial.

But Tony didn't have a chance to reply, before Bill rushed forward and split them apart.

'Where's Mum?' he demanded.

Tony stared at Rachel and then he looked at Bill. 'I'm so sorry,' he whispered.

She stared at him, trying to grasp what he was telling her. She could tell from the look in his eyes that it was the worst possible news.

'What?' Rachel asked, taking a step backwards.

'I couldn't . . . I didn't get to her in time.'

'What do you mean? She must be here somewhere,' Bill said, trying to shove past Tony.

Tony grabbed him by the shoulder. 'No, it's too late.'

'What do you mean?' Rachel asked.

'The house. I saw it go when the flood hit. I was trying to reach it. The whole shop. It's gone.'

'Gone?' Rachel gasped.

'I managed to climb to the top of the old oak tree at the

alley before the waves hit. That's where they rescued me from just now.'

Bill was shaking his head. Rachel could see in the dim light that his face was white with rage. 'You got to the tree? If you got as far as the tree, you could have got as far as Mum. You . . . you fucking coward!'

'No, Bill, no,' Tony said. 'No, I tried, honestly –'

'You're lying. You just saved yourself, didn't you? You left her there to die.'

'You! Calm down,' said a policeman who had heard the commotion. 'I'm sure the poor lad did his best. You saw the conditions out there yourself. He was lucky to get away with his life. He was up that tree all night.'

Rachel couldn't believe what she was hearing. Her mother had gone. And Rachel had wished it on her. The last thing she'd said to Tony yesterday was that she hated her mother and wanted her dead. If it was anyone's fault, it was hers.

'You might as well have killed her yourself,' Bill shouted, pressing his face up against Tony's.

Through her tears, Rachel saw Tony flinch and back away.

'He doesn't mean that, Tony,' she said, stepping in between them and breaking them apart.

'I should never have trusted you,' Bill shouted. 'I should have gone to her myself. You're just like your brother . . . you . . . you murderer!' Bill punched him in the face. Rachel screamed, as Tony staggered backwards. Bill launched himself at Tony and they fell to the wet road, gasping.

'Stop it!' Rachel yelled at Bill. 'Stop it.'

She fell to her knees beside them. They were both gasping for air, Bill grabbed Tony's wet shirt bunching it up around his neck. The policemen struggled to separate them.

447

Rachel pulled at Bill's shoulder. 'Let him go, Bill. Let him go!'

'I wanted to save her, I swear it,' Tony managed, through the stranglehold.

'You're lying. I can see it in your eyes.'

Two more policemen descended on them and dragged them all apart. 'That's enough. Any more and you're under arrest.'

Bill stood upright and shook himself. He put his hands to his hair and bunched them into fists, his face contorted with grief and fury.

Tony was still lying on the road. His hair had fallen into his face. He touched his cheek where Bill had punched him.

Rachel stared up at Bill. 'What are you doing?' she screamed at him. 'It's not Tony's fault.'

Bill walked away from her and then walked back, trying to calm down. Then he held out his hand to her.

'Get away from him, Rachel,' Bill said. 'Come now. Come on.'

But Rachel stayed next to Tony, supporting him to his feet.

'I'm not coming anywhere,' she sobbed. 'Not with you. How could you say those dreadful things?'

Bill stepped in close. 'Now!'

She clutched on to Tony's arm.

'If you don't get away from him, this minute, then you're no longer my sister. Do you understand?' Bill's tone was icy cold as he stared at her. 'It's because of him I came to you in the first place when I should have been with Mum. I could have saved them both. Mum and Emily. I shouldn't have had to be with you, because of your stupidity, your, your . . .'

'I'm sorry,' Rachel cried. 'I'm sorry.'

'Then come on. Come now!'

'No,' Rachel sobbed.

'Then I will never speak to you again.'

And then he was walking away. Rachel rushed after him and tried to grab his arm, but he shook her off.

'Leave him,' Tony said, catching up with her and putting his arms around her. Through her tears, Rachel watched Bill forcing his way through the crowd, down Summerglade Hill to the town below.

# Chapter XXIX

**Mallorca, Present Day**

In the late afternoon, the heat seemed almost unbearable. It felt as if everything was being burnt by an invisible fire. Laurie, who'd always felt things intuitively, felt as if the air was charged with violence. And yet all around her everything was eerily silent.

She was sitting in the only shady part of the garden she could find, at the corner of the swimming pool, her feet dangling in the warm water. She was in the circle of shade cast by one of the rattan umbrellas, but it hardly helped. She was keeping as still as she possibly could, but could feel perspiration flicking out all over her – even her fingertips, as if she were running a marathon. It felt as if she was suffocating.

She squinted out at the view, seeing the sunshine reflecting off the shimmering surface of the flat sea, like a swathe of tinfoil. It was almost too painful to look at. In the distance she could see a yacht far away on the horizon. She thought about the day she'd spent sailing on *Flight* with Sam. She'd been so happy. So clear. But now?

Laurie pulled her feet from the water and hunched up her knees, resting her temple on her kneecaps. There was still no word from Sam. At first she'd wondered whether the call inside had been from him, but she'd soon changed her mind. She was just being paranoid. It could have been anyone ringing Rachel.

Sam was probably telling Claire right now, she reasoned with herself. Maybe that was why she was feeling like this. She felt her ears burning and remembered the childish rhyme. What was it? Left for love, right for spite? Well, her right ear was on fire.

She touched her earlobe tentatively, wishing she could tune in to whatever was being said about her. She felt so helpless. And so nervous. It was her conversation with her father that had done it. Now she was alone and had time to mull over what he'd said, his hard-hitting comments about her not knowing the truth about Sam and Claire's marriage and his scepticism about Sam's promise to leave Claire, stung more and more.

Laurie remembered the wedding photo she'd seen of Sam and Claire together when she'd first arrived at the villa and how betrayed she'd felt. She'd been focused on Sam, but next to him Claire had looked so happy. Happy and delighted. Perhaps her father was right, Laurie pondered, watching two butterflies battle over the surface of the pool. She knew how Sam felt and how things were from his point of view, but she didn't have a clue about how Claire felt about their marriage. After all, her wedding vows to Sam probably had been sacred. She hadn't had a clue that Sam was harbouring a guilty secret, that his heart might not have been 100 per cent in it.

And now three years after that picture had been taken, they were still married. Laurie thought about the times she'd seen Claire and Sam together, how Claire teased him and tried to ruffle his feathers in public. Each time, Laurie had been blinkered by jealousy and irritation, but what if all it had really been was Claire's way of showing her affection?

Laurie imagined herself in Claire's shoes. She was going

to be devastated when Sam told her he was leaving. It would come as an absolute bolt out of the blue. She couldn't begin to imagine the hatred Claire would feel towards her. And Claire would be right to hate her, wouldn't she? After all, this was Laurie's fault. She'd stolen Claire's husband away. That was how Claire would see it. She wouldn't see that there was love involved. She would only ever see deceit and lies.

And what had Claire ever done to Laurie, apart from want to be her friend? All she'd done from the moment they'd been introduced was try and include her and to make her feel like part of the family. And in return, Laurie had betrayed her. She'd thrown their family connection back in her face.

Laurie buried her face in her hands. She felt so wicked. So tainted. All that was good and pure and noble about her love for Sam when they'd been together, now seemed soiled and she felt wretched with guilt. Now she'd seen her father's view of Sam, as a traitor, she felt like an outcast herself. It wasn't only Claire but the rest of the world who would never see the truth about her and Sam.

It was all such a journey into the unknown. It was all such a risk. Christ, she didn't even know whether she and Sam would be compatible living together. He hadn't met many of her friends and the ones he had met, like Roz, distrusted him for what had happened three years ago. Would any of Laurie's friends ever be able to see that her and Sam's bond was amazing and magical? Or, like Laurie's family, would they only see two people who had fallen from grace, who had been selfish and thoughtless? It seemed so unfair. She didn't want to be a selfish person, she wanted everyone to be happy.

But now she could see how naive that hope was. The

truth was that she didn't really know anything. Her father's revelations had made her see that. Laurie glanced towards the back doors of the villa, wondering what was happening in there. Her father had seemed insistent on going to confront Rachel alone and Laurie had known better than to prevent him. And now she didn't dare interrupt, despite the fact that she was longing to go inside and get her things and leave.

As if reading her thoughts, she heard the swish of the terrace doors sliding open. She scrambled up from the edge of the pool and put on her shoes. The soles of them burnt her feet. Her father and Rachel stepped out on to the terrace together in silence. Laurie shaded her eyes from the sun.

She could tell from the grim look on both of their faces that the reunion hadn't gone well. Yet, oddly, they both walked side by side down the steps together, their strides perfectly matched, and even from a distance she could see a family resemblance between them.

Yet up close, as she stopped in front of them on the other side of the pool, Laurie was in for a shock. Rachel had been crying. More than that, she looked as if she'd been through a horrible trauma. Her eyes were bloodshot and her face wrinkled, as if she'd aged twenty years in just twenty minutes.

Laurie felt terrible. She wanted to hug her, to try and make things better. She knew how furious her father had been. Had he taken his wrath out on Rachel? Had he reduced her to this humbled shadow of her former self? Rachel had been so excited this morning, now she looked utterly wrecked. Laurie tried to smile at her, but Rachel avoided looking at her.

It was her father who spoke first.

'You didn't tell me the truth about Sam, Laurel,' he said. He never called her Laurel.

Laurie opened her mouth, staring between Rachel and her father.

'You didn't tell me that he was related to my sister,' he continued. 'That he was married to her granddaughter.'

It was Rachel's turn to speak. Her voice shook as she glared at Laurie. 'Is it true?'

Her father had told Rachel about Sam, then. That's how she'd found out. How bizarre that she'd assumed they were talking about their own past, when all this time they'd been in there talking about her and Sam. No wonder her ears had been burning.

'Rachel, I didn't mean to –' she began, but the look in Rachel's eyes silenced Laurie and made her stomach lurch.

'You came here knowing you would be near Sam. And you . . .' Rachel faltered. 'I trusted you.'

Laurie stared at them both. She was at a total loss as to how to defend herself. In every possible showdown scenario she'd imagined, either Sam or her father had been by her side, supporting her. She hadn't expected her father to be with Rachel, taking some moral high ground, being so weirdly protective of her. Now she felt cornered.

'But . . . but –' she stumbled.

'You're just a liar!' Rachel choked and Laurie saw that whatever she said, she'd already been judged. The disgust in her aunt's voice terrified her. She appealed to her father.

'Look, I'm sorry, but if you'd have been honest with me and told me about Rachel in the first place, instead of keeping our family a secret for all these years, then I would have known who Sam was. I would have known he was in the same family as me when I fell in love with him *three years ago* in France.'

454

'He wasn't yours to fall in love with,' Rachel snapped.

'Maybe, Rachel. But . . . but Sam's a person. Not your property.'

'He's not yours either. I want you to get out of my house. I want you to leave before you do any more damage.'

Laurie felt utterly stricken by Rachel's venom. 'Oh, Rachel. Do you really think that's why I came here? To make people unhappy? That's not who I am.'

'Oh, isn't it?'

'No! I didn't mean . . . I didn't want it to happen like this –'

'Might I remind you that Sam is married to Claire,' Rachel cut in.

It was pointless trying to explain to Rachel, but Laurie tried one last time.

'Yes, I know that. And he's been nothing but loyal. He's stayed with Claire and he's made a home for Archie. He's done everything right for you, but he's sacrificed his own happiness in the process. He didn't want this to happen, either.'

'How dare you! He was perfectly happy until you came along. You're not going to get him. Do you hear me? I won't allow it.'

Laurie could tell she meant every word. She felt like a beaten dog. But still she wouldn't give up. She had to defend her feelings for Sam. She had to try and make them understand. 'I'm sorry if it goes against your morals, Dad, and I'm sorry it's turned out like this for you, Rachel, but I'm not going to apologise for falling in love. To either of you. I didn't choose for it to be like this, but it is. And I'm not going to pretend I don't feel how I do, just to please you two.' She stopped. From the hard looks on their faces, she could see she was getting nowhere. Her words were falling on deaf ears. 'You know what? This is my life. It's none of your goddamned business.'

'She's right, Rachel.'

It was Sam. He must have come through the house. Like an apparition, he was now standing behind Rachel and her father above them on the terrace. She had no idea how long he'd been listening.

Sam took off his sunglasses and it was then that Laurie saw how ashen he looked. He stared through the gap between Rachel and Bill directly at Laurie and the tears that were so close to the surface came rushing out of her in a sob.

'Oh, Sam,' she cried, running to him.

He seemed too shaken to say anything. Instead, he held her briefly to him and kissed her forehead. In that moment, she knew he'd told Claire.

'You can't do this, Sam!' Rachel said, her voice shaking.

'I'm sorry, Rachel, but I already have.' His voice was barely more than a whisper.

'Don't you dare –' Rachel thundered.

He gripped Laurie's hand. She knew that he loved Rachel and that turning his back on her was one of the hardest parts of what they had to do.

'Dad?' Laurie asked, brushing away her tears. But her father turned away and put his hands in his pockets. He didn't even look at Sam.

'Bill?' Rachel shouted. 'Aren't you going to do anything?'

'I can't stop them, Rachel. You know I can't. You of all people should know that.'

Rachel stared at him in astonishment.

'Are you ready?' Sam whispered, turning to Laurie. He looked harrowed, as if he'd had something knocked out of him.

She nodded.

'If you go through that door then it's all over, Sam,' Rachel called out. 'If you leave, then you leave everything. You're fired. I'm warning you –'

But Sam squeezed Laurie's hand. Turning their backs on Rachel, they walked quickly into the house.

Inside, Laurie made it to the hall before she threw her arms around Sam and held him.

'Oh, God, Sam, that was so awful,' she said, shaking. 'Hideous.'

'Are you OK? I've been so worried.'

He held her face, staring into her eyes. 'Oh, Laurie, I love you so much.'

He kissed her again, then he pulled away.

'What happened?' Laurie asked. 'What about Archie?'

Sam shook his head. She could see the tears he'd been holding back welling up in his eyes. 'Claire . . . she . . . I had to leave him.'

'Oh, darling, I'm so sorry.'

Why was this so hard? She had no idea what to say to take away Sam's pain.

'I can't bear it,' he said. 'Just the thought of him not having a father . . . or calling someone else "Dad".' Sam covered his eyes.

'You're his dad,' Laurie said, firmly, taking his hand so that she forced him to look at her. 'Whatever happens, Archie will always know that, Sam, no matter what. He'll grow up knowing the truth. Not like me. We'll see him. And we'll tell him everything. We'll make him understand.'

Sam interlaced his fingers with hers and squeezed both of her hands.

'We've got each other now,' she said.

Sam nodded. 'Let's just get the hell out of here, shall we?'

They ran up the stairs and collected all her bags. 'What about the paintings?' Sam asked.

'Leave them. I can do more. Let's just go.'

On the driveway, Laurie dumped the bags by her feet. 'Whose car?' she asked. 'I hired this one, but it doesn't matter.'

Sam took the car keys of the Porsche out of his pocket and left them in the car door. 'I don't work for the company any more, so I guess we'll take yours.'

He didn't look back as he walked towards the Fiesta, opened the door and flung Laurie's bags in the back seat. She watched him, amazed that he was being so brave. He looked at her over the top of the car.

'I feel so bad about Dad.' Laurie hesitated, glancing back towards the house.

'Do you really want to go back in there?'

Laurie shook her head and stared at the house one last time, but she still felt guilty for abandoning her father. She thought about everything he'd told her about his and Rachel's past. Laurie couldn't bear the thought that he wouldn't forgive her for what she'd done. But maybe, once he'd got over the shock of what had happened, he'd understand that she had to make this clean break, just as he had done all those years ago. She had to have a go at making her own family with Sam – even if it meant hurting the people she loved.

'Laurie?' Sam asked, gently.

Laurie shook her head and hurried into the car and Sam got in next to her. It was unbearably hot, but she didn't care. She leant across and kissed him, over and over again. Then she stopped and stared into his eyes.

'Oh, Laurie,' Sam said, with a long sigh, as he leant back against the headrest. 'How could we ever have taken this long to get here?'

'Hang on,' she said, with a battle-weary smile as she started the engine. 'We haven't got there yet.'

# Chapter XXX

**Stepmouth, 23 August 1953**

The short blast of a hand-cranked air-raid siren rose up into the pale blue skies. It was meant to act as a warning, but it was the last of so many that no one in the Salvation Army food queue, including Tony Glover, so much as flinched. Then came the boom of the high explosive detonating. Away in the distance, a plume of dust and stone splinters burst into the air above where the town hall had once stood.

A whistle blew and the roar of bulldozers and shouting soldiers filled the air as work resumed. Wherever you looked, uniformed people were on the move: members of the army, the civil defence, the RAF, the AA, the RAC and the Women's Voluntary Service.

There was still so much left to do. The sixty-ton boulder which the army engineers had just exploded was only one tiny part of the estimated fifteen thousand tons of rock which the River Step had swept into town on the night of the flood.

Eight days had passed since then. Yesterday afternoon, Tony had gathered with Rachel and the rest of the remaining townspeople over at the St Jude Cemetery on the grassy, seaward-facing slope to the right of the harbour, as a service for the dead had been held.

Thirty-six people were now known to have been killed in the streets of Stepmouth and the surrounding villages during the night of 15 August. The eldest victim had been an eighty-year-old woman, the youngest a baby boy of barely three months. Four adults remained missing, presumed dead. A solitary Scottish piper had played 'Flowers of the Forest' in final tribute to them all. The sad notes had drifted up from the cemetery and into the hills.

A memorial was to be built, inscribed with the names of the dead. The Duke of Edinburgh had promised to visit.

According to a newspaper report Tony had read, on the night of 15 August nine inches of rain had fallen, of which five inches had fallen during the cloudburst which occurred between seven and eight thirty. With no one but nature to blame for what had happened, there was talk now of making representation to the Ministry of Defence with regard to the cloud-seeding operations which had been carried out in the preceding months over the moors.

A BBC television crew had been stationed here all week and had broadcast the service live to the nation. The flood had been the first British disaster to be relayed from country to country, so that now the whole world knew the fate of the town.

Stepmouth had been devastated. Its streets had been choked with rubble and its buildings assaulted and knocked down. Worst hit had been the town centre. Windows hung splintered and smashed. Broken furniture blocked doorways and lay jammed in the mud, which had been dumped nine feet high in between some of the houses that remained. Whole floors of properties had been packed with mud and detritus, or simply swept away. Solitary walls now teetered where two- and three-storey buildings had once stood.

People who'd lived in London had described it as on a par with the damage inflicted on the capital during the Blitz.

461

The carnage continued inland. This morning, Tony and Rachel had caught a lift in an army truck with the soldiers who'd been billeted in Brookford village. They'd travelled along the West Step valley and down Summerglade Hill and into the town.

A filthy tidemark scorched the valley where the waters had risen. Almost all of the foot and road bridges had been torn down, including the one at Watersbind. That Bill had found one safe enough to cross after the flood had hit, had been a miracle. The hydroelectric power station had also been destroyed. Tony's stepfather, Don, had slavishly worked there on the night of the flood to keep the power to the town switched on, until he'd finally being forced to flee. Two of Don's friends had failed to make it out, but Don himself had survived.

Tony reached the counter of the Salvation Army's mobile canteen.

'Tony, isn't it?' one of the men working there asked.

'That's right.'

'Still collecting for your family and' – the smartly uniformed man scanned the list before him – 'Rachel Vale?'

'Yes.'

The man filled Tony's water bottle with clean water for him, before lifting up a cardboard box on to the counter. The box was marked: GLOVER & VALE FAMILIES (STAYING TOGETHER).

Only three houses still stood in the row in which Tony had been born. The engorged West Step had torn the others down on its way past. But Tony's family had been lucky. His mother's house, where she and the twins had huddled together in her bedroom, had escaped intact.

Good, then, as well as evil had come from the flood. Tony's previous disputes with his mother had evaporated

462

in the face of the greater tragedy. He'd moved back home the day after the waters had retreated. His mother had been wonderful with Rachel, too, helping her to come to terms with what had happened. She'd offered to let Rachel stay – at least until the baby was born.

It made sense. Now that Mrs Vale was dead and the possibility of Tony and Rachel staying together in the town had reopened. And it certainly made sense for the next two years, during which time Tony and Rachel would have to spend most of their time apart.

One of the few items not swept away by the flood had been Tony's call-up papers, which had arrived on the morning of the fourteenth. He'd been summoned to a medical in Barnstaple the following week. Two years in the army would follow. He'd try for married quarters in time, but he'd heard that they were rare.

'There should be enough for two days there,' the Salvation Army man said kindly, pushing the brown cardboard box over the counter towards Tony, 'but let us know if you need any more.'

Something inside the box caught Tony's eye and he rummaged through it, before pulling out what looked like a giant yellow claw. 'Are these –'

'Bananas,' the man confirmed. 'Sent over from Jamaica as part of the relief effort.'

'I've never seen them like this before,' Tony said. 'Only black. You know, the way they are when they've been preserved.'

'Aye, well, that's what they look like when they're fresh.'

The man smiled at him and Tony smiled back. Fresh, he thought. A new beginning. The world was changing. He could feel it all around.

'Tony!' it was Rachel's voice.

He turned to see her walking slowly towards him from the high street. Unlike Tony, who still had some clothes at his mother's house, Rachel was dressed in donated too-big black leather shoes, too-long striped woollen leggings and a too-warm woollen dress.

Beneath the dress, her ribs were still bandaged tight to encourage them to heal. She was meant to be in bed, but had insisted on coming into town with him. To see her friend Pearl, she'd said. To check that she was OK.

Thanking the man behind the counter, Tony picked up the box and walked across the uneven ground towards Rachel.

'Look!' she said as she reached him. Her eyes were on fire, her shoes caked in mud. She held out her hands to show him what she'd found. 'It's Mum's,' she said.

He knew exactly what it was: the plain silver crucifix that Mrs Vale had dropped on the floor of Bill's room on the night of the flood. He was staggered to see it in Rachel's hands, and how she'd come by it, he had no idea.

'You said you weren't going to look.' At the house, he meant. She'd said it the morning after the flood, as the waters had still been receding and they'd stared at the rank drift of mud where Vale Supplies and the ironmongery had once stood. Nothing had remained of the home in which Rachel and Bill had grown up.

'I couldn't help myself,' she said. 'I had to say goodbye. Not like at the service yesterday. But there, where it happened. And then I saw it, hanging from the side of the bus stop . . . like she'd left it there for me . . .' He expected her to start crying, but she smiled at him instead. 'I'm so glad I've got it to remember her by.' She pushed it into his hands. 'Will you look after it for me? I broke the chain when I pulled it free and this dress hasn't got any pockets.'

He lowered the cardboard box on to the ground. The crucifix seemed to burn into his skin as he took it from her.

'We should get going,' he said, slipping it into his trouser pocket and picking up the box again.

But Rachel didn't move. 'Let's not go straight back,' she said.

'But there's nowhere else to go.'

'Let's pretend,' she said, reaching up to touch his bruised face. An insane hopefulness filled her eyes. 'Just for a while, let's pretend that everything's normal.'

'How?'

Because it was impossible, wasn't it? To be normal. Because, after all the destruction, now the work of rebuilding had begun. Roadblocks had been positioned on the roads into the town, keeping unwanted visitors out. A mains electricity cable had been fired across the valley using a rocket to restore power. Rickety buildings were being demolished and torn down with steel cables by bulldozers. Giant Scammel lorries crawled up the roads around Summerglade Hill, bearing the debris away. Council workers had set about mending the smashed and exposed sewerage pipes. The stink of the disinfectant sprayed by firemen as a precaution against disease drifted in the breeze across the town.

'We'll walk to the beach,' Rachel said, 'where all we can hear is the waves.' She stared at him, determined. 'We'll walk there and we'll turn our backs to the town until we can't see it any more.'

'All right,' he agreed, willing to try anything that might help her wash away the pain.

She slipped her arm into his and they set out together in silence towards the east side of town. The harbour was

465

strewn with boulders and its walls had crumbled like those of a sandcastle into the sea. Soldiers were working frantically while the tide was still out, bulldozing rubble and ploughing out mud and sand, in an effort to shore up the harbour's defences against the sea.

The river channel which had once bisected the town was now being excavated, cleared and widened, so that nothing like this could ever happen again. The stones which had made up both South Bridge and Harbour Bridge had either been swept out into the estuary, or swallowed by mud. In their places, two shining new Bailey bridges stood, erected by the Royal Engineers who'd been sent to help rebuild the town. On the green metal bridge which had taken Harbour Bridge's place, and towards which Tony and Rachel now walked, a Union Jack flag had been set into a steel oil drum, and now fluttered in the breeze.

Tony's heart went out to Rachel in her despair. But a different emotion entirely had hold of him. Lucky, that's how he felt. Lucky to have survived. Lucky that his family – his mother and Don and the twins – had survived. Lucky that his new family – Rachel and the baby – had, too. Lucky that they weren't dead, not like so many of those who Tony had grown up with and around.

Wilfred Lee, who Tony had last seen when he'd spoken to him through the letter box, had died. His body had been found half buried in a mudbank the following morning. His house was still standing and Tony could only think that he'd stayed true to his word and attempted to cross the high street to help save Mrs Vale. Only to have then been swept away.

Tony's oldest friend, Pete Booth, had also been killed, along with his father and mother, as the second – and now universally acknowledged, larger – wall of water had

466

ploughed through the centre of the town. His tiny terraced house had been torn to pieces. Pete's body was one of those missing. His parents had been found among the rubble of their home.

Tony still held out hope that Pete would somehow show up alive.

But it had been Emily's death which had hit Tony hardest of all. According to Bill's friend Richard Horner, it had been Bill who'd discovered her body, dishevelled and bruised, washed up on the seashore near where the Bathers' Pavilion had once looked out across the waves. No one knew what he'd been doing down there to begin with, but he'd carried her body all the way to the churchyard on his own.

It had been Emily who Tony had thought of at the cemetery as the lone piper had played.

Tony glanced up what was left of the high street as they walked past its end. It was no longer straight, but warped and smashed. At the far end, the old oak tree stood firm, its leaves shimmering now in the warm summer breeze.

Lucky to have survived . . . by Christ, he'd been that.

Unlike Mrs Vale, whose body had been one of the first to be found, broken and twisted in the branches of a sycamore tree by the quayside. The same police launch which had rescued Tony had spent twenty minutes trying to coax her down, before they'd realised that she was already dead.

Tony pictured the crucifix falling once more to the floor in Bill's bedroom, and remembered how Mrs Vale had screamed at him to get out.

As Mrs Vale had sunk beneath the water at the bottom of the stairs and the thunder outside had gathered and rolled towards him, Tony had snapped himself out of his trance and leapt to his feet.

No time to think. No time to think about what he'd done.

That's when the first wave of water had hit the house. He'd watched from the landing as Bill's room had literally been torn from the side of the building. A wave rushed in at him, hurling him back against the wall. The lamp shimmered and died. But already Tony had seen the ladder, leading up to Rachel's room . . .

He scrambled up through the onslaught of spray and into the attic, slamming the trapdoor down behind him. Darkness all around. He fumbled across the groaning floorboards. Rafters cracked beneath him. Waves roared outside.

All he could think of was what Bill had said about the foundations. The house was going to collapse beneath him. He could feel it breaking up. Any second now and it would be gone.

A flash of lightning and there, he saw it – a block of white leapt out of the darkness – the skylight leading on to the roof.

In the same instant, he remembered the oak tree he'd climbed that night back in June. Would it still be there? Would it have stood its ground as the river had tried to wrench it free?

It was the only chance he had.

As he opened the skylight, a great hissing sound filled his ears. Water – as high as the second floor – raged and foamed below. But the oak had held firm. As the roof creaked below him, Tony hauled himself up into the branches – first two, then three feet higher – until he could climb no more.

He tore his leather belt from round his waist and lashed his arm to the strongest branch he could find.

He thought it was over. The river had begun to drop. But then the noise of thunder rolling towards him down the valley picked up again. He thought of Rachel, alone in the van. He prayed she was beyond the river's reach. Take me, he thought. Take me, but keep her safe.

As the thunder rose, he stared down through the furiously quivering mesh of branches and into the swathing, swirling black mass of water. It was like the end of the world, like the mouth of hell, devouring everything before it, sucking down everything in its path. A black soup of black souls. And his was darkened too, now, wasn't it? He was going to die, damned and alone.

He bit down the whimpers he wanted to release and raise like a howl into the wind. He'd killed her. He hadn't wanted to – hadn't meant to – but he had. *It was an accident,* a voice inside him cried. But the result was the same. He'd killed Rachel's mother, just as surely as his brother had killed her father.

He'd lose her. He knew he'd lose Rachel if he told her the truth.

The thunder was upon him now and the second great wave hit him like a punch to the back of the head. The tree screamed out, buckled under the strain. Then flexed back, dragging Tony upwards with it as it reared up out of the water.

Sheet lightning flashed again. The house swayed below. For an instant, Tony thought it would rock back on to its foundations and hold. But then it was falling away, vanishing into the raging torrent below him.

Vanishing, vanished: the house was gone, Mrs Vale's body with it. Everything that had happened had been erased.

Tony was seized by the idea: no one need ever know

469

what had gone on. He'd tell Rachel and Bill that he hadn't got there in time. He'd claim he'd never set foot in the house.

Why would Rachel ever leave him if he'd done nothing wrong?

The tree cried out again, as another wave slammed into it. None of his scheming mattered. He'd be dead by morning for sure. And if this was the end of the world, then he'd see his brother in hell. He hadn't even said goodbye to Rachel . . . Rachel . . . Let her be the last image in his head.

'There's something wrong, isn't there?' Rachel now said. 'Tell me. Tell me what it is.'

Guilt. That's what it was. That's what she was reading in his eyes now as they stopped and he turned to face her. It had kicked in the instant he'd lied to her and Bill about what had happened. And Bill had seen through him, hadn't he? And since then it had only got worse. He wasn't afraid he'd get caught. He wouldn't.

But he didn't want to lie to Rachel. Trust her. That's what he should do. If he couldn't do that, then what was the point in any of this? What good was love if it was based on lies?

They were standing on the east side of town, at the start of the rocky beach. Cars littered the foreshore like tin cans washed up by the tide, just some of the many which had been reported lost. Out to sea, a helicopter flew low over the waves.

'There's something I need to tell you.' He sat down on a wide, flat rock. It was warm from the sun and smooth as steel, polished by the sea.

'What?' She sat down beside him.

470

Putting the box of supplies to one side, he took the necklace from this pocket. He wanted everything out in the open. The sooner the better, for them both. Trust her, he told himself again. Believe in her. Believe that she'll forgive you.

'It's about your mother. It's about the way she died. About what happened between me and her.'

Rachel's face sank into uncertainty. 'What do you mean, *between* you? You said you didn't get to her in time.'

Tears filled his eyes, the same tears he'd been crying as he'd clung to the oak tree on the night of the flood and waited to die. That was the first time he remembered crying in his whole life, and this was the second. He began telling her the truth, about how he did make it inside the house after all, and about how Mrs Vale refused to come with him.

'She screamed at me,' he told her. 'She screamed at me to leave. She screamed at me because of who I am, because she was scared . . .'

'But you're Tony,' Rachel said, holding his shoulders now, looking deep into his eyes. 'My Tony. You'd never do her any harm.'

It was there – in that sentence, in that faith Rachel had placed in him – that his own faith in her ability to forgive him suddenly died. *You'd never do her any harm.* That's what Rachel believed. That he wouldn't, that he couldn't. Tell her the truth – that he'd fought with her mother, that he'd toppled her down the stairs – and that belief would be shattered. Then whose Tony would he be? Still hers? Or a different Tony, the one she'd used to think he was, the scumbag she'd used to cross the street to avoid? The one who could harm. The one who now had.

The truth? What good was the truth when it might only

destroy them? Guilt, he decided there and then, he could live with. His fear of losing her was greater.

He started to lie again, the same as he'd done when the police launch had rescued him from the oak tree, the same as he'd done when he'd found Rachel and Bill up at the encampment.

He now invented a different ending to the real one. He softened the facts so that they'd be easier for Rachel to swallow.

'Your mother was still in Bill's room when the first wall of water came through,' he said. 'She was swept away with the side of the house.'

Rachel stared at him in astonishment. 'But why didn't you tell me before? Why did you lie?'

See: already his lie was taking on a life of its own. Already it was growing between them, like an evil seed which might one day rise up between them and force them apart.

'Because I watched her die,' he answered, making it up now as he went along, blending facts with lies, embellishing and improvising, until it all rang true. 'I watched your mother die and I didn't want you to know . . . I didn't want you to know that the last thing she was thinking was how much she hated me . . . how she was prepared to die rather than trust me . . .'

'But I love you. None of that would have made any difference. I knew she hated you. I told you what she said about the baby. What I should do with it. Because it was yours . . .'

Caught out already, his lie ran on. 'I thought that if I told Bill how close I'd got, he'd only hate me more . . . for having terrified her in her last moments. And blame himself. For sending me to get her. Knowing that if it had been the other way round then she would have gone with him the moment he'd arrived. I thought that I could save him the guilt . . .' he implored Rachel, willing her now to believe him. 'And because she was already dead, I didn't think it would matter what I said . . .'

'But the truth always matters.'

'I know. That's why I'm telling you now.'

'And if Bill *had* known before . . . he might not have left. If he'd known how hard you *tried* to save her.' She was speaking faster, thinking aloud. 'If he'd seen that it wasn't your fault she died at all, but her own . . . Don't you see that?'

Relief washed over him. She wasn't going to leave him. She believed what he'd said. And if she believed it – she was right, why wouldn't Bill? He cursed himself, wishing now that the story he'd just told Rachel was the one he'd told Bill.

But how was he to know his original story of not reaching Mrs Vale in time to save her wouldn't wash with Bill? And would have instead led Bill to conclude that it was Tony's cowardice which had caused her death? Why would Tony have ever imagined that when the only act of cowardice Tony had ever committed in his life was just now when he'd failed to tell Rachel the truth?

She scrabbled to her feet. 'I've got to tell him. He's got to know.'

'But how?' Tony asked, standing, too. They hadn't seen Bill since the argument. Richard Horner had come to see them two days afterwards to tell them that Bill had been staying with his family, but that now he'd gone. He wouldn't be returning, Richard had said. There was nothing for him here any more. Bill had sworn as much.

'He'll come back,' she said. Her eyes shone with optimism. 'For Mum's funeral . . . for –'

'But what if he doesn't?' Tony asked. 'What if he meant what he said to Richard?'

'Then I'll track him down.' Again, that look of determination. 'Somehow. Then . . . then I'll write to him. I'll tell him everything you've just told me. I'll make him see sense . . .'

Tony looked past her at the bare patch of bulldozed ground near the new Harbour Bridge. Not a single brick of the Bathers' Pavilion remained. All that had survived the great storm of 1933 had succumbed to that of the night of the fifteenth. Tony remembered the drawing of it which he'd seen in Bill's room, in the moments before that had been swept away. Perhaps Bill was right, to have left. Perhaps there really was nothing for him here any more.

'What about me?' Tony asked. 'Can you forgive me for lying to you?'

'You've told me the truth now. How can I not?'

He wrapped his arms around her and stared over her shoulder at the devastated town. He'd miss them all, the people who'd died here. But, as with his brother Keith, in time he'd learn to live without them. He and Rachel were survivors. Nothing would ever change that. It was there in their natures, for ever now. Their future stretched before them, vast and unknowable. They'd run together towards it, he knew, holding hands, like children to the sea.

# Chapter XXXI

**Mallorca, Present Day**

In central Palma, Rachel hurried across the Costa de la Seu, with its row of yellow taxis and smart, red, horse-drawn *galeras*, towards La Seu, the Gothic cathedral. Mercifully, the heat had subsided and now, at nine thirty in the morning, the breezy sea air was clear and refreshing after yesterday's roasting. She stopped in the middle of the road at the crossing, watching the horses swish flies away with their tails. Behind them the fountains in the waterside lakes plumed upwards into the air.

The cathedral stood majestic against the sky. It was odd that she'd become so used to it, but now that she was about to visit it as a tourist for the first time in years, Rachel stopped for a second to marvel at its proportions. Wasn't it strange, she thought, that something so huge could be such a feature in the landscape of her life and yet she hadn't really acknowledged it before? It was the second such epiphany she'd had today and she shook her head, a perplexed smile on her face.

She glanced at her watch. She'd been due to meet Bill inside the cathedral five minutes ago, but she couldn't help that she was running late. Besides, she hoped their break from each other this morning had made a difference to his mood. But maybe she would find him just as uncommunicative and stubborn as he had been earlier.

It was crazy that they still hadn't talked properly, but

475

as Rachel crossed over to the pavement, smelling the sweet sugared peanuts from the stall in the square and hearing the busker pattering out a tune on his steel drum, she felt vital and alive. Somehow, the conversation with Bill about the past, which had seemed so important a few hours ago, had now lost its significance.

She thought back to their showdown in the house yesterday afternoon. Rachel could hardly believe now that she'd broken down so thoroughly. Of course, she hadn't meant to, she'd meant to stay in control of the situation, but his verbal attack on the stairs had tipped her over the edge. And once she'd started talking about Laurie, it had been as if she'd come completely undone.

She couldn't even remember now whether she'd made any sense, but her earlier strength had utterly deserted her, and she'd told Bill everything. She'd told him about her relationship with Laurie and how betrayed she felt. She told him about Sam and Claire and Archie. Then she told him of the pain of losing Anna and how she and Tony had adopted Claire. And then she'd told him about Tony, about their marriage, about the loss she now felt.

It had all come out as a painful, jumbled mess, punctuated by uncontrollable sobs. It was only now, in the clearness of a new day, that Rachel could see that her breakdown had been the final flush of grief. It was as if it had been at that moment that she'd finally realised that Tony had gone. Now she found it strange that it had taken her so long.

At first, Bill had been dismissive, but as Rachel's outpouring had progressed, he'd had no choice but to comfort her. He hadn't tried to interrupt until it was all out. He'd waited until she'd regained her composure. Then he'd made her sit down and drink a glass of water, watching her intently, his face pained until she'd finally told him that she was better. It was only then that he'd suggested that they go outside together and talk to Laurie.

Poor Bill. He must have been so shocked by her outburst. She could see now that he'd wanted to mediate, to try and fix the situation with Laurie, but as Rachel had confronted his daughter, he must have seen that it was pointless. He'd looked completely out of his depth. And after Laurie and Sam had left, he'd remained quiet and withdrawn.

She'd managed to persuade Bill to stay the night on the understanding that she'd take him to the airport this morning. She had been unable to look him in the eye as she'd shown him to the guest room. She'd felt too churned up, too embarrassed about her earlier breakdown and Bill hadn't seemed to want to mention it, let alone forgive her for it. With nothing else to lose, she'd hastily collected all the letters she'd once written to him, and left them on the bed in his room.

And then she'd left him to go and comfort Claire. When Rachel had returned from a harrowing evening at Claire's apartment, Bill had already retired to bed. She'd waited for ages outside his door, her knuckle poised to rap on the door and wake him, but in the end, she'd tiptoed away.

This morning, she'd been ravaged by lack of sleep. Bill had been up when she'd appeared for breakfast and his greeting had been impersonal, yet courteous enough, as if he'd been staying at a bed and breakfast. They'd both retreated into detached politeness. She'd had no idea whether he'd bothered to read the letters she'd left in his room. He'd certainly given nothing away. As they'd driven out of the villa together, she had realised that she didn't know him at all.

She'd felt too distant from him to suggest accompanying him on his tour of the cathedral, which he'd decided to do over breakfast, as they had time to kill before the flight home he'd arranged. Instead, she'd left him to it and had taken the opportunity to go to the Ararat office on a damage-limitation exercise.

She'd wanted to ensure that she played Sam's sudden absence shrewdly. There was no point in upsetting the staff. They'd had enough to deal with having lost Tony. During the previous night, she'd tossed and turned in her bed, trying to work out a solution. She hadn't been able to separate her anger towards Sam on a personal level from her panic that he'd let her business down. Could the business really survive without Sam? She'd given him everything and now he'd walked away as if it didn't mean anything.

It had all seemed such a muddle and a mess, but as she'd entered the cool reception area, with its pale carpet and sleek pictures of all Ararat's hotels, Rachel had felt suddenly clear-headed, as if she were suddenly back on familiar turf.

Being the weekend, there'd hardly been any staff in so early. Still, it had taken quite a bit of persuasion before the new receptionist had relented and let Rachel into Sam's office. Rachel had had to resort to explaining to her that she owned the company.

*She owned the company.* Apart from Sam's 5 per cent holding, which she'd be seeing her lawyer about as soon as was possible. Rachel spread her hands out on the desk, looking around the room which reminded her so strongly of Sam. Maybe there was no need to create a drama. Maybe she was going about this all wrong. Maybe she should keep Sam's misdemeanours within the family. Perhaps she should just tell the staff for now that he'd taken extended leave and buy herself some time.

But then she thought about the last time she'd been in these very offices a few weeks ago and her feelings of exclusion. Only now did she recognise that she'd also been envious. This was her and Tony's baby – a business that they'd nurtured and loved together. Maybe, after all, she wasn't ready to take a back seat and hand it all over to somebody else. Maybe Sam's shattering news had a positive side after all. Maybe it was a wake-up call for her. Was she really ready to retire?

And do what? she asked herself. She wasn't young, but she wouldn't consider herself old. Not yet, anyway. And she was fit. What on earth would she do with her time if she didn't continue working? The one thing she'd learnt in the past few months was that focusing her energy on her children and grandchildren was certainly not the way forward.

Even Claire hadn't really needed her when it came to it. By the time Rachel had arrived at the apartment the night before, Claire had already been comforted by several girlfriends. Rachel had been so full of anger and vitriol. She'd felt so betrayed and ready to fight Sam on Claire's behalf, but as she'd listened to Claire talk to yet another friend on the phone, it had become apparent to Rachel that, unbeknown to her, Claire and Sam had been leading virtually separate lives. She'd come away with the conclusion that Claire's fury wasn't so much that Sam had left her, but that she hadn't left him first. It was more a matter of battered pride than a broken heart.

And Archie . . . poor Archie had been asleep. No one had explained to him what had happened yet.

Yes, Rachel concluded, as she sat in Sam's chair in the

Ararat headquarters, her family were like a hall of distorted mirrors, where the truth didn't ever seem to be reflected. What she needed was something real. Something solid. Something to focus on. And here it was. Right in front of her all this time.

She thought about Tony and how much she'd felt she'd betrayed him yesterday. And then how much she'd mourned him. Was that it? Was she just going to let him go? Was she going to walk away from all he cared about in his business, too?

No, damn it, she wasn't. If she'd died and Tony had still been alive, he would have thrown himself into work. Yes, she thought, it was time to wake up and start her life again. This was her business, and if there were tricky times ahead, it was up to her, as the captain, to steer it through.

Inside the lofty splendour of La Seu, it was cool and dark. The sounds of hushed, shuffling tourists reverberated around the vast shadowy chambers along with the echoing monotone of priests at their prayers. It took a while to locate Bill, but Rachel finally found him sitting on one of the rows of densely packed pews in the central aisle, consulting a guidebook through half-moon spectacles.

'Do you know this place is an astonishing feat of engineering?' he asked, by way of greeting, as she squeezed past a praying nun and sat down next to him.

She'd forgotten that he'd been so interested in architecture. She knew from Laurie that he'd spent his life as a teacher. She wondered how many of his other dreams had gone unrealised.

'It took hundreds of years to build. And they kept having to reinforce it. Shore it up with buttress after buttress. But they never gave up. Amazing to have that kind of vision.'

Rachel followed his gaze up the nave with its pencil-thin pillars soaring up to at least twenty metres, before branching out like palm fronds to the rib-vaulted ceiling. She'd been expecting Bill to be cold and unfriendly and she'd wanted to hurry him out of the cathedral and get him to the airport. But the atmosphere in here was so serene that now she felt her thoughts floating away, until the volume of tranquil space above them calmed her racing mind.

'Fifty years has gone so fast, hasn't it?' he said, eventually.

Rachel turned to him.

'Why didn't you come back? For the funeral?' she asked, before she'd even realised she was going to bring up the past.

It took a while for him to answer. 'I thought about it, but it was too hard. I felt as if I'd failed everyone and going back would have seemed . . . I don't know. I couldn't face it. I wanted to be free of that place.'

'I kept in touch with Richard for years afterwards,' she said. 'That's one of the ways I knew where you were. Where to send the letters . . .' she prompted.

Bill quietly shut his guidebook and rested it on his knees.

'Why did Tony lie?' he asked. 'About not having reached the house in time to save Mum?'

So he had read the letters after all! Rachel felt a shimmer of hope light up inside her.

'I suppose he said what was easiest on the spur of the moment. He was frightened and shocked, traumatised by what he'd seen. He thought he was making it easier for me. And for you.'

'But he did try? He did get to the house in time? What you wrote in the letters . . . it's all true?'

Rachel could see that, for Bill, knowing that an attempt to save their mother had been made and had failed, was so much harder than believing what he'd believed all these years: that Tony Glover had been a coward who hadn't tried.

Rachel wanted to punish him for being so obstinate and for ignoring her for all this time. If he'd only listened to her back then . . . if he'd only opened and read just one of her letters, instead of sending them back, then everything would have been different. But she could see now that there was no point in recriminations.

'Yes, but the point is, Mum didn't want to be saved. Not by Tony, anyway. It was her stubbornness that killed her, not the flood,' she said. 'She refused to forgive him. She refused to see that he was trying to rescue her.'

'I still should have saved her.'

Rachel sighed. 'You know, it's so sad we both feel so guilty. It was just what Tony wanted to avoid. For us both.'

'Why do you feel guilty?' Bill sounded surprised.

'Because I wished it upon her. We had a terrible argument just before the flood. That was why I ran away with Tony. I was so angry, I wanted her dead.'

'You were in trouble. You were just a kid, Rachel. You couldn't have predicted the way things were going to turn out.'

'I suppose.'

'She was my responsibility.'

Rachel turned to him. 'But don't you see? You mustn't feel guilty either. You did the right thing. You went to try and save Emily.'

'And failed.'

'It was an accident, Bill. It was a freak of nature.'

'But I left Mum to die.'

'Oh, Bill, I know you didn't want Mum to die, you just wanted Emily to live more. That's why you chose to go after her. Emily was your future and Mum was your past. You did the right thing, you must see that?'

They were silent for a while and then Bill stretched and delved his hand into his back pocket. He pulled out his wallet.

'I never forgot her, you know,' he said. He leafed through one of the leather slots and pulled out a tiny brown envelope. Inside was an ancient photograph of Emily.

Rachel was amazed, as he handed it over. The photo was so worn, and the light in the cathedral was so dim that she didn't know what he was showing her at first. And then she recognised Emily's features. She stared at the tiny image, feeling a surge of nostalgia.

'She was so pretty, wasn't she? I think I was a little bit in love with her myself.' Rachel smiled sadly at Bill. 'I can't believe it. You've kept this all the time? What did your wife say?'

'She never knew. Not really. Besides, with her it was . . . different. We were older. You're the first person who's ever seen this.'

Rachel knew that him showing her the photo was his way of acknowledging all the time that had passed. She handed it back in silence.

Bill sighed and glanced at it once more before he put it back in his wallet. 'I don't know why I've kept it. Silly, really. But I've always felt that having it kept a bit of her spirit with me. Like a lucky charm, I suppose.'

'She was always so positive, wasn't she? She would have . . .'

Rachel stopped. She didn't know what to say. Emily staying alive would have what? Changed everything, she supposed. Would have meant that they'd have all stayed together?

'Ah,' Bill said, lightening up. 'There's no point in regretting what should have been. I realised that a long time ago. If Emily hadn't have gone, then I wouldn't have met Jean. We were happy, you know.'

There was a long pause.

'So were we,' Rachel said.

'I said some things I didn't mean, yesterday, Rachel. I can see that Tony was a good husband to you. Now I know he did his best, I can see that perhaps I shouldn't have left the way I did . . .'

'I wish it had all been different. I wish I hadn't been caught between you both. You could have known him.'

'Yes, but not knowing him made it easier for me to blame him. Oh, I know I made out that I hated him, but just for the record, I didn't really. Emily made me see the light on that one. Maybe if the flood hadn't have hit, I'd have landed up friends with him, who knows? But at the time, I guess I was jealous of him.'

'Jealous? Of Tony?'

'Yes, I suppose. Jealous and angry. Because he took my little sister away and that meant I'd failed.'

'Failed? How do you mean?'

'Because I promised Dad. I promised him that I'd always look after you. After you and Mum. And I didn't. I let him down. I let you get involved with Tony and then when it came down to it, I left you both.'

'I don't think you let Dad down,' she said, quietly.

'Tell me. Did you ever see Keith Glover again?'

Rachel sighed. 'No I didn't. He died in a bar brawl, soon after he got out – before Tony could get to see him.'

'I know. I heard about it.'

'So we never told the kids about him. About what he'd done. We put it behind us. We put it all behind us.'

Rachel stared up at the kaleidoscope of light in the distant stained-glass rose window. She'd been wondering what it would feel like to have this conversation and she'd been expecting it to be much harder. Now in the vast cathedral, her and Bill's ancient emotions seemed so irrelevant. She felt as if something in the cathedral was healing them both. As if they were both letting go and that, underneath, forgiveness had been there all along.

She suddenly remembered her mother's crucifix around her neck. She reached behind her and took off the tiny clasp.

'I found this afterwards,' she said, handing it to Bill. 'I want you to have it.'

Bill stared at the small necklace in his hand. She could see that the sight of it moved him.

'Poor old Mum. I guess we're both more like her than we care to admit,' he said, looking up at her. His eyes were soft with tears. She felt as if they were children again.

'I'm not,' Rachel said. 'I've spent my whole life trying not to be like her.'

'I'm admitting I'm stubborn, it won't kill you to admit you're a control freak like her,' he said.

Suddenly, they both laughed.

But then Bill turned to her, his face serious. 'Don't make the same mistake, Rachel. Don't do what Mum did to you and Tony with Laurie and Sam.'

Rachel waved her hand to dismiss him, annoyed that he'd brought up Laurie and Sam just when they were having a breakthrough. 'It's totally different.'

'Is it? Laurie's a good girl, Rachel,' Bill said. 'Believe me. She's like her mother. She feels things deeply. And she deserves a chance at happiness. From what she said, I know she and Sam love each other.'

Rachel sighed. 'But I thought Claire and Sam were so happy together,' she said. 'I thought they were the perfect family.'

'Oh, Rachel. There's no such thing. You must know that by now. You can't blame yourself for not seeing the truth. Isn't it true that people lie to their families more than anyone else? I've learnt that. I never thought Laurie would trick me like she did. I never thought she'd have brought me to this.'

Rachel glanced at him. 'I made her do it.'

Bill put his hand around their mother's crucifix and held it in his fist. 'Let them go, Rachel. Forgive them, otherwise it'll kill you. It'll make you old and bitter.'

He didn't say, 'like Mum,' but Rachel could sense that he wanted to.

She felt as if she didn't know anything any more. 'I only wanted what was best.'

'You don't know what best is. Accept it. Give it up. Can Sam and Laurie and Claire really do any worse than we did?'

'I suppose not.'

Rachel placed her hand over Bill's.

'Come on,' he said. 'We should get going.'

Outside the cathedral, the bright sunlight hurt Rachel's eyes. She put her sunglasses on. She was unsure of what had passed between them. Whether everything had really been resolved, or whether they'd both accepted that it couldn't be. Whatever had happened, she felt much lighter without her mother's crucifix around her neck. She felt as if she'd stopped being responsible for what had happened so long ago.

Bill looked out at the horizon and she followed his gaze to the row of palm trees before the road, then the harbour and the white yachts sailing far into the distance across the bay. She wondered whether Laurie and Sam were together on *Flight*. She could suddenly picture them laughing and the image reminded her so strongly of her and Tony that she stopped at the top of the steps.

And suddenly, she felt free. Maybe Bill was right. Maybe she should let go of the past and of her family. Maybe she should start pleasing herself.

'Listen, Bill, do you really have to go?' she asked, suddenly. 'There's so much more left to see. I've got to get back to work in a couple of days, but –'

Bill turned to face her. 'You want me to stay?'

Slowly, she nodded. 'Only if you want to?'

He looked out at the view, smelling the air. And then he looked back at her. 'Well, I suppose a couple more days wouldn't hurt.'

And with that he offered her his arm, squeezing her hand gently as she took it. And then they walked down the white stone steps together into the sunshine.

ABERDEEN CITY LIBRARIES

# Authors' Note

The events in this novel were partly inspired by the Lynmouth Flood Disaster of 1952, in which thirty-four people lost their lives. We're grateful to the following authors, whose books provided invaluable information concerning the night of the flood, as well as background for the period:

Delderfield, Eric R., *The Lynmouth Flood Disaster*, E.R.D. Publications Ltd, 1953

Haynes, Richard, *The Day that the Rain Came Down*, Mediaworld PR, 2002

Hesp, Martin, *Snow, Storm & Flood on Exmoor*, Exmoor Press, 1999

Prosser, Tim, *The Lynmouth Flood Disaster*, Lyndale Photographic Publications, 2001